Yesterday's Sky

—⁓—

novel

A Magic Window on Italian Life During the Fifties

Angela Sciddurlo Rago

Acknowledgments

For all the love my father gave me in his short life…

I would like to thank Lisa Tuvalo, my husband Vito, my son Leonardo, my daughter Rossella, Dr. Corina Rios and Professor Mario Fratti, who have believed in me and have encouraged me to write *Yesterday's Sky*. A special thank you to Dr. Emelise Aleandri, whom I consider to be the Godmother of my novel.

Preface

W hen they say, "You can never go home again," nowhere is that more true than as it pertains to the little town of this nostalgic story. A physical trip to the setting of this novel may be impossible, but the virtual voyage this story provides is real and tangible; so much so, that one can touch it, taste it, smell it, and fully experience it in the here and now, effecting a time travel to a distant location and era. Only in this novel written by actress, screenwriter, playwright, and artist, Angela Sciddurlo Rago, does the former world of a small southern Italian town now still exist, the town that once moved in orbit under the Yesterday's Sky of more than half a century ago. The "Sky" of the title is the metaphor for the fate or destiny that hovers above each individual in the daily struggle for survival in the little village of Vocevero. The "Yesterday" of the title places this reminiscence squarely and irrevocably in the past. At the center of this struggle are Norina Voltini, an impoverished widow desperately conniving in every possible way to feed her large, fatherless family, and her beautiful young daughter, Grazia, in whom is invested all hopes for saving the family's future. The intricacies of plot navigate the reader through a typical year in the life of this family living on Saint Peter Street, and of a town peopled by a vast array of colorful characters with intriguing names that illustrate their idiosyncratic behavior or physical characteristics. The reader will be glued to these pages because they introduce an intoxicating cast of neighbors and townspeople. Among them are Bellina the Good Deed; Pino the Red Eye; the Dumb Brothers; Anna the Heavyweight;

Lina the Warm House; Titina the Alligator; Giacomino the Blind Man; American Wives called White Flies; Lillino the Vendor; Angela the Crazy Head; Franchino the Bird Nest; Carolina the Good Life; Carlo the Broken Neck; Annibale the Announcer; Doctor Polo the Married Priest; Filomena the Grave Heart; Ciriaco the Tower; Laura the White Flower; Saveria the Midwife; Fiorella Torre the mysterious Contessa; Olga the Scared Cat; Tommasino the Donkey Ears; Colombina the Farmer's Wife; and Antonio the Devil, and many more. This litany of names alone provides the imagination with endless possibilities for comedy and drama, as the characters intermingle, each with their own beliefs and agendas. Together, the population creates a distinct personality for the town itself as a backdrop and matrix for the passions that boil within it. The town is a theatre, its streets are the stage, and the townspeople are the actors, vestiges of the ancient Commedia dell'arte. Each person is as specialized and distinct as are the masks of Arlecchino and Pulcinella and Colombina. Just as the traveling troops of the commedia dell'arte followed an itinerary from town to town based on the liturgical calendar, the fascinating actors of Sciddurlo Rago's small town celebrate their farces, dramas, and tragedies throughout the yearly festivals of their lives: Carnevale, Christmas, Easter, weddings, funerals, Saints' feast days, and even the visit of a traveling circus. This epic depiction is successfully and eminently entertaining, but the more important underlying dramatic conflict is not the battle for the basic needs of survival, food, and shelter, but the struggle experienced and personified by the principal character, Grazia, who wrangles spiritually and psychologically against ancient customs and superstitious attitudes, leftovers from centuries of old habits and restrictive rules and beliefs. Although vestiges of former times, the old traditions are still at play now in Grazia's lifetime, wreaking havoc on her hopes for love and a better future. The excitement of Yesterday's Sky is watching the peeling away of these layers of the past for Grazia and the revelation of her own potential for a more liberated life. Apart from her art and her performances as an actress, Angela Sciddurlo Rago's body of literary works, consisting of several plays (A Little More, The Value of Money, Honor and Dishonor, Life On Hold, Widow and Lover, Those Who Love You, More of a Man) and film scripts (Sister Italy, The Psychic, and Mme. Soraya), are manifestations of a worldview that celebrates small town Italian culture, whether the town is located in southern Italy or in Bensonhurst, Brooklyn. But, her works are also a worldview that illuminates a larger picture, the encompassing psychological and sociological contexts in which her memorable characters circulate.

Dr. Emelise Aleandri

Yesterday's Sky

I

"The beauty of a woman is like a blooming rose… You have to immortalize it before it withers," the people of Vocevero often said. In small-town southern Italy, it was considered a rite of passage for young women to have their portraits taken when they turned sixteen.

Norina Voltini would have loved to have such a testimonial of her daughter Grazia's beauty, but unfortunately, she couldn't afford the expense of the photographs. Norina's husband had passed away, leaving her and her six children in dire need. In their little town, Grazia was considered a great beauty.

"Grazia should have her portrait taken. She is seventeen years old. She should have taken her portrait last year," Clotilde, Norina's late husband's sister, would always say.

Clotilde would have loved to pay for her niece's portrait, but she couldn't afford it either. She was a widow, and her only source of income was a small pension.

"If I get a big job, I'll pay for Grazia's portrait," Norina's brother Vituccio would always say.

Vituccio was a taxi driver with a big heart who gave free rides to the less fortunate people in town. He considered himself lucky whenever he got paid for his work.

Norina couldn't rely on her sister Ada, who was married to a wealthy landowner. Ada's control freak husband had forbidden her from giving any money to her relatives. Norina kept her faith, praying to the Madonna to grant her the means to take her daughter to the photographer. While she recited her prayers, Norina visualized a rich man admiring her daughter's picture on display in the window of the photo studio.

Norina would often visit the photo studio and admire the pictures in the window. In the fifties, it was mostly the wealthy people in town who had their portraits taken, and so it was mainly their portraits exhibited in the window. The Four Season Contessas, appropriately named: Primavera, Autunno, Estate, and Inverno, always had their portraits on display. Norina liked the customers of the photo studio. They were all elegantly dressed, and always appeared highly sophisticated. They were high-class people, the kind with whom Norina loved to associate whenever she could.

When Norina saw Mrs. Matilde Fatti in front of the photo studio one afternoon, she smiled at her. "*Buongiorno, Signora* Matilde."

"Good to see you, Norina," Mrs. Fatti said. She then indicated the pictures in the window. "The portrait of your daughter, Grazia, should be there. She's one of the most beautiful girls in town. A lot of American men look at the portraits of young women. You never know, an American may notice Grazia's beauty and propose marriage to her."

Norina thought that American men were more prone to marrying poor women. They were so rich that they didn't care if a girl had a dowry. An American would have been a blessing from the sky. He could have helped the whole family.

Norina's eyes sparkled at the idea that her daughter could marry an American. "I'm going to take Grazia to the photographer soon."

"I haven't seen Grazia in a while," Mrs. Fatti said. "Is she working out of town?"

"Oh yes, Grazia has a very important job. She's a secretary in the city."

"I'm glad. I have always liked Grazia. She's smart and well-mannered."

Grazia wasn't a secretary, but a simple part-time maid. Norina lied to get a bit of respect and admiration. Mrs. Fatti was a wealthy neighbor. She was one of the many wives in town who had husbands working in

America and received big checks every month. These wealthy women were referred to as the American Wives. They distinguished themselves by the flashy outfits they wore, their puffy hairdos stiffened with hair spray, and the magical scents of American candies and chocolates they carried with them. They were also known as White Flies, a rare species because they, like the aristocrats and the professionals, were able to afford many luxuries. They were the best customers of butcher shops. Meat was a luxury, and only the White Flies were able to afford it on a daily basis.

The American Wives were considered *signore*, and were some of the most highly respected women of the town. The American Wives were the most generous among the White Flies. Mrs. Fatti had often hired Norina to do the laundry and bake cookies and had compensated her bigheartedly.

"Before I forget, I'm going to need you to do some ironing and beat the mattress," Mrs. Fatti said.

Norina's face lit up at the thought of earning a considerable amount of money and being tipped with lots of American goodies. "When do you want me to come?"

"You can come tomorrow morning, if you want. You can bring one of your daughters to help you with the mattress. It's quite heavy."

"I'm going to bring Grazia with me, but don't tell anybody because she doesn't do cleaning. She's going to do it just for you, because you are a very respectable person."

"I won't tell a soul," Mrs. Fatti whispered, waving good-bye.

Flashing a light smile, Norina waved back. As Mrs. Fatti walked gracefully away, the scent of the American chocolates and candies vanished into the air.

The luminous sky was more captivating than ever. The sun was beating down on the houses and projecting oversize shadows on the paved street. Norina looked at her own shadow and followed it with childlike interest all the way to a green house on Regina Street. To

Norina's relief, the door was open and no one was waiting by the sidewalk. The main entrance of the house was screened by a fish-net curtain that was used to keep out the flies. Through the curtain, Norina saw Maria the Purple Rose talking to an obese woman. Norina waited patiently. As soon as the obese woman walked out, Norina dashed into the house.

Maria the Purple Rose was considered the best fortune teller in town. She was an old woman with gray hair and a deep set of purple eyes. She was always dressed in black and always wore a purple silk rose on her chest.

"I came to ask about my daughter Grazia's fortune," Norina said, handing Maria two hundred lire. "Last time you told me that Grazia's sky was going to change."

"The colors of the sky change. The sky cannot be dark forever. Grazia's sky will get brighter soon." Maria closed her eyes and crossed her arms on her chest. "I see a man proposing marriage to Grazia. I can hear him talk, but he doesn't speak good Italian."

"Is he rich?" Norina asked.

"Very rich." Maria opened her eyes and uncrossed her arms.

Norina knew that Maria would require more money to reveal more details. Unfortunately, Norina didn't have any more to give her.

"I'm going to come back some other time," Norina said, walking out of the house.

Strolling down the street, Norina kept on repeating Maria's words in her mind. *"Very rich." The man doesn't speak good Italian. He is certainly going to be a man who didn't go to school.*

Norina didn't care if her future son-in-law was ignorant, as long as he was rich. Filled with unbounded vitality, she headed to her house.

Most of the poor people living on Saint Peter Street occupied a single walk-in room on the ground floor. Very few of them had an extra room on the second floor. Wealthy people had larger homes, which consisted of several rooms on the second floor and on the third floor.

The street was so narrow that it didn't give access to any noisy cars, and was a perfect playground for the poor children. Wealthy children were not allowed to play in the street. Their parents considered themselves better than their impoverished neighbors and refrained from associating with them. Wealthy people were rarely seen outside. They kept to themselves.

Poor people, on the other hand, carried out their work and their daily chores in the sidewalk or the street. The street was also a workshop for the poor. Ninuccio the Painter had placed a door on an easel and was scraping it. Onofrio the Umbrella Repair Man was patching up an umbrella. His daughter, Carmela, was crocheting a blanket.

The old women of the street, seated by their front doors, were watching the children play. They were the guardians of the street. Thanks to them, children were never unattended. When poor mothers left their children alone in the street, there was always a guardian who provided lots of love and tenderness to the children.

Norina looked at her children, Olimpia, Mario, and Pasquale, who were having fun. Pasquale and Mario were playing "Hide and Seek." Olimpia and her girlfriends were holding hands, dancing in a circle, singing "Let's Go Around the World." Norina's youngest son, Little Donato, was in the comfort of Old Veronica's lap. The old woman was combing his hair.

Old Veronica was a lonely woman who made her living reciting prayers. Since she had a lot of free time on her hands, she often took care of Little Donato. The baby called the old woman, *Nonna* Veronica, because he considered her his grandmother.

The old woman burst with delight when she finally succeeded in making two curls fall on Little Donato's forehead. She planted a kiss on the baby's rosy cheek. She then picked up the baby and showed him off to Norina. "He looks just like an American kid."

Norina nodded, smiling at her baby, who kept on indicating his curls with his tiny fingers. In her imagination, Norina pictured herself as one of those American Wives she admired whenever they walked down the street, pompously holding their children by the hand. Their children looked like dolls, and always had their hair meticulously combed.

"Let's go and feed the chickens," Old Veronica said to Little Donato.

Norina watched her baby as he walked away holding the old woman's hand. Her eyes became gloomy. *Little Donato couldn't possibly look like an American child. The children of the American Wives are always perfectly dressed. They wear custom-made outfits. Little Donato is wearing clothes handed down by his older brothers Pasquale and Mario.*

The sight of Nannino the Vendor wheeling his cart distracted Norina from her thoughts.

"Colorful fabrics at a discount price. Come and look at my beautiful fabrics," the vendor shouted over and over.

Nannino was a short and chunky old man who used to sell the remnants of fine fabrics. Many neighbors surrounded him, eager to buy his fabrics at an affordable price. Norina wished she could afford those fabrics. She would have loved to sew new clothes for her children.

Giovanni the Farmer, a tall man with a prominent red nose, caught Norina's attention. Giovanni was the wealthiest farmer on Saint Peter Street. As Norina waved at him, he responded with a timid nod.

Norina flashed her most charming grin. "Don't forget to call me and my boys when you pick the apples."

"I won't forget," Giovanni said.

Suddenly, his wife, Colombina, a chubby woman with curly hair, popped out of the house. Colombina gave Norina a harsh look. Norina ignored her and walked towards her house.

The Voltinis' house was tiny. It had a walk-in room on the ground floor and a room on the second floor. The kitchen was poorly furnished with a table, eight chairs, a credenza, and a hand basin. The furniture, the walls, and the fireplace were old and decrepit. The fishnet curtain hanging on the front entrance had many patches. At the back of the kitchen there was a faded, wall–to-wall flower print curtain that screened off the bed where the boys slept. Everything seemed to be falling apart with the exception of the shining new white stove with two burners.

Caterina, Norina's fifteen year-old daughter, had the duty of keeping the kitchen clean. After cleaning for hours, she had sunk into a chair to give herself some rest. Caterina sprang from the chair when she saw her mother's image behind the fishnet curtain. She rapidly reached for a cloth, and pretended to wipe the table. As soon as Norina walked into the house, she inspected the floor to make sure it had been scrubbed properly.

"I cleaned everything," Caterina said. "I even mopped the floor with vinegar and water."

"We have to start cooking," Norina said. "I'm going to wash the zucchini. You can chop the onions in the meantime."

Obediently, Caterina followed her mother's order. She reached for a knife and the onions. While Caterina began peeling the onions, Norina took the zucchini from a wicker basket. When her kind, loving Gino was alive, he would often bring home many baskets of zucchini from the local fields. As she rinsed the vegetables in a steel bucket, the murky water mirrored her sullen face. Her life would have been so different if her husband were alive.

A house where a man doesn't set foot is a miserable house. A poor husband is better than no husband at all. Norina startled at the sight of Grazia bounding into the house. She set her eyes on Grazia's bag. "What did you bring?"

Grazia drew two bundles wrapped in a towel from her bag and handed them to her mother. "I brought hard bread."

Norina placed the bundles furtively in the fireplace. "Tomorrow, you are going to work with me at Mrs. Fatti's house. She's going to pay us well and give us American goodies for sure."

Grazia smiled in agreement.

"Can I come?" Caterina asked as she chopped the onions.

Norina shook her head. "You can't come."

"You always pick Grazia to help you out when you get a good job." Caterina bit her lower lip as she slashed an onion. "You should pick me."

"The American Wife asked me to bring one of my daughters, and I picked Grazia because she's stronger and older."

"Grazia has a job. I don't have a job." Caterina's eyes gleamed with tears due to the onions. "I deserve a job."

Pasquale, Mario, Olimpia, and Little Donato popping into the house interrupted their conversation.

Pasquale stamped his foot. "I'm starving."

Grazia promptly began to slice the zucchini. "Dinner will be ready soon."

Norina sprinkled oil in a pan, and then situated it on the burner of the stove. She was fond of the new gas stove her brother Vituccio had given her. It was the only modern appliance she had and was easy to use. Norina lit up a match and placed it by the burner. As she turned a dial, the flame magically appeared.

Olimpia approached her mother. "Let me blow out the match. Please... please."

As Norina drew the match by Olimpia's lips, Olimpia closed her eyes and blew out the little flame.

"Did you make a wish?" Caterina asked.

Olimpia nodded as she placed the dead match on the stove.

"What was your wish?"

Olimpia twisted her lips. "It's supposed to be a secret."

"I won't tell anybody."

"I wished that one day we would all go to America."

Caterina scrunched her forehead. "That's an impossible wish."

Grazia positioned a cauldron filled with water on the burner. To avoid wasting another match, she lit the dead match on the flame of the lit burner and used it to light the second burner.

Norina placed the chopped onions into the golden oil in the pan. The sizzling noise of the frying onions was music to the children's ears. They gathered by the stove and watched, enthralled by the onions caramelizing. As soon as Norina dumped the zucchini slices in the pan, the sizzling noise got louder. The children jumped cheerfully.

Pasquale indicated the cauldron. "The water is boiling."

Grazia quickly immersed the pasta and poured a full glass of seawater into the boiling water. Pasquale and Olimpia paced back and forth, their senses intoxicated by the aroma of the zucchini and sautéed onions. As soon as Grazia drained the pasta, the children congregated around her to enjoy the warmth of the steam.

Olimpia picked up Little Donato and indicated the steam to him. "It looks like a cloud."

The baby extended his hands to touch the little cloud. His face drooped when he realized that the little cloud had disappeared.

Caterina spread a worn tablecloth on the table and placed spoons, glasses, and a bottle of water. Norina arranged the pasta with zucchini into a large plate. They all took a seat around the table when Norina placed the large plate on the table.

"Before we start eating, you have to pray." Norina joined the palms of her hands. "Repeat after me: God bless the Madonna, Our Lady of Sorrows for giving us this food. Amen."

Reluctantly, the children joined the palms of their hands and repeated the prayer after their mother.

Norina drummed her fingers on the table. "We can eat now."

They all shoveled spoonfuls from the huge plate of steaming food. It was like a race. Whoever was faster had a chance to eat more. Caterina and Pasquale were the ones who ate the most. Mario couldn't keep up with the others, and ate scantily. Olimpia ate moderately. Little Donato scarcely ate. Norina and Grazia ate the least, to allow the children to have more. As soon as they were done eating the main course, Norina surprised the children with hard bread and homemade marmalade for dessert. The Voltinis had dessert only on special occasions. The children ate the treat with delight.

"Mrs. Fatti, the American Wife, gave me and Grazia a big job for tomorrow," Norina said.

"We are going to get American chocolates and candies," Pasquale said.

Olimpia bounced up and down.

Grazia flashed her magical smile. "You are going to have a taste of America."

II

Shades of pink and purple seemed to be dancing in the sky when Norina woke up the following morning. *The sky is serene,* she thought, peering out of the window.

Saint Peter Street was deserted and absorbed in a deep silence. Everybody was asleep. The houses appeared to be asleep with their windows and doors shut. In their intimate closeness, it looked as if they were huddling together for warmth in the morning's chill.

Norina smiled at the statue of the Madonna, Our Lady of Sorrows, in her black lace gown with gold trim, standing majestically on the dresser. "Thank you for the job," she whispered, blowing the Madonna a kiss.

The Madonna seemed to be gazing at the children: Grazia, Caterina, Olimpia, and Little Donato, who were sleeping peacefully.

Our Lady of Sorrows keeps an eye on my children, Norina thought. She startled as she heard shouts coming from the street. It was Tommasino the Donkey Ears' voice.

Tommasino was a tall and lean man with huge ears. He was usually the first vendor wheeling his cart through Saint Peter Street in the morning. "Who wants eggs?" he kept shouting.

He's going to wake up the children. Norina sprang open the shutters and poked her head out. "Hey, Tommasino the Donkey Ears, you'd better stop yelling. My children are still sleeping. You think you have the right to wake up everybody just because you want to sell your eggs? People have better things to do than buy your eggs."

The shutters of the house across the street flew open. Titina the Alligator, a petite woman in her late fifties, with thick eyeglasses and crocodilian teeth popped out of the window. "Norì, you should throw urine on his head."

Norina had threatened many times to throw urine on Tommasino the Donkey Ears, but she never had the courage to do it. The poor vendor had a crippled leg, and struggled forlornly to push his cart.

"If I dump urine on him, he is going to yell like a maniac and wake up my children." Norina slammed the shutters. To her dismay, the children had woken up from their sleep. Norina directed a stern look at the girls. "Get dressed and make the beds."

Obediently, Grazia, Caterina, and Olimpia donned their black mourning garb. Throughout southern Italy, it was a tradition for bereaved women to demonstrate their grief by continuing to wear solid black clothes for months or even years. Such garb was called *il lutto,* and it signified that the wearer was still in full mourning. Men were not expected to dress in black. They simply wore a black button on their collar. Little Donato didn't have to wear a sign of mourning since he was a baby.

Caterina dressed Little Donato in his day colorful clothes. In the meantime, Grazia and Olimpia made the beds. As soon as Norina exited, Olimpia placed a porcelain doll neatly between the pillows on the big bed. Norina only kept the doll for show. Her daughters were not allowed to play with it. Olimpia couldn't resist the impulse to rearrange the doll's hair.

"Let's go," Grazia said.

They all went down the stairs. Once they bounded into the kitchen, they were faced with their mother's harsh look.

"Pasquale and Mario are still sleeping," Norina said. "I'm going to throw some water on their faces."

"I'll wake them up," Grazia said, dashing into the back room.

Pasquale and Mario were sleeping peacefully in the full-size bed. As usual, Pasquale was taking up most of the blanket and space, while Mario lay, barely covered, on the edge of the bed.

Poor Mario, he must have been cold during the night, Grazia thought as she shook his shoulder tenderly.

Mario awoke instantly. Grazia had to shake Pasquale's shoulders vigorously to wake him up.

Pasquale compressed his lips. "I have to get dressed."

Grazia leaped out of the back room and stepped into the kitchen.

"Fresh ricotta," a voice from the street yelled.

Caterina's face lit up. It was the voice of Rocco, Carmine the Shepherd's son. He was making his rounds, spreading the news that the ricotta cheese was ready. Caterina peered outside, but to her disappointment, Rocco was nowhere to be seen. The wealthy neighbors were going to the shepherd's house, eager to buy fresh, steaming ricotta and its whey.

Rocco must be selling the ricotta inside, Caterina thought. "*Mamma,* we have no milk for breakfast."

Norina drew money from her brassiere and handed it to Caterina. "Buy a liter of milk."

Caterina rushed out of the house. Mario and Pasquale popped out of the back room, eager to have breakfast. They watched Grazia as she set the table with five bowls and five spoons. Olimpia stood by the front door, intoxicated by the aroma of the fresh ricotta cheese that permeated the street. She stared at her neighbors drinking their bowls of ricotta. Ricotta cheese was a luxury the Voltinis couldn't have for themselves.

Pasquale stamped his foot. "*Mamma,* you should get the sugar."

The children jumped cheerfully as Norina unlocked the credenza and took out a jar of sugar. They reached for their bowls and gathered around the table, watching their mother dump one spoonful of sugar into each bowl.

"Caterina hasn't come back with the milk," Olimpia said.

Pasquale raised an eyebrow. "Caterina likes to spend time at the shepherd's house."

Grazia knew what kept her sister over at Carmine the Shepherd's house. Caterina had a crush on his son Rocco, who was considered the most handsome teenage boy on Saint Peter Street. Grazia kept it a secret, knowing Caterina would never be allowed to go out on her own if their mother ever found out. Finally, Caterina appeared in the house carrying a bottle of milk.

"What took you so long?" Pasquale asked.

Caterina revealed a trace of a smile. "There were a lot of people in the shepherd's house buying ricotta."

Pasquale narrowed his eyes. "You tasted the ricotta."

Caterina crossed her hands on her chest. "I swear on my aunt's grave that I didn't taste the ricotta."

Rocco did give her a cup of ricotta, Grazia thought. She always knew it when her sister told a lie. She decided to remain silent; realizing that Pasquale would be envious if he knew Caterina had eaten such a delicacy.

Olimpia sighed. "I wish one day we'd have ricotta for breakfast."

"The sky can't always be dark for us. Sooner or later, our sky is going to shine," Norina said as she poured equal shares of milk, hard bread and water into each bowl.

As the children ate, they carefully watched their mother lock the sugar in the credenza, and entertained the hope she would forget to keep the key. To their disappointment, she quickly placed the key in her pocket.

Norina turned to her children. "Get ready to go to school."

Dutifully, Mario, Pasquale, and Olimpia slipped on their school uniforms and walked out of the house.

Mario always has a sad look in his eyes when he has to get ready to go to school, Grazia thought.

Mario was repeating the second grade for the third time and was in the same class with Olimpia, even though she was four years younger. It was humiliating for Mario to have his younger sister in his class. For his schoolmates, it was just one more reason to pick on him. Norina wanted him to drop out of school, but her sister-in-law Clotilde talked her out of it. Clotilde believed Mario was better off in school than out roaming the streets, since there were hardly any jobs for a boy like him. Olimpia was doing better in school than Mario, having been left back only once. Pasquale was the smartest one in the family. He had always been promoted and was attending middle school.

Grazia stepped outside and gazed at her siblings as they walked down the street. They looked indigent in their worn, black public school uniforms. The children attending Catholic school were sporting their immaculate blue uniforms with white collars and matching ribbons. They resembled little dolls.

Grazia spotted Serafina the Maid escorting Mrs. Fatti's son, Robertino. Serafina was as short as the child. As usual, she was carrying the boy's school bag on her hunched back. She was so old and feeble that she could hardly walk, but always insisted on carrying his school bag. She feared the child would develop a crooked spine if he were to carry the bag himself.

Serafina is so gnarled it seems like she's going to collapse under the weight, Grazia thought.

"It's time to go," Norina said, popping out of the house.

"Fine, we'll go now," Grazia said.

Norina led Grazia to the American Wife's sumptuous dwelling. The front of the house was paneled with splendid marble tiles.

When Norina rang the bell, she received no response. "The American Wife forgot all about us. These rich women have too many things on their minds," she said, ringing the bell a second time.

"Mrs. Fatti may get annoyed," Grazia said. "Don't ring the bell again."

They waited impatiently, pacing back and forth. Finally, the door sprang open and Mrs. Matilde Fatti appeared, clad in an emerald green silk robe. To their relief, Mrs. Fatti flashed a smile, exposing her perfect white fake teeth. "Come in. I didn't expect you so early."

Norina and Grazia walked eagerly into the house as if it were a palace owned by a queen.

"You haven't been here since I remodeled the house. Let me show you around. I bought everything new," Mrs. Fatti said, escorting them into a spacious room furnished with a red velvet living room set. A television set stood on top of a white marble table.

Norina's jaw dropped as her eyes darted around the room. "I never saw a living room like this."

Grazia was not impressed at all. She thought the furniture was too gaudy.

Mrs. Fatti indicated the adjoining room. "I also bought a new dining room set."

The furniture was made of glistening wood. The chairs were upholstered in gold velvet. A giant radio stood prominently in the back of the big room. There was a golden china closet exhibiting silverware and sparkling glasses. A chandelier filled with countless ornaments of resplendent glass was suspended from the ceiling.

"The furniture comes from America?" Norina asked.

"I bought it in the city. It's an American-style dining room set. I also remodeled the kitchen," Mrs. Fatti said, leading Norina and Grazia into the new kitchen paneled with black and white lustrous ceramic tiles.

"It's beautiful," Norina kept saying.

Gratified by Norina's reaction, Mrs. Fatti beamed. "I put in a wet sink. Serafina the Maid can no longer go to the community fountain. She's gotten too old to carry heavy buckets of water. I have drapes that need to be washed. You can wash them in the wet sink."

Norina bounced. She was thrilled by the thought of washing the drapery under the running water.

Mrs. Fatti pointed towards a large white box. "I also bought a refrigerator."

The American Wife seizes every opportunity to show off, Grazia thought.

"You got the 'refrigidade' from America?" Norina asked.

"No, I bought it in the city. It's an American-style refrigerator."

"I heard that in America all the people have a 'refrigidade,'" Norina said.

Mrs. Fatti nodded. "My husband says that in America everyone has a refrigerator, a wet sink, and a television set."

Norina flashed a light smile as she pictured the American houses filled with gleaming furniture, wet sinks, television sets, and refrigerators. "In America, people must make a lot of money."

Mrs. Fatti spread her arms wide open. "God bless America. America has changed my life."

America changed her life for sure, Norina thought.

Mrs. Matilde Fatti had once been a poor woman herself. Her sky changed when her husband went to America. Thanks to the dollars he sent home, she bought the two houses next-door, sparkling modern furniture, and all those new appliances. America changed Mrs. Fatti's social status as well. She became a White Fly and gained lots of respect from the people in town.

"Would you like a cup of coffee?" Mrs. Fatti asked.

"No, don't go out of your way," Norina responded, although she craved that cup of coffee.

"*Signora* Fatti, you should not trouble yourself," Grazia said.

It was customary to refuse any sort of food the first time it was offered. The guest only accepted when the host insisted out of courtesy.

"It's no trouble at all. A cup of coffee is the best thing in the morning. Sit down. Make yourselves comfortable," Mrs. Fatti said as she started the coffee.

Norina and Grazia sat down by the table, eager to have coffee. They rarely had coffee at home. It was a luxury reserved for guests.

Mrs. Fatti reached for a big jar filled with peanut brittles from the credenza. "My husband sent these brittles from America."

Norina's eyes sparkled as Mrs. Fatti arranged the brittles on a gold plate. Norina was so elated to be treated with such respect she did not realize Mrs. Fatti was overjoyed by the impression she had made.

Mrs. Fatti placed the plate filled with peanut brittles ceremoniously on the table. "Excuse me a minute. I want to go upstairs and change. Keep an eye on the coffee pot," she said, heading towards the stairs.

Norina sat still on the chair until she heard the sound of Mrs. Fatti's footsteps going up the stairs. She then sprang from the chair, grabbed a handful of peanut brittles, and placed them in her pocket.

"Don't take too many. Mrs. Fatti may notice," Grazia said.

"The American Wife has so many, she's not going to notice," Norina mumbled, eating a peanut brittle with gusto. Her eyes lit up as she took another handful of peanut brittles. She leaped when she heard a bursting noise.

"It's the coffee pot." Grazia ran to the stove and turned off the flame.

Norina gave a sigh of relief and slipped the peanut brittles into her other pocket. She was intoxicated by the coffee aroma circulating into the air. At the sound of footsteps, Norina stood still, like a schoolgirl. Mrs. Fatti appeared in the room wearing a gaudy royal blue housedress.

"The coffee is ready," Grazia said.

Mrs. Fatti poured the hot coffee slowly into the demitasse cups. "How much sugar do you take?"

Norina tapped her feet. "I like it sweet, put four spoons."

"I'll have one," Grazia said.

Mrs. Fatti shoveled generous spoonfuls of sugar into the demitasse cups with finesse. "I go easy on the sugar. I don't want to gain any weight. My husband says that American women watch their weight."

How can they watch their weight if there is so much food in America? Norina thought, gulping her sweet coffee all in one shot.

Grazia sipped her coffee in a ladylike manner.

Grazia behaves like a signora. If her mother were not around her, no one would guess that she was a Voltini, Mrs. Fatti thought.

"I'm going to start washing the drapes," Norina said.

"Don't tell Serafina the Maid that I hired you to wash the drapes," Mrs. Fatti said.

Norina raised her finger to her lips. "I won't say a word."

"Grazia can do some dusting in the meantime." Mrs. Fatti walked out of the room.

While Grazia dusted the furniture, Norina enjoyed washing the drapes with soap in the sink. She was marvelously enchanted by the running water sprinkling the drapery. She couldn't resist the temptation of adding more soap. The running water converted the soap into foam. She played with the foam with childlike interest.

"I love the wet sink," Norina said. "It's like having the town fountain in the house."

Grazia bobbed her head in agreement.

Filled with delight, Norina kept on sniffing the fragrance of the soap as she rinsed the drapes and drained the water out. When she was done, she placed the drapery in a zinc basket. Grazia helped her mother carry the heavy basket to the terrace.

They admired the sky which seemed to be painted with various shades of blue and yellow as they hung the drapes out on the terrace. The sunrays dappled the little attached terraces. A flock of white pigeons flying in the bright sky caught Grazia's eyes. She followed the direction of the birds and saw them landing on the terrace that belonged to Baronessa Rosa, the best opera singer in town.

As usual, the baronessa welcomed her pigeons home with joy. "Come here, my little angels," she said, feeding them peanuts. She directed her gaze at Norina and Grazia. "Did you see how well my pigeons dance in the sky?"

"They are beautiful," Grazia responded.

Norina contorted her face. "The pigeons better not shit on the drapes."

"Don't worry. They only dance around my terrace and Count Torre's terrace. We are the only ones who feed them. Nobody else cares about my pigeons." The baronessa walked back into her house.

Norina giggled. "What is the matter with her? She thinks that people are going to feed her pigeons? She's out of her mind. People don't have enough food to feed their own children."

"Mrs. Fatti can afford to feed the pigeons, but she doesn't bother," Grazia said, watching the pigeons landing on Count Torre's terrace.

Count Torre was the richest man on the street. His residence was so large that it looked like a palace. People called it *il palazzo*.

Grazia's thoughts shifted to the count's wife, Contessa Fiorella Torre. *She's such an unhappy creature. She's imprisoned in her own house and hasn't been outside for the past ten years. A woman is not forgiven when she makes a mistake. She pays a high price.* "Count Torre cannot be the one who feeds the pigeons. A person that is so cruel to his own wife cannot possibly be kind to animals."

"I heard that the contessa feeds the pigeons."

Loud yells coming from the street interrupted their conversation. They suddenly recognized Tommasino the Donkey Ears' voice, and they looked down the street, intrigued. The poor vendor was arguing with Titina the Alligator. Norina figured out what had happened immediately. Her neighbor was stingy, and always tried to buy Tommasino's eggs at a discount price.

The poor vendor smashed the eggs onto the ground. "Are you happy now? Nothing for you and nothing for me."

Norina burst out laughing. She watched the scene with great fascination. She was driven by the secret thrill of witnessing what would happen next. The action revolved around Tommasino and Titina playing the leading roles as many curious neighbors gathered around them.

"You are a cheap, greedy bitch," the vendor shouted. "You come from generations of cheap, greedy bitches. It's like a blood disease that runs in your family. I have more respect for my old chickens than you."

Titina turned to the neighbors. "I want the satisfaction of smacking and biting this retard. He has the nerve to badmouth my relatives, and compares me to his stupid chickens."

Tommasino waved his hands up in the air. "Go ahead, bite me. I'm not afraid of your alligator teeth. You are so short that you have to get on a chair to smack me."

Titina placed her hands on her hips. "I may be short, but I'm smart. You are tall and stupid. You are only useful for picking fruit from the trees."

Norina spotted Mrs. Fatti among the neighbors. She figured Mrs. Fatti would empathize with Tommasino. The American Wives were his best customers. They loved his eggs, and had them delivered every day. They would beat the yolks with sugar, add a few drops of Marsala wine, and have them for breakfast or dessert. The taste was delicious.

Norina sprang back with excitement when Titina grabbed a chair and threw it at the vendor. "She missed," she whispered to herself. She pursed her lips. If the chair had knocked down Tommasino, the scene would have been much more exhilarating.

"Leave him alone," Mrs. Fatti shouted.

Mrs. Fatti never took part in street discussions since becoming a White Fly. She had made an exception for the poor vendor.

Tommasino's *eggs must be exceptional*, Norina thought.

"Mind your business," Titina bellowed. "Who do you think you are? You have no right to get mixed up in my business."

Mrs. Fatti held her head up high. "I'm a *signora*, and it's my duty to teach you some manners."

Titina laughed. "A real *signora* is born a *signora*. No one becomes a *signora*. You think that you're a *signora* just because your husband was lucky to go to America. If it weren't for Saint America, you'd be just like me."

Mrs. Fatti shrugged her shoulders. "I'm not going to answer you back because I know how to behave like a real *signora*."

Titina showed her fists to Mrs. Fatti. "If I pull out that stupid sprayed hair of yours, you are not going to look like a *signora* anymore."

Colombina the Farmer's Wife and Ninuccio the Painter grabbed Titina by the arms and dragged her away.

"It's over," Norina said, tapping her fingertips on the railing.

My mother always enjoys a bit of drama at other people's expense, Grazia thought.

Norina noticed that the neighbors were whispering to Mrs. Fatti. "I wonder what they are saying. I'm going to ask the American Wife."

Grazia twisted her face. "Save your breath. Mrs. Fatti has learned how to behave like a *signora*. A *signora* doesn't squeal when something embarrassing happens to her."

"You're right," Norina said, leading Grazia down the stairs.

Once they entered the bedroom, they saw Serafina the Maid dusting the furniture. She was so small that she looked like a child from a distance.

Serafina gave them a stern look. "What are you doing here?"

"Mrs. Fatti hired us to help you beat the mattress," Grazia said. "I can also help you strip the bed."

Serafina shook her head. "I don't need your help."

Norina and Grazia sat on the sofa while the old maid undid the bed. She moved so slowly that they grew annoyed watching. Serafina's face turned red when she lifted the mattress from one side.

"She's going to drop dead if she carries the mattress. We better help her out," Norina whispered to Grazia.

Norina and Grazia lifted the mattress from the opposite side and made the effort to lug most of the weight. When Serafina carried her side of the mattress, to her surprise, it was light.

They transported the mattress all the way to the balcony and leaned it over the railing.

"I want to make one thing clear," Serafina said. "I'm the maid. Mrs. Fatti promised me on my mother's deathbed that I'm going to be her maid for the rest of my life and no one is going to take my place."

"My daughter has a very important job in the city," Norina said. "She doesn't need your job. Today, she came to give me a hand beating the mattress."

"Mrs. Fatti doesn't need you to beat the mattresses," Serafina said. "I can do it myself."

She's going to drop dead for sure if she tries to lift a mattress by herself, Norina thought.

Grazia patted Serafina's hunched back. "We have no intention of taking your job."

Serafina revealed a glint of a smile as she exhaled heavily.

"Let's beat the mattress," Norina said.

They armed themselves with carpet beaters and beat the dust out of the mattress with all their strength.

"There they are," they heard a voice from below. They promptly looked down on the street and spotted Caterina holding Little Donato by his hand.

"Grazia, *Mamma*," the child yelled, jumping up and down.

Little Donato's legs caught Serafina's attention. "The boy has bowed legs."

I wonder why his legs are so curved. All my other children have straight legs. Thank God he's not a girl, Norina thought. "He's a boy, his legs don't really matter."

"People are going to nickname him 'Bow-legs'," Serafina said.

Grazia bit her lower lip. Norina gave Serafina a harsh look.

"Grazia, come home," Little Donato shouted.

Grazia waved at her little brother. "I'll come home soon."

"Let's bring the mattress back," Norina said.

Little Donato watched his mother and his motherly sister disappear behind the mattress. "Grazia, *Mamma*," he kept calling out.

"This time let's not carry all the weight. The old bitch can carry her fair share of the mattress," Norina whispered in Grazia's ear.

They held back from lugging most of the weight and allowed Serafina to carry an equal share. By the time they placed the mattress back on the frame, the old maid was out of breath. She sank into a chair and gasped for air. Her face had turned scarlet.

The old bitch deserves to be punished. No one makes fun of my son's legs, Norina thought.

Serafina had other things on her mind. Her beady eyes had noticed a peanut brittle sticking out of Norina's bulging pocket. "I don't think Mrs. Fatti is going to like it when she finds out that you stole her peanut brittles."

"Mrs. Fatti gave me the peanut brittles with all her heart," Norina said. "I didn't eat them because I wasn't hungry so I saved some for later."

Norina turned her back on Serafina and escorted Grazia down the stairs. "The stupid old maid is getting on my nerves." Norina clenched her fists. "I feel like pulling out the few strands of hair she has left on her head."

"Serafina is old, weak, and small." Grazia tapped her mother's arm. "You should have pity on her."

As they bounded into the kitchen they heard a child's voice say, "I don't want another spoonful."

Mrs. Fatti was walking after her son Robertino eager to feed him a spoonful of egg yolks beaten with sugar. Robertino cringed as he swallowed it.

"He has no appetite. I have to beg him to eat," Mrs. Fatti said. "I let him come home on his lunch break because in school he doesn't eat at all."

What a waste! Grazia thought as she looked at the cup filled with sweet egg yolks. *My siblings would devour it in a split second.*

"Grazia, you can go home now," Norina said. "I can do all the ironing."

My mother is releasing me because she wants the glory of bringing home the American goodies, Grazia thought. She turned to Mrs. Fatti. "It has been a pleasure coming to your house."

Mrs. Fatti grinned. "The pleasure has been all mine. Thank you for coming."

Grazia dashed out of the house.

"Grazia is so well-mannered," Mrs. Fatti said.

Norina smiled in agreement. Her smile turned into a grimace when she saw Serafina the Maid entering the room. *She's a ghost. She's everywhere.*

The old maid ignored Norina. She gave her attention to Mrs. Fatti. "Is Robertino ready to go back to school?"

"He's almost ready," Mrs. Fatti said as she drew another spoonful of sweet egg yolks by her son's mouth.

Robertino shut his mouth against the spoon.

Mrs. Fatti dumped the spoon of egg yolks into the cup. "Serafina, you can go to church after you take Robertino to school."

Serafina reached for the youngster's school bag. "I'm going to come back with Robertino when he gets out of school."

Norina watched Serafina carrying the school bag as she dragged Robertino out of the house. *How weird! Serafina looks like an old woman going to school.* "I want to start the ironing. I better light the coals in the warming pan and heat up the iron."

Mrs. Fatti couldn't help but laugh. "There's no need for all of that. I have an electric iron." She placed her son's egg cup in the sink. "I'll get the iron. You can wash the cup in the meantime."

As soon as Mrs. Fatti disappeared in the stairway, Norina downed the sweet egg yolks thirstily. *What a delight! The White Flies are right. Tommasino's eggs are the best in town,* she thought as she washed the cup.

Minutes later, Mrs. Fatti returned carrying a stack of clothes and a shiny electric iron. She plugged in the iron. "You just have to wait a few minutes until it gets hot. I can't trust Serafina when it comes to fine linens."

Get rid of her and give me the job, Norina thought.

Mrs. Fatti read Norina's mind. "I can't get rid of her. She's alone. She has no living relatives."

"I feel very sorry for Serafina." *It's about time that she drops dead. Serafina has lived long enough,* Norina thought. "Do they live long in her family?"

"Serafina's mother died at the age of one hundred and two, and she wasn't sick one day in her life. Even Serafina never gets sick."

Norina compressed her lips. *I'm never going to get Serafina's job.*

"I'm embroidering my initials on my scarf. I love embroidery. It calms me down." Mrs. Fatti walked out of the room.

She says that embroidery calms her down, Norina thought. *She never said that when she was poor, she had to do it to make ends meet.*

Norina felt privileged to use an electric iron. She loved sliding the gadget over the linens. It was like magic. The wrinkles disappeared instantly. Norina worked slowly. She wanted to take up as much time as possible. She enjoyed every hour that went by, and more time meant more money. As she labored, she beamed at the thought of bringing home a considerable sum of money. She was excited about putting away some lire for Grazia's portrait. Norina bounced when Mrs. Fatti suddenly appeared in the room.

"Would you like a veal steak?" Mrs. Fatti asked.

"Oh no, never mind. I don't want you to go out of your way. It's too much trouble," Norina responded.

"It's no trouble at all."

Norina flashed a hint of a smile. "If you insist, I'm going to have the veal."

As Norina continued her ironing, she enjoyed the sizzling sound of the steak cooking in the pan and the delicious aroma.

Mrs. Fatti served the steak in a fancy plate along with a rich green salad and a glass filled with *aranciata,* a carbonated orange drink. "You can cook a steak in no time. In America, people eat a lot of steak. American women don't like to spend much time in the kitchen."

If I had the money to buy veal, I would spend a whole day in the kitchen cooking it, Norina thought, eating the steak with gusto. Her mind shifted to her children, who were having hard bread soaked in water for lunch. *I'm going to treat the children with meat,* Norina promised to herself, drinking the *aranciata.*

When they finished eating, Mrs. Fatti turned on the radio. Norina continued her tasks, listening to the music. A radio was an extravagance she couldn't even imagine granting herself. She smiled, enchanted, every time she heard one of her favorite songs. She couldn't resist the impulse to sing along. Between one song and the next, she pictured the cash and the American treats she was about to receive. The radio was blasting a waltz tune when Norina was done with the ironing. Mrs. Fatti compensated her generously with one thousand and two hundred lire and a basket filled with American goodies.

When Norina got home, she happily gave the children Mrs. Fatti's American chocolates and candies. The children ate the sweets with delight.

"We got a taste of America," Pasquale said.

III

The sunrays washed over Norina's and Grazia's happy faces as they strolled down the street. Grocery shopping was a social event for them. They always met people they knew and heard the latest gossip.

Norina made a list in her mind of the food she intended to buy. "I don't have to buy bread. You can bring home some bread tomorrow."

Grazia clenched her teeth. *She wants me to steal from my boss.*

It's not a sin to steal from rich people, Norina thought. *They have plenty of food.*

Their minds were distracted by Carolina the Good Life, emerging on the street. As she wheeled a blue baby carriage towards them, Carolina waved.

Grazia directed her attention to the newborn baby. "He's so cute."

"He's my Little Gianni." Carolina smiled. "He's the prince of the family. After four girls, I finally got a boy. My husband was obsessed with having a son. He wanted someone to carry on the family name. Too bad he didn't get to see Little Gianni yet. He can't wait to see him."

He can't wait to see him because he's a boy, Grazia thought. *I remember how disappointed he was when his daughters were born.*

Norina turned to Carolina. "When is your husband coming back from Venezuela?"

"In six months. He cannot afford to come home often. Venezuela is not like America. My husband has to work hard to make his money."

Women whose husbands worked in Venezuela didn't get the title of White Flies. They couldn't grant themselves the same luxuries as the American Wives, and had a much more modest life. It still was considered a good life, since they didn't have to struggle. When Carolina was single, she was poverty-stricken, but when she got married, Carolina acquired the nickname of the Good Life.

The owner of the bottega was a buxom woman named Teresina. She had the misfortune of having ten daughters. It was a disgrace to have many daughters. For mothers who produced only girls, fathers were often mortified to the point of refusing to see their newborns for days. For the poor, it was a tragedy. Daughters were considered worthless and a burden. They didn't even carry on the family name. What's more, the parents had to produce a dowry to marry a girl off, if they were even lucky enough to find someone who wanted her. Fortunately, two of Teresina's daughters were already married. Her first-born had moved to Germany, and her second-born had moved to Argentina, but Teresina had eight more daughters to marry off. Teresina had adopted her husband's nephew, Peppino, to carry on the family name. Peppino was treated like a prince in a kingdom of worthless girls.

The bottega was crowded. As usual, there were two lines: one for the paying customers and one for the credit customers. The line for the paying customers was always shorter than the one for the credit customers. Consequently, Teresina's business wasn't doing well. The woman had a big heart. She gave credit to the needy, even though most of them already owed her money.

The credit customers were intoxicated by the scent of American chocolates and candies in the air. The delightful aroma originated from Mrs. Gisella Maori, an American Wife with a puffy hairdo. The White Fly was being served by Teresina and three of her daughters: Pasquina, Chiara and Costanza. Mrs. Maori was a paying customer and was granted the privilege to be served before the credit customers. She was buying all sorts of expensive groceries: olives, sugar, Parmesan cheese, prosciutto, salami, and coffee. Teresina and her daughters were extremely polite with Mrs. Maori.

"The American Wife has dollars. She gets the royal treatment," a short credit customer whispered.

A tall credit customer nodded.

Norina and Grazia stood proudly on the line of the paying customers. They eyed Angela the Crazy Head, who was having a conversation with Anna the Heavyweight in the line of the credit customers. Grazia had great admiration for those two women. Angela was nicknamed Crazy Head because she was highly intelligent and well-educated. She made her living writing letters for the illiterates in town. Anna was nicknamed Heavyweight because she had the strength of a beast. No one wanted to mess around with either of these infamous women. They both were considered equally dangerous. One could intimidate any man in town with her fists, while the other needed only her words. There were rumors that Angela the Crazy Head gave memorable speeches that would put a lawyer to shame. Once, she had sued a man for fraud and won the case in court, acting as her own lawyer. There were also reports that Anna the Heavyweight gave memorable beatings that would put a boxer to shame. She had sent a lot of men to the hospital, and had always gotten away with it because her victims were too humiliated to admit they had been beaten up by a woman.

Flashing a smile, Norina waved at the two notorious women.

My mother is hoping to be included in their conversation, Grazia thought.

As soon as Anna and Angela returned the smile, Norina took Grazia by the arm and dragged her towards them. Grazia listened, intrigued.

"I just had a big fight with my daughter," Anna the Heavyweight said. "I told her that she's a whore, and that she's never going to get married."

"But Margherita is so beautiful," Angela the Crazy Head said. "She'll find someone who will marry her."

Anna shook her head. "There's no hope for her. She has ruined her reputation and not even a crippled man is going to marry her."

"Why?" Norina asked.

Anna widened her eyes. "You know why. Everybody in town knows."

Norina shrugged.

My mother is pretending not to know, Grazia thought. *It's not wise to know something bad that involves Anna the Heavyweight or her family.*

"Margherita is having an affair with Franchino the Bird's Nest," Anna said.

"The good-looking vendor who cries when he sees a bird's nest?" Angela asked.

"Yes, he's the one. Jesus, Joseph and Mary… he is married and has eleven children."

"Can you do anything to stop him?" Angela asked.

Anna bit her finger. "I can't do anything."

"Why?" Norina and Angela asked in unison.

"That stupid daughter of mine swore on her father's grave that she's going to kill herself if I beat him up," Anna whispered, keeping an eye on the American Wife leaving the store with her wicker carriage filled with costly merchandise. "Look at her. She didn't even say good-bye. Who the hell does she think she is? I'm going to give her a beating one of these days."

"If you do that, you are going to end up in jail," Norina said. "She's a woman. She's going to call the guards for sure."

Anna raised her voice. "I don't mind spending a couple of days in jail."

"You can go ahead of me," Norina said.

Anna turned to Teresina. "Give me a quarter-kilogram of salami."

Reluctantly, Teresina reached for the salami and began to slice it. When she was done, she wrapped the salami in a sheet of white paper.

Anna dipped her hand into her sweater, drew a small black booklet from her brassiere, and handed it to Teresina. "Write the amount."

As soon as Teresina scribbled the amount on the booklet, Anna wrote an X next to it. The X stood for her signature. She then stuffed the booklet back into her brassiere and grabbed the salami. Waving good-bye to all the credit customers, she scrambled outside, eager to eat the delicacy.

The tall credit customer scrunched his forehead and stared at Teresina. "You give her salami on credit?"

Teresina clasped and twisted her hands together. "What do you want me to do? It's been two years that I've been giving her credit, and she hasn't come up with a lira. She says that she'll pay me once her cousin sends her money from Switzerland."

"Don't give her any more credit," the tall paying customer said. "I heard that her cousin from Switzerland passed away."

"If I stop giving her credit, she's never going to pay me," Teresina said.

"If she hasn't paid you in two years, she's already never going to pay you," the tall paying customer said.

Teresina's face blushed. "It pays to be on good terms with her. She can be dangerous."

"True, she might give you a hell of a beating if you cross her," the short credit customer said.

"Let's change the subject," Teresina said. "Let's talk about the good news."

"What news?" Norina asked.

"My daughter is marrying an American," Teresina responded.

Suddenly, Teresina had the undivided attention of every customer in the store.

"It was love at first sight." Teresina flashed a radiant smile. "An American millionaire came into the bottega and bought a whole kilogram of prosciutto. My daughter Chiara sliced the prosciutto for him and he fell in love with her."

"And?" the short credit customer asked.

"The following day, the American sent his cousin to the house with a marriage proposal."

"What did he say?" the tall credit customer asked.

"He said: Teresina, the American that bought a whole kilogram of prosciutto yesterday wants to marry your daughter. He wants an answer in two days."

The short credit customer closed her eyes as she grinned. "It's very romantic."

"We had a family meeting, and we all decided it was a good marriage for Chiara," Teresina said. "He comes from a good family. His father had the good fortune of going to America many years ago. He sent his son back to find a bride."

"A lot of Italians who move to America send their sons to Italy to find a wife," the short credit customer said.

The tall credit customer bobbed his head in agreement. "They prefer to have Italian daughters-in-law."

"Is the American paying for the wedding?" the short credit customer asked.

"He's paying for all the expenses," Teresina said, spreading her arms wide open. "He doesn't want me to spend a lira."

The short credit customer's mouth fell open.

The tall credit customer sighed happily. "It sounds like a fairy tale wedding."

It sounds like an arranged marriage. Did you ask your daughter before consulting the whole family? Grazia wanted to question Teresina, but remained silent.

"I can't believe Chiara is going to be an American Wife," Norina said.

Teresina shook her head. "Chiara is not becoming an American Wife. He's taking her to America with him. She's planning on becoming an American citizen so she'll be able to bring the whole family to America. We're sick of the bottega. Very few people pay us."

Norina drew lira bills from her brassiere and waved them up in the air. "I have money."

Teresina's eyes lit up. "You have the cash to pay your old debt?"

"I have enough money to pay for all the food that I'm going to buy today."

Teresina bit her lower lip. "I shouldn't allow you to buy food if you won't pay your old debt."

Angela patted Teresina's shoulder. "Come on, close one eye. You can't complain about Norina. She only owes a little. She's not like Anna the Heavyweight."

Teresina exhaled heavily. "Thank God she's not like Anna the Heavyweight. Otherwise, I'd go broke."

Norina crossed her hands on her chest. "I swear on my sister's grave that I'm going to pay the old debt when Grazia gets paid."

As Contessa Primavera entered the store, Teresina shifted her attention to her daughter, Pasquina. "Take care of Norina. Give her what she wants. I'll take care of the White Fly."

Pasquina sniffed as she looked at Norina. "What do you need?"

Norina rubbed her chin. "Give me seven kilograms of spaghetti, a liter of oil, and half a kilogram of sugar."

Pasquina was the most unattractive of Teresina's daughters. She was petite, with blemished skin, a long nose, and bulging eyes. She weighed the spaghetti and wrapped them in a sheet of brown paper. She walked out of the room and returned a few minutes later with a bottle of olive oil.

"You also want half a kilogram of sugar?" Pasquina asked, casting a harsh look.

Norina nodded yes.

Pasquina narrowed her eyes. "You shouldn't waste your money on sugar."

"I only buy it once in a while."

Pasquina placed a sheet of brown paper on the scale and dumped a heaping scoop of sugar on it. After she had consulted the scale, she took several spoonfuls of sugar out. She then wrapped the sugar, directing her stare at Grazia. "When you get paid, you'd better bring us the money to settle the old debt."

Grazia's face paled as she bobbed her head in agreement. It was beyond her control. She always gave all the money she earned to her mother.

Norina paid for the groceries and walked out of the bottega, escorted by Grazia and Angela the Crazy Head.

"Teresina got a kiss from the sky," Norina said. "Her daughter is going to marry a millionaire."

"Since one of her daughters is marrying an American, all of Teresina's daughters are going to marry well," Angela said.

Grazia tilted her head and expanded her eyes.

"They're no longer common girls," Angela said. "They've been upgraded. They've become candidates to go to America. Everyone in town is going to want to marry them so they can go to America. You'll see. Even Pasquina might get engaged soon."

Norina wrinkled her nose. "Who the hell is going to marry Pasquina? She's uglier than an old debt. Not even penicillin can save her. She's so ugly that not even a *palazzo* under her name can be enough to convince a man to marry her."

It's so hard to be a woman, Grazia thought. *If a woman is ugly, people hold it against her. I wonder how Pasquina feels about being ugly.*

"The opportunity to go to America is worth more than beauty," Angela said. "You'll see. I'm sure Pasquina will marry a handsome man."

They stopped in front of the Seven Fountains. There were many women fetching water with their buckets. Angela drew a bottle from her fishnet bag and placed it under the faucet. She watched the scintillating water with fascination.

"Mrs. Fatti has a fountain in her kitchen," Norina said.

"She's an American Wife," Angela said. "She can afford luxuries."

"I don't understand why Mrs. Fatti doesn't go to America to live with her husband," Grazia said.

"Mrs. Fatti will never go to America," Angela said.

"Why?" Grazia asked.

Angela flashed a hint of a smile. "Mrs. Fatti is a show-off. In Italy, she derives gratification from showing off her wealth to all the poor people she grew up with. She has a large audience to impress. If she went to America, she'd have no audience. She would be a nobody."

Norina lowered her head and clenched her hands. "We can't impress anyone. We have nothing to show off."

"I can hardly make ends meet," Angela said. "I have a husband in Germany who's living the good life and doesn't send me a lira."

"You're still better off than I am." Norina tapped Angela's arm. "You only have two daughters. You don't have six mouths to feed. Plus, you make money writing letters."

"Things are getting harder these days." Angela sighed. "More children are going to school and people have them write letters."

"Children don't know how to write letters like you do," Norina said.

Angela drew her bottle away from the faucet. "Most of the farmers don't care about quality. They let their children write letters. My best customers are the American Wives. They have the cash, and they want to improve themselves. They even call me to read them novels."

"I loved all the novels you read us about Lucrezia Borgia," Grazia said.

"I'm fond of Lucrezia Borgia." Angela stamped her foot. "She poisoned her lovers. My husband deserves a lover like her."

"A lot of men have come back to town," Norina said. "I'm sure your husband is going to come back too."

Angela raised her voice. "A lot of men who have abandoned their wives come back from abroad when they get old and decrepit, and it breaks my heart that their wives take them back."

The poor women have no choice, Grazia thought. *They have no jobs and, no money, and they need a husband to support them. It's so hard being a woman.*

"Any husband is better than no husband at all," Norina said. "They say that a house where a man doesn't set foot is a miserable house."

"Reheated cabbage and recycled lovers have never been to my taste." Angela shook her head. "I don't want my husband to come back."

Grazia nodded. "If a woman had a choice, she would never take back a husband who betrayed her."

"The problem is most of the women in this town don't have a choice." Angela's eyes dimmed. "They have to live and die with their husbands. Being married is just a way to survive. A woman is like her husband's employee."

The sight of Bellina the Good Deed carrying her bucket captured their attention. Bellina had polio when she was a child, and it had left her with a crippled leg. They called her the Good Deed because she was always willing to help others despite her disability.

"Bellina is struggling to carry the bucket, but she still does it," Grazia said.

"Bellina doesn't have a place of her own. She lives with her mean cousin, Filomena the Grave Heart," Angela said. "Bellina wants to feel useful, but her cousin Filomena treats her like a slave. Women need real jobs, but in this country, there's barely any work for us. Our sky is dark."

"We can't live under a dark sky forever." Norina looked up in the sky. "The colors of the sky are going to change one day or another. Chiara's sky got bright overnight. She's marrying an American."

"I wish I could find my brother in America," Angela said. "If I could get ahold of him, my sky would change. I'll be able to emigrate to America and live under a better sky, an American sky. America is a better place for women. Women can be independent."

"*Mamma*, I have to go to work," Grazia said. "I can't be late."

"I have to go too," Angela said. "I have a letter to write for an American Wife."

Grazia and Angela treaded down the street. Norina watched them until they disappeared into the distance before she proceeded down the street.

Norina entered the butcher shop and ordered six veal cutlets. Domenico the Butcher gave her an amazed look, which intensified when Norina took the six hundred lire out of her brassiere to pay for the meat in full.

In a hundred years, I would have never thought that I would see Norina purchasing veal, Domenico thought. *People like her usually buy horsemeat. Maybe one of her daughters got engaged.* He looked at Norina as she sauntered out of the shop, and remembered the crush he had on her when they were young. He flashed a light smile. *She's still a beautiful woman.*

When Norina entered Saint Peter Street, she waved at Titina the Alligator who was seated by her front door, knitting a sock.

"I went to the bottega and the butcher," Norina said, shaking her fishnet bag.

Titina placed her work aside and fixed her eyes on Norina's bag.

She's envious, Norina thought, looking at Titina's stunned face.

Norina loved to attract envy. It gave her the illusion of being rich. Rich people were envied. Poor people received nothing but pity.

Once inside her house, Norina placed the groceries daintily on the table. Streams of sunlight filtered through the glass door and reflected on the goodies. She locked the sugar and the bottle of oil in the credenza. She had to keep such treasures out of the reach of the children.

Humming a song, Norina busied herself cooking the precious veal. Even though she enjoyed the delicious aroma that filled the whole kitchen, she opened the door to allow the fragrance to diffuse onto the street as well.

As soon as she finished cooking, Norina stepped out of the house and waved at her children playing down the street. "Come and eat the veal," she yelled.

The children stopped playing and ran towards the house, eager to eat the delicacy.

"We're having veal," Pasquale shouted, exposing a bright smile.

Colombina the Farmer's Wife and Titina the Alligator widened their eyes as they exchanged looks.

"How can Norina afford veal?" Colombina asked.

"She's got a rich lover for sure," Titina responded.

Colombina raised an eyebrow. "God knows what people do to afford meat."

The children gorged themselves on the veal. It was tender and full of flavor. Norina thought Grazia was not entitled to the meat, since she got plenty to eat at her employer's home. Besides, Grazia would have disapproved of such extravagance if she found out. Norina felt she had the right to a few luxuries in life.

IV

S tands topped with colorful umbrellas were brightened by the sun. Vendors advertised their fruits and vegetables with loud and harmonious calls. The poor, searching for bargains with their fishnet bags, circulated through the street like bees in a honeycomb. The wealthy, wheeling their wicker carriages, were greeted respectfully by merchants selling top quality fresh produce.

Grazia walked with her head down, attempting to avoid the gazes of vendors who had given her credit in the past. Her mother had a balance due with many vendors. A chill swept over Grazia as she recalled creditors that had barked at her demanding payment of her family's debts. To her relief, the greengrocer market was overcrowded and none of the creditors noticed her.

Grazia stopped in front of Olga the Scared Cat's stand. Olga had the look of a scared cat. She had brownish marks on her face, her white hair was permanently disheveled, and her blue eyes had a wild stare. She always dressed in black and wandered forlornly through the fields at all hours of the night. There were rumors that she stole the superlative fruits and vegetables during the night and sold them during the day. Many people suspected that was why her prices were unbeatable. Even though Olga offered the poor people affordable quality produce, many people were afraid of her and didn't give her any business. They were convinced she was some sort of witch who gave the evil eye, the *malocchio*.

Olga was always kind to the children. She spent most of the money she earned buying candies for poverty-stricken children and liquor for herself. Many of the children believed Olga the Scared Cat was a good witch. They called her their Fairy Godmother.

Olga gave Grazia a harsh look. "You are a Voltini. Your mother has debts with many vendors."

Grazia drew one hundred lire from her purse and showed it to the spooky vendor. "Give me a bunch of broccoli-rabe."

Olga grabbed the money and placed it furtively in her pocket. She reached for a bunch of broccoli-rabe and wrapped it in a sheet of newspaper. When she was done, she tossed the bundle into Grazia's hands.

As soon as Grazia walked into the house, Norina approached her and asked, "The vendors didn't ask about old debts?"

"No, I bought the broccoli-rabe from Olga the Scared Cat." Grazia exhaled. "You don't have any debts with her."

"I never bought anything from Olga the Scared Cat." Norina slammed her hands on the table. "I stay away from her. She gives the *malocchio*."

"The *malocchio* is superstitious nonsense. I don't believe anyone can just give a person a curse." Grazia placed the broccoli-rabe in a bucket filled with water. "I'm going to work," she said, scrambling out of the house.

The broccoli-rabe standing in the bucket looked like a composition of green flowers. Humming a song, Norina washed and chopped the broccoli-rabe. When she was done, she placed a cauldron filled with water on the stove. She lit a match and attempted to turn on the burner until the match died out. Her whole body trembled as she came to the devastating realization the tank was out of gas. She couldn't cook.

Norina's eyes brimmed with tears. *Olga the Scared Cat did give Grazia the malocchio and Grazia passed it on to me.* She threw herself onto a chair and laid her head on the table. Tears were streaming down her face. *What am I going to give my children for dinner?*

Besides the sugar, Norina had no food in the house that could be eaten uncooked. If she had only bought bread instead of pasta, she could have fed her children. They loved fresh bread dipped in water and oil. It had a rich taste. Norina calculated she didn't have enough money to buy a new gas tank. Regretfully, she concluded that she would have to use the money she had aside for Grazia's portrait to buy something that could be eaten raw. Pasquale popped into the house, startling her. Norina hastily wiped away her tears with the backs of her hands.

"*Mamma*, is dinner ready? I'm starved," Pasquale shouted.

"I'm going to cook when Grazia comes home," Norina said. "Go back to playing."

Pasquale scrambled out of the house.

Norina stepped outside and sat by her door. She wished Grazia would bring some food home from work. Titina the Alligator walked by with a basket full of fennel.

Norina forced a smile. "Where did you get the fennel?"

"From Giovanni the Farmer." Titina raised her chin. "You buy veal from the butcher and goodies from the bottega. I settle for fennel."

She's envious, but she doesn't know that I wish I had her fennel right now, Norina thought.

"I also got a whole kilogram of fennel for Carolina the Good Life because she doesn't want to cook. Her baby boy is sick and she's taking care of him." Titina lowered her voice. "That baby is always sick. I don't think he's going to live long."

"*Mamma mia!* Don't say that." Norina's eyes became gloomy. *I can't ask Carolina to use her stove. Carolina is busy taking care of her sick son.*

Norina headed to Mrs. Fatti's house, entertaining the hope that the American Wife would let her use her stove.

Mrs. Fatti knows how to behave like a signora. She's not going to tell anybody if I used her stove, Norina thought. Once she reached the house, she saw Serafina the Maid seated by the front door.

Serafina gave Norina a stern look.

"Is Mrs. Fatti home?" Norina asked.

"No, she's out of town. Her sister is getting married tomorrow. Baronessa Rosa went with Mrs. Fatti because she's going to sing in church." Serafina raised an eyebrow. "What do you want from Mrs. Fatti?"

"I wanted to ask her if her husband knows my cousin who lives in America."

Serafina twisted her face. "Everybody says that they have relatives in America."

Norina walked away. She didn't bother to retort to Serafina. Her mind was filled with worries, and she had no one to turn to. Her brother Vituccio and her sisters-in-law were out of town. Norina couldn't possibly use her poor neighbors' gas ranges after showing them she had granted herself the luxury of buying veal.

"You wasted all your money on veal and you want to use our stoves? You should have used the money for a gas tank," Norina imagined Titina the Alligator would say.

The sunset gradually dimmed the brightness of the day. The sky turned muddy gray. Many people on the street appeared saddened by the gloomy dusk sky. The street was a world at once cheered by the poor children's bustle and oppressed by the mute worries of their poor parents.

Seated by her front door, Old Veronica had Little Donato on her lap. The baby applauded with joy as the old woman began to sing his favorite song. Old Veronica's eyes released intense warmth. The image of the old woman and Little Donato faded under the sky, which had become a deep gray as the evening descended on the town.

Even the houses had been absorbed by the shades of the sky. They looked murky in that obscurity. Norina felt lost in the dark. People on the street seemed to be intimidated by the darkness as well and retired into their homes. They looked like walking shadows, swallowed by their doorways.

Suddenly, feeble lights, coming from many windows illuminated the street. People were having dinner. Norina felt disheartened. She was the only one who couldn't cook the evening meal.

One by one, the lights emanating from the houses disappeared. When supper was done the poor walked out of their dwellings and sat by their front entrances. The street had gotten so obscure that the houses and the people were barely visible.

All at once, the small street lamps lit up, projecting a gleam on the houses and the people. To Norina's relief, a small figure emerged down the street. She recognized Grazia's black dress fluttering in harmony with her movement. Norina's face brightened when she noticed her daughter was carrying a bag.

"I brought something," Grazia whispered as she walked forward.

Norina followed her daughter inside the house.

"My boss gave me a slice of cheese because she didn't like the taste of it," Grazia said. "We can grate it over the pasta."

Norina scrunched her forehead. A slice of cheese wouldn't satisfy her children's appetite. "I want you to go to Giovanni the Farmer and buy a kilogram of fennel."

"We have plenty of food."

"We have no gas in the tank. We can't even boil water. We can't use Aunt Clotilde's and Aunt Marta's stoves because they're both away on the pilgrimage. The children are hungry." Norina reached for the lira coins and handed them to Grazia.

Reluctantly, Grazia headed to Giovanni the Farmer's house. She wished fervently for his son Giorgio to answer the door instead of his wife. Colombina treated her like a worm. Giorgio, on the other hand, treated her kindly, and had asked her out many times. Though

Grazia had a soft spot for Giorgio, she had always refused to date him, knowing his mother had absolutely forbidden him to go out with a Voltini girl.

"Those girls are nothing but worms. They're so poor that they don't even have the eyes to cry," she had heard Colombina say.

"A guy who has serious intentions has to ask your mother's permission to go out with you," Grazia's mother had always told her.

Giorgio had never asked Norina's permission to date Grazia. Consequently, Grazia assumed he just wanted to fool around with her.

A bright light radiated from the farmer's quarters. When Grazia reached the house, she peered through the window and saw the whole family seated at the table around a cake. They were probably celebrating a birthday. It was the most inappropriate possible time to disturb them. Her heart pounded as she waited in front of the door, attempting to muster the courage to knock. She felt like an intruder. As Giorgio caught sight of her through the window he instantly got up from the table, elated and surprised.

"There's someone standing by the door. I'll go and see who it is," Grazia heard him say.

As soon as Colombina eyed Grazia she grabbed Giorgio by the arm and shouted, "Don't you dare open that door. Stay where you are."

Immediately, Grazia was faced with Colombina's stern look. Grazia clasped her hands together to keep them from shaking.

"This is no time to disturb people," Colombina bellowed.

Grazia's face blushed. "I need a kilogram of fennel."

Colombina rubbed her thumb against her index finger and middle finger. "Show me the money."

Grazia promptly handed Colombina the lira coins.

Colombina giggled as she placed the coins in her brassiere. "Remind your mother that she owes me five hundred lire for the tomatoes. What you just gave me isn't even enough to pay for the old debt. If you want fennel, you have to give me more money."

"I don't have any more money." Grazia bit her lower lip so as not to cry. She felt humiliated. Her humiliation intensified when she looked thought the window and met Giorgio's stare. She read compassion in his eyes. His compassion made her feel even worse than a worm.

"Come back when you have enough money," Colombina shouted. "I can't give you any more credit."

Grazia squeezed her eyes as Colombina slammed the door in her face. She walked away, relieved to be out of Colombina's sight. Grazia heard hollering coming from inside the house. It was Colombina chastising her son for staring at a Voltini girl. Grazia felt so mortified that tears rolled down her cheeks. When she saw Titina the Alligator, she hastily dried her tears with the backs of her hands.

Titina indicated the children standing by their front door. "Your brothers and sisters are waiting for you."

A pale light from the street lamp bathed the children. Eager for food, they waved at their motherly sister. Their faces drooped as soon as they noticed Grazia was empty-handed.

"We're hungry," Pasquale whispered.

"What are we having for dinner?" Olimpia asked.

Grazia patted Olimpia's arm. "Let's go inside."

Grazia entered the house. She was followed immediately by her siblings. Once inside the house, they all gathered around Grazia.

"What happened?" Norina asked.

Grazia twisted her face. "Colombina took the money. She refused to give me any more credit. She said you owe her money for the tomatoes. Why didn't you tell me about the tomatoes?"

Norina placed her palm on her forehead. "I forgot about the tomatoes. It was a long time ago."

"What are we having for dinner?" Pasquale asked.

Norina drew the key to the credenza from her pocket and waved it in the air. "There's a solution for everything. Only dead people don't have any solutions. We can have sugar and water."

"Only sugar and water?" Pasquale asked as Norina unlocked the credenza.

"You can also have the cheese my boss gave me. Sugar and cheese give you a lot of energy." Grazia widened her eyes, surprised by her own words.

Grazia promptly sliced the cheese into equal shares and gave it to her siblings. The children ate the cheese and drank glasses of sugar and water to wash it down.

"Is there anything else to eat?" Olimpia asked.

Norina forced a smile. "Tomorrow, we're going to get the new gas tank and we're going to eat like queens and kings."

The children smiled at the prospect of getting a good meal.

"Go out and play," Grazia said to her siblings. *If they have fun playing, maybe they'll forget about being hungry.*

Norina gave it a lot of thought, but she couldn't find a way to come up with the money to buy the gas tank. Her last resort was praying. It broke Grazia's heart to see her mother down on her knees before Our Lady of Sorrows. Norina was begging the statue to provide her with the money for the gas tank.

Grazia's eyes lit up as an idea came to her mind. "*Mamma,* did you use the bottle of oil that you bought from the bottega?"

Norina shook her head. "I didn't open the bottle."

"We can sell the bottle of oil to Carolina the Good Life. We sold her a bottle of oil Uncle Vituccio gave us once, remember?"

Norina joined the palms of her hands. "The Madonna has answered my prayers."

Grazia led Norina down the stairs. Norina quickly unlocked the credenza, took out the bottle of oil and handed it to Grazia. Grazia covered the bottle with a cloth and dashed out of the house. She walked swiftly to Carolina's house and knocked on the front door. The door sprang open and Carolina appeared.

"What brings you here in the evening?" Carolina asked as she led Grazia into her house.

Grazia forced a light smile. "A bottle of oil."

Carolina scrunched her forehead. "A bottle of oil?"

Grazia placed the bottle on the table. "I bought a bottle of oil from the bottega, but my Uncle Vituccio brought us one just like it. We don't want to keep too much oil in the house. My sisters will waste it. Olimpia and Caterina play a game with the oil."

"What kind of game?"

"They make rings in the water with drops of oil and whoever gets the bigger ring wins." Grazia's mouth fell open. She was astounded by her own words. She couldn't believe how she came up with all those lies.

"What your sisters do is not a game." Carolina narrowed her eyes. "It's a way to find out if they have the *malocchio*."

"The *malocchio*?"

"My son has the *malocchio*." Carolina's eyes shone with tears. "Was my son sick when you saw him?"

"Not at all, he looked so healthy and adorable."

"People who complimented my Little Gianni were jealous. They wished bad things on him. That's why he got sick so suddenly." Carolina let out a long sigh. "My baby boy is precious. He has been a blessing from the sky. He saved my marriage."

"How did he save your marriage?"

"My husband was so obsessed with a son that when I had my fourth girl, he lost interest in me. He was convinced that I wasn't capable of having a boy, so he hardly sent me any money from Venezuela. I was afraid that he was going to find a lover in Venezuela just to get the son he wanted."

"That's terrible."

"Zina the Silk Stockings's husband went to Venezuela and abandoned her because she had five girls. People say he lives with a woman that gave him three boys."

"I heard Zina works very hard repairing silk stockings with her little mending machine, and she can barely feed her children."

"She's still young and beautiful. Sometimes she has affairs. I heard that she has a lover who buys her a lot of gifts. I also heard he's so ugly that she's ashamed to be seen with him."

It's so hard to be a woman, Grazia thought. *Zina sleeps with men that repulse her, just to survive.*

"Come and see my Little Gianni." Carolina escorted Grazia into the back room.

The baby was lying in a cradle surrounded by his four sisters.

"Look how red his face is." Carolina touched the baby's forehead. "He has a high fever."

"Did you call the doctor?"

"I call the doctor every time he gets sick. The doctor doesn't know where the fever comes from."

"You should hire Old Veronica to pray for his well-being."

Carolina flashed a glint of a smile. "Good idea."

Grazia blew a kiss at the baby. "I hope he gets well soon."

"Thank you for your good wishes. I can sense that they come from your heart."

Grazia compressed her lips. *Carolina forgot all about the bottle of oil.* "It's late. I have to go home."

"I didn't even offer you a glass of almond milk. My head is not in the right place."

Carolina led Grazia out of the room. Once into the front room, she noticed the bottle of oil standing on the table.

"I'll buy the oil." Carolina reached for the money and handed it to Grazia. "I'll need plenty of oil to test for the *malocchio*."

Grazia's eyes sparkled as she pranced out of the house.

Little Donato had fallen asleep in Norina's arms. She carried the baby to the bedroom. A chill swept over her as she hugged his little body. He was so skinny.

He's not getting the right food. He needs to be fed like the American Wife's son, with plenty of milk, eggs, and meat, Norina thought, placing her baby in the crib. She covered Little Donato with a blanket and gave him a light kiss on the cheek. She was accustomed to kissing her children when they were asleep. "If Carolina the Good Life buys the oil, I'm going to get the gas tank. I'm going to cook, and I'm going to give you lots of pasta and broccoli-rabe," she whispered, caressing her baby's face. She stiffened up when Grazia bounded into the room.

"Carolina gave me four hundred lire," Grazia said, handing the coins to her mother. "She gave me more than what we paid for the oil."

Norina beamed. She swiftly placed the coins in her brassiere. "That's enough for the down payment on the gas tank."

Grazia gritted her teeth. "What are you going to do if Paolino the Gas Man wants the payment in full?"

Norina flapped her hands. "I'm going to convince him that I have the money."

In the evening, the poor would sit outside their front doors and catch up on the latest gossip. As they passed by, Norina and Grazia nodded hello to friends and acquaintances. As soon as they turned their backs, people whispered among themselves. They were surprised to see two women walking the streets in the late evening, and wondered where they were going.

The gas store was located in the old part of town. It was situated in the front room of a house. In the back, where the family lived, were the kitchen and the bedroom. The owner of the store was a short and lean man named Paolino. Paolino's wife, Ninetta, a heavy and tall woman, was in the store most of the time, since Paolino was busy delivering the gas tanks. Because Paolino turned his feet out when he walked, he always gave the impression that he was about to fall. Many people wondered how Paolino managed to lift the tanks without tumbling.

They thought his wife should have delivered the tanks on his behalf, but since the woman was always pregnant, she couldn't possibly carry the heavy containers.

When Norina and Grazia walked into the store, Ninetta greeted them warmly. Norina pulled the coins out of her brassiere and waved them around enthusiastically.

Ninetta flashed a smile as she followed the trail of the glittering coins. "You need a new gas tank?"

Norina nodded.

"Paolino is not here. He's doing an emergency delivery for an American Wife."

Norina gave Ninetta the coins. "This is the deposit for the gas tank. I need the tank as soon as possible. I bought two kilograms of broccoli-rabe and ten kilograms of pasta and I can't cook."

Ninetta's mouth fell open. "You bought ten kilograms of pasta?"

"Yes, I hate to go back and forth to the bottega. So when I go, I buy a lot of food. I also bought two kilograms of sugar. It's good to have sugar in the house."

Someone who buys all that food has the money to pay for a gas tank, Ninetta thought. "I'll send my husband to your house tomorrow morning to install the new gas tank, but make sure you have the money to pay the balance."

"I have the rest of the money." Norina dipped her hand into her brassiere. "If you want, I can give it to you right now. Sooner or later, I have to pay."

Grazia's face paled. *If Ninetta wants the full amount, we're going to look like fools.*

"You don't have to," Ninetta said, entertaining the hope Norina would insist out of courtesy.

Grazia gave a sigh of relief.

In a fraction of a second, Norina pulled her empty hand from her brassiere. "I'm going to give Paolino the rest of the money tomorrow."

Grazia noticed the disappointment on Ninetta's face.

The only source of light in the black sky was the moon. The night had descended on the streets, which were deserted and absorbed in a deep silence. All the doors and windows were shut now, and Norina and Grazia were the only people on the street. Consumed with worry about the gas tank, they were not afraid to walk into the dark night.

"We don't have the money to pay the balance," Grazia said. "What if Paolino refuses to install the gas tank?"

"I'm not going to tell him that I don't have the money till after he puts the tank in." Norina's lips quivered. "Do you think that he's going to take the tank back if I don't give him the rest of the money?"

"I hope he doesn't. He did take Titina the Alligator's tank back once."

"Titina has no manners." Norina twisted her lips. "She cursed out Paolino. That's why he took the tank back."

Grazia raised her eyebrows. "The least one should do is be courteous to one's creditors."

V

Sewing and embroidery were skills girls would learn for their own needs and ostensibly to have something to fall back on in the future.

"Learn a trade and put it aside. One day you may use it," an Italian proverb said.

Many women who weren't lucky enough to get married, made a living with the skills they had acquired during their youth. Two unwed middle-aged women supervised the Sewing School: Miss Ombretta Beffi and Miss Aria Levigni. Miss Ombretta taught sewing while Miss Aria taught embroidery. Since they had dedicated their entire lives to their trade, which was considered a form of art, they were bestowed the title of Maestra. Together they were the Maestre.

Ombretta the Maestra was considered the best dressmaker in town. The garments she crafted were so expensive that only the White Flies were able to afford them. Among the White Flies, she preferred the American Wives because they were more generous than the aristocratic women. The American Wives also had the most fashionable styles made, favoring modern looks with dazzling colors. Just the opposite, the aristocratic women were conservative, always picking old-fashioned patterns and dull shades.

In the little town, the school was attended by girls eager to learn how to sew their own clothes and embroider their own linens as a trousseau for their marriages. The school girls who couldn't afford to pay the tuition all worked as assistants. Grazia was the best part-time assistant.

The Maestre wanted to hire Grazia as a full-time member of the staff with no pay for two years, and minimal pay for the following years. Though Grazia loved the fine arts of sewing and embroidery, she refused the offer. She couldn't give up her day job. She needed to earn money to help her family.

Grazia honed her artistry on what fabrics she was able to obtain from the clothes her employer gave her. She nourished the wish that one day she would be able to select and buy new fabrics and linens. She needed at least four sets of sheets and tablecloths for a trousseau. A young lady had to own a dowry and a trousseau to marry well. A rich girl's trousseau consisted of a dozen sets of sheets, towels, tablecloths, nightgowns, and fine outfits. The entire trousseau would be displayed in the bride-to-be's house traditionally a few weeks prior to the wedding.

The young apprentices loved high fashion apparel. When the Maestre were not around, they took the opportunity to try on the American Wives' attire. They derived great gratification from adorning themselves in those outfits. It gave them the illusion of being American spouses. Marrying an American was the dream of many eligible *signorine* in town.

Grazia looked forward to going to the Sewing School. It was the only time she got to spend with her girlfriends: Tonia, Patrizia, and Orsola. Grazia's girlfriends always boasted about having boyfriends who whistled when they passed by their houses, wrote them love letters and had flowers delivered to them. Grazia had only dreamed of any kind of romance. She secretly wished she could have a boyfriend.

Tonia, Patrizia, and Orsola had busy social lives. They went to parties and went dancing. They always encouraged Grazia to go dancing with them. At times, Grazia was tempted to accept their invitations, but once she gave it a serious thought, she always refused because her mother's objections were so deeply ingrained in her mind.

Grazia woke up early in the morning and dressed in her best black clothes. After combing her hair with care, she looked at herself in the mirror. Her hair looked fine, but her black frock made her look awkward.

Her image disappeared off the mirror as she ran down the stairs.

I'll try out something colorful at school, Grazia thought, flashing a glint of a grin. Once she set foot into the kitchen, she was faced with her mother.

"What is Ombretta the Maestra sewing lately?" Norina asked.

"The Maestra is sewing the wedding gown and eight outfits for Chiara, Teresina's daughter," Grazia replied.

It was a custom for a newlywed woman to wear a new ensemble every day, for eight days in a row. The bride would show off her wardrobe strolling on the streets, escorted by her husband. The newlyweds would visit a different relative each day. It was a way of showing the relatives respect, and gratitude for their wedding gifts.

Norina exhaled. "Chiara received a blessing from the sky."

"The wedding gown is made of French satin. The train is the longest one I've ever seen. When Chiara came for the fitting, they all looked at her as if she were some sort of princess."

"She is a princess. She's marrying an American."

"The eight outfits Ombretta the Maestra is sewing for Chiara are marvelous, and they all have matching hats."

"For my eight days of the bride, I only had four outfits, but they were the most beautiful ones in town." Norina closed her eyes and smiled. "People waited on their balconies for me to come out of my house."

"I know. A lot of people have told me your garments were stunning."

Norina's smile faded as she opened her eyes. *Those days are gone.* Now she would dress in rags if it weren't for the clothes Grazia's employer gave her.

"I'm going to the Sewing School." Grazia rushed out of the house.

At the Sewing School, Chiara's wedding gown was on display. It was the most beautiful nuptial dress the Maestre had ever designed.

"Fine fabric makes a dress precious," Ombretta the Maestra said.

"Fine embroidery transforms a dress into a work of art," Aria the Maestra said.

The wedding gown was indeed treated like a priceless work of art. Whenever the Maestre were not around, a student assumed responsibility for guarding the gown.

Ombretta the Maestra pointed at Grazia. "Today, you are responsible for guarding the wedding gown."

"Thank you," Grazia said. "It's an honor."

Aria the Maestra turned to the students. "Now we must go. We won't be out long. You'd better behave. I don't want any complaints from the neighbors."

"We won't make a sound," Patrizia said.

The Maestre walked out of the room. They headed to the flea market that took place in the *piazza* every Saturday. The students remained still until the Maestre's steps faded into silence.

Patrizia jumped up. "Now we can play."

The students cheered with ecstasy.

"What game are we playing today?" Tonia asked.

"We have to stage the wedding. Orsola can play the groom, since she's big and tall, and Grazia can play the bride."

Grazia's face flushed. "I have to wear the wedding gown?"

Patrizia couldn't help but laugh. "Of course. What kind of bride would you be without a wedding gown?"

Grazia shook her head. "I can't do that."

Patrizia scrunched her forehead. "Why not?"

"The wedding gown could get dirty."

Orsola giggled. "Nonsense, we've always tried dresses on. They've never gotten dirty."

"Tonia can wear the dress of the mother of the bride," Patrizia said. "I need volunteers to wear the outfits of the sisters of the bride."

Eagerly, the volunteers raised their hands. Patrizia picked seven girls willing to play the sisters.

"What about the girls that didn't get picked?" Orsola asked.

"Whoever didn't get picked can play the wedding guests," Patrizia said. "You can wear the costumes you like."

"What are you wearing?" Tonia asked.

"I don't have to get dressed up," Patrizia said. "I'm going to play the role of a relative who has not been invited to the wedding and I'm going to make a scene."

"Good idea." Tonia slipped on Teresina's frock. Since the dress was huge in the bosom, she used two throw pillows to fill in her breasts. "How do I look?"

"You look great," Orsola said.

"You have to mimic Teresina's voice," Patrizia said.

"Of course," Tonia said, imitating Teresina's high-pitched voice. "This is the most important day of my life. I'm getting rid of my third daughter. Too bad I have seven more daughters to go. It's not going to be easy to get rid of all of them. I should put them on sale."

"Thank God you have a bottega," Patrizia said. "You should put them on display with your salami."

The girls laughed.

"Quiet," Patrizia shouted. Let's start the wedding scene."

Seven girls donned the bride's sisters' garb. Since Orsola played the groom, she pulled her hair back and painted a mustache on her lips. Two girls helped Grazia slip on the bride's wedding gown. Grazia looked spectacular. It looked as if it was shaped to fit her body.

"The wedding gown looks better on you than on Chiara," Tonia said. "You're much prettier than the actual bride."

Grazia's jaw dropped. She had never imagined being considered prettier than Chiara.

As soon as Patrizia hummed the nuptial march the girls, sporting their new dresses, walked down the imaginary aisle. The girls clad in the wedding guests' outfits amused themselves, making fun of the sisters and the mother of the bride. Grazia was the only one who was more scared than amused.

Grazia sat on a chair. "I can't do this. The Maestre could come at any minute."

"Don't be a chicken," Patrizia said. "They won't come back for at least an hour."

"We have plenty of time to have fun," Orsola said.

A rumble came from the stairs. The girls immediately stopped their pageantry.

Orsola wiped her lips with the backs of her hands, attempting to remove the painted mustache. "Who could that be?"

Grazia's whole body trembled as she got up from the chair. "What should I do?"

"You should all hide in the fitting room and change back into your clothes," Patrizia said.

After the girls ran into the fitting room, Patrizia headed towards the entrance and opened the door. To her relief, she was faced with Mrs. Matilde Fatti.

Patrizia forced a smile. "Good to see you, *Signora* Fatti. I heard a strange noise coming from outside."

"A bucket fell down the stairs," Mrs. Fatti said. "I saw a cat running away. He must have pushed the bucket."

Patrizia exhaled heavily. "It was only a cat."

"I want to have a dress made. I've decided to wear something new for Chiara's wedding."

"Ombretta the Maestra is not here. She went to the flea market."

"To tell the truth, I also came for a peek at Chiara's wedding gown. May I see it?"

"The wedding gown is in the fitting room. Grazia is guarding it." Patrizia winked. "I'll see if I can persuade Grazia to show you the gown."

Mrs. Fatti watched Patrizia walk into the fitting room and resisted the urge to follow her.

As soon as Patrizia entered the fitting room, Grazia asked, "Who was at the door?"

Patrizia shrugged. "It was just an American Wife. Did you hang the wedding gown?"

"Of course."

"Bring it into the front room. Mrs. Fatti wants to see it."

Grazia bit her lower lip. "Does she know?"

"Know what?"

"That I tried on the wedding gown?"

"Of course not."

Grazia lifted up the wedding gown and carried it out to the front room. She felt so guilty for wearing it that she was relieved the gown covered her face. She was followed immediately by the girls who were hiding in the fitting room. It seemed like a small procession led by the wedding gown.

"It's a masterpiece," Mrs. Fatti said all in one sigh.

"We usually don't show it to anyone," Patrizia said. "We're making an exception for you."

The American Wife flashed a smile. She felt honored to have been privileged to see the nuptial dress.

Grazia set down the gown and gasped for air.

"Good to see you, Grazia," Mrs. Fatti said.

"Please don't tell anybody that we have shown you the wedding gown," Grazia said.

"I won't say a word. When is Ombretta the Maestra coming back?"

"It may take her awhile," Patrizia said. "You're better off coming back later."

"I'll come back some another time." Mrs. Fatti exited the room.

Grazia took a close look at the precious gown and sighed with relief. "Thank God it didn't get dirty."

"I have an important announcement to make," Patrizia shouted. "Tonight, my cousin Alvaro is having a party at his house. You are all invited."

The girls bounced up and down, waving their hands up in air.

Grazia took Patrizia aside. "I can't come. My mother won't let me."

"I'll come and talk to your mother." Patrizia patted Grazia's arm. "Plenty of boys like you. You shouldn't miss out on the opportunity. If you come to the dance, you'll find a boyfriend in no time."

Showing a bright smile, Norina welcomed Paolino the Gas Man. Paolino responded with a timid nod as he wheeled the gas tank into the house on a dolly. He staggered as he lifted the tank and placed it underneath the stove. He looked like he was going to fall under the tank.

I can't figure out how he can walk with those weird feet, Norina thought. *Thank God he didn't fall down.*

Despite his disability, Paolino was a fast worker. He removed the empty tank and installed the new one in ten minutes.

"I'm done," Paolino said.

Norina's face blushed. "I'm going to give you the rest of the money for the gas tank as soon as my daughter gets paid. She has a high-class job. She works in the city for a lawyer."

"But you told my wife that you had the money for the balance." Paolino tapped on the handle of his dolly with his fingertips. "You said that you were even willing to give her the money yesterday."

"I did have the money, but I gave it to a friend in need."

"I hope you don't wait until you need another gas tank to give me the money."

"I'm going to give you the money soon." Norina crossed her hands on her chest. "I give you my word of honor."

"Your word of honor isn't worth anything," Paolino wanted to say, but he remained silent. He was tempted to take the gas tank back, but he refrained from doing so as he realized he had to deliver a tank to a White Fly who was a good customer. He didn't want to be late and disappoint her.

As Paolino wheeled his dolly in a hurry, he stumbled so much that Norina had the impression he was going to collapse. To her relief, Paolino didn't tumble, but shuffled out of the house. Norina sensed he was in great need of money. She freed herself of the guilt in her con-science by promising herself she would pay him as soon as possible.

Norina cooked while humming a song. She felt rich as she thought about her seven kilograms of pasta.

At lunch, Norina served abundant portions of spaghetti and broccoli-rabe to her children. As soon as they were finished eating, the children scrambled out of the house, eager to play. Norina sat outside by her front door. She huffed when she saw her sister-in-law Clotilde walking forward. She gave Clotilde a welcoming grin even though she was not happy to see her. Since Clotilde was her late husband's sister, Norina felt she had to pay her respect.

"I just got back from the pilgrimage," Clotilde said.

"Sit down," Norina said, indicating a chair.

As Clotilde sank her heavy body onto the chair that groaned due to her weight, she handed Norina an envelope. "I came to give you a letter of condolence from my cousin Tettina who lives in America."

Norina tore open the envelope. Her face drooped. "She didn't send any money. American relatives send money with a letter of condolence."

"I'm surprised my cousin didn't send any money. I'm going to write to my Aunt Elvira to inform that my brother passed away. I'm sure she'll send a letter of condolences and money."

Norina gave the envelope to Clotilde. "You can keep the letter. I don't even know how to read it."

"I can read it for you."

"Never mind." Sensing hot flashes on her face, Norina drew her fan from her pocket and fanned herself vigorously. She felt relieved as the soft wind caressed her face.

Clotilde noticed the fan was mended on one side. "The mending is too visible. Don't bring the fan to church."

"I never bring my mended fan to church."

At the sight of Grazia and her companion emerging down the street, Norina closed her fan. "Grazia is coming with her friend Patrizia."

"I'm glad Grazia associates with a good girl like Patrizia. A proverb says: 'Tell me who your friends are and I'll tell you who you are.'"

The girls waved as they walked forward.

"It's a pleasure to see you, *Signora* Norina and *Signora* Clotilde," Patrizia said.

Norina and Clotilde smiled.

"*Signora* Norina, my cousin Alvaro is having a party at his house," Patrizia said. "May Grazia come?"

Clotilde raised an eyebrow. "I heard Alvaro has wild parties at his house when his parents go out of town."

Norina got up from the chair. "My daughter is not allowed to go to parties." She gave Patrizia a stern look. "If you dare to take Grazia to a party behind my back, I'm going to forbid her to go to the Sewing School."

Patrizia didn't respond. She waved good-bye and walked speedily away.

"I cannot believe she had the courage to ask me such a thing," Norina shouted.

"Let's talk inside," Clotilde whispered. "I don't want the neighbors to hear our conversation."

Clotilde and Norina dragged Grazia inside the house.

"A girl who goes to parties without her parents can only ruin her reputation," Clotilde said.

"But my cousins Mariella and Catia always go to their friends' parties without their parents and have a lot of fun dancing," Grazia said.

"There's a big difference between you and your cousins. They were born under a better sky." Norina banged the fan on the table. "Our sky is dark."

Grazia's eyes brimmed with tears. "It's not fair. Just because I'm poor, I can't have any fun."

"Rich girls can have fun. They got nothing to lose. Sooner or later, someone in town is going to marry them." Norina pointed the fan at

Grazia. She looked like a mean teacher threatening her with a baton. "You are so poor that you don't even have the eyes to cry. You only have a good reputation, and you can't afford to ruin it."

"Once you ruin your reputation, you're lost forever," Clotilde said. "You are not going to find a single soul to marry you."

Norina turned to Clotilde. "You remember Rina, the daughter of Goffredo the Stray Dog?

Clotilde nodded. "I remember her. Rina got engaged with Renato the Horseback. Renato refused to marry her two days before the wedding because he found out she had ruined her reputation."

"Rina ended up marrying an old man with a crooked eye. And because of her bad reputation, the entire family suffered. Her younger sisters didn't marry well, because people thought they were bad like Rina. Her younger sisters ended up marrying poor farmers, who take them to work in the fields every day." Norina stared at Grazia. "You are the oldest of your sisters. It's all up to you."

Grazia's mouth fell open. "All up to me?"

Norina waved the fan. "You have your sisters' fate in your hands. If you ruin your reputation, people are going to think that your sisters are like you, and they are not going to marry well."

Clotilde glared at Grazia. "You don't have the right to ruin your sisters' futures."

Norina firmly believed Grazia would have a good chance of marrying well if she kept her reputation intact. Grazia was the only daughter who was blessed with beauty. Caterina and Olimpia were common looking. Norina was sure that if Grazia could only get her portrait exhibited in the window of the photo studio, a rich man might see it, and fall in love at first sight.

Grazia confined herself to her bedroom and wept until her tears ran dry. She felt imprisoned by her poverty. Life was unfair. She couldn't have fun because she was born under a dark sky, and her girlfriends were entitled to have fun, because they were born under better skies.

The poor girl was terrified by the thought that her sky would be dark forever.

Cheers coming from the street caught Grazia's attention. As she looked out the window, she spotted her brothers, Pasquale and Mario playing "Knights and Ladies" with the neighborhood kids. The game involved the girls picking the boys they wanted to marry. She was glad Mario was playing. However, as she watched the game, she realized to her disappointment that no girls ever picked him to be their knight. Mario had a speech disability and preferred to remain silent. He only spoke when it was absolutely necessary. On those occasions, Mario was so embarrassed that he blushed and only a few simple words would come out of his mouth. People made fun of him. He was never going to be taken seriously, and no one was going to give him a real job. Men who didn't have a real job had nothing to offer in a marriage. Only people who had something to offer got married. A man was expected to be a good provider for the family. No one was ever going to marry Mario.

Mario is less fortunate than I am. His sky will never change. At least I have a chance of getting married and changing my sky. Her friend Patrizia's words came to Grazia's mind, "Plenty of boys like you. If you come to the dance, you'll find a boyfriend in no time." *If I go to the dance I may find a boyfriend,* Grazia thought as she ran down the stairs.

When she bounded into the kitchen, Grazia made up an excuse to go out. "Ombretta the Maestra wants me to help her sew the buttons. May I go back to the Sewing School?"

As soon as Norina nodded, Grazia walked out of the house. Once on the street, Grazia quickened her pace, driven by the secret thrill of spending time with her privileged girlfriends who lived under a better sky.

At the Sewing School, all the young ladies were excited about the dance at Alvaro's house. Grazia was the only one who didn't get her mother's permission to attend the dance.

Tonia patted Grazia's arm. "You should come to the dance."

Grazia pictured her mother's look of anger. If her mother found out, she was destined to get a whipping with her father's belt. "I'm afraid people might tell my mother."

"Your friends will never tell your mother," Patrizia said.

Grazia smiled. Her smile faded when she looked at her dress. "I feel awkward going in my mourning dress."

"You can wear one of my dresses," Patrizia said.

Grazia thanked Patrizia with a hug.

Grazia donned Patrizia's dress with delight. It was a beautiful flower print dress. Fearing someone would recognize her, she walked in the street with her head down. To her relief, no one acknowledged her. Clad in the pretty colorful dress, Grazia felt the sensation of a woman living under a better sky.

The party took place in a sumptuous *palazzo*. When Grazia entered the ballroom, she was noticed on the spot. All eyes were on her. She was the beauty of the ball. Giorgio couldn't resist the impulse to approach her. Before she knew it, she found herself dancing with him to a romantic song. Suddenly, the lights went off and the room was clouded in darkness.

"What's going on?" came some scattered voices.

It was one of Alvaro's tricks: he would usually turn the lights off for a few minutes to allow the couples to kiss. Giorgio took the opportunity to give Grazia a kiss. Though Grazia was shocked, she didn't dodge the kiss. She savored it. The kiss gave her a weird and wonderful sensation. It made her shiver! As soon as the lights went back on, a sense of uneasiness swept over Grazia. She pictured her mother's face fuming with rage, and was consumed with panic.

"I can't stay here," Grazia said. "If my mother finds out, she'll be furious." She darted out of the room.

Giorgio followed her outside. "Grazia," he kept calling out.

"Go away! I'll get in trouble if I'm seen with you. I'll get a whipping with my father's belt. Do you want me to get whipped?"

"No, I love you too much to ever let you get hurt," Giorgio said, watching her run away.

Grazia disappeared quickly into the distance. She was a vision to him. Giorgio was confused and overwhelmed with wonder. He didn't know if he had kissed her in real life or in a dream.

Grazia hurried back to the Sewing School and changed into her mourning dress. In her black dress, she again felt like the same miserable Grazia Voltini who lived under a dark sky and was not allowed to enjoy her youth.

On her way home, Grazia mused about Giorgio. He was so exceptionally handsome. His kiss had made her shiver. It had given her a split second of intense happiness. However, it was a bliss that couldn't last because she wasn't entitled to it.

"Giorgio is never going to marry a Voltini girl with no dowry and no trousseau," her mother had said scores of times.

I should cross him out of my mind, Grazia thought. She startled at the sight of Ninetta the Gas Man's Wife, and three of her children emerging on the street. *Ninetta is going to ask for the balance for the gas tank.*

Ninetta was in fact paying visits to customers who owed her money. She waved at Grazia as she walked forward with her children. "I'll pass by your house shortly."

"See you later," Grazia said, quickening her pace.

As soon as Grazia got home, she told her mother Ninetta was going to pay them a visit.

"Ninetta wants the rest of the money for sure." Norina flapped her hands. "I'm going upstairs. When Ninetta comes, tell her that I went to see a sick relative. When she asks for the money, swear that you're going to give it to her as soon as you get paid."

Grazia's face flushed. "I hope she believes me."

"You have to behave like a Voltini." Norina banged her fist on the table. "You have to be convincing when you promise to pay a debt."

Behaving like a Voltini was the last thing Grazia wanted to do. "It's not fair to take merchandise and not pay for it."

"It is fair," Norina bellowed. "We have the right to survive." She took a pause and lowered her voice. "You can also say that your uncle, Vituccio, is wealthy and that he can pay for the gas tank."

Grazia's whole body trembled as her mother disappeared behind the door that led to the stairs. She wished she could disappear as well. She paced back and forth, rehearsing in her mind the lines she was going to recite to Ninetta. The sight of images behind the fishnet curtain made her leap.

Ninetta pulled the curtain aside and entered the house with her children. One of the children started to cry. The poor mother picked him up and held him in her arms.

"I need to talk to your mother," Ninetta said. "It's important."

"My mother went to visit a sick relative," Grazia said, closing the curtain.

Ninetta rocked her crying toddler in her arms. Finally, the baby stopped crying. She set the baby on the floor and turned to Grazia. "I need the money." Her eyes became gloomy. "My husband doesn't have the money to get new gas tanks from the warehouse. If he doesn't get the tanks, he can't do any business."

Grazia crossed her hands on her chest. "I swear on my aunt's grave I'll give you the money as soon as I get paid."

"Please, give me the money as soon as possible. Most of the people who owe us money wait to pay until they need another gas tank. We can't wait that long. The business is doing badly because a lot of people don't pay us."

"I have a wealthy uncle, Vituccio the Taxi Driver. He's known for his good heart. I'll borrow from him, and I'll give you the money before I get paid."

Ninetta gave a sigh of relief. "I trust you more than your mother."

I don't deserve Ninetta's trust, Grazia thought.

As Ninetta walked out of the house, hauling her three children, Grazia noticed the children were poorly dressed. *Ninetta must need the money as much as we do,* Grazia thought. As soon as their steps faded into silence, Grazia opened the door that led to the stairs. "*Mamma*, you can come downstairs."

Norina ran down the stairs and bounded into the kitchen. "Did she believe you?"

Grazia's face drooped as she nodded.

Norina exhaled. "If I get a job, I'm going to pay Ninetta."

"*Mamma*, you should pay Ninetta as soon as I get my wages. I promised her."

Norina ignored Grazia's words. She pulled the curtain aside and peered outside. The sky had turned black and was bare of stars. Her lips quivered as she calculated she had a lot of debts. Her mind was distracted by an image standing by the house of Carmela the Daughter of the Umbrella Repair Man.

"Grazia, come and see. There's a man by Carmela's house."

Grazia dashed to the front entrance and gazed at the man. "I wonder who he is."

"Look, the man is entering Carmela's house." Norina raised an eyebrow. "Can it be that Carmela has a lover?"

"*Mamma*, it's so dark we can't identify the man. We only saw a glimpse of a man."

"A glimpse of a man," Norina whispered.

Perhaps a man could have helped them in their desperate situation.

VI

A glimpse of a man behind the fishnet curtain startled Norina. She ran to the front entrance and pulled the curtain aside. She was faced with Giovanni the Farmer. He was carrying a case of eggplant topped with many heads of garlic and a bunch of fresh mint.

Norina tilted her head and stared at him.

"The eggplants are from Count Torre," the farmer said, walking into the house. "He wants you to jar them. He has the jars if you need them."

Norina flashed a smile. "I'm going to send my boys to the *palazzo* to pick up the jars."

The farmer placed the case of eggplant on the floor and handed her a white booklet. "You can go to the bottega, get the vinegar and oil that you need, and have it put on Count Torre's account."

"God bless you," Norina mumbled.

He looked at her and blushed.

"Keep me in mind when it's time to pick the olives."

"I'll keep you in mind." The farmer stepped outside and closed the fishnet curtain. He suddenly disappeared.

Norina placed the white booklet in her brassiere. With unbounded vitality, she then ran up the stairs. She was excited at the thought of making an income. The eggplant job was a blessing from the sky!

Once into the bedroom, Norina kneeled in front of the statue of Our Lady of Sorrows and recited two Hail Mary's with devotion and gratitude. "Thank you for getting me another job."

As soon as Caterina staggered into the room, Norina got off her knees and blew a kiss to the Madonna. She then directed her gaze at her daughter. "Water. I need water."

"You want a glass of water?" Caterina asked.

"I need a lot of water," Norina shouted.

"*Mamma*, we have two buckets of water in the kitchen."

"Two buckets are not enough. I need more water."

"Why do you need more?"

"I got the job of jarring the eggplants for Count Torre. I'm going to need a lot of water to rinse the jars."

Caterina's eyes lit up at the prospect of an eggplant dinner. "I'll ask Olimpia to come with me to the fountain, I can use her help."

Caterina dashed out of the room. Norina opened the shutters and poked her head out. Mario and Pasquale were playing a game called "The Bell." The game consisted of pushing an old shoe heel with one's foot within the borders of squares drawn on the ground. Mario was comfortable playing any sort of game where he didn't need to speak.

"Mario, Pasquale," Norina called out.

"We're in the middle of the game," Pasquale shouted.

"You have to go to Count Torre's *palazzo* and pick up some jars."

"I'm going to the *palazzo*," Pasquale said to his friends. I'm going to meet Contessa Fiorella for sure."

"Can I come with you?" a thin boy named Biagino asked.

"I want to go too," a chubby boy named Luigino said.

Pasquale turned to his mother. "Can my friends come with me? They want to give me a hand carrying the jars."

Norina shook her head. "I can't send an army there. Two boys are enough." The shutters slammed shut.

Pasquale shrugged as he looked at his friends.

"Let me know what Contessa Fiorella looks like," Biagino said.

Pasquale winked. "You'll be the first one to know."

Pasquale took Mario by the arm and yanked him away.

The boys watched Pasquale and Mario until they vanished down the street.

Norina started her prep eagerly, washing and slicing the eggplants. As she worked, she entertained herself with the thought of visiting once more the opulent *palazzo* where Count Torre lived. Every time she had the opportunity to visit Count Torre's *palazzo*, she hoped for a chance to catch a glimpse of the miserable and famous Contessa Fiorella Torre. Norina had not seen the contessa since the day her husband, Count Torre had caught her in bed with another man. It was unusual for a woman to betray a husband who was a good provider. He inflicted a harsh punishment on her: he shaved all her hair and kept her a prisoner in the *palazzo*. The poor victim wasn't allowed to appear in public. She participated passively in the life that surrounded her by peering through the shutters of her window.

A woman blessed with the luck of marrying a count shouldn't betray him for the world, Norina thought. *She had luck in her hands and didn't know how to appreciate it. What a fool! She set her eyes on a lover who was so poor that he didn't even have the eyes to cry.* Suddenly, Norina closed her eyes and revealed a glint of a smile as she pictured herself having the good fortune of marrying a count. She would have treated him like a king. Norina opened her eyes and jumped up at the sound of steps.

Grazia popped into the house.

"You scared me," Norina said. "Since you're here, I want you to go to the bottega."

"I can't ask for credit there." Grazia twisted her lips. "You didn't pay the old debt."

"You have to shop for Count Torre." Norina drew the white booklet from her brassiere and handed it to Grazia. "Get one bottle of vinegar and four liters of oil."

With the white booklet, I'm going to be treated like a White Fly. Grazia reached for her fishnet bag and dashed outside.

As Norina continued her work, she realized she had run out of water. The girls hadn't come back with the buckets of water. *It takes them forever every time they go to the fountains. They're talking to their friends for sure,* Norina thought, rushing out of the house.

Norina passed by the Seven Fountains to check on the girls. She gritted her teeth when she saw them talking to their girlfriends.

"Caterina, Olimpia," Norina shouted.

The girls froze when they eyed their mother.

Norina glared at them. "Go home right now. Start washing the jars as soon as Pasquale and Mario bring them."

The girls hastily reached for the filled buckets and headed home. In the meantime, Norina bumped into Carolina the Good Life and started a conversation with her. Carolina informed her she had used the oil she had purchased from Grazia to test the baby for the *malocchio*. She had hired Old Veronica to pray for the curse on her little son to be lifted. The baby was finally *malocchio*-free and in better health.

Mario and Pasquale stopped in front of a door adorned with golden leaves.

Pasquale rang the bell with a grin. "If I get to see Contessa Fiorella, I'll become the most popular boy on Saint Peter Street."

Mario beamed at the thought of seeing the contessa. He was sorry that she was a prisoner in her own *palazzo*. He had dreamt about her being a beautiful princess. He and Pasquale waited anxiously in front of the majestic door. Minutes later, the door sprang open and a tall maid appeared.

She immediately saw the two boys as rascals. "What do you want?" the maid asked, wrinkling her nose.

Mario stared at his brother, entertaining the hope he would talk on his behalf.

"We're Norina's sons," Pasquale said. "We're here to pick up the jars."

The maid led the boys upstairs to the kitchen. The boys were amazed. They had never seen such an enormous room. There were flowers painted on the walls, so many chairs, and a huge table.

The maid indicated two cases of jars on the floor. "Take the cases and go straight downstairs. Don't go wandering around the house."

The boys nodded. They picked up the cases and walked out of the kitchen.

Once into the hallway, Pasquale placed his case on the floor.

"Wait here. Call me if you see the maid coming."

Mario's face turned red. "I'm, I'm a-a-a-afraid."

Pasquale huffed. "Don't be a chicken."

Pasquale headed down the hallway. He stopped in front of each door and peeped into the keyhole, eager to see Contessa Fiorella.

Mario's whole body began to shake. "The-the maid is-is co-co-coming."

"Let's get out of here." Pasquale picked up his case. "I don't want that witch to see us," he whispered, running away.

Mario followed his brother. Driven by intense fear, he had to stop many times to gasp for air. Mario couldn't keep up with Pasquale's pace. "Wait-wait-wait for me-me."

When they finally reached the ground floor, they let out a deep sigh.

"We'll get to see the contessa next time we come to the *palazzo*," Pasquale said.

Mario nodded.

The bottega was packed. Pasquina and her sister Costanza were serving the customers. Pasquina was extremely genteel. She was taking care of Saveria the Midwife, who was considered a White Fly. Saveria was an attractive woman in her early thirties. She was tall and slim, with blond hair and a deep set of green eyes. Saveria was born in Germany and had come to Italy at an early age. She had married Don Calogero, a crippled man twice her age. He encouraged her to study and paid for her education. However, once she achieved her independence, she granted herself the same freedom as a man. She had so many love affairs that people wondered if her husband had fathered even one of her children. Although she didn't have a good reputation due to her many extramarital activities, she was highly respected in town due to her profession. There were people who trusted her more than their own doctor.

"Hurry up," Saveria said. "I have a woman in labor. She's so big I'd be surprised if she didn't have twins."

"Who's the woman giving birth?" a petite credit customer asked.

"Laura the White Flower."

"I know who she is. They call her the White Flower because her wedding gown was adorned with white silk flowers."

"Laura the White Flower keeps me very busy. She has a child every year." The midwife contorted her face. "I told her husband not to get her pregnant anymore, but he doesn't listen. She should stop having children or she'll jeopardize her health."

"Laura's husband is a very busy man." *How does he find the time to keep up with his lover and get his wife pregnant?*

Saveria read the customer's mind. "Laura's husband is the last man a woman should marry."

Pasquina handed Saveria a sandwich generously stuffed with prosciutto and Swiss cheese. Saveria scrambled out of the bottega eating the sandwich.

Saveria the Midwife is a professional, Grazia thought. *Her profession has allowed her to be a free woman. She's just like a man. She does what she likes without suffering consequences.*

As usual, there was a short line for the paying customers and a long one for the credit customers.

To Pasquina's surprise, Grazia stood among the paying customers. *She has some nerve to stand with the cash customers,* Pasquina thought. She contorted her face when Grazia's turn came. "You're in the wrong line."

Grazia displayed the white booklet. "I'm shopping for Count Torre. My mother is jarring eggplant for him."

"Since you're shopping for Count Torre, I suppose you're in the right line." Pasquina flashed a smile exhibiting her prominent pink gums. "What do you need?"

"I need four liters of olive oil and a bottle of vinegar."

"Come with me to the back room."

Grazia followed Pasquina into a huge room filled with barrels of olive oil and bottles of vinegar. Pasquina reached for a bottle of vinegar and handed it to Grazia.

"Your mother brags that you work as a secretary for a lawyer in the city." Pasquina twisted her lips as she poured oil in a bottle. "You should use your wages to pay your old debt."

Grazia's face blushed. "We have to use my wages to pay for the gas tank."

"It's an old excuse. Many bad credit customers use the excuse of the gas tank. Don't expect me to give you more credit."

"I don't want more credit from a witch like you," Grazia wanted to say, but she chose to remain silent.

Pasquina gave Grazia a harsh look as she filled another bottle with oil. "When your mother gets paid by Count Torre, she'd better pay her debt to us. If we could collect all the money that people owe us, we'd be millionaires."

"I'll make sure she pays you. But, it's not fair..."

"What's not fair?"

Grazia overcame her embarrassment and followed through on her impulse to speak her mind. "You give Anna the Heavyweight credit for two years, and you don't dare tell her anything. But, you always remind my mother and me of the debt. We've only been on credit for the past six months."

Pasquina revealed a hint of a grin. "Anna is paying us back in other ways."

"What do you mean?"

"She's helping us collect from the other credit customers."

"Are you going to send Anna to my house to collect money?"

Pasquina stamped her foot. "I won't have to send her if you settle your debt."

Grazia crossed her hands on her chest. "I promise I'll pay it off."

Pasquina narrowed her eyes. "You'd better keep your word. Otherwise you and your mother are going to get a beating from Anna the Heavyweight."

Grazia bit her lower lip so as not to cry as she followed Pasquina to the front room.

Pasquina turned to the credit customers. "Olga the Scared Cat is banned from the bottega."

"Why?" a chubby credit customer asked.

"Anna the Heavyweight caught Olga hiding four eggs in her brassiere. Anna punched the Scared Cat in the chest, squashed the eggs, and kicked her out of the bottega."

"Olga steals from rich people and buys candies for the poor children," the petite credit customer said.

"I don't understand why she is so kind to the children," Grazia said.

"Olga is kind to children because she didn't get to enjoy her children. Her husband kidnapped them and took them to Germany to live with his mother." The petite credit customer sighed. "Her husband paid a high price."

Grazia scrunched her forehead. "A high price?"

"She killed him."

Grazia widened her eyes. "How did she kill him?"

"I heard that she poisoned him."

"I heard that she killed him with black magic," the chubby credit customer said. "Olga has the power of giving the *malocchio*. She gives the *malocchio* to adults, but she'll never give it to kids because she loves them."

"The Scared Cat never stopped looking for her children," the petite credit customer said. "She thinks that many poor children look like her own children. She gives away all that she has to poor children."

"The Scared Cat is not allowed in this store anymore. We don't tolerate thieves." Pasquina rubbed her hands together. "Soon, we'll be collecting from all the bad credit customers. Whoever doesn't pay us won't get any more merchandise."

Grazia placed the bottles hurriedly in her fishnet bag and dashed out of the bottega.

When Norina walked into her house, she saw glittering clean jars standing on the table.

Caterina and Olimpia washed the jars, Norina thought, flashing a light smile. She promptly reached for a cloth and busied herself drying the jars. She felt overcome with joy every time she had a little job. It made her feel like the breadwinner of the family.

Grazia trudged into the room, carrying her fishnet bag. She gave a sigh of relief as she placed the bag of heavy bottles on the floor.

"What took you so long?" Norina asked.

"The bottega was packed," Grazia responded. "Pasquina insisted on the money of the old debt. She said she'll send Anna the Heavyweight after us."

"Anna is a good friend of mine." Norina giggled. "She's never going to beat me up."

"I promised Pasquina to pay her for the old debt."

"That witch deserves nothing but false promises. I don't know if I'm going to have enough money to pay the old debt."

Grazia's face drooped. She wanted to keep her pledge, but didn't dare say anything to her mother.

Norina handed Grazia three heads of garlic. "Peel the garlic."

Obediently, Grazia began to peel the bulbs. "Pasquina said she won't give us any more credit."

"Well then I'm going to ask her mother. Teresina is kindhearted."

Norina concentrated on her work. She soaked the eggplant slices in a bucket filled with vinegar. Eager to get remunerated, she wanted to finish as soon as possible. She jumped up as she heard yells from Ercole the Ragman, wheeling his cart on the street.

"New things for old things. Trade in your old rags for new pots and pans," Ercole kept shouting.

Ercole the Ragman would come by Saint Peter Street once every two weeks with his cart of pots and pans. He was always polite to his customers, though he was known for cursing furiously whenever he would pass by the house of Anita, his estranged wife. Anita had dumped him for the notary of the town. She claimed Ercole was physically abusive. Ercole proclaimed to everyone in town that Anita was a whore and insulted her at every given opportunity. Anita always ignored his slurs. Her lover was an important man, so she felt Ercole was beneath her now. She was considered a White Fly. She lived in a *palazzo*. Ercole was simply a ragman who lived in a tiny house.

"Rags are valuable," Ercole yelled. "They're better than my whore wife."

"Anita is going to end up like a carriage horse," Norina said.

Carriage horses were known for having a glamorous youth and a miserable old age. They were in high demand when they were young and beautiful since they were able to perform. No one wanted them when they became elderly and decrepit because they were no longer functional.

"Why?" Grazia asked.

"A poor husband gives you more security than a rich lover does," Norina said. "Anita has put her survival at risk by choosing her lover over her husband. When she gets old, she's going to lose her beauty. Her lover is going to get tired of her for sure and is going to kick her out on the street."

Anita did the right thing, Grazia thought. *A woman must react when she finds an abusive husband, or she may end up going crazy*. She peered through the fishnet curtain and saw many neighbors scrambling out of their houses, willing to trade their old cloths for new pots and pans. She felt disappointed that she didn't have the material to trade in. She loved to get new things without spending money.

Excited to make money, Norina continued her work with zeal. She filled the jars with eggplant, added small portions of garlic, mint, and then poured the olive oil on top. The oil preserved the eggplant. The jars seemed to sparkle with glittering gold flecks.

"I wish I could jar my own eggplant," Norina said.

Grazia smiled in agreement. "The children love eggplant."

Their ears were overcome by Franchino the Bird's Nest's loud voice. "Magic wine, magic oil, the best oil and wine in town."

Franchino the Bird's Nest advertised wine and oil. He also sold seawater, but couldn't publicize it because it was illegal. The poor used seawater instead of salt for cooking. It was much cheaper and still tasteful. Salt was expensive, since the government had a monopoly on it.

"Go and get a bottle of seawater," Norina said. "Franchino is a good guy. He's going to give you credit."

Grazia scrambled out of the house. Rich people bought wine and oil. Poor people formed a long line to buy the seawater. Franchino was serving his customers with a bright smile. He was a tall and muscular man with a handsome face, framed by a mass of black hair. He was both feared and highly respected due to his incredible physical strength. He was the only vendor in town who had a motorized cart, which was loaded with bottles of wine, oil and seawater. He was fond of his cart. He boasted he had the best cart in town. He called himself the King of the Sea, claiming he knew a secret spot where the water was pure, salty, and clear. Anybody could have taken water from the sea and sold it, but nobody dared give Franchino any competition.

Grazia waited until Franchino served all the people in line before she approached him. "Please give me a bottle of seawater. I'll pay you when I have the money."

Franchino knew no one would ever refuse to pay him a debt. He gave Grazia a big bottle of seawater and bowed. "Allow me to carry the bottle to your house, *signorina*."

"No, thank you," Grazia said. "I can handle it."

"I won't insist," Franchino said. "I never contradict women."

As Franchino turned on the engine of his cart, Grazia noticed the neighbors' eyes were all fixed on him. Franchino the Bird's Nest was like the leading character of a romantic film. Everybody knew he was in love with Margherita, Anna the Heavyweight's daughter. People were curious to find out how the romance was progressing. As usual, Franchino stopped his cart by Margherita's house and whistled loudly. The loud whistle further emphasized his masculinity.

"Things are going smoothly," Ninuccio the Painter said. "They're still in love."

Children were impressed by the vendor's thunderous whistle.

"Nobody knows how to whistle like Franchino the Bird's Nest," Olimpia said.

The children agreed. They were not aware that through that loud whistle, Franchino was acknowledging his sweetheart. Margherita appeared at her window and waved at Franchino. He blew her a kiss that made her heart pound at a roaring rate. The nosy neighbors watched Franchino's cart go further down the street. When the cart finally disappeared into the distance, they gathered to gossip about the love affair. Grazia approached the neighbors, eager to listen to their comments.

"I think it's a platonic relationship," Baronessa Rosa said. "They hardly see each other."

Titina the Alligator raised an eyebrow. "They hardly see each other because he's married and has eleven children."

"They love each other," Grazia said.

"They're crazy about each other," Ninuccio said. "You can tell by the way they stare at each other."

Carmela the Daughter of the Umbrella Repair Man nodded. "No wonder people call Margherita and Franchino the lovers of Saint Peter Street."

The Voltinis had eggplant sautéed in garlic and oil for lunch.

When they finished eating, Norina turned to the children. "It's time to take your nap."

Obediently, Mario retired to the back room. Though Pasquale didn't like to nap in the afternoon, he reluctantly followed his brother. Caterina and Olimpia took Little Donato to the bedroom upstairs. They had the duty of quieting the baby down and coaxing him into falling asleep. Grazia went to work.

During the siesta, Saint Peter Street was deserted and absorbed in deep silence. Children were put to sleep against their will so they wouldn't make any noise playing on the street. It was a matter of respect not to disturb the neighbors during the siesta. The houses, with their shadows lying comfortably on the white stone pavement, seemed to be resting like their residents.

Norina continued her work, enjoying the silence and the sunrays filtering through the fishnet curtain. She was driven by the elation of earning money. When she completed her work, she stepped back and looked at the eggplant jars with great satisfaction.

A rumbling sound from the back room made her hop. "Mario, Pasquale," Norina called out, fearing they'd fallen from the bed.

The boys bounded into the kitchen.

Norina gave them a stern look. "You weren't sleeping."

Mario lowered his head and remained silent.

"*Mamma*, the siesta is over," Pasquale said. "Can we go out now?"

Norina realized the midday nap time was over. "You can go."

As the boys scrambled outside, Norina went up the stairs.

Once into her bedroom, she changed into her Sunday black outfit. She then combed her hair meticulously. She was going to a count's *palazzo*. She didn't want to look sloppy.

Norina went downstairs and walked out of the house. Her boys were playing ball with their friends.

"Pasquale, Mario, get the cases," Norina shouted. "We have to go to Count Torre's *palazzo*."

The boys rushed into the house. They returned a minute later carrying the cases.

"Let me know what happens," an obese boy named Albertino whispered to Pasquale.

Pasquale winked. "You'll be the first to know."

Carrying the cases, Pasquale and Mario followed their mother.

On their way to Count Torre's *palazzo*, they heard the squealing noise of Olga the Scared Cat's cart. The boys set down the cases and ran towards Olga. Norina grinned as the spooky vendor gave a handful of candies to her boys.

"Olga the Scared Cat is here," a child yelled.

In a fraction of a second, a crowd of poor children congregated around the vendor. Olga distributed the candies, with a wide smile exposing her missing front teeth. It was the first time Norina had seen her smile.

Olga is not so scary looking when she smiles, Norina thought.

Savoring their candies, the children watched their Fairy Godmother walk away.

Norina turned to her boys. "Let's go."

Promptly, the boys picked up the cases.

Norina led them to Count Torre's opulent *palazzo*. She rang the bell and waited impatiently. A minute later, the door swung open and the tall maid appeared.

"I brought the eggplant jars," Norina said.

"Come with me," the maid said, escorting them upstairs into the hallway.

"Leave the cases in the kitchen and wait there," the maid said to the boys, pointing out a door with her long fingers. She then turned to

Norina. "Come with me into the library. Count Torre left an envelope for you."

Norina followed the maid to the library. The boys went into the kitchen and placed the cases on the floor. They then walked down the hallway.

Pasquale peeped hastily through the keyhole of a door and whispered, "People say the contessa is the most beautiful woman on earth."

Mario remained silent, standing on his trembling legs.

Pasquale compressed his lips. There was no sight of Contessa Fiorella. *I heard she's always in her bedroom,* he thought as he squinted through the keyhole of the bedroom door. "It's her! She's wearing a black cape on her head."

Mario tiptoed towards the door. "Let-let-let me see-see."

Pasquale moved away from the door and allowed Mario to peep through the keyhole.

"I-I don-don't-don't see her-her-her face."

"She probably turned. I got to see her face." Pasquale flashed a smile. "She's stunning."

Mario had no notion that his brother was lying. Pasquale had lied because he intended to tell his friends he had witnessed the face of the woman every boy in town wanted to see. Mario gasped at the sound of approaching strides. Norina and the tall maid appeared in the hallway.

The maid glared at the boys. "What are you doing here?"

Mario's lips quivered. He didn't dare speak.

"We got lost," Pasquale said. "We were looking for the stairs."

"The stairs are that way," the maid yelled, pointing at the opposite side of the hallway. "I told you to wait in the kitchen."

"These boys get lost easily in a *palazzo,*" Norina said, rubbing and twisting her hands together. "We live in a small house. Please don't tell Count Torre."

The maid narrowed her eyes. "If I tell Count Torre, you'll never jar vegetables for him again."

Norina got down on her knees. "Please don't tell him."

The maid remained speechless.

Norina folded her hands as if she were praying. "I'm a poor widow, and I need to work."

"I won't tell Count Torre," the maid finally said.

"Thank you." Taking a deep breath, Norina got off her knees. "You're such a good person. I knew your mother, and she was a good person too. It runs in the family."

The maid revealed a hint of a grin.

"Let's go." Norina clutched the boys by the arms and hauled them away.

When they exited the *palazzo*, Norina grabbed the boys by their shirts and shook their shoulders. "I know what you were doing. You were looking for Contessa Fiorella. You're lucky that you didn't get caught. Count Torre doesn't want anyone to see his wife. You both deserve a beating right now. You're lucky I don't want to make a scene on the street."

The boys freed themselves from their mother's grip and scurried away. Norina didn't chase the boys. She had other things on her mind than beating them.

Norina went to the photo studio and admired the pictures on display. Her eyes sparkled at the thought that she had earned some money. *One day I'm going to have enough money to take my daughter to the photographer.*

On her way home, Norina kept on placing her hand in her brassiere to feel the banknotes Count Torre had given her. It felt good to have money! Norina felt as if an oppressive weight had been taken off her shoulders. It was a serene feeling to put her worries to rest. Invigorated, she smiled vibrantly at all the friends and acquaintances she passed on the street. People thought something extraordinary had happened to her. The cash lifted Norina's spirits so high that when she arrived at home, she forgot all about her boys spying on Contessa Fiorella.

Pasquale and Mario were the celebrities of the day. A group of boys were waiting for them on the corner of Saint Peter Street.

"Did you get to see Contessa Fiorella?" Albertino asked.

Pasquale leaped as he beamed.

"How is she?" Biagino asked.

"She's the most beautiful woman I've ever seen in my life."

Albertino turned to Mario. "Did you see her?"

Mario nodded yes.

"He saw her from the back," Pasquale said. "I saw her face."

Mario wanted to tell his friends he didn't get a chance to see the contessa's face because the maid arrived in the hallway as soon as he looked in the keyhole. As he gave it a second thought, he decided against it. It would have been too much hassle. They were probably going to laugh at him anyway.

Mario is too dumb to see anything good, Albertino thought.

A car rumbled at the intersection of Saint Peter Street and sped away. It alarmed the boys. A few minutes later, Grazia emerged down the street. Grazia waved at Pasquale and Mario as she walked forward.

"I got a lift from my boss, Mrs. Francesca Zordi," Grazia said. "She parked on Saint Rita Street because the car couldn't go through Saint Peter Street."

Pasquale raised his eyebrows. In the little town, he had never seen a woman driving an automobile.

Grazia flashed a light grin. "I'll show you the car and I'll introduce you to her. She went to the shoemaker. She should be out in a minute. Come with me."

Pasquale and Mario followed Grazia to Mrs. Zordi's vehicle.

Pasquale's jaw dropped as he saw the car. "This is a Mercedes. I've seen this car in movies. This is the car I want to buy one day."

When Mrs. Francesca Zordi walked out of the shop, the boys stared at her. She was a tall, magnificent woman with platinum blond hair and a deep set of emerald eyes. She was elegantly dressed in a shiny green suit.

She's a woman and a half, Pasquale thought.

Mario couldn't keep his eyes off Mrs. Zordi. She looked like an American movie star he had seen on posters.

"I want to introduce you to my brothers, Pasquale and Mario," Grazia said.

Pasquale gave Mrs. Zordi a handshake. "It's a pleasure to meet a beautiful woman who can drive."

"Grazia, your brothers are a handsome pair of boys," Mrs. Zordi said, showcasing her gorgeous red lips with a wide smile.

Pasquale's face blushed. He had never gotten a compliment from a stunning *signora*. Mario didn't realize the accolade was also addressed to him. He didn't dare give Mrs. Zordi a handshake. She was too precious to be touched by him. He kept staring at her with his mouth open. She was the most beautiful woman he had ever seen. Mrs. Zordi got into the car and revved the engine. The boys watched the car until it melted into the horizon.

"I guess they make exceptions. They give licenses to beautiful women." Pasquale set his eyes on Grazia's empty bag. "You didn't bring any food?"

Grazia winked. "I brought something that's more valuable than food."

Grazia had brought home her wages.

Norina used her daughter's money and her money to clear her debts. Once she paid Teresina from the bottega, Franchino the Bird's Nest, Carmine the Shepherd, Paolino the Gas Man, and five fruit vendors she was left with no money, but she had gained trust and was able to renew her lines of credit. A line of credit was worth just as much as cash. Norina calculated that if she got ten jarring jobs in a year, she would be able to save enough money to pay for Grazia's portrait. Only a miracle would give her so many jobs in a year... but Norina believed in miracles.

VII

Norina twisted her lips when she saw Clotilde, standing behind the fishnet curtain.

Clotilde pulled the curtain aside and stepped into the house, flashing a smile. "I have a letter for you."

Norina's face drooped. "Another letter of condolence?"

Clotilde closed the curtain and sank her heavy body onto a chair, which groaned from her weight. "I received a letter with a five-dollar bill from Aunt Elvira," she said, handing Norina the money. "I exchanged the American bill and I got three thousand lire. You can use the money for Grazia's portrait."

Norina spread her arms wide open. "Our Lady of Sorrows gave me a miracle."

Clotilde exhaled. "No, no... Saint Joseph performed the miracle."

"Our Lady of Sorrows did it. The Madonna helps me all the time. Saint Joseph never did anything for me."

"We should go to the photographer and make an appointment instead of arguing. The beauty of a woman is like a blooming rose. It must be immortalized before it withers. Grazia should have had her portrait taken when she was sixteen. We've waited too long already."

Filled with unbounded vitality, Norina ran up the stairs. She returned a few minutes later, wearing her best black Sunday attire. Clotilde got up from the chair, took Norina by the arm and led her out of the house.

With his white hair, a salt and pepper goatee, and black-framed eye-glasses, Ubaldo the Photographer had the look of an intellectual. He was surprised to see indigent women like Norina and Clotilde in his studio. Norina took a deep breath to summon the strength to do the talking, but once she spotted a disapproving look from Clotilde, she remained silent.

"I want to schedule an appointment for a photography session with my niece," Clotilde said.

The photographer checked his calendar. "I'm booked for the next two weeks, unless you want to come tomorrow morning at nine thirty."

"We'd be delighted to come tomorrow morning."

"I have all the money to pay now," Norina said as she drew the lira bills from her brassiere.

"You can pay me when I take the photographs," the photographer said.

As Norina placed the money back in her brassiere, Clotilde took her by the arm and dragged her away.

Once they exited the photo studio, Clotilde glared at Norina. "You have no etiquette. You should not keep money in your brassiere. And most of all, you should never take money out of your brassiere in front of a man."

Norina didn't pay any attention to Clotilde's comments. She smiled, imagining herself as one of the wealthy *signore* in town, accustomed to taking her children to the photographer.

Clotilde interpreted Norina's smile as an insult. "Are you making fun of me?"

Norina remained silent and continued to smile.

"If you wash a donkey's head, you end up wasting your time and your soap," Clotilde mumbled, marching away.

Clotilde looks like a whale when she walks, Norina thought, keeping her smile.

When Norina went home, she gave Grazia the great news: "Tomorrow you are going to have your picture taken."

"My picture taken?" Grazia asked. "With what money?"

"Aunt Clotilde gave me the money. She got a five-dollar bill from her aunt who lives in America."

"*Mamma*, it's such a waste to spend money on pictures. We should save the money for a rainy day."

"Aunt Clotilde wants to use the dollars for your portrait. She thinks a woman should have her portrait taken when she is young, while her beauty is like a blooming rose."

Grazia didn't protest. She knew she couldn't possibly persuade her mother to change her mind.

The following morning, as soon as Norina woke up, she looked out the window. The sky was filled with various shades of pink.

The sky is serene. It's a good sign, Norina thought. Infused with a sudden joy, she approached Grazia, who was sleeping peacefully.

"Get up," Norina whispered, shaking Grazia's shoulder vigorously.

Grazia woke up and got out of bed.

"Let's get the bathtub."

Grazia followed her mother down the stairs. Once on the ground floor, they went into the back room where Mario and Pasquale slept. They lifted the bathtub and carried it into the kitchen, careful not to make any noise that would wake up the boys.

As Grazia started the fire in the warming pan, Norina watched with fascination as the black charcoal turned phosphorescent crimson. Norina trotted around the room, reached for the curling iron, and placed it reverently on the warming pan. In the meantime, Grazia poured buckets of water into the bathtub. When she finally filled the bathtub, she slipped off her nightgown all in one motion. The crystal-clear water mirrored her beautiful naked body.

Norina took a bar of soap from the credenza and handed it to Grazia. "The soap smells like roses."

Inebriated by the floral scent, Grazia sat in the bathtub and enjoyed sliding the slippery soap over her body. At the sound of a knock, she sprung back. "Who could that be?"

"It's Aunt Clotilde," Norina said as she opened the door.

Clotilde, dressed in her best black nun-like attire, stepped into the house.

Norina fixed her eyes on the bag Clotilde was carrying. "What did you bring?" she asked, closing the door.

"I'll tell you later." Clotilde glared at Grazia. "You aren't ready?"

Grazia caressed her neck with the soap. "I'm almost done." As she felt a hand grabbing the soap, she was faced with her mother's stern look.

"The soap is melting," Norina said, wiping the bar of soap on Grazia's head. "You don't keep the soap in the water." Norina promptly locked the soap in the credenza.

Clotilde placed a chair by the hand basin. "Grazia, it's time to wash your hair."

Grazia jumped out of the bathtub. She wrapped a towel around her body and sat down by the hand basin. Clotilde pulled and scrubbed Grazia's hair. Grazia gave a sigh of relief when she felt water splashing on her head. Clotilde vigorously wiped Grazia's hair with a towel. She then reached for the hot curling iron and twisted Grazia's hair meticulously into banana curls. When she finally finished, Clotilde admired the strawberry blond curls framing her niece's striking features.

"I'll wear my black Sunday dress," Grazia said. "It's the best dress I have."

"The photographs are going to last forever, and you should not be remembered in black," Clotilde said, drawing a flowing silky lavender dress with lace trimming from her bag.

Norina's mouth fell open. "The dress is *spettacolare!* Where did you get this dress?"

"Aunt Elvira sent me the dress from America. She wrote in the letter that she bought it from a place called the Salvation Army. It must be a fancy boutique." Clotilde folded her hands. "God bless my aunt!"

Norina beamed. "No wonder the dress is so beautiful. It comes from America."

Grazia donned the lavender dress. She was thrilled to wear a colorful dress rather than the black frock she was accustomed to. Clotilde and Norina stepped back to have a full view of the dress on Grazia.

"Grazia looks like a White Fly," Clotilde said.

Norina smiled in agreement.

"Grazia could use a little lipstick."

Norina promptly reached for a red lipstick and applied it on Grazia's lips. She then headed to the stairs. "I'm going to get dressed."

"Make sure you put your money in your purse," Clotilde said. "It's vulgar to keep it in your brassiere."

Norina nodded and went up the stairs. She bounded into the bedroom and slipped on a tailored black satin dress that had been given to her by Mrs. Francesca Zordi, Grazia's employer. Mrs. Zordi met all the requirements of a White Fly: she was well educated, and married to a rich lawyer. Norina relished sporting outfits that had been previously worn by a *signora* of Mrs. Zordi's stature. Possessed by a secret thrill, Norina paraded in front of the mirror and sneaked a smile at her image. She looked like a *signora!* Her smile faded when she leveled her gaze at her hair. Her hair was pulled back in a simple bun. It was the common style among peasant women. *Signore* had their hair done professionally, and wore it elaborate and puffy. She hadn't been to a hair stylist since her wedding day. Norina's image disappeared from the mirror as she took her money out of her brassiere and transferred it to her purse.

When Norina stepped into the kitchen, Clotilde scrutinized Norina's outfit. "It's chilly. You should wear a jacket."

"This is the best black dress I have," Norina said. "I'm not going to wear my old jacket just because it's chilly."

"I could use a light jacket," Grazia said.

Norina shook her head. "You don't need a jacket."

"A jacket will hide the beauty of the dress," Clotilde said.

Norina and Clotilde took Grazia by the arms and led her out of the house. The poor girl felt like a puppet maneuvered by her aunt and her mother.

The blues and pinks of the sky were brightened by the luminosity of the sun. The three women were revitalized by the nourishing sun's rays.

Norina looked at the glittering sky. "It was written in the sky that Grazia was going to get her picture taken today."

"Everything is written in the sky," Clotilde said. "Having the portrait taken is part of Grazia's destiny."

It was unusual to see people sauntering on Saint Peter Street in their best attire at nine o'clock in the morning. The neighbors suddenly stopped in their tracks when they noticed the three elegant women. Lina the Warm House, a buxom woman with gray hair, was taking her brother Giacomino the Blind Man for a walk. Lina was known for keeping her house warm in the winter, when times were good. She waved at the elegant women.

"We're going to the photography studio," Norina said. "Grazia is going to have her portrait taken."

How can they afford a portrait? Lina thought while staring at Grazia. "I love your dress."

"My aunt sent the dress from America," Clotilde said. "She bought it from a high-class boutique called the Salvation Army."

Clotilde, Grazia and Norina walked away.

"I remember Grazia when I was still able to see," Giacomino said. "She was so pretty. She had strawberry blond hair, green eyes, rosy cheeks, and a magical smile. Is she as pretty as she was when she was a little girl?"

"She's even prettier," Lina said.

"Describe to me the dress she's wearing."

"It's a lavender silk dress with lace trimming."

Giacomino sighed. "I used to make lots of silk dresses with lace trimming when I was able to see." In his better days, Giacomino was a great tailor.

Titina the Alligator walked by like a hungry pigeon that had spotted food. "Where are they going?"

"They're going to the photographer," Giacomino said. "Grazia is going to have her picture taken."

"Where the hell did they get the money to pay for pictures?" Titina asked.

Lina shrugged. "I don't know."

Titina compressed her lips. "What about Grazia wearing a colorful dress?"

"Her father has only been dead one year," Lina said. "People wear black for three years when a parent dies."

"There's no respect these days," Giacomino said, watching the three *signore* look-alikes fade into the distance.

As they turned the corner onto Saint Rita Street, the three women bumped into Pino the Red Eye wheeling his cart. As usual, he had donned a torn green jacket and a red hat that matched the red cyst on his droopy left eyelid. Pino looked like a clown straight out of the circus.

"Fresh fish-fish-fish," Pino yelled out. "Who-who wants fresh-fresh-fresh fish? *Es muy-muy-muy bonito.*"

Pino the Red Eye was known as the idiot vendor of the town, and he had a soft spot for attractive women. As soon as he saw Grazia, he stopped his cart and stared at her with his mouth agape. He took off his hat and bowed. "Are-are-are you Gra-zia?"

Touched by his kindness, Grazia granted him her magical smile.

"She's my daughter," Norina said.

"I-I-I can't-can't-can't believe-believe it. She-she became very-very-very tall. I-I-I remember-remember her-her when she-she-she was this-this-this little." Pino gestured her height with his hat. He then turned to Grazia. "You-you look *muy-muy-muy bonita*. You-you look like-like a-a-a cont-contessa."

It was the best compliment one could have paid to a peasant girl, but Clotilde didn't appreciate it coming from a man like Pino, who she considered a lowlife.

"We're in a rush," Clotilde said, taking Grazia and Norina by their arms and dragging them away.

She's a star in the sky, Pino thought as he turned his head to have a last look at Grazia. She was like a vision to him.

"These men have no manners." Clotilde snorted. "They don't know it's not polite to stare at women."

"Many years ago, Pino got a lot of money from a rich aunt that lived in Argentina," Norina said. "He gave all the money to a whore who told him that the Argentian bills had no value in Italy."

"As soon as his father died in Argentina, his stepmother took all the money and kicked him out of the house. Pino was such a fool that he didn't even claim his father's inheritance. He came back to town with no luggage." Clotilde glared at Grazia. "Avoid looking at such worthless people."

As they passed by the *piazza*, they eyed the wealthy people of the town strolling by the central fountain, sporting their high fashion attire. Clotilde felt quite at home. These were the sort of people with whom she preferred to associate. Her face lit up when she saw Contessa Gildawalking forwards. The contessa greeted Clotilde, smiled at Grazia, and completely ignored Norina. Clotilde was accepted by the local high society because she was the President of the Catholic League of Saint Maria's Church. She had earned the position thanks to her knowledge. Since she could read and speak Latin and Italian correctly, she was considered a respectable woman.

Norina, however, was not accepted by the high society of the town. She was known as a common, ignorant peasant who could barely speak proper Italian. Her means of expression was the local dialect, which was considered a coarse and vulgar form of the Italian language. Aware of her ignorance, she always refrained from speaking whenever she encountered educated people. The local dialect was prevalent among the poor. The wealthy utterly refused to speak it, and often pretended they didn't understand it at all.

Norina listened carefully to the conversation her sister-in-law was having with Contessa Gilda, and tried to understand the meaning of the difficult words they were saying. Her face brightened when her daughter was included in their conversation.

Grazia can keep up with them, Norina thought. She felt extremely honored that a contessa was having a conversation with Grazia.

When they passed through the old part of town, where the poor lived, Norina was well-received. Many friends and acquaintances greeted her warmly. Clotilde felt uneasy among these underprivileged people. To her eyes, they were nothing but a bunch of lowlifes. The sidewalks were so narrow that people seated by their front doors occupied most of the space, and didn't leave any room for the passersby. The Dumb Brothers got up from their seats and waved at Norina. They bowed and moved their chairs away to allow the three women to pass by.

"Don't go out of your way," Norina said. "We can walk on the street."

"We never let women walk on the street," the elder Dumb Brother said.

"We feel important when we behave like gentlemen," the younger Dumb Brother said.

The Dumb Brothers were very popular in town. The younger brother didn't dare speak if the elder brother didn't start the conversation. The elder brother demanded respect from his younger brother for the simple reason that he was older. Their parents had died when they were children, and they had spent many years in an orphanage supervised by strict nuns. The Dumb Brothers were like eternal children, because they always had something naïve and silly to say. They always generated laughter.

Clotilde pretended they didn't exist. *How can my sister-in-law talk to such stupid people?*

Norina smiled at her friends, Gina and Giovanna Margassi. The two women waved at her in recognition. The Margassi Sisters used to be great dressmakers in better days, when they were young and beautiful. Through the years, the women had lost both their beauty and their prestigious jobs. The poor women's haute couture clothes were so worn out that they looked almost like rags. Clotilde wrinkled her nose as she looked at them.

Gina Margassi flashed a wide smile showing her rotten teeth. "Nori, you look elegant."

"Grazia is going to have her portrait taken," Norina said.

"Grazia looks like a princess," Giovanna Margassi said.

Clotilde grabbed Norina and Grazia by their arms and pulled them away. "I don't want people to notice you know them."

Despite her aunt's disapproval, Grazia sneaked a smile at the Margassi Sisters. They were considered outcasts due to their bad reputation. Though they were great dressmakers, women didn't give them work to avoid associating with them. The Margassi Sisters had been raped by a landowner while they were working in the fields. Consequently, no one wanted to marry them. Not only did they get no sympathy for being raped, but many people even blamed them.

The peasants' creed was: "Men are hunters. Women have to protect themselves. An unwed woman who works in the fields is just asking to be raped."

People didn't consider the fact that the Margassi Sisters worked in the fields during the war out of necessity, because their dressmaking business had fallen on hard times. The poor women were subjected to more abuse through the years. They were considered no better than a butcher's towel, where all the men wiped their hands.

"I have no respect for women who have one lover after the other," Clotilde said. "If you associate with them, people will think you're just like them. Tell me who your friends are, and I'll tell you who you are."

Grazia felt sorry for the Margassi Sisters. *"Those two women are nothing but innocent victims,"* she wanted to blurt out, but caught herself and chose to remain silent.

Norina remained silent as well, not wishing to start a quarrel about the redeeming qualities of her friends. Gina and Giovanna were kind-hearted, and always willing to help others. She recalled how romantic they were when they were young. They dreamt of an idyllic Prince Charming, but they only ended up being used for sex.

Clotilde, Norina and Grazia quickened their pace as they bumped into a gang of teenage boys by an abandoned castle. The town had never had the money to restore the old castle, though it was considered an important monument. The castle had become a place overrun with rats, street boys, drunkards, and gypsies. There were rumors that prostitutes used it during the night to ply their trade. The boys were astounded by Grazia's beauty, to the point that they couldn't keep their eyes off her. They followed her closely.

"She must be a movie star," one of the boys said.

"Go away," Clotilde shouted.

The boys ignored her request and continued to follow Grazia.

Clotilde flapped her hands. "I'm going to call a municipal guard."

A barefoot boy dressed in a patchy blue jacket turned to Grazia. "Can I have a word with you?"

Grazia didn't respond.

Clotilde gave the boy a harsh look. "Disappear!"

"I have the right to walk on the street," the boy said.

Clotilde kept looking around, hoping for a municipal guard to appear. To her dismay, the guards were nowhere to be found.

"Let's go even faster," Grazia said.

The women literally ran to the photo studio.

When they finally arrived, Clotilde gave a sigh of relief. "Those boys can't come in here."

Ubaldo the Photographer welcomed Clotilde, Grazia, and Norina with a bright grin.

Clotilde introduced Grazia to the photographer. "My niece is delighted to have her portrait taken."

The photographer stared at Grazia. "She's a great subject, an enchanting creature."

Norina raised an eyebrow. She was not able to comprehend the meaning of the word "subject." As she was about to inquire, Clotilde silenced her with a stern look. She then gestured with her hands to draw the money out of the purse. Norina hastily fished lira bills out of her purse.

"I have all the money," Norina said, fanning herself with the lira bills.

She's so vulgar! A woman should never fan herself with money, Clotilde thought, clasping and twisting her hands together.

The photographer paid no attention to Norina. His eyes were focused on Grazia, who looked like a goddess to him. He placed the money in his pocket without even bothering to count it. He then led the women to the studio, which was decorated with all sorts of flowers and a huge hand-painted mural depicting a spring landscape.

The photographer directed Grazia to stand in front of the mural. "Right there, that's the perfect spot," he said, as Grazia stood next to a hand painted tree. Stroking his goatee, he exhaled heavily. "She's a graceful creature. She looks like a Renaissance woman."

Once again, Norina didn't understand what the photographer meant. She pinched her fingertips together and shook her hands up and down.

"*Mamma*, he's saying that I look like a woman from the past," Grazia said.

Norina nodded and rehearsed in her mind Italian words she wanted to say to avoid dialect words. "Grazia looks just like my grandmother.

They called her Eleonora of the Daisies because she always had daisies in the house."

"My father probably knew her." The photographer was still concentrated on Grazia. "I want you to smile lightly."

As Grazia flashed a delicate smile, the photographer immortalized it by snapping a photograph. Norina and Clotilde preferred a broader smile, and they mimicked it. To their disappointment, Grazia ignored their suggestions and kept smiling lightly.

Norina summoned her courage and said, "Grazia is not smiling enough. She has to smile much more."

"I don't want a forced smile," the photographer said, staring at Grazia, who flashed another spontaneous light smile. "Her light smile is so powerful it brightens up her whole face. It's perfect." He snapped several additional shots. "I've captured her essence."

Beaming with the satisfaction of an artist aware of having completed a masterpiece, the photographer escorted the women to the front room. He released them each with a kiss on the hand. Norina was reluctant to leave. She was fond of being in that high-class place and she wanted to be seen there by as many people as possible. Her face radiated when she smelled the aroma of cocoa. Mrs. Matilde Fatti entered the studio. Norina couldn't resist the impulse to approach her.

"The photographer took a lot of pictures of Grazia," Norina said, indicating her daughter.

"Grazia looks *bellissima*." Mrs. Fatti grinned. "Her portrait will definitely be exhibited in the window."

Norina's eyes sparkled. Her dearest wish of the photo in the shop front had come more than half way true. As Mrs. Fatti sauntered gracefully away, the scent of American chocolates evaporated into the air. Norina stepped towards Clotilde and Grazia.

"There's a meeting at the Catholic League. I'm planning a pilgrimage to Saint Michael." Clotilde waved and rushed out of the photo studio.

"*Mamma*, we have to feed the children," Grazia said, dragging her mother outside.

The sky was as luminous as ever. The streets were completely deserted and filled with all sorts of delicious aromas. People had retired into their houses to have lunch. Norina and Grazia passed by Giovanni the Farmer's house.

"I wish Colombina the Farmer's Wife could see you in this dress," Norina said.

Grazia nodded, though she would rather have been seen by Colombina's son, Giorgio.

The Voltinis enjoyed big portions of pasta and potatoes for lunch. As soon as they were done eating the main course, Norina gave her children hard bread and marmalade for dessert, to celebrate Grazia's portrait.

"*Mamma*, we should have taken a family portrait instead of just my portrait," Grazia said.

What's the use of taking a family picture if we don't have the head of the family? Norina thought. *A family without a father is like a tree without a trunk.* "I'd rather have pictures of each of my children when their beauty is like a rose in bloom." She had learned that phrase from Clotilde and loved to repeat it.

"*Mamma*, am I going to have a photograph taken when I turn sixteen?" Caterina asked.

"I'm going to take you to the photographer when the time comes," Norina said. "Now, you're only fifteen."

Olimpia asked, "How many years do I have to wait to have my picture taken?"

Caterina giggled. "You're only nine years old. You have to wait seven years."

"I would love to have my portrait taken," Pasquale said.

"Boys have their portrait taken when they reach the age of eighteen," Caterina said. "You have four years to go."

"By then I'll have enough money to pay for my own portrait, and the family's portrait."

Mario didn't ask to have his photograph taken. He doesn't feel worthy of it, Grazia thought. "When Mario turns eighteen, he'll have his portrait taken as well."

Mario felt many eyes on him. He covered his face with his hands.

He's ashamed whenever he receives any sort of attention, Grazia thought.

"Mario is only thirteen years old," Pasquale said. "He has a long way to go."

"Little Donato should have his photograph taken." Grazia hugged her baby brother. "He's so cute!"

Little Donato was a three year-old boy with a set of big green eyes, curly blond hair, and rosy cheeks.

"If our sky gets brighter, I'm going to take my baby to the photographer too," Norina said.

They all smiled at Little Donato as they all wished for a brighter sky.

VIII

Warm golden rays pelted both poor and wealthy alike as they entered Saint Maria's Church. The house of worship was overcrowded. People were eager to see Teresina's daughter, Chiara marry the American.

The aisle was adorned with flowing white garlands of flowers. The immediate family was seated prominently in the front row. Teresina, bursting with elation, pompously sported a silver lace cocktail dress. She had cut her hair, and had a puffy hairdo just for the ostentatious occasion. She looked ten years younger. Her daughters looked their best in their high fashion outfits and matching posh hats.

The distant cousins of the groom, the only relatives he had in Italy, felt honored to be seated in the very front row. They gave themselves airs of importance for being related to the American.

Many White Flies had been invited to the wedding as well. The aristocratic women sporting their finely tailored, conservative ensembles were seated in the second row of the church. The Four Seasons Contessas demonstrated their status with high-priced jewelry and newly made couture dresses. The American Wives looked fashionable in their gaudy and brightly colored outfits. Aria the Maestra and Ombretta the Maestra were seated among their customers.

Though Teresina had invited only her paying customers to the wedding, she had made an exception for Anna the Heavyweight. The fortress of a woman was clad in what looked like a faded black lace dress, which horrified the two Maestre. Anna was not aware that the extra fabric she had used to enlarge the dress was quite noticeable, since it was not as faded as the old dress. Anna the Heavyweight felt like a million lira in her lace garb. She kept directing friendly glances at the White Flies, as if she were one of their social peers.

Norina, Grazia, and Angela the Crazy Head considered themselves lucky to have found seats in the last row. Many credit customers were standing. Grazia spotted Giorgio and his mother seated far ahead, among the paying customers.

As soon as the American groom appeared, escorted by his best man, the attention of many women in the church focused on him.

"He's not bad for an American," a young woman said. "Most of them I've seen looked like nightmares."

"They sure don't send the handsome Americans home to marry Italian girls," an old woman said.

"The American girls keep the handsome ones for themselves." Lina the Warm House raised an eyebrow. "They aren't stupid."

"Tell me how the bride looks," Giacomino the Blind Man said.

Lina patted Giacomino's arm. "The bride hasn't arrived yet."

"Teresina's daughters look like White Flies," Norina said.

"They'll soon become White Flies themselves," Angela said.

Grazia had her eyes fixed on the clothing Ombretta the Maestra had made. Though Grazia had only sewn the buttonholes, she felt proud to have given her small contribution to the creation of such masterpieces. "The outfits the American Wives are wearing are gorgeous."

Angela nodded. "They're breathtaking."

"The bride has arrived," Lina said.

Chiara looked more beautiful than ever in her wedding frock. She majestically walked down the aisle, escorted by her adopted brother Peppino. People's eyes were transfixed on her. The women scrutinized the gown. The train was so long that it had to be held by six flower girls. When Peppino gave her away to the American groom, many unmarried women got so emotional that their eyes gleamed with tears. Marrying an American was the dream of most of the unmarried women in town.

"How does the bride look?" Giacomino asked.

"She looks like a princess," Lina replied.

"What about her dress?"

"Her dress is made of shiny satin with delicate roses embroidered on the sleeves and the waistcoat."

"How's the headpiece?"

Angela drew her index finger to her lips and tapped Lina's arm.

"I can't talk now," Lina whispered.

The blind man had to rely on his imagination. He relished the mental image as he fancied the bride in his mind. He recalled Chiara as the prettiest of Teresina's daughters. He pictured her donning a headpiece inlaid with pearls and tulle.

At the sound of the bells, people directed their undivided attention to Father Camillo, who began celebrating the Mass. As usual, when he read the Gospel in Latin, very few people bothered to listen. But when he spoke Italian, he regained the attention of the audience.

"Love between a man and a woman is sharing, understanding, compassion, and fidelity. Marriage is the symbol of endless love. Marriages are made in Heaven. They are preordained by the sky."

Many people seemed to be touched by the speech. Several women were weeping. When the priest pronounced the couple husband and wife, Teresina gave a sigh of relief. One more daughter was married, but she was dismayed at the realization that she still had seven more daughters to marry off.

The people lined up to receive communion. As they walked slowly down the aisle, the guests haughtily gave a better display of their new clothes. As soon as Father Camillo announced the Mass had ended, Baronessa Rosa sang Schubert's "Ave Maria." Her voice was powerful, and she sang like an angel. At the sound of the wedding march, the bride and the groom walked down the aisle. Everyone in the church looked at them. They were the stars of the day.

In the foyer of the church, everyone stood in line to congratulate the newlyweds and their immediate family. Saveria the Midwife was granted the privilege of skipping the line. She quickly gave her best wishes to the newlyweds.

"I passed by to see the bride," Saveria said, giving Teresina a hug. "I don't know if I'll make it to the reception. I have a pregnant woman who's due any minute. If she gives birth before the party is over, I'll come."

"I hope you can come to the party," Teresina said as the midwife scurried away.

Norina couldn't find the proper words to say to Teresina and, allowed Angela to do the talking. "Congratulations! I'm charmed and captivated. I've never seen a bride so ethereal, so spectacular, and so refined."

Teresina tilted her head and widened her eyes. She didn't comprehend Angela's erudite flattery.

"Luck waits behind your door and comes to you when you least expect it," Mrs. Fatti said.

Teresina nodded. Her eyes coruscated. It was the happiest day of her life. "I can't believe it happened so fast," she kept saying.

Norina, Angela, and Grazia gave their congratulations to the newlyweds. Revealing a white toothy grin, the groom expressed his gratitude to everyone in English.

"What is he saying?" Norina asked.

"The groom is thanking people for their kindness and for coming to church," Angela said.

The groom's distant cousins were accepting congratulations from the attendees. "We are real cousins," they kept saying.

"They probably had never seen the groom in their lives before he came to this country," Angela said.

"They all want to be associated with Americans," Grazia said.

People were also standing on line to compliment Aria the Maestra and Ombretta the Maestra on the wedding gown and all the dresses they had designed.

"Thanks to you, most of the people in church have high fashion outfits," Mrs. Fatti said.

"Some people think a church is a runway," Grazia whispered.

"They go to church to show off and compare their new clothes," Angela whispered back. "They have no notion Jesus Christ would find them utterly repugnant."

Angela, Norina and Grazia joined the people waiting outside the church. As the bride and the groom descended the church steps, poor and wealthy people alike cheered with joy.

Children shouted in unison, "Hurrah to the newlyweds. *Viva gli sposi.*"

Pino the Red Eye kept staring at the bride with his mouth wide open. "I-I-I can't believe she's-she's-she's Chiara, Ter-esina's daughter-daughter. Chiara is-is a-a-a *muchachita muy-muy linda*. She's a-a-a star in-in-in the sky."

The Dumb Brothers smiled in agreement. They were all formally dressed in their Sunday suits out of respect for the newlyweds, even though they had not been invited to the wedding reception.

"We're lucky to have such a beautiful woman in our town," the elder Dumb Brother said.

"It's like having a movie star in the town," the younger Dumb Brother said.

Serafina the Maid was standing in the crowd. With her eyes wide open, she was admiring the latest married couple. Though the poor woman had never been invited to a wedding, she would always sport her baby blue lace garb to see any newlywed couple in the church.

"I heard that Serafina had that dress made to wear at her funeral," Titina the Alligator said.

"She shouldn't wear it to see the brides," Lina the Warm House said.

"They live long in her family." Norina giggled. "That dress is going to be down to strands of thread before Serafina dies."

Titina and Lina couldn't help but laugh.

Carmela the Daughter of the Umbrella Repair Man was searching for the man she loved among the guests. She beamed when she finally saw him entering a car. Entertaining the hope that he would greet her, she hurried towards him, but he didn't even bother to acknowledge her.

Titina noticed the whole scene. "Carmela's lover doesn't greet her in public."

"He's making a fool out of her." Lina said. "She thinks that her lover is going to marry her, but why buy the house if the rent is free?"

"Carmela has a lover?" Norina asked.

Titina nodded. "He visits her in the night. Carmela's parents are always out of town, and let their deaf aunt stay at the house with Carmela. The aunt doesn't hear him when he sneaks into the house."

Lina pointed out Franchino the Bird's Nest. He looked sharp! He was wearing a black suit, his hair was neatly combed, and he had a white rose in his hand. Unexpectedly, Franchino threw the rose at Margherita.

Margherita caught the rose and smiled. "It's a good sign. It means that he's going to marry me."

Titina pinched her fingertips together and moved her hands up and down. "How the hell is he going to marry you if he's already married? You're lucky that his wife is a little slow and doesn't give you a beating."

Margherita remained speechless. The sobering statement snapped her back to reality. She frantically looked for Franchino, but to her disappointment, he had disappeared into the crowd.

The Margassi Sisters approached Norina and Grazia.

"The wedding gown is so well made," Giovanna Margassi said.

"The bride looks stunning," Gina Margassi said.

God knows how many times they've dreamt of being brides, Grazia thought.

"I got engaged," Giovanna said, showing off her ring. She was not aware that her presumed fiancé was already married, and that the ring he had given her was fake.

Gina beamed. "My boyfriend said that he's going to give me an engagement ring on my birthday." Gina didn't know her boyfriend had no intention of giving her a ring, and wasn't going to see her on her birthday because he was dating another woman.

"The two whores have new lovers," Titina whispered. "They don't give up. They still think that men are going to marry them."

"Men just want to have a good time with them," Lina whispered back.

As three photographers snapped pictures, people grinned, hoping to show up in the background of the photos. They all watched the newlyweds as they entered a glittering white Mercedes convertible. The affluent guests got into luxury cars as well. Anna the Heavyweight was thrilled to have the privilege of going for a ride in a fancy vehicle provided for the guests. She beamed and waved at all the credit customers as she was driven off.

Giorgio eyed Grazia while he was helping his mother get into one of the luxury cars. He didn't greet Grazia, though he did sneak a smile at her. Grazia, however, looked away.

Grazia's eyes became gloomy. *He doesn't have the guts to say hello to me when his mother is around, but he's bold enough to kiss me when the lights are off.*

A long line of luxury cars followed the newlyweds' car beeping their horns loudly. Many bystanders gazed at the cars with their mouth open. They had never seen so many magnificent automobiles!

Angela, Norina, and Grazia ambled away, enchanted to have witnessed a fairy tale wedding.

"Chiara is no longer a small-town girl," Angela said. "She's about to go to America. Thanks to her, all the members of her family have been upgraded. They've become candidates to go to America. The prospect of a better sky is ahead of them."

"I'm surprised that Teresina's daughter who lives in Argentina didn't show up for the wedding," Norina said. "Teresina's second-born daughter came, the one that lives in Germany. She was seated in the first row with her husband and her son."

"I heard Teresina's daughter who lives in Argentina married a man who doesn't like to work, and couldn't afford the ship fare," Angela said. "She was too ashamed to ask her mother for money."

"I know a lot of girls that have gotten married, then gone off to a foreign country and never come back," Norina said. "Their mothers never saw them again."

It must be terrible to leave your homeland and not be able to see your loved ones, Grazia thought.

"The newlyweds are having the reception at a hall," Angela said. "It's not even just sandwiches. They're having a complete dinner."

Norina's jaw dropped. "A whole dinner?"

"They're having an American style reception. They can afford it." Angela winked. "The groom is paying for all the expenses."

"The groom is much older than the bride," Grazia said. "He must be at least fifteen years older."

Norina waved her hands up in the air. "Who cares, as long he's an American. At least he's decent looking. Finella, the daughter of Gloria the Widow, married a man with a hunchback because he was an American. At least Chiara's husband looks presentable."

Grazia turned to Angela. "Why don't you come over to my house and read the novel about America? My neighbors would love to hear you read. Giacomino the Blind Man asks me all the time."

"I'll come tomorrow afternoon," Angela said. "I should finally have some free time on my hands. I've been very busy lately. A lot of people have called me to write their wills since the notary charges a fortune."

Norina patted Angela's shoulder. "I'm glad you made some money."

Angela gave a sigh of relief. "At least I was able to pay some of my debts."

Norina's eyes lit up as she looked at Ubaldo the Photographer's studio into the distance. "Let's go and see the photographs in the window. I want to ask the photographer if Grazia's pictures are ready."

Norina led Grazia and Angela to the photo studio. They admired the photographs on display in the storefront.

Angela indicated an oversize portrait of the Four Seasons Contessas. "The four sisters had a lot of suitors, but they refused to get married because they didn't find true love. They were beauties when they were young, but now they're old ladies."

"I don't see why they bother to take portraits," Norina said. "Young people should take portraits. I'm old. I'm never going to waste my money on a picture for myself."

"You aren't old." Angela smiled at Norina. "You're still young and beautiful."

"I was beautiful when I was young," Norina said, tippy-toeing into the studio.

Ubaldo the Photographer bowed and kissed Norina's hand. "*Signora* Norina, you remind me of your daughter. Your daughter got her beauty from you."

For a moment, Norina felt beautiful again. It left her speechless. She couldn't find the proper words to say in formal Italian, nor did Norina want to speak dialect to him.

"You didn't bring your lovely daughter?" the photographer asked.

"Grazia is waiting outside," Norina mumbled.

The photographer sneaked a look out the window and got a clear view of Grazia. She appeared like a vision to him. "Grazia is one of the best subjects I've ever photographed."

Again, Norina didn't comprehend what the word "subject" meant. She changed the topic and asked, "Are Grazia's pictures ready?"

"I'll bring them over to the house on Saturday afternoon." The photographer's eyes were fixed on Grazia.

Norina waived merrily at Angela and Grazia as she scrambled out of the photo studio. "The photographer is going to bring the pictures on Saturday. I have to invite Clotilde; otherwise she's going to get offended."

"Let's pay your sister-in-law a visit," Angela said. "I'm in the mood for a fresh cup of coffee."

Norina flashed a light smile. "Clotilde is going to give us a cup of coffee for sure if you come with us."

Clotilde offered coffee only to guests as respectable as Angela the Crazy Head. She had never wasted a cup of coffee on the likes of Norina and Grazia.

They headed to Clotilde's house. When they reached the house, Angela knocked. The door jolted open and Clotilde appeared.

"It is always a pleasure to see you, Angela," Clotilde said.

Angela gave Clotilde an embrace. "I'm always honored to see you."

Grazia kissed Clotilde on the cheek. Norina greeted Clotilde with a nod.

Clotilde led them inside the house and indicated the table. "Make yourselves comfortable."

Norina, Angela, and Grazia sat by the table. The kitchen was small, tidy, and spotless.

Clotilde turned to Angela. "Would you care for a cup of coffee?"

"No," Angela said. "Don't go out of your way."

Clotilde flashed a glint of a grin. "It's no trouble at all." She reached for the coffee mill and turned the crank repeatedly, mincing the coffee beans.

They all enjoyed the smell of fresh ground coffee that circulated into the air.

Norina's eyes radiated as she watched Clotilde fixing the coffee. "The photographer is going to bring Grazia's pictures to the house on Saturday afternoon."

"I'll come to your house then." Clotilde reached for a plate of dried figs and placed it on the table.

Angela and Grazia only took one fig each. Norina couldn't resist the impulse to grab a handful of figs. Aware that Clotilde would launch one of her trademark reproachful looks, she avoided eye contact as she placed the figs in her pocket. Instead, she fixed her eyes on the percolating espresso pot.

Clotilde served the coffee in demitasse cups. "Angela, how many spoonfuls of sugar would you like?"

Angela held up her index finger. "Just one, please."

Clotilde shoveled a heaping spoonful into Angela's cup. She refrained from asking Norina if she wanted any sugar, hoping she wouldn't have the audacity to ask for it and thus force her to give it up. She had anticipated incorrectly. Norina took the sugar pot and dumped a lot of sugar into her cup. Though Clotilde threw her a disapproving look, Norina managed to ignore her. Norina drank her cup of coffee all in one shot. Grazia respectfully poured only a tiny spoonful of sugar into her coffee.

Thank God Grazia is not like her mother, Clotilde thought. *She's well-mannered. She took after my side of the family.*

"We'd better go. It's getting late," Angela said.

"Wait a minute. I have bananas for the children." Clotilde headed into the back room and returned a minute later with a bundle wrapped in newspaper.

Norina took the bundle and placed it furtively into her fishnet bag.

Angela gave Clotilde a hug. "Thank you for the coffee. You make the best coffee in town. It's been a pleasure seeing you."

"The pleasure has been all mine," Clotilde said. She gave Grazia a kiss on the forehead and dismissed Norina with a stern look. She was upset at her for wasting so much sugar.

Strolling down the street, Norina, Grazia, and Angela greeted their friends and acquaintances. Norina unwrapped the bananas in her fishnet bag.

"I'm surprised Clotilde bought bananas for the children," Angela said. "Bananas are imported, and are very expensive."

"Clotilde got them for free from one of her friends at the Catholic League," Norina said. "I'm sure she didn't buy them."

"You must want to show off the exotic fruit," Angela said. "Why else would you unwrap the bananas?"

"I want to make my neighbors jealous."

Angela couldn't help but laugh.

"*Mamma*, I don't understand why you want your neighbors to be envious," Grazia said.

Angela winked at Grazia. "It fulfills her fantasy of being a White Fly."

They bumped into Flora the Duchess, who was one of the richest White Flies in town. She greeted them with a smile. Pleased, they smiled back at her.

"I'm surprised that the Duchess smiled at me at all," Norina said.

Grazia refrained from telling her mother the truth. The Duchess had merely smiled at Grazia, not Norina. Recently, Grazia had embroidered the Duchess' nightgown, and she had been very satisfied with her work.

"I think that Flora the Duchess showed me respect because I'm carrying the expensive bananas," Norina said.

Angela giggled. "She probably thought you became an American Wife."

"No one is ever going to marry a widow with six children," Norina said. "When American men come to Italy to get married, they pick the youngest and most beautiful girls."

"Grazia could be chosen," Angela said.

Norina revealed a glint of a grin. "I wish!"

Grazia scrunched her forehead. She felt uneasy at the thought of marrying a foreigner.

"I have to go. I have to do some tutoring for an American Wife's son." Angela walked away.

Norina and Grazia headed home. Once they arrived on Saint Peter Street, they spotted the children and waved at them.

"I brought bananas," Norina yelled, shaking her fishnet bag.

"*Mamma* brought bananas," Olimpia shouted.

The children waved their hands up in the air as they ran towards their mother.

Norina gave them each a banana. To Norina's disappointment, the neighbors weren't around. As she looked down the street, she noticed a group of people seated by Titina the Alligator's front door.

"Something must have happened." Norina tapped her feet. "Let's go and see what's going on."

Norina and Grazia joined the neighbors standing by Titina's door. "What happened?" Norina asked.

"We're waiting for Anna the Heavyweight to come back from the wedding reception," Lina the Warm House responded.

"What about Clombina the Farmer's Wife? She didn't come back from the reception?"

"Colombina came back, but she didn't give us any satisfaction. You know Colombina, she doesn't like to gossip when her husband is around. The only information she gave us is that there were two hundred people at the reception."

Giacomino the Blind Man sighed. "I wish I'd been invited to the reception."

Lina patted Giacomino's arm. "It's more than fair that we don't get invited. We're credit customers. We should consider ourselves lucky that we even get credit."

"Anna the Heavyweight is the lucky one," the blind man said. "She's the only credit customer who was invited."

"Anna deserved to be invited," Ninuccio the Painter said. "She's forced a lot of customers to pay their debts. Teresina recouped a lot of money thanks to her."

Lina folded her hands. "Thank God Anna hasn't forced us to pay our debt."

"Anna paid us respect," Giacomino said. "We're neighbors."

Titina the Alligator twisted her face. "You never know. Anna can change her mind any minute."

"I'm always nice to her," Lina said.

"Pasquina said she's not going to give any more credit to people that haven't paid their balances," Grazia said.

Lina's lips trembled. "Then Pasquina will probably refuse to give me more credit."

"How old is your debt?" Ninuccio asked.

"Two months. I always pay her every two months when I collect Giacomino's pension check."

Old Veronica shrugged. "Your debt is not so old. She's going to give you some credit. I'm sure she's going to feel sorry for your brother because he's blind."

Lina exhaled in relief.

"See, I'm worth something," the blind man said.

As Anna the Heavyweight finally emerged down the street, Titina pointed at her. "She's coming."

The neighbors couldn't help noticing the strong woman was stumbling as she walked forward.

"She's drunk," Lina said.

Ninuccio laughed. "Anna gets drunk every time she goes to a party."

They all walked towards Anna, eager to ask questions about the wedding reception.

"How was the reception?" Titina asked.

"It was like those parties you see in the American movies," Anna replied. "They had a band that played all day long."

"A full band?" Lina and Titina asked in unison.

Anna nodded. "A real band. The same band that plays at the funerals."

Old Veronica's mouth fell open. "That must have cost a lot of money."

"What about the food?" Ninuccio asked.

"It was out of this world." Anna shut her eyes and smiled. "I've never seen so much food in my life. They had half a chicken per person, lasagne, prosciutto, salami, Parmesan cheese, mozzarella, olives and…"

Giacomino's face glowed as he pictured the food in his mind. "What else?"

Anna pulled a tray wrapped with white tulle out of her bag and showed it off. "They also gave a tray filled with cookies to each guest."

Titina's jaw dropped. "A whole tray!"

"What about the drinks?" Ninuccio asked.

Anna shut her eyes and grinned. "They had wine, *aranciata*, and champagne."

Giacomino licked his lips. "I wish I was invited."

"You weren't invited," Lina raised her voice. "Stop whining."

"What about the cake?" Old Veronica asked.

The fortress of a woman spread her arms wide open. "The cake was this big. I saved a piece for Margherita. And they also gave a tray filled with American chocolates and candies to each guest."

Many neighbors widened their eyes as they exchanged looks.

"I have to go," Anna said, faltering away.

They all followed Anna to the front door of her house.

"Colombina told us that there were two hundred people at the reception," Titina said. "Is it true?"

"Colombina doesn't know how to count," Anna said. "There were two hundred and fifty people. She's so stupid. She didn't even bring a bag to take food home. She wanted to behave like a White Fly. She kept encouraging her son to dance with a White Fly."

A flush spread over Grazia's face. "*Did he dance with her?*" she wanted to ask.

"Which White Fly did he dance with?" Titina asked.

"Oh no, he didn't dance with the White Fly. I don't blame Giorgio." Anna giggled. "The White Fly was as ugly as a real fly."

Grazia gave a sigh of relief.

"Did Saveria the Midwife come?" Norina asked.

Anna nodded. "She came."

"Did she bring her husband?" Titina asked.

Anna yawned. "She did."

"She always takes her husband to parties," Lina said. "He sits in a corner because he can't walk."

"Who did she dance with?" Titina asked with an insinuating tone.

Anna winked. "The Midwife danced the entire time with the notary's son, the handsome one."

"She sure knows how to pick the good-looking ones," Lina said.

Carmela the Daughter of the Umbrella Repair Man was tempted to ask if her lover had danced with anyone. As she gave it a second thought, she refrained. He was her secret lover. She didn't want anyone to be suspicious of her relationship with him.

"What about the favors?" Titina asked.

As the strong woman stretched her arms, numerous neighbors moved away. Anything could be expected from such a woman, especially when she was drunk. "They gave a silver rose."

Titina tapped her feet. "Show it to us."

"It's wrapped up with the chicken. I'm not in the mood to unwrap it." Anna exhaled. "I'll show it to you some other time."

"Stay with us for a little more," Giacomino said. "Come on, we want to know more."

"I'm tired," Anna shouted. "I want to go to sleep."

No one dared to contradict Anna the Heavyweight. Even drunk, they knew her strength was not to be challenged. They all retired to their homes, and went to sleep, dreaming of the sumptuous and delicious food served at the wedding reception.

Norina, for her part, dreamed of Grazia marrying a rich man and having a wedding like that for her own daughter.

IX

The doors and shutters blew open as if they were yawning. People were awakening from the siesta. The poor came out of their houses and placed their chairs by their front doors. They sat lazily outside in search of something to do or someone to talk to. They seemed sluggish after their afternoon nap with the exception of the children, who were happy to be free to play in the street. The children created their own excitement by inventing games.

When Angela the Crazy Head was seen on Saint Peter Street entering the Voltinis' house with a folder in her hands, the neighbors reckoned she was about to read a novel. The news spread fast throughout the vicinity. Many neighbors readied themselves to pay the Voltinis a visit. Most of the poor people were illiterate, and loved to be read to. Listening to a novel was unusual and exciting. It was like going to the movies.

Norina saw two figures standing behind the fishnet curtain. She ran to the front entrance and welcomed Lina the Warm House and Giacomino the Blind Man. To Norina's delight, they brought a heaping plate of green olives.

"We heard that Angela the Crazy Head is going to read a novel," Lina said, placing the plate of olives on the table. "Norina, do you mind if we listen?"

Norina flashed a light smile. "I don't mind at all."

Grazia helped Giacomino find a seat.

"Norina, you don't mind if I invite Anna the Heavyweight, do you?" Lina asked. "She loves novels."

Norina giggled. "How can I say no to Anna the Heavyweight?"

"Anna's daughter would want to come as well, and so would Old Veronica and Carmela the Daughter of the Umbrella Repair Man."

"Invite whoever wants to come," Norina said.

Lina was elated. Norina managed to hide her contentment, affecting a nonchalant expression. She didn't want to give the impression she was eager to host as many people as possible for the reading, since they all brought treats. She preferred for people to beg to be invited. Lina walked out of the house. She returned ten minutes later, escorted by twelve people.

Grazia's heart skipped a beat when she saw Giorgio standing next to Giovanni the Farmer. She restrained herself from looking at him, afraid to give away her feelings. Though Giorgio wanted to talk to Grazia, he couldn't do so in his father's presence.

Many people brought their own chairs, knowing the Voltinis didn't have enough chairs to accommodate everyone. They all brought goodies: roasted chickpeas, dried sunflower seeds, dried figs, and almonds. Baronessa Rosa brought a whole box of mint candies and placed it on the table. The children rapidly opened the box.

"The candies are for the guests," Norina shouted.

The children ignored their mother. They grabbed handfuls of candies and dashed outside, eager to show the candies to their friends.

"I try to teach my children good manners, but they don't listen," Norina said.

Nobody paid any attention to her comment. They were anxious to hear the reading of the novel.

"Angela, why don't you start?" Giacomino tapped his feet. "What are you waiting for?"

Angela turned to Norina. "Are we expecting more people?"

"The room is packed," Carmine the Shepherd said. "If more people come, they have to sit in the back room."

When Angela opened the folder with the manuscript, a deep silence overtook the room. Everyone stared at her. Angela finally said, "Today I'm going to read a love story entitled *Going to America*."

Many listeners grinned. The title was appealing. As Angela began, the audience gave her their undivided attention. She was a great storyteller. She would raise and lower her voice, changing her tone according to the characters and situation. Angela sounded just like a radio play. The listeners couldn't stop themselves from exchanging enthralled glances.

"Angela should have been an actress," Baronessa Rosa said.

Several listeners smiled in agreement. Angela made it possible for everyone to understand the plot of the romance. Whenever she encountered a difficult word, she translated it into dialect.

"Angela should have been a teacher," Old Veronica said.

Numerous spectators signaled in agreement.

The leading characters of the novel were two young peasants: Nardo and Vincenza, who were passionately in love. The impoverished couple struggled to survive in a small town in southern Italy, never abandoning their dreams of a better future. Nardo, to improve himself, found a job working on an ocean liner. On one of the trips to America, he had the opportunity to jump ship. He decided not to return home, opting instead to stay in the land of opportunity. He found a good paying job, but being an illegal alien, he feared deportation back to Italy. He wanted to stay in America as long as possible, hoping eventually to save enough money to marry Vincenza. The story of the star-crossed lovers captivated all the listeners. At the end of the first chapter, Angela paused for a small intermission.

"Nardo is an illegal alien," Ninuccio the Painter said. "If the American government finds out, he'll be forced to go back to Italy, and he'll never set foot in America again."

"Angela, go on," Giacomino said. "We want to know more."

Angela began reading the second chapter. Nardo got greedy. He didn't want to give up the money he earned in America. If he married an American woman, he would be able to reside in America, but would have to give up the woman he loved. Nardo had to make the most crucial decision in his life. He had to choose between his sweetheart in Italy or his new life in America. At the end of the chapter Angela took another intermission to allow the listeners to make their comments.

"If Nardo marries an American citizen, he gets to stay in America legally," Giovanni the Farmer said.

"I feel sorry for Vincenza." Margherita's eyes glittered with tears. "She'll lose the love of her life if Nardo finds another girlfriend."

Old Veronica folded her hands in prayer. "God is going to provide another boyfriend for Vincenza."

"It won't be the same," Grazia said.

"He should choose the woman he loves over America," Giorgio said, gazing at Grazia.

Men don't choose the women they love in real life, Grazia thought, revealing a somber look.

Norina contorted her face. "If Nardo chooses the woman he loves, he is going to starve with her in Italy."

"But romance is more important than life," Margherita said.

Many listeners widened their eyes as they exchanged looks.

"You can't eat romance for dinner," Anna said.

Several listeners laughed under their breath.

Lina turned to Angela. "Who does Nardo choose, Vincenza or America?"

Angela shook her head. "I can't tell you."

"He'll definitely choose Vincenza," Margherita exhaled. "He's devoted to her."

"Nardo is not stupid." Titina raised an eyebrow. "He's never going to give up America for a woman who is so poor that she doesn't even have the eyes to cry."

"If a man is in love with a woman, he should most definitely pick her," Grazia said.

Giorgio's eyes sparkled. *I wish my mother would give me permission to marry Grazia,* he thought.

"Angela, go on with the reading." Giacomino stamped his foot. "We want to know more."

Angela began the third chapter. Her voice once again became the only sound in the room. The audience was thrilled to know what was going to happen next. Suddenly without warning, loud yells disturbed everyone's concentration.

"Who's shouting outside?" Norina asked.

Grazia leaped out of her chair. "A woman is crying for help."

"Let's go and see what's going on," Giorgio said.

"Help! Help!" They heard more screams from a woman's voice.

People rushed out of the house.

"Where's everybody going?" Giacomino asked. "Don't leave me alone. Don't forget that I'm blind!"

"Come with me." Grazia took Giacomino by the arm, and led him to follow the mob.

"For God's sake! Somebody should help me," the woman shouted.

"I hear Maddalena's voice," the blind man said. "What's happening to her?"

"I don't know," Grazia said. "I see many people are standing by Maddalena's house."

"Help!" Maddalena kept screaming.

"Grazia, go and see, but come back every now and then and let me know what goes on," the blind man said.

As Grazia merged into the crowd, she felt a hand holding her hand. It was Giorgio's hand. She revealed a trace of a smile at the comfort of his grip. She wished it would last forever. As soon as she eyed Caterina walking forward with Little Donato in her arms, Grazia blushed and regretfully slipped her hand out of Giorgio's.

"The wolf," Little Donato said.

Grazia caressed the baby's face. "There's no wolf."

Maddalena's shrieks got louder. Maddalena had a drunken husband, and was used to fleeing the house whenever he thrashed and threatened her. Every time there was a scene, the neighbors scrambled out of their houses to be an audience for the live theater."

"You've been with another man," Maddalena's husband Arturo, yelled. "You're nothing but a whore. You're a *puttana* just like your mother and your sister. You're going to end up in a whorehouse."

"You're crazy," Maddalena yelled back. "You don't know what you're saying. You're just a washed-up drunk."

"Explain to me who left the cigarette butts in the ashtray. I want to know who smoked in my house."

"My friend Claretta smoked."

"I don't believe you. Your friend doesn't smoke. You're screwing another man. You're a streetwalker. I want to know who was in my home. Tell me!"

"No man was in the house. I swear on my mother's grave."

"Your mother was a whore. You can't swear on a whore's grave."

"I can swear on my mother because she was a good mother."

Arturo's tone grew frantic. "I want to kill that son of a bitch. If you don't tell me his name, I'll kill you."

What followed was a brief silence. The listeners wondered what would happen. At the sound of approaching footsteps, the listeners ran away like frightened pigeons, and withdrew back into the security of their own dwellings. They were enthralled by their ability to witness the scene as it happened without getting involved. They simply had to peer outside to get a view of the action. The only people still on the street were Grazia, Giorgio, and Giacomino.

"What's happening to Maddalena this time?" Giacomino kept asking, flapping his arms like a wild fowl.

As Grazia and Giorgio walked towards the blind man, a hand clenched Grazia's arm. It was her mother's hand. Norina had come to rescue Grazia.

"Get inside," Norina shouted.

"*Mamma*, we should help Maddalena," Grazia said.

"I don't want you to get involved," Norina said, yanking Grazia in the direction of her house. "People who get caught up in things like this always come out the worst. You are going to get a beating from Maddalena's husband for sure. I stopped Angela from getting mixed up. She wanted to go to Maddalena's house."

Angela is such a good person, Grazia thought.

"Giorgio, you better come inside," Colombina the Farmer's Wife shouted.

Giorgio walked into his house with his head down, knowing his mother was about to reprimand him for standing next to Grazia.

"Help! Somebody help me, for God's sake. He wants to kill me," Maddalena yelled.

A loud rumble suddenly muffled the voice of the victim. Many people figured Maddalena had fallen down the stairs, or her husband had thrown her into a wall. The silence continued as numerous people imagined the violence that must have been inflicted on Maddalena. To their surprise, Maddalena popped out of her house in one piece. The spectators saw her panting figure hurrying away, while Arturo ran after her with a bottle of liquor and a box of matches in his hands.

"She doesn't deserve to live," Arturo bellowed. "She's a whore. I'll break this goddamn bottle of whisky over her head and light her up with a match."

"Help! He wants to burn me alive," Maddalena screamed, running down the street.

Maddalena felt relieved when she saw a man on the street. "Please, help me!" she shouted, but as she recognized Giacomino the Blind Man, she realized the disabled man couldn't help her.

The cowardly, fearful neighbors remained confined in the security of their houses. Not a single soul aided the defenseless woman. Peering through the shutters of her window, Contessa Fiorella's eyes expressed pity and concern as she watched Maddalena run down the street with her furious husband chasing her. The scene brought back painful memories from her past.

The neighbors finally came out of their homes. Like the enthralled bystanders they were, they watched the bodies of Maddalena and Arturo get smaller and smaller until they faded and completely disappeared into the distance, just like the ending of a film. The onlookers gathered like birds sharing a meal in the middle of the street.

"I didn't want to get involved," Lina the Warm House said. "I mind my own business."

"Is it true that Maddalena has a lover?" Norina asked.

Old Veronica shook her head. "I've never seen Maddalena with another man."

"I've seen her talking to a man at ten o'clock at night," Colombina the Farmer's Wife said.

Titina the Alligator raised an eyebrow. "Maddalena wears lipstick, even when she goes shopping."

"If her husband beats her up, he must have a good reason," Colombina said.

"He only beats her up when he's drunk," Norina said.

"He must have a good reason to get drunk," Titina said.

"He drinks because of her," Colombina said. "I think Maddalena is just like her sister."

"Maddalena's sister is a whore. Her mother was a whore. It runs in the family. Maddalena comes from generations of whores." Titina twisted her face. "It's like a family disease."

"A pear cannot fall far from the tree," Colombina said.

"I feel sorry for Maddalena," Carmela the Daughter of the Umbrella Repair Man said. "I hope Arturo doesn't get ahold of her."

"Arturo is an animal," Angela the Crazy Head said.

Grazia bobbed her head in agreement.

"Arturo spoiled the reading of the novel. I didn't chase him because he runs faster than me." Anna the Heavyweight clenched her fists. "He deserves a beating. Arturo is such a jerk."

"I'm going to report Arturo to the *carabinieri*," Angela said.

"Can you at least tell us how the novel ends?" Lina asked.

"You'll have to find out next time," Angela responded, waving good-bye.

As they watched Angela the Crazy Head walk away, they wondered what the conclusion of the novel would be.

"Nardo is going to dump Vincenza and marry an American woman for sure," Titina said.

"I hope he marries Vincenza, she's the love of his life," Carmela said.

Lina and Titina exchanged looks. As soon as Carmela walked away, they began to talk about her behind her back.

"I heard that Carmela and her lover are still seeing each other," Lina said. "He visits her every night."

"He's having a good time with her for sure," Titina said.

Colombina narrowed her eyes. "If he gets her pregnant, he's going to refuse to marry her, no question about it."

"It's a sin if he gets her pregnant and refuses to marry her," Old Veronica said.

"It's a sin if a woman opens her legs." Colombina glared at Grazia. "If my son got a lowlife girl pregnant, I'd never give him my blessing to marry her."

Grazia's face flushed. "*I know you don't consider me worthy of your son. I'll try my best to get him out of my mind,*" she wanted to say, but chose to remain silent.

Titina raised her voice. "It's all up to the woman. If the woman doesn't open her legs, she has nothing to fear."

Titina is so ignorant. She's always ready to condemn women. Grazia thought. She resisted the urge to retort to Titina.

After they filled their heads with gossip, the neighbors, eager to fill their stomachs, withdrew to their homes.

Meanwhile Angela the Crazy Head went to visit the *carabinieri*, the local police in town, who highly respected her for her intellect. On many occasions, the *carabinieri* had even asked her for advice.

"What brings you here, *Signora* Angela?" Mino the Carabiniere asked.

"I want to report Mr. Arturo Fossini for battering his wife and threatening to kill her," Angela replied.

"It's not the first time Arturo has done that."

"He deserves to be punished. He's a beast."

"I know, but nobody in town ever has testified against him, his own wife never pressed charges. Once, Anna the Heavyweight punched Arturo in the nose to defend Maddalena. I couldn't arrest him because Maddalena denied that her husband had given her a beating. I didn't arrest Anna since I felt that Arturo deserved more than a punch in the nose."

"Maddalena never presses charges because she's afraid of him." Angela patted her chest. "I'm willing to testify against him."

Mino crossed his arms. "What have you seen?"

"I've seen him pursuing and terrorizing his wife. He was holding a bottle of whisky and a box of matches in his hands, and was threatening to douse Maddalena and to light her on fire."

"And did he do it?"

"No."

"*Signora* Angela, you are a smart woman." Mino pinched his fingertips together and moved his hands up and down. "You should know that's only hearsay. There's no legitimate evidence to convict Mr. Fossini."

Angela stared directly into his eyes. "You should stop him. He might do something crazy."

Mino the Carabiniere winked. "We'll keep an eye on him out of respect for you."

Angela thanked him with a smile.

That evening, the Voltini family had a great dinner. Grazia made *cialledda,* hard bread dipped in seawater and topped with tomatoes, oil, and oregano. They also had side dishes of green olives and dried sunflower seeds with their main course. Dessert consisted of dried figs, almonds, and mint candies. The children ate with their usual fervor. By the time dinner was over, an onyx night had descended on the town. As soon as the street lamps glowed, the Voltinis dashed out of the house. Grazia asked the neighbors if they had seen Maddalena, but no one knew her whereabouts.

"Arturo will never catch Maddalena," Old Veronica said. "She runs faster than he does."

"When it comes to husbands and wives, you should never get in the middle," Carolina the Good Life said.

"They always fight. Sometimes they rough each other up, but in the end, they always make up." Old Veronica flashed a light smile. "Last week I saw Maddalena and Arturo arm in arm, going to the cinema."

"I heard that he buys her jewelry and flowers every time he lays a hand on her," Colombina the Farmer's Wife said.

"If they always make up, there's no need for these theatrics," Carolina said. "It's shameful for them to run around like characters in a play."

"We get to watch live theater right outside." Old Veronica indicated Mrs. Fatti's house. "Rich people only get to see films on television."

They all turned their gaze to Mrs. Fatti's house. The American Wife was the only neighbor nearby who had a television set on the ground floor.

"I prefer watching movies on Mrs. Fatti's television set." Ninuccio the Painter said, joining the group of people gathered by the American Wife's house.

Grazia noticed Pasquale was among the boys standing on the chairs in the back. Being one of the tallest boys, he was able to enjoy a great view of the film through the glass door, which radiated an opalescent light.

The younger children were satisfied to sit on the steps of the side entrance, where they enjoyed the voices and the musical score of the motion picture entitled *Love and Jealousy*. Mario was always among the children seated on the steps. To Grazia's delight, he had an amused look in his eyes.

From time to time, Pasquale called Mario and allowed him to get on his chair and take a quick glance at the screen. Mario was enchanted by the television set. He thought it was a magic box since it showed amazing pictures that moved so fast.

Giacomino the Blind Man always had a privileged seat by the glass door of the American Wife's opulent house. Although he couldn't see the television screen, he listened carefully and envisioned the scenes in his mind. When there were long pauses, and he couldn't figure out what was going on, he would ask people close to him.

Many neighbors were more interested in the live theater that happened on the street earlier in the day.

"Did you see a woman running?" Lina the Warm House asked a circle of adolescent lads who lived on a lane nearby.

"We've seen that woman from Saint Peter Street running," one of the lads responded. "She was yelling like a maniac."

"Did you see which way she went?"

The lad nodded. "We followed her for a while. She was heading towards the river. A crazy guy was chasing her."

Grazia's eyes dimmed. *Maddalena is a victim of a crazy man.* "Can you look for her?"

"We'll find her," the lad said. "We're strong. We can protect the *signora*."

Grazia gave a sigh of relief as she watched the gang of adolescent lads walking away.

The television set was blasting a dramatic musical score when the spectators saw a woman emerging towards them on the street.

"She's coming," Titina the Alligator shouted as Maddalena walked forward.

Everyone was confronted with Maddalena. She had bruises all over her face. She sneered and completely ignored anyone who attempted to greet her. She quickly opened the door and went straight into her house. Many spectators winced as Maddalena slammed the door behind her.

"I don't understand why she behaves that way." Lina the Warm House shrugged. "We haven't done anything to her."

We were a bunch of cowards. None of us lifted a finger to help Maddalena, Grazia thought, but she refrained from expressing herself. It would have been pointless. *You can't contradict the ignorant. They think they're always right.*

"Maddalena got what she deserves," Titina the Alligator said. "A woman should never cheat on her husband. I wonder how she got away."

Giacomino the Blind Man focused his attention on the voices coming from the television set and to anything people said. "How did she get away?" he asked.

The television screen showed a woman hiding under a car.

"She was able to hide from him," Ninuccio said, although he was alluding to the movie. "That's why he didn't get the chance to kill her. He should have killed her, after what she did to him."

Giacomino expanded his eyes, since he thought Ninuccio was talking about Maddalena. "What did she do?"

"She kissed another man," Ninuccio replied, referring to the movie.

Giacomino's jaw dropped. "They saw her kissing another man?"

"Did you see the bruises on Maddalena's face?" Norina asked.

"He must have given her a hell of a beating," Titina said.

The blind man figured Maddalena had been caught in *flagrante delicto* with a lover. To make sure, he kept asking, "Who saw Maddalena with another man?"

No one paid attention to his questions. The television screen showed the leading actor robbing a bank. He was pointing the gun at two women.

Lina indicated the actor on the screen. "What about him? He's no saint. Someone should kill the husband."

"People are afraid of him," Ninuccio said.

"He has a gun," Carolina the Good Life said.

Giacomino's mouth fell open. "Maddalena's husband has a gun?"

No one bothered to give the blind man an explanation.

"He's killing her," Lina shouted, as the actor in the movie pointed the gun at the bank teller.

In the television screen, a lady looked through the window and waved at the passersby to seek help.

"Oh my God!" Carolina yelled. "Someone should help her. She could end up dead."

"Oh God!" Giacomino threw his hands up in the air. "What happened?"

Again, no one bothered to give the blind man an explanation.

"You should go to the *carabinieri* and tell them that Arturo has a gun," Giacomino shouted. "He's dangerous! He should be arrested."

For Giacomino the Blind Man, the movie and reality had become hopelessly intertwined.

X

It was Norina's habit to clean the house meticulously whenever she expected important visitors. On those occasions, she used the soap her sister Ada had given her. Humming a song, Norina scoured the floor, enchanted by the scent of the soap. When she was done, she pulled the fishnet curtain open and dashed outside. She admired her kitchen floor, dotted with glittering wet spots. She smiled at passersby overtaken by the fragrance of the soap permeating the street. When the wet spots disappeared, she returned inside the house and pulled the curtain closed.

Bursting with vitality, Norina dressed the kitchen table with an embroidered tablecloth that belonged to her mother. The tablecloth was torn, and it had plenty of patches. Norina placed an ashtray on top of the biggest patch and then centered a vase with plastic yellow roses. She stepped back to get a better view of the flowers. They looked charming! She smiled serenely as she pictured Grazia's beautiful face printed on a postcard she could proudly show to her friends and relatives. The church bell melodically chiming the hour startled her. She had to get ready. Ubaldo the Photographer could walk in at any time. She didn't want to be seen in her housedress by such an important visitor.

Norina ran up the stairs and went into the bedroom. She donned her black Sunday frock. The dress gave her the semblance of being a *signora*. She happily pirouetted in front of the mirror and looked at herself. She still had a nice figure. When she was young she had been a beauty, pursued by scores of suitors. If she had been able to afford a dowry, she would have married well. Unfortunately, she had to settle for a working farmer who didn't even have a plot of land to his name. Numerous rich men had asked her out on dates, even though their parents didn't approve of her because she was poor. Three prosperous men had asked her to elope, but she had refused. She had always been afraid to take such risks. Women that eloped with men had no real guarantee of marriage.

Her sister Ada had eloped with a rich guy and gotten pregnant. Ada had taken a big risk. She could have ruined her life! She could have ended up abandoned with a baby to support. Of course, no one would ever have married her then. Ada was fortunate when the well-off man married her. She presumed he must be a good man. She was not aware he was a despot who was occasionally prone to beating her, and forbade contact with her family. Nevertheless, Norina considered her sister fortunate. Ada lived in a big house, always had food on the table, and had nice clothes. Ada had another advantage: she didn't have to worry about her daughters' futures at all. They had good dowries, and therefore were destined to marry well.

Norina had three daughters. It wasn't going to be easy to marry them off without dowries. It was a disadvantage to have many children. White Flies had fewer children. They feared that by birthing many children, they would end up destitute.

"If you divide wealth into too many shares, you end up with poverty," an old proverb said.

Norina often fantasized about having wed a rich spouse: a man who would have given her plenty of sumptuous food and a posh wardrobe.

Norina perked up when she saw Grazia's image in the mirror. "How did you get here?"

Grazia shrugged. "I walked."

Norina drew lira coins from her brassiere and handed it to Grazia. "Go to the bottega and buy six rolls each with one slice of *mortadella*."

"We shouldn't waste our money on cold cuts," Grazia said.

Norina flashed a bit of a grin. "We have to grant ourselves some luxuries once in a while."

As Grazia went downstairs, Norina combed her hair neatly. When she was done, she took one last look at her reflection in the mirror and headed to the stairs. Once on the ground floor, Norina went outside and smiled as she looked up at the luminous sky. It was a momentous day. She was going to receive Grazia's pictures! She was so content that she couldn't stop smiling. Norina's smile swiftly faded when she saw Clotilde emerging on the street. Clotilde's shadow moved rapidly on the ground. Norina's eyes lit up as she noticed Clotilde was carrying a bag.

Norina led Clotilde inside the house. "What do you have in the bag?"

"Something useful." Clotilde pulled a small plate filled with almond cookies, a bottle of homemade lemon liqueur, and a little crystal glass out of the bag and placed them reverently on the table. "I'll pour the liqueur for the photographer. You're messy when you fill glasses."

Norina compressed her lips. *Clotilde thinks I can't do anything right.*

Pasquale, Olimpia, and Mario popped into the house. They greeted Clotilde with a hug. Pleased, Clotilde grinned. Then she suddenly gave them a stern look. "I brought cookies for the photographer. Don't you dare touch one. You can only have them if he doesn't eat them. Is that clear?"

The children's faces drooped as they nodded.

Grazia walked into the house carrying her fishnet bag. She greeted her Aunt Clotilde by giving her a kiss on the cheek.

Pasquale turned to Grazia. "What do you have in the bag?"

"I bought rolls stuffed with *mortadella*," Grazia said.

"*Mortadella*," Olimpia shouted, jumping up and down.

"Eat outside, so you don't get the house dirty," Norina said.

As soon as Grazia handed the children the sandwiches, they scrambled out of the house. It was an extravagance to have a sandwich with a slice of *mortadella*.

Norina has the audacity to buy cold cuts for lunch, Clotilde thought. *No wonder she runs out of money.*

Grazia didn't allow herself a *mortadella* sandwich. She considered it a waste of money since she was going to work and would have access to plenty of food at the Zordi residence. Grazia kissed Aunt Clotilde's cheek again and exited the house.

Clotilde scrutinized the kitchen to make sure everything was in place. The tablecloth's patches caught Clotilde's eye. "Norina, you should have told me to bring one of my tablecloths. The patches on your tablecloth are too visible."

"The photographer is not going to notice," Norina said. "He wears eyeglasses."

"He'll notice because he wears eyeglasses. People see better when they wear eyeglasses."

"That's not true. Titina the Alligator wears eyeglasses and she can hardly see. You want me to call Titina and ask her if she sees the patches?"

Clotilde flared her nostrils. *"The photographer has good eyeglasses. Titina is using the eyeglasses that belonged to her dead aunt,"* she wanted to say. Clotilde regained her composure and decided not to argue with Norina. The last thing she needed was Titina's intervention. It would have created the latest performance of the Saint Peter Street live theater.

Caterina pulled the fishnet curtain out of the way and peered inside the house. "What does the photographer look like?"

"He's got white hair and black eyeglasses." Clotilde pushed Caterina outside and closed the curtain. "You're letting all the flies into the house."

At the sight of the flies meandering in the kitchen, Clotilde stamped her foot, wringing her hands together. "Norina, you should get rid of those flies. It's not good to have flies in the home when you have guests. They make the whole place look filthy."

Norina reached for a cloth. "I'm going to take care of the flies." Norina loved to chase flies around the room. "I got him," she yelled with childlike delight every time she caught one.

"I see a man with white hair and black eyeglasses down the street," Caterina shouted, popping into the house.

"Pull the curtain aside and hold it for him when he walks in," Clotilde said.

"I know how to show respect to guests." Looking at a fly on the table, Caterina tapped her feet. "I want to catch the flies. I'm good at it."

"No one is faster than me when it comes to catching flies," Norina said, capturing the fly with a cloth.

"He's almost here," they heard Olimpia's voice say.

Norina instantly disposed of the cloth and the dead flies. Pasquale, Olimpia, Mario, and Little Donato walked into the house. Caterina held the curtain aside to welcome the important visitor. Finally, he appeared. Caterina released the curtain as soon as Ubaldo the Photographer entered. He looked very distinguished in his gray suit and maroon tie. He bowed and gave the women kisses on their hands. Clotilde was overwhelmed by his gentility. She moved a chair away from the table and gestured for him to sit down. As was the proper etiquette, the photographer handed Norina the envelope containing Grazia's portraits before he sat on the chair. Norina tore open the envelope. The minute she pulled out the photographs, the children promptly gathered around her.

Pasquale's face glowed. "My sister looks like an actress."

Olimpia jumped and beamed. "Grazia looks like a *signorina* I saw on Mrs. Fatti's television set."

Caterina's jaw dropped. "Grazia is stunning."

Norina nodded with a grin. "She's very beautiful."

"Grazia looks very refined," Clotilde said.

Olimpia climbed on a chair to take a better look. Just as she attempted to reach for a photograph with her little hand, Clotilde gave her a stern look and snatched the photographs away. Clotilde couldn't help but burst into a smile when Little Donato pointed at the photographs and sang: "Grazia!" in his childlike voice.

Mario stared at Grazia's image, speechless. He thought his sister looked absolutely beautiful, even more beautiful than Mrs. Francesca Zordi. As usual, however, Mario lacked the confidence to express his opinion, reluctant to reveal his speech disability to the special guest. The photographer was the hero of the day.

Norina started the coffee. Though there wasn't any need to make coffee for the guest, since Clotilde had brought liqueur, Norina decided to have coffee to treat herself. Grazia's portrait was a major event to celebrate. She unlocked the credenza and took out the sugar pot.

Clotilde indicated the cookies to the photographer. "Would you care for a cookie?"

"No, thank you," the photographer responded. "I have sensitive teeth. I don't eat sweets."

It was exactly what the children wanted to hear. They attacked the plate and filched all the cookies except one, just in case the important visitor changed his mind. Clotilde managed to hide her disappointment by forcing a grin at the honored guest. She then reached for the lemon liqueur and poured it gracefully into the small crystal glass.

Ubaldo drank the alcohol all in one shot. He twisted his finger into his cheek. "The lemon liqueur is exquisite."

"I made it myself." Clotilde poured more lemon liqueur into his glass.

In the meantime, Norina placed a tray containing three steaming demitasses cups of coffee and the sugar pot on the table.

Clotilde turned to the special guest. "How many spoons of sugar would you like?"

"None," the photographer replied. "I take my coffee without sugar."

"Put four spoons in my cup," Norina said.

Clotilde shoveled two spoonfuls of sugar into Norina's cup and one into her cup.

The photographer sipped his coffee. "If you don't mind, I'd like to ask your permission to exhibit one of Grazia's photographs in the window of my studio."

"You want to show off my niece to everyone?" Clotilde asked. "A respectable unwed woman should not have her photograph on display."

Norina was grateful to Clotilde for providing the money for Grazia's portrait, and she didn't want to disagree with Clotilde in the photographer's presence. She remained silent, even though she was desperate to have her daughter's portrait on display. She was confident the photographer would win Clotilde over.

"*Signora* Clotilde, you should take great pride in Grazia's beauty." Ubaldo showed a glint of a grin. "Look at her delicate features. Look at her smile. It's magical. It illuminates the whole image. Showing her photograph in the window would be like showing a work of art."

Norina tilted her head. She didn't understand why her daughter's portrait was compared to a work of art. Before Norina could ask him for an explanation, Clotilde silenced her with a stern Look.

Clotilde shifted her attention to the photographer. "There is a difference between art and photography," she said with the air of an expert.

"At times, you can create art with photography," the photographer said. "In as much, photography can become art."

Norina's eyes lit up. "Now I understand. My daughter's portrait is like a painting."

Ubaldo nodded. "It's a piece of fine art that deserves to be displayed. Many mothers beg me to put their daughters' photographs in the window. Most of the time, I refuse because I'd rather show the most photogenic ones. Even Contessa Gilda asked to have her daughter's photo displayed. I had to make up excuses, because I'd rather exhibit a photograph of someone like Grazia. You shouldn't hesitate to give me permission to display your daughter's portrait."

Norina fixed her eyes on Clotilde to seek her approval. Clotilde's face was impassive. It seemed she couldn't make up her mind. After a minute that seemed to last forever, Clotilde finally approved with a slow smirk.

Norina promptly turned to Ubaldo. "I give you permission to show Grazia's portrait."

Norina's eyes sparkled as she envisaged her beautiful daughter on display in the window of the photo studio. She couldn't wait to show Grazia's portrait to friends and acquaintances as well as strangers.

"The girl in the picture is my daughter. Her name is Grazia, Grazia Voltini." Norina planned just what to say in case she happened upon a rich man looking at her daughter's portrait.

"I'm going to put Grazia's portrait on display as soon as I get back to the studio," Ubaldo the Photographer said as he got up from the chair. He then bowed and gave Clotilde and Norina each a kiss on the hand.

Enchanted, they watched him stride out of the house.

"He's very refined," Clotilde said. "He's a real gentleman, an intellectual."

Norina bobbed her head in agreement, though she didn't know what the word "intellectual" meant. *He's also a good-looking man,* she thought, revealing a trace of a smile.

Sensing the children's eyes on the sugar, Clotilde hastily stored the sugar pot in the credenza before they could attack it. She directed a stern look to the children. "If you ever do that again, you're going to get punished."

"What did we do?" Pasquale asked.

"You behaved like animals," Clotilde shouted. "You snatched all the cookies from the plate."

"You told us we were allowed to eat the cookies if the photographer didn't eat them. He said he had bad teeth and couldn't have sweets. We were polite. We left him one cookie, just in case he changed his mind."

Clotilde broke into a grin. "You should become a lawyer. You have an answer for everything."

The children set their eyes on the last cookie lying on the plate.

Clotilde pointed at Mario. "You should eat the last one because you only took a single cookie."

Mario remained speechless. He was astonished that his aunt had chosen him.

"Mario, take the last cookie," Clotilde said.

Obediently, Mario took the cookie. He blushed as he sensed all eyes on him. He felt as if he were stealing it. He confined himself in the corner and munched it, savoring every crumb.

Clotilde retrieved the empty plate, the liqueur, and the little crystal glass. She wrapped them in towels and placed them in her bag.

"I have no use for liqueur." Norina said. "My head spins when I drink."

"A woman shouldn't drink. I only keep a bottle in the house for when Father Camillo comes to visit."

The priest drinks good wine when he preaches in church and good liqueur at Clotilde's house, Norina thought.

Clotilde placed one of Grazia's photographs in her purse and gave a parting homily to the children: "May Jesus Christ be praised."

"May he always be praised," the children replied in unison.

As soon as Clotilde departed, Norina reached for her daughter's portraits and stepped outside. She waved the photos in the air. "I got Grazia's photographs."

Norina captured the attention of all the neighbors seated at their front doors. In a fraction of a second, they congregated around her.

"Can I see them?" Lina the Warm House asked.

Anna the Heavyweight took the photographs from Norina's hands. "I want to see them first." She smiled as she looked at the photographs. "Grazia is a doll." She then switched her attention in the direction of her house and shouted, "Margherita, come and see Grazia's photographs."

"Please, let me see them in the meantime," Lina said.

The strong woman pushed her away with one hand. "My daughter has to see them first."

A line of neighbors, anxious to see the photographs, formed behind Lina. They all waited impatiently for Anna's daughter. When Margherita finally popped out of the house, they all cheered. Anna handed her daughter the photographs.

"Grazia looks gorgeous," Margherita said.

Lina promptly took the photographs from Margherita's hands and gazed at them. "Grazia looks like a White Fly."

The neighbors congregated around Lina to look at the photos.

"She looks like an angel," Old Veronica said.

Baronessa Rosa flashed a grin. "Grazia looks divine."

Titina the Alligator narrowed her eyes when she looked at the photographs. Due to her poor eyesight, she had only a blurry view of Grazia. "She looks more beautiful in person."

Many neighbors gave her stern looks.

"You say that because you can hardly see," Old Veronica said.

Titina lifted her chin. "I can see more than you because I'm much younger and I wear glasses."

"I see so well that I don't even need eyeglasses."

Titina placed her hands on her hips. "You don't have the money to buy glasses."

"I have a rich niece who is happy to buy me eyeglasses any time I want."

"You don't have a rich niece. All your relatives are so poor that they don't even have the eyes to cry."

"I don't want you to fight in front of my daughter's pictures," Norina yelled.

Anna clenched her fists. "If you don't stop, I'm going to give you both a beating."

Intimidated by the strong woman, Titina and Old Veronica remained silent.

"I remember Grazia from when I was able to see, and I can imagine how she must appear in the photographs," Giacomino the Blind Man said. "She's so breathtaking that she could marry an American."

Norina's eyes coruscated. She derived immense gratification from the captivated expressions and by the comments of everyone who viewed Grazia's portrait.

Norina informed the viewers that Ubaldo the Photographer was going to display Grazia's portrait. "He picked my daughter's photograph out of all the girls in town. To tell the truth, I didn't want to put Grazia's picture in the window, but he insisted."

"It's an honor to have a portrait on display," Baronessa Rosa said. "You should be proud."

Norina revealed a smile. She was proud and honored to have her daughter's beauty grandstanded.

As soon as Norina returned to the house, she placed one of the photographs on top of the mantle of the fireplace. Like a star in the sky, Grazia's photograph illuminated the whole kitchen. Norina thought Grazia was the most precious possession she had. She was certain her daughter's portrait would be noticed at the photo studio. She hoped a rich man would become enraptured by Grazia's beauty and ask for her hand in marriage. Her whole face lit up at the idea of having a wealthy son-in-law who could uplift the entire family.

When Grazia came home from work, she was faced with her own portrait standing on top of the mantle of the fireplace.

"Do you like the picture?" Norina asked.

"It's nice," Grazia replied. She didn't show any emotion. She felt her mother should have spent the money on something more useful, like food, instead of wasting it on the photographs.

Norina beamed. "I showed the photograph to the neighbors and they all liked it. Giacomino the Blind Man said that you look beautiful enough to marry an American."

My mother is so excited that she's lost touch with reality, Grazia thought. *She forgot that Giacomino can't see.*

XI

Norina couldn't personally deliver Grazia's portrait to her only sister, Ada. She wasn't on speaking terms with Ada's husband Rodolfo, and consequently wasn't allowed in his house. The trouble between Norina and her brother-in-law went back eighteen years to when Ada eloped with Rodolfo. He was considered *un buon partito*, a good catch, since his family owned large expanses of land. Rodolfo's family utterly disapproved of his relationship with Ada, who was a poor peasant girl with no dowry. When Rodolfo's parents found out Ada was pregnant, they forbade their son to wed her. Suddenly, Rodolfo disappeared. Norina's brother Vituccio went looking for him, but Rodolfo was nowhere to be found.

"I'm going to be forced to put my child in an orphanage and work as a maid for the rest of my life," Ada said as tears streamed down her face. "No one is ever going to want to marry me."

"There's a solution for everything," Norina said.

Norina summoned the doctor and convinced him to exaggerate the severity of Ada's condition. She also begged Father Camillo to persuade Rodolfo to marry her sister. The priest and the doctor went along with Norina's plan, driven by the belief they could greatly improve two lives: those of both Ada and her baby. The doctor got ahold of Rodolfo somehow, and informed him that Ada was terminally ill. In spite of this, Rodolfo didn't seem to care.

"It's God's will," Rodolfo said, as if he were a priest.

Father Camillo finally convinced Rodolfo to marry Ada as an act of charity, since she didn't have long to live.

I can kill two birds with one stone, Rodolfo had thought. *I'll save my reputation, and I'll become a free man.*

Once Ada married Rodolfo, she came back to life.

"It's a miracle," Father Camillo said to the congregation in church.

Six months later, Ada gave birth to their daughter, Mariella. A year later, another daughter named Catia was born. Rodolfo was obliged to acknowledge his wife in light of the fact she had made him a father. He took pains to transform her into a *signora.* He taught her how to read, write, and speak Italian correctly, as well as the rudiments of etiquette.

Rodolfo was nicknamed Great Shoulders due to his physically imposing frame. He didn't have any respect for his indigent in-laws, whom he considered lowlifes, especially Norina. He forbade his wife and daughters to see Norina and her children, or give them any pecuniary assistance.

Rodolfo considered himself a White Fly. He was so filled with himself that he didn't want to have nothing to do with lesser people. "They're nothing but dirty black flies," he would say. "We can't put all the herbage in one bunch."

Though Ada felt sorry for her needy sister, she was dreadfully terrified of her husband. Thus, she rarely helped Norina financially. Norina was confident that her only brother, Vituccio, would give her a gift once she gave him Grazia's photograph. It was customary to give out photographs to one's relatives, and recipients usually expressed their gratitude with a gift. Norina needed a gift of money or food.

Vituccio Senzi was a popular taxi driver in town. He and his wife, Marta, lived on a cul-de-sac nicknamed Horseshoe Street since it was shaped like a horseshoe. Due to his line of work, Vituccio was often seen in the company of women whose reputations had been sullied. Everybody assumed he was having a good time with one or more of them.

All the gossip about Vituccio ended up reaching the ears of his wife Marta, who didn't think twice about throwing fits and scolding him loudly with accusations. Even though Vituccio always managed to turn the radio to its highest volume, attempting to camouflage his wife's hysterical yells, the whole neighborhood could hear the battle anyway. Because of her ear-splitting screams, Marta had been nicknamed the Screamer of Horseshoe Street.

When Norina entered Horseshoe Street, she heard yells and assumed they were coming from her brother's house. Norina nodded "Hello," to Candida the Rosy Cheeks, who was standing by her door listening to the commotion.

Candida greeted Norina with a trace of a smirk. "You missed the first act of *La Traviata*."

"What happened?" Norina asked as she admired Candida's rosy cheeks.

"This morning they had a big fight, and your brother managed to play the musical score of *La Traviata* as background music."

"I'm going to try to calm them down."

Norina headed towards the Senzi's house. As soon as she reached the front entrance, the cacophony ceased. Marta appeared and forced a smile.

"I brought Grazia's photographs," Norina said as she passed Marta and walked into the house.

Vituccio tapped his feet. "Let me see them."

Norina withdrew two photographs from her purse and handed them to him.

Vituccio was so proud that he couldn't contain his joy. He trotted around the room, staring at the picture.

Coming back in, Marta looked at the photographs with a half-smile, but declined to offer any compliments.

"Grazia is the jewel of our family," Vituccio said. "I'm going to frame the picture and put it on my dining room table."

"Vituccio, I want you to give a photograph to Ada," Norina said.

"I'll visit Ada when Rodolfo is not around and give her the pho-tograph." Vituccio turned to his wife. "We have lots of onions that a customer gave me. Where are they?"

Marta bit her lower lip. "They're in the back room."

Vituccio went into the back room and returned a minute later with a basket filled with onions. He placed the basket on the table. "I got them from a farmer I drove to Naples. The poor man didn't have any money to pay me, so he compensated me with lots of onions."

Marta stamped her foot. "Next time, you should ask your customer to show you the money before you drive them anywhere."

"The man was desperate. He had an urgent situation. He had to visit his dying mother. I couldn't ask him to show me money."

Marta raised her voice. "Do you think you're the priest of this town?"

Vituccio shrugged. "Onions are better than nothing."

Norina bobbed her head in agreement. "Onions are better than nothing. I love to have raw onions with bread."

Marta gave Norina a stern look.

Norina decided to leave before Marta started a quarrel. "I have to go home."

"You just got here. Stay a little longer," Vituccio said. He wanted his sister to stay so he could have a break from his wife's torment.

"I have to make dinner for the children." Norina took the basket of onions and dashed outside with her head down.

Norina was disappointed. She had been flirting with the prospect that Vituccio would have given her some money or pasta. Unfortunately, she had to settle for onions. She quickened her pace as she heard bick-ering coming from her brother's house.

Marta kicked a chair and shouted, "You're not bringing home any money. You can't afford to give your sister a whole basket of onions."

"It's just the two of us here. We had too many onions," Vituccio said. "We have to consider ourselves lucky we don't have six children to feed."

"Thank God you don't have any children to feed." Marta huffed. "All the other taxi drivers in town make good money. You're the only one that brings home onions instead."

Vituccio's face flushed. "I have bad luck. It's not my fault."

Marta pointed her index finger at Vituccio. "It is your fault. I know why you're always broke."

Vituccio tilted his head and expanded his eyes.

"A lot of people have told me that you don't charge women for rides."

Vituccio turned the radio on at its highest volume. The radio station blasted a tango tune.

Marta clenched her teeth. "Yesterday you saw Lisetta, the Madame of the whorehouse, and you gave her a free ride."

"I had to take her to a doctor in the city. I didn't charge her because she didn't even have one lira."

Marta narrowed her eyes. "How can a whore be broke?"

"She's no longer a lady of the night. She gives free services to most of her customers. She believes in sexual charity."

Marta's jaw dropped. "Sexual charity?"

"Lisetta claims that she's become charitable."

Marta banged her fist on the table. "She's charitable with you for sure. Whores and criminals. Those are the people who are seen in your company."

"I can't force the women that ride in my car to show me a certificate of good behavior. I can't ask all the people I take to the lawyer if they're guilty of the crimes they've been accused of. I make a living driving people around."

"You can ask them if they have the money to pay you before you drive them anywhere."

"I can't do that. Most of the time it's an emergency. I feel bad."

"You feel bad for your *puttane* because you care for them. I'm sure they pay you in other ways."

Vituccio Senzi was a good man, filled with love and compassion. He didn't realize he was always broke because of his generosity. He firmly believed it was because fate was cruel to him.

Vituccio placed his hand on his chest. "Believe me. I've never had an affair with one of those kinds of women. I'm not that type of guy."

Marta remained silent. Vituccio's words were lost on his wife.

Unduly, Marta had built such an unethical reputation for Vituccio that no one believed his words. He was considered the most famous womanizer in town. It was a judgment shared by his brother-in-law Rodolfo, so Vituccio could never rely on him. Rodolfo was always ready to insult him. His wife's accusations and his brother-in-law's harassment had created a difficult situation for Vituccio, whose conciliatory attempts to preserve his dignity were always useless.

Tired of his wife's badgering, Vituccio took one of Grazia's photos, placed it in an envelope, and headed to the front door.

Marta's eyes flushed. "Where are you going?"

Vituccio sighed. "I'm going over to Ada's house to bring her the photograph."

"Her husband might be home, and you know he'd love to kick you out. Rodolfo said you've disgraced the entire family with your dirty reputation."

Vituccio refused to retort and stormed out of the house.

Marta took another basket filled with onions and followed him outside. "I know where you're really going. You're going to see your whores."

Vituccio exhaled. "I need some fresh air."

"I know what sort of fresh air you're getting with your whores."

Suspecting that anything else he said would meet with a similar riposte, Vituccio remained speechless.

Marta began to throw onions at him, one by one. "You should give your *puttane* some onions instead of giving them all your money," she screamed as she sensed sympathy from the neighbors.

The curious neighbors sat by their front doors, anticipating the stirring drama of the Vituccio and Marta Senzi Show. The theatrics gave them something to gossip about. They gathered into little groups and started conversations.

Vituccio scurried away, mortified, sensing the glares of the locals. To his disappointment, the neighbors refused to acknowledge him. The jury of the small-town scandalmongers had convicted him without a trial.

Vituccio decided to avoid walking all the way down Horseshoe Street, to get away from his neighbors' view. He felt relieved once he reached Stella Street, but to his dismay, he overheard people whispering behind his back. Apparently, even people living in the lanes nearby knew everything about him.

"A womanizer like him must make his wife's life impossible," he heard a voice say.

"He deserves a whipping," he heard another voice say.

Vituccio didn't bother to respond or to defend himself. It wasn't worth the effort.

As Vituccio passed by the *piazza* he bumped into Lisetta, the ex-Madame of the whorehouse. Though she was no longer a prostitute, she still looked like one with her heavy makeup and garish attire. Obsessed with the color red, Lisetta always wore low-cut red dresses. The ex-Madame was seen alone most of the time. Fearful of ruining their reputations, none of the women in town wanted to associate with her, except her fellow prostitutes. Men who had slept with her, pretended not to know her whenever they encountered her in public. On the contrary, Vituccio was a true friend, and wasn't ashamed of her. He greeted her warmly with a handshake.

Lisetta kissed him on the cheek. "I'm so happy to see you."

"I'm happy to see you too," Vituccio said.

She flashed a glint of a grin when she noticed Vituccio had an impression of her scarlet lips on his face. "Can you keep a secret?"

"Of course."

"I'm having sex with Pino the Red Eye. I'm not charging him any money. I feel sorry for him. He hardly makes any money selling fish. Do you know that he was a virgin?" Lisetta whispered in Vituccio's ear.

Vituccio couldn't help but laugh.

Lisetta waved at Vituccio. "I'll see you Saturday."

They have an appointment. His wife is right. He does have a good time with whores, a nosy neighbor that happened to pass by thought as he witnessed the scene.

The neighbor didn't know Vituccio's appointment was to drive Lisetta to her doctor in the city, and of course, immediately assumed the worst. A platonic friendship between a former prostitute and a man of Vituccio's reputation was beyond his imagining. He didn't know Vituccio was a gentleman, and had never had sex with a prostitute. Vituccio had compassion for them, and treated them as if they were as respectable as any other woman in town.

Sensing people's scorn on him, Vituccio staggered away.

When Vituccio passed by the fish market, he was greeted warmly by the vendors, several of whom he had given free trips.

Pino the Red Eye welcomed Vituccio with a radiant face. "Would you-you-you like-like some free-free-free fish?"

"I'll get some fish next time," Vituccio said.

Vituccio had no intention of taking complimentary fish from the beleaguered vendor. Pino would often run out of money to buy fish from the sailors and be unable to work for weeks. To go back to business he would borrow from friends, including Vituccio, who had helped him out a couple of times. Pino had always paid him back. He was an honest man who could be trusted.

"You-you-you have-have been very-very-very kind to-to-to my-my Lisetta. You-you gave her-her free-free-free rides." Pino shut his eyes and smiled. Lisetta is-is a-a woman and a-a-a half."

Vituccio nodded. "She's a good woman."

"I want to-to-to have a-a-a big wedding when-when I-I-I marry Lisetta, and-and I-I-I want you-you-you to-to be my best-best-best man."

Vituccio shook Pino's hand. "I would be honored."

"Thank you-you. You are-are-are my best-best-best friend."

Vituccio grinned. "I'm privileged to be your friend."

Vituccio didn't take Pino seriously. He didn't believe the poor vendor was ever going to make enough money to afford a wedding reception. Nevertheless, he was flattered that Pino considered him his best friend.

Pino the Red Eye needed a good friend. The only living relative he had was a half-sister in Argentina, Cecilia, and she was so ashamed of him that she pretended he didn't exist. Once Pino unexpectedly received a package with five shirts and a note that read:

From the only person who loves you.

Pino assumed his half-sister had sent him the package. He was so thrilled that he wore all five shirts, one on top of the other, and paraded on the street to show them off.

"My-my sister-sister has-has sent me-me five-five-five shirts-shirts from-from Argentina," Pino said to all his acquaintances.

Pino wanted to spread the news that he had a person who cared for him. He hired Angela the Crazy Head to write his half-sister a thank you letter. Cecilia never responded to Pino's letter. There were people in town who believed someone had played a prank on Pino by sending him the shirts and wondered who would waste their money to buy five new shirts for Pino the Red Eye.

Vituccio hoped his wife would never find out that Pino the Red Eye wanted to marry Lisetta and had asked him to be the best man. He knew Marta would be furious. Marta felt she was superior to both Pino and Lisetta, and didn't want to associate with whores and lowlifes.

As Vituccio headed to Ada's house, he entertained the hope that Rodolfo would not be there. Rodolfo had a bad temper, and was much bigger than him. The last thing he needed was to bump into his brother-in-law and be send home with loud accusations and possibly a bloody nose or a black eye. Vituccio's thoughts shifted to Lisetta. She had made Pino very happy by giving him her services free. No other prostitute would have ever slept with Pino the Red Eye even for a fair price. They were too repulsed by his physical appearance. Lisetta wasn't an uncompassionate person, after all. She had become a sex worker because she'd had a rough life. There were rumors that her husband Alfredo had forced her into prostitution.

That man was the scum of the earth, Vituccio thought.

Lisetta's husband had died mysteriously in Germany.

"Whoever lives miserably, dies miserably," many people said when they heard the news of his death.

When Vituccio arrived at his sister's house, he rang the bell and waited impatiently.

The door opened and Ada appeared. Her face lit up. "Vituccio."

"Is your husband home?" Vituccio asked.

"No, he went to the social club." Ada led him inside the house. "What brings you here?"

"My wife's nagging. She accuses me of having all sorts of affairs with ladies of the night."

"She's jealous. She's afraid to lose you."

"She's fanatical. She yells like a maniac and throws onions at me."

"Marta loses her mind whenever she gets upset. But deep down, she's a good person." Ada noticed the envelope in Vituccio's hands. "What is it, a letter?"

Vituccio drew the picture out of the envelope and handed it to Ada.

Ada flashed a bright smile. "Oh. Grazia is… *bellissima.*" Suddenly, her smile faded. "I can't put it on display. I'll have to hide it. If my husband sees it, I'll be in big trouble."

"Norina told me to bring it to you. She couldn't drop it off herself since she's not welcome in this house by order of the tyrant."

"You know how much I'd love to see her. Rodolfo doesn't listen to reason. I have to accept him the way he is. How's Norina doing?"

"She hardly has the money to buy food. I gave her some onions today. I felt bad that I didn't have more to give her."

"You don't know how much I would love to help my sister, but I can't. My husband gives me no money because he's afraid I'll give it to Norina. If I gave you some food to give to her, it'd get back to him. I really can't trust anybody. News travels so fast in this town. Rodolfo pays people to spy on me."

"He's another crazy person I have to deal with. Did you know that he tries to fuel my wife's jealousy?"

"I know. Rodolfo thinks you're the biggest womanizer in town. You're a victim of living in such a closed-minded place. I've tried to tell people that you're faithful, but no one believes me. Once you spill a handful of flour on the floor, it's hard to pick it up."

Vituccio's eyes became gloomy. "I am a victim."

Ada saw a red mark on his cheek. "What happened to your cheek? You got hurt?"

"No."

Ada took a closer look at the red mark. "It's the impression of lipstick." She reached for a towel and wiped it off. "I'm glad I noticed. Your wife would have thought the worst."

Vituccio contorted his face. "She would have strangled me." He crossed his hands on his chest. "Believe me, I'm innocent. I don't know how it got there."

"A woman wearing lipstick kissed you on the cheek." Ada shrugged. "I don't see anything wrong with that. Would you like a cup of coffee?"

"No, I'd better go. I don't want to bump into your husband. The last thing I need is to hear how much I've disgraced the family. I wish I were a Casanova. At least then I'd have some fun."

As Vituccio exited the house, Ada took another gaze at Grazia's photograph and beamed. Grazia looked like a younger version of Norina. Ada went to her bedroom and hid the picture under the mattress. Rodolfo would have given her a thrashing if he saw Grazia's photograph in his house. In his judgment, Grazia was a Voltini, and even printed on paper she was not worthy of being in his house.

On her way home, Norina passed by the old town and couldn't resist the impulse to stop by the photography studio. Her eyes gleamed with joy when she saw Grazia's photograph standing triumphantly in the center of the window. Norina waited there, entertaining the prospect that people she knew would pass by, but to her disappointment, she didn't know anyone who passed. When she saw a woman wearing dark sunglasses, she figured it was her neighbor, Maddalena. Norina waved to draw her attention. As soon as Maddalena waved back, Norina gestured to her to come forward.

Intrigued, Maddalena approached Norina. "What happened?"

"Nothing, I just want to show you my daughter's picture." Norina pointed towards the window.

As Maddalena removed her sunglasses to take a better look at the photograph, she exposed the bruises on her eyes.

"Grazia looks breathtaking," Maddalena said.

Norina smiled. "Ubaldo the Photographer begged me to put Grazia's portrait in the window. I really didn't want to do it, but he insisted so much."

"Grazia's portrait deserves to be in the front of the shop. Grazia is the beauty of Saint Peter Street." Maddalena exhaled. "I hope she finds a good husband."

"How's your husband?"

"Arturo is a plague on my life. He always accuses me of fooling around."

"He's very jealous."

"He'll never change. After he throws a fit and hits me, he always goes to confession and repents. He apologizes to me and buys me flowers and jewelry." Maddalena fingered the earrings dangling from her ears. "Last week, he bought me these."

Norina scrutinized the earrings. "They are very nice. They look expensive. At least he's thoughtful."

"I have no choice. I have to accept Arturo the way he is." Maddalena fiddled with her earrings. "What could I do? Where could I go? I have no place to stay. I don't have a job so I can't leave him. I don't want to end up like my sister Lisetta."

Norina widened her eyes. "God forbid!"

Maddalena put her sunglasses back on. "Arturo thinks that I'm like my sister. He thinks it's a family disease that we carry in our blood."

"Lisetta was such a good girl. I remember when she got married to Alfredo. Her husband seemed to be a good man."

"Marriage is a risk. It can ruin your life. Everyone believed that my sister's husband was a gentleman. No one knew that he was a monster. He destroyed my Lisetta. He was nothing but a pimp."

"Arturo is not as bad as Alfredo was, at least."

Maddalena's eyebrows curled against each other. "But he's worse in other ways."

"A husband who puts food on the table is better than no husband at all. I wish my Gino were still alive."

"Your Gino was a good man. He would never have hit you in public." Maddalena clasped her hands and looked up. "God takes away all the good husbands."

Even if her husband gives her a beating once in a while, he at least buys her jewelry. What's more important, he puts food on the table, Norina thought as she watched Maddalena skulk away.

The sunset had obscured the sky. People had retired to their houses to have dinner. Norina smelled the aroma of all sorts of food drifting through the air as she headed home. To her dismay, she only had onions to give to her children.

Onions are better than nothing, Norina thought. *I can make a delicious onion soup.*

XII

Delicate sunrays emerged from the purple-gray sky as Grazia headed to the train station. The sanitation workers were sweeping the streets with huge wicker brooms. Some farmers were riding bikes, tractors, motorcycles, or wagons pulled by mules. Grazia spotted Carmela the Daughter of the Umbrella Repair Man riding a bicycle. As Grazia waved, she noticed that Carmela was dressed like a man. Carmela's face turned beet red as she looked away. She pedaled furiously, rapidly disappearing into the distance.

What is Carmela doing dressed as a man? Grazia asked herself.

"What's a pretty girl like you doing out on the streets at this time of day?" Grazia heard a lecherous voice ask.

As Grazia turned her head, she was faced with Antonio the Devil, an obese street sweeper who had rotten teeth, sunburnt skin, and a reputation across town for his perversity. Grazia was petrified, but managed to hide her fear behind a stern look.

"If you're looking for adventure, I can give you all the adventure you want," Antonio the Devil said. All at once, he pulled down his pants. He wore a sardonic smile as he showed off his manhood.

Grazia ran away, horrified. The malicious street sweeper burst out laughing. He would often expose himself to young women. He always got away with it because the girls were too ashamed to say they had seen the intimate anatomy of a man.

Grazia gave a sigh of relief when she finally arrived at the train station. To her disappointment, the train was running late. She paced the platform back and forth. She was dismayed when Antonio the Devil reappeared. He kept pointing at her and chuckling hysterically.

Grazia gritted her teeth. *He followed me all the way to the train station. He senses I'm afraid and enjoys it. He's a depraved man.*

Grazia exhaled heavily when she heard the screeching sound of the approaching locomotive. As soon as the train came to a halt, the doors opened and Grazia jumped in. Her eyes filled with tears as she threw herself onto a seat. Impulsively, she withdrew a book from her bag and held it in front of her face. She didn't want to give Antonio the Devil an opportunity to look at her through the window. She rapidly wiped her eyes with the backs of her hands as she saw drops of tears on the book. She had borrowed the book from Mrs. Francesca Zordi, and didn't want to damage it.

When Grazia walked into the Zordi's house, her somber look revealed her mood.

"What happened to you? You look like you saw a ghost," Mrs. Francesca Zordi asked, leading Grazia into the living room.

"I saw a disgusting man. He showed me his private parts and followed me all the way to the station. I was so relieved when I got on the train."

Mrs. Zordi gave Grazia a hug. "You should report him to the *carabinieri.*"

Grazia remained silent.

"We create monsters because we don't have the courage to stop them. No man has the right to treat women like objects."

"I got so scared," Grazia mumbled, bursting into tears.

Mrs. Zordi reached for a handkerchief and handed it to Grazia. "Sit down and relax."

As Grazia sat down a tall, handsome man sauntered into the room. He smiled at Grazia, mesmerized by her beauty.

"This is my friend Sallustio," Mrs. Zordi said.

Grazia nervously wiped her tears with the handkerchief. She forced a smile, though she didn't recognize his name.

"You look upset. You should drink some chamomile tea," Mrs. Zordi said. "Make a whole pot and bring it to the living room. You'll have tea with us."

It was the first time Grazia was invited to have tea with Mrs. Zordi. *You'll have tea with us*, she kept repeating to herself as she headed to the kitchen.

"Who's that girl?" Sallustio asked.

"She's my favorite maid," Mrs. Zordi responded.

"She looked distraught."

"She saw a revolting pig on her way to the train station. He exposed himself and followed her."

"That can be upsetting for a woman."

"I feel sorry for her. She's a good person. She works hard to help her family out. She's not a common peasant girl. She's intelligent, and she seizes any opportunity to improve herself. She often borrows my books."

A beautiful and intelligent young woman like her should be more than a maid, Sallustio thought.

Grazia entered the room carrying a tray containing hot cups of chamomile tea, a sugar pot, and silver spoons. She placed the tray on the coffee table.

"I don't want any sugar," Mrs. Zordi said, taking a cup of chamomile tea.

Grazia directed her attention to the guest. "How many sugars would you like?"

"I'll take care of it," he replied. "Enjoy your tea." He was so captivated by Grazia's beauty that he forgot to put any sugar in his tea. He kept staring at her as he sipped it.

Overwhelmed by his courtesy, Grazia forgot to take any sugar as well. She apprehensively took a sip of her tea.

Mrs. Zordi turned to Grazia. "Do you know the person who followed you?"

Grazia blushed and lowered her head as she realized Mrs. Zordi had told the distinguished man she had gotten an eyeful of Antonio the Devil's private parts. "His name is Antonio. He's nicknamed the Devil because he acts like one."

"I heard about him," Mrs. Zordi said. "He is the one who raped the Gorgeous Woman. People named her that because she was the most beautiful woman in town in those days."

Sallustio looked at Grazia. "You should definitely report him to the *carabinieri*. A vicious animal like that should not be on the loose. If you don't want to do it, I'd be happy to do it."

"I'll report him." Grazia widened her eyes, surprised by her own prompt words.

Mrs. Zordi lit a cigarette. "I remember the story. Antonio the Devil wanted to marry the woman he had raped."

"It must be doubly traumatic for a woman to wed a degenerate who has raped her," Sallustio said.

"Lots of men who rape women marry them." Grazia twisted her face. "The victims accept marriage to their rapists because they know no other man would have them."

"That's terrible," Sallustio said.

Mrs. Zordi took a drag of her cigarette. "People thought the Gorgeous Woman would have no choice but to marry her rapist, but to everyone's surprise, she steadfastly refused."

"Now there was a woman with principles, and a lot of courage," Grazia said.

Mrs. Zordi puffed smoke into the air. "The Gorgeous Woman tried to take legal action against Antonio the Devil, but his father had influential friends who were able to cover things up and have him acquitted of all charges. The poor woman didn't have the money for a good lawyer, and Antonio the Devil was left on the loose."

"She had a miserable life," Grazia said. "No one ever married her. To support herself, she ended up working in the fields. She was only in her thirties when she died."

It would be a shame if Grazia ended up just like the Gorgeous Woman, Sallustio thought. *She deserves to be loved and protected.*

Mrs. Zordi scrunched her cigarette into the ashtray. "Antonio the Devil was never punished, though he probably felt it was punishment enough that he didn't marry the woman he loved to abuse."

"The Gorgeous Woman made an effort to change things," Sallustio said. "She certainly made a difference."

Grazia flashed a glint of a grin. She liked this gentleman. He was distinguished, intelligent, and refreshingly sensitive. He was also attractive. He had piercing eyes that inspired trust. She could feel her body responding to the physical attraction.

Later in the day, Grazia fantasized about the distinguished man while she cleaned the Zordi residence. She figured he must be a foreigner, since he had an accent. She wondered what country he came from. When Grazia finished working, she wanted to say good-bye to the mysterious distinguished man, but she didn't have the courage. She told herself he was probably too important to pay her any more attention. She was nothing but a common maid. Immersed in her thoughts, she headed to the train station.

As soon as Grazia boarded the railcar, she opened her book and began to read, attempting to distract herself from thinking about the distinguished man. When the train took off, Grazia didn't notice that the distinguished man was on the platform, waving vivaciously at her.

She's too divine to pay me any attention, Sallustio thought, watching the train recede into the panorama.

Grazia couldn't concentrate on her reading, since thoughts of Antonio the Devil kept invading her mind. As she closed the book, she decided not to tell her mother about the incident. Grazia recalled when her mother blamed Caterina for being witness to the pervert's private parts.

"It's your fault," Norina yelled. "You were looking at him."

"Why would I be looking at an ugly thing like him?" Caterina yelled back.

Norina lowered her voice. "Don't tell anybody. People twist things around. They're going to think that you provoked him, or perhaps that you're having an affair with him. You have a reputation to save."

Grazia decided to tell Anna the Heavyweight about Antonio the Devil. Anna was the only person in town who could give him a thrashing and get away with it. On her way home, she realized she had forgotten to bring home any food for her family.

The children were disappointed when Grazia walked into the house empty-handed.

"I didn't get a chance to take anything from the Zordi's house," Grazia said.

Pasquale stamped his foot. "We can't even ask Aunt Clotilde for food. She's away on another pilgrimage."

Norina forced a smile. "You can have milk and water for lunch."

"Milk and water without any bread doesn't fill you up," Pasquale shouted.

Norina unlocked the credenza. "I have some sugar," she said as she withdrew the jar of sugar.

Norina patiently filled three bowls with milk and water. She then added one spoonful of sugar to each bowl to enhance the taste. Pasquale, Mario, and Olimpia slurped down the sugared milk and water voraciously.

Grazia read the despair on their faces. *They're hungry. If they have fun playing, they'll forget about being hungry.* She turned to the children. "Go out and play."

The children walked out of the house.

Caterina bounded into the kitchen carrying Little Donato in her arms and set him on the floor. "*Mamma*, the baby is hungry. Should I give him some milk?"

Norina placed her hands on her cheeks as she realized she had forgotten to leave any milk for Little Donato. She turned to Grazia. "We're out of milk. Go to Carmine the Shepherd and get half a liter of milk. Tell him that I'm going to pay him later."

"I'll give it a try," Grazia said, walking out of the house.

Norina reached for a cloth and busied herself catching flies.

"I'll help you catch the flies," Caterina said.

"I don't need your help," Norina yelled.

Caterina scrambled out of the house.

Norina imagined herself hunting the White Flies. They were the lucky ones. They had no worries in the world. She derived a particular satisfaction when she smashed one of those flies. But as she gave it a second thought, however, she realized she was killing her own kind. The flies were black. She was considered a black fly, a common fly.

When Grazia walked into the house empty-handed, Norina bit her lip so as not to cry.

"Carmine the Shepherd doesn't want to give me any more credit," Grazia said.

Norina reached for the sugar pot reserved for the guests. "We're going to give Little Donato water and sugar."

Norina couldn't resist the impulse to dump all the sugar into a bowl. Her eyes gleamed with tears as she looked at the empty pot. She was left with nothing.

Little Donato avidly drank the sugared water, but it didn't satisfy his hunger. He cried hysterically while his tiny stomach rumbled.

Grazia attempted to calm him down by rocking him in her arms, but Little Donato wouldn't stop crying.

Norina placed her hands on her head. "He's giving me a headache."

"I'll take him to old Veronica's house," Grazia said, leading the baby outside.

Norina's mood brightened when she recalled she didn't have any debts with the bottega at the moment. *I'm sure Teresina is going to give me credit*, she thought. She reached for her fishnet bag and rushed out of the house.

When Norina entered the bottega, to her disappointment, Pasquina was the only one serving customers. Norina waited patiently, standing in the line for the credit customers for a half an hour until her turn finally arrived. Pasquina gave her a harsh look.

"Where is Teresina?" Norina asked.

"She went with my sister Costanza to Ombretta the Maestra to pick the pattern for the engagement dress."

"Costanza is getting engaged?"

Pasquina smiled. "Oh yes."

"Give her my congratulations."

Pasquina's smile faded. *My sister has no use for Norina's congratulations.* "What do you need?"

"I need a kilogram of pasta and a kilogram of bread."

Pasquina narrowed her eyes. "Do you have one hundred and five lire?"

Norina's face blushed. "I'm going to pay you when Grazia gets paid."

Pasquina shook her head. "I can't give you credit."

"You gave Titina the Alligator credit."

Pasquina raised her voice. "I'm taking legal action against Titina because she bought a radio as big as a dresser and didn't pay her old debt to us."

"Who gave Titina the money to buy a radio?" a fat credit customer asked.

"Her son gave her the money for sure," Norina said. "He works in Switzerland."

Pasquina rubbed her hands together. "We called the marshal."

The fat credit customer's mouth fell open. "The marshal?"

"The marshal is going to Titina's house to take the radio away. My brother-in-law has taught me that business is business. In America, nobody gives anybody credit."

Norina dashed out of the bottega. Tears shone in her eyes. She walked down the street with her head bowed, to avoid looking at people. She didn't want to reveal her desperation. As she passed by Good

Health Street, she heard loud wails. She instantly turned in the direction of the noise and saw a black velvet drape hanging by the front door of a house.

"Where are you?" Norina heard a voice say.

Someone has died and people are crying, Norina thought. *People don't cry when you're starving. They only cry when you drop dead. They call all the dead people buon anime even if their souls are rotten.*

Norina approached an old woman seated by her front door and asked, "Who died?"

"Laura the White Flower," the old woman responded.

"Laura and I went to elementary school together."

"We live under the sky, anything can happen." The old woman shrugged her shoulders. "You're lucky it wasn't you."

Norina glared at the old woman. *She has some nerve. She's lucky it wasn't her. She's old enough to drop dead.* Her thoughts were distracted by the sight of a man standing precariously on the edge of a balcony.

"I'm going to kill myself," the man yelled. "I can't live without my wife."

Norina suddenly recognized the man. It was Fabrizio, Laura's husband. Two men appeared on the balcony and grabbed Fabrizio by the arms.

"Fabrizio, calm down," one of the men holding him back said.

"They should let him go," the old woman said. "He's never going to jump anyway."

"They all pretend to be devastated when they lose their wives," Norina said. "It's all an act. He's going to recover. He's going to pick out his new wife at the funeral for sure."

The old woman bobbed her head in agreement. "He was not good to his wife. He used to yell at her all the time."

Men who become widowed wed in a short span of time even if they have a dozen children, Norina thought as she walked away. *A widowed woman with children has hardly any chance of getting married again.*

She was worthless to a man. She had nothing to offer besides six children to feed. There was no chance she would ever be a wife again.

Norina spotted Baronessa Rosa. The opera singer appeared to be as desperate as Norina was.

"Have you seen Bianchina?" the baronessa asked.

Norina tilted her head. "Who's Bianchina?"

"One of my white pigeons has disappeared. Her name is Bianchina. Have you seen her?"

"No. I haven't seen any pigeons." Norina pursed her lips. *I wish the loss of a pigeon was my only problem.*

"You don't know how much my Bianchina means to me." Baronessa Rosa burst into tears. "She was given to me by my husband. Bianchina was two days old when he brought her home. He didn't even get to enjoy our pigeons. He died three days later. If you happen to see Bianchina, please let me know."

Norina nodded. *At least her husband left her with pigeons instead of children to feed. Someone got ahold of her bird and had it for dinner for sure. I'd do the same if I could grab one of her pigeons, but they're hard to catch.*

Norina was in desperate need of food to feed her children. As she gave it some thought, she realized the only person who could have helped her was her brother. She decided to send Grazia over to her brother's house to ask for food. As soon as Norina arrived home, she gave Grazia the orders: "Go to Uncle Vituccio's house and ask for a kilogram of pasta."

Grazia reached for her fishnet bag and dashed out of the house like a good soldier.

Marta gritted her teeth when Grazia stepped into her house.

"Is Uncle Vituccio home?" Grazia asked.

"He's not home. He's supposed to be working." Marta kicked a chair. "He's spending time with his whores for sure."

She's upset, Grazia thought. "When will he be back?"

Marta shrugged. "God knows."

Grazia summoned up her courage and said, "I came to ask for a kilogram of pasta. We're short on pasta."

Marta slammed her hands on the table. "Do I look like a bottega?"

"No, but I know Uncle Vituccio buys a lot of pasta."

"Not anymore. Lately, he's been bringing home nothing but onions."

Grazia flashed a hint of a smile. "Onions are better than nothing."

Marta scrambled into the back room and returned a minute later with a basket filled with onions. "This is the only food I can give you. Your uncle isn't bringing in any money lately. He's too busy fooling around with his whores."

Grazia rapidly filled her fishnet bag with onions. She refrained from saying anything in her uncle's defense. It was a waste of time. She was never going to be able to convince Aunt Marta her husband was innocent, and the last thing she wanted to do was antagonize her any further.

"Thank you for the onions," Grazia said, rushing out of the house.

Grazia has some nerve to ask me for pasta after her mother wasted money on a portrait. I didn't even have a portrait taken when I got married. She's just like her mother. She even talks like her. "Onions are better than nothing." Marta contorted her lips. *Her whole family should bathe their asses with those onions.*

Grazia fought back tears as she walked down the street. *If Uncle Vituccio were home, he would definitely have given me the money to buy pasta,* she thought.

She saw the photo studio from a distance. She didn't even stop to look at herself on display.

That damned portrait! My mother should have saved the money for a rainy day instead of wasting it on photographs.

Her eyes lit up when Angela the Crazy Head came to her mind. She decided to go to Angela's house.

Angela the Crazy Head welcomed Grazia with sincere joy.

"I asked Aunt Marta for some pasta, but she only had onions to spare," Grazia said. "I can give you some onions if you like."

Angela patted Grazia's arm. "You should keep the onions for your family."

Grazia gave Angela three onions. "I have lots of onions."

Angela thanked Grazia with a smile.

"I have to ask you for a favor."

"What favor?"

"If you have another reading of the novel in my house, I'm sure my neighbors would come and bring some goodies. I only have onions to give to the children, and they're tired of eating onion soup without any bread or pasta."

"I'll come as soon as I have some spare time." Angela took a piece of hard bread and handed it to Grazia. "It's not much, but it's better than nothing."

"You should keep the bread for yourself."

"Your siblings need it more than I do. Luckily, I only have two mouths to feed."

Grazia accepted the bread from Angela and dashed out of the house.

Once Grazia reached Saint Peter Street, she saw a crowd gathered in front of Titina the Alligator's house. Grazia joined the crowd.

"What happened?" Grazia asked.

"The marshal and Teresina from the bottega came to take Titina's radio," Lina said.

"Our Lady of Sorrows," a voice hollered.

Teresina and the marshal emerged from the house.

Teresina waved her hands in the air. "Guess what we found instead of the radio?"

"What?" Old Veronica asked.

Teresina covered her eyes with her hand. "A mouse on a plate eating tomato sauce."

"This is a waste of time," the marshal said.

Grazia saw her mother watching the scene with delight. *I'm glad she's having some fun.* "What happened to the new radio?"

"You think Titina is stupid?" Lina whispered. "Her cousin took the radio in the middle of the night and brought it to his house."

"What if Teresina finds out?" Grazia asked.

"Nobody will tell her. We're all in the same boat. We're all credit customers, so we have to protect each other."

Titina made her appearance. She felt as if she were on stage. The spectators moved away and granted her the best spot in the middle of the street.

Titina placed her hands on her hips and faced the marshal. "This is all I've got. If you want to take my broken chairs and my cracked chamber pot, you're welcome to take it."

Teresina huffed. "I didn't know that the new radio had disappeared."

Titina crossed her hands on her chest. "I swear on my aunt's grave that I never had a new radio."

The marshal turned to Teresina. "This indigent woman doesn't have anything valuable. We have nothing to gain."

As soon as the marshal and Teresina faded away into the distance, the neighbors gathered around Titina to laugh it off.

Ninuccio the Painter chuckled. "I didn't know that you were able to outsmart a marshal."

Titina chortled and spread her arms wide open. She felt like the leading character of Saint Peter Street's live theater."

When Grazia went home, she told her siblings Angela the Crazy Head was going to do another reading of the novel.

Olimpia swung her arms. "We're going to get Baronessa Rosa's mint candies."

The children skipped merrily around the house. Even though they had onion soup with hard bread for dinner, they didn't complain. They ate thinking of all the goodies they were going to have when Angela read the novel. To the children Angela the Crazy Head had become another fairy Godmother, with the power to magically conjure food and treats.

XIII

Norina's eyes welled up with tears as she kneeled before the statue of Our Lady of Sorrows.

"I'm desperate. Pasquina from the bottega and Carmine the Shepherd don't want to give me credit anymore. Clotilde is out of town and Marta only has onions to give me. I'm hungry. I've only eaten onion soup for days. You're the only one who can help me. Please, you have to help me."

To Norina's relief, the Madonna had a concerned expression on her face. She seemed to be listening to the prayer. Suddenly, she heard a voice inside her saying: *"Go to the wake."*

Norina called to mind her friend who had just passed away, and part of her wished she had died instead.

"Go to the wake," the voice said again.

Norina heard her belly groaning from hunger when she finally realized what the voice was suggesting. By going to the wake, she could stuff her stomach! They always served coffee and cookies at those functions. Overtaken by a sudden glee, Norina sprang off her knees and dried her tears with her sleeve. Filled with vitality, she got dressed in her black Sunday clothes and ran downstairs.

Once into the kitchen, Norina bumped into Grazia.

"Why are you all dressed up?" Grazia asked.

Norina flashed a smile. "I'm going to a wake. You have to come with me."

"Who died?"

"Laura the White Flower."

"I remember her. You stopped talking to her a long time ago."

"You have to make up with people when they die." Norina took Grazia by the arm and dragged her out of the house.

People didn't take naps during the siesta when there was a death in the family, nor did they hold back their morose moans of grief. Loud cries were coming from Laura the White Flower's house. The neighbors didn't complain out of respect for the deceased.

A skinny girl dressed in gray greeted Norina and Grazia as they entered the house. She escorted them into the bedroom. The deceased lay in a coffin clad in her wedding gown. Her husband Fabrizio was surrounded by friends and relatives, who were comforting him.

Norina produced some tears. "Laura," she shouted. She turned to an elderly woman. "I can't believe Laura is gone. She was such a good friend. When we were young, we were always together. We were in the same school in the first and the second grade. Laura was so smart. She was the best student in the class."

The elderly woman twisted her lips. *Laura was a disaster when it came to school. She repeated the first grade four times and never made it to the second grade.* She produced a half smile. "Yes... Laura was a good student."

"My wife was very smart," Fabrizio bellowed.

Grazia recalled that Fabrizio had called Laura stupid on many occasions.

"We also used to go to the Sewing School together," Norina said. "Laura was the best seamstress. She had hands of gold."

A middle-aged woman scrunched her forehead. *Laura never learned how to sew. She got kicked out of the Sewing School.* She exposed a glint of a grin. "Laura was very talented."

Fabrizio burst into tears. "My wife was wonderful. She knew how to do everything. I've lost the love of my life."

Norina opened her arms and threw them above her head. "I've lost a great friend. Laura! Why did you have to die? I don't understand why God takes all the good people."

The elderly woman folded her hands in prayer. "God doesn't want the bad people. He doesn't like them."

Norina stared at the deceased. "Laura, answer me. Talk to me."

Grazia's mouth fell open. *My mother is quite an actress.*

The skinny girl took Norina by the arm and helped her into a chair. The girl patted Norina's shoulder. "You're taking it too hard. You have to calm down. I'll give you some chamomile tea."

Norina shook her head. "How can I even think of tea?"

To Norina's relief, the girl insisted. "Have some chamomile tea, it'll calm you down."

"Ask for a cup of tea," Norina whispered in Grazia's ear as the girl walked away.

"I'm not thirsty," Grazia said.

Minutes later, the girl brought Norina a cup of chamomile tea. "How many sugars?" the girl asked.

"Put five," Norina responded.

Promptly the girl shoveled five teaspoons of sugar into the cup. Norina drank the sweet tea all in one shot.

"You probably didn't eat anything. Have some cookies."

"I'm too upset. I can't eat," Norina said, knowing the girl would persist out of courtesy. "I got so agitated today that I didn't have any food. My stomach shut down."

The girl reached for a tray filled with cookies. "Have some cookies. People say that if you eat and drink, you can drown your sorrows."

"How can I drown my sorrows?" Norina produced more tears as she grabbed a cookie. "Laura was such a good friend. She was so young!"

The girl gave Norina a handkerchief. Norina swiftly used it to wipe her tears.

"My daughter was too young to die," Laura's mother, Albina, yelled like a maniac. "Her children still need her."

"God should not take the young people," the middle-aged woman said. "God should take the old people."

The elderly woman gave her a stern look.

"God should have taken me instead of my daughter." Albina smacked herself in the face. "Why didn't he take me?"

"How did she die?" Grazia asked.

"A miscarriage. It was her eleventh pregnancy," the elderly woman responded.

"Poor Laura! She died over a miscarriage," Norina mumbled, eating her cookie.

Grazia remembered Saveria the Midwife had told Laura's husband that another pregnancy could have been fatal. *These men don't care. They only care about their pleasure.*

Loud prayers coming from the adjoining room caught Norina's attention. She jumped out of the chair and peered into the room. Old Veronica was reciting prayers with a group of elderly women.

Norina spotted Serafina the Maid sporting her black Sunday outfit. *She's a ghost,* Norina thought. *She's everywhere! Serafina always wears her best clothes whenever she goes to weddings and funerals.* Attracted by Laura's mother's shrill wails, Norina went back to sit on her chair.

"God says to have many children, but he didn't look after my daughter… and what about Saint Anna?" Albina shouted. "Saint Anna is supposed to take care of all pregnant women. How come she didn't take care of my daughter? I've been devoted to Saint Anna all my life. I begged her so much to look after my daughter. And what did she do for me? She didn't even bother to listen to my prayers. Saint Anna is not a real saint. A real saint helps you out."

Serafina poked her head into the room. She seemed absorbed by the drama.

Serafina thinks she's watching a tragic play, Grazia thought.

Old Veronica walked into the room and gave Laura's mother a severe look. "This is no time for sacrilege. You should not dare to criticize a saint."

"My daughter died because Saint Anna didn't help her out," Albina yelled.

Old Veronica looked up at the ceiling. "It was God's will. We have no control over what is written in the sky. We can only accept our destiny."

"Saint Anna can control the sky, but she didn't protect my daughter." Albina stamped her foot. "What kind of a saint is she? I treated her well. I bought her so many candles, so many flowers. I even donated my thick gold necklace to her. I'm never going to buy her another candle. I'm never going to give her flowers. I'm never going to give her another piece of jewelry. Saint Anna doesn't deserve anything. She's an ungrateful saint."

"Stop it," a woman from the Catholic League said. "If you keep blaming Saint Anna, the priest won't allow you in the church."

The Dumb Brothers entered the room. They began sobbing instantly. Several people surrounded them, eager to hear their comments.

The elder Dumb Brother waved at the deceased. "*Ciao* Laura... you look so pretty in your wedding gown. You look like you're getting married again."

"I can't believe you're wearing your wedding gown in the coffin," the younger Dumb Brother said. "I never saw you in a coffin. I hope you are comfortable in the coffin."

"How can she be comfortable? She's dead," the middle-aged woman said. "You don't feel anything when you die."

The elder brother shook his head. "That's not true. The priest said that bad people burn in Hell after they die. How can they not feel anything when they burn?"

"You should never talk about Hell at a wake," Old Veronica said. "Laura is in Heaven, surrounded by angels."

"I'm glad Laura is having a good time in Heaven with the angels," the younger brother said. "Laura worked so hard during her life. She deserves to have a good time."

Most of the people refrained from laughing, out of respect for the departed.

Norina didn't pay any attention to them. She had other things on her mind. "The children need food. Bring whatever you can from the Zordi's house," she whispered to Grazia.

Grazia pursed her lips as she nodded.

Anna the Heavyweight walked into the room. "Now it's my turn to pay my respects," she shouted. She pushed the Dumb Brothers away from the coffin and looked at the corpse. "Laura, you were a good mother, a good daughter and a good friend. You had a lot of patience with your children. You never beat them. You took good care of your mother when she got sick. And, you were very generous to me. You always gave me wine when I visited you. One time you even gave me a piece of chicken. I don't understand why God took you. You didn't deserve to die. God should only take those who are cheap, bloodsuckers and evil. They're the ones who deserve to die. I hope they die soon."

Anna went on and on with her crying. People were impressed by her energy. When she grew tired, she sat down and waved at the skinny girl who had been handing out food and drinks. The girl promptly approached her. Anna asked the girl to bring her coffee and cookies. She felt she had earned the treats since she had done so much blubbering, and the girl swiftly brought them.

Grazia discerned it was the right time to tell the strong woman about her encounter with Antonio the Devil. She sat next to Anna and told her that Antonio had exposed his private parts, and had laughed at her on top of it.

Anna contorted her face. "He laughed at you after he did that?"

Grazia nodded.

Anna's eyes flushed. "I'm going to take care of him."

Grazia thanked her with a hug.

People are afraid of Anna. She's more effective than the carabinieri, Grazia thought as she scurried out of the house to go to work.

Norina sat next to Anna, knowing she would have a better chance to get more cookies.

"Are the cookies good?" Norina asked.

Anna twisted her finger into her cheek. "They are very good." She promptly asked the girl for more cookies, and received a lot of them.

Anna shared the cookies with Norina.

On her way home, Norina saw Maddalena and Arturo riding in a glittering green car. Norina waved vivaciously at Maddalena. She was proud to know people who owned cars.

As Arturo stopped the car, Maddalena poked her head out of the window. "We're going to the opera."

Norina's jaw dropped. "To the opera?"

Maddalena smiled. "We're going to see *La Tosca*."

"Have fun." *Norina* watched the car until it disappeared into the distance. *Maddalena's husband isn't so bad after all. He smacks her around from time to time, but he treats her like a signora. He even takes her to the opera.*

Norina had never been to the opera. The closest she had ever come was hearing musicians playing opera music and singers singing arias during the town's annual feast in the *piazza*. The musicians and singers performed in a gazebo decorated with many lights and ornaments, which had been built for the occasion. Many of the poor people brought their own chairs from home to sit by the gazebo. They enjoyed the music and the arias as if they were in a theater. Norina had heard that real opera performances were glorious! They took place in a big, majestic theater with comfortable plush red velvet seats, elaborate hand-painted backdrops, and singers dressed in ornate costumes.

Norina grinned as she pictured the scene. *That must be spettacolare.*

When Grazia arrived for work at the Zordi's house, she was eager to see the distinguished man. She searched for him in every room of the house, but he was nowhere to be found. Filled with disappointment, she went into the kitchen and reached for the broom. While she swept the floor, she wondered who and where he was. She had a frantic desire to ask her employer many questions about him. She kept rehearsing in her mind how she was going to pose those questions. She didn't want to give away that she liked him. After giving it a lot of consideration, she decided not to ask Mrs. Zordi about him. The distinguished man was probably very important. Grazia didn't feel worthy of him. She was nothing but a simple maid with nothing to offer. Besides, he was too good to be true. He was handsome and intelligent, and had respect for women. She had never met someone like him face-to face. Sometimes she had to remind herself that he was real, and not a prince she had met in her dreams. Grazia was startled as she saw Mrs. Zordi entering the kitchen.

"Did you report Antonio the Devil to the *carabinieri*?" Mrs. Zordi asked.

"I told Anna the Heavyweight to give him a warning." Grazia winked. "He's afraid of her."

Mrs. Zordi laughed heartily. "I'm going to write to my friend and tell him how clever you are. He was worried about you. I'll tell him you are safe. If Anna gets involved, Antonio the Devil will be afraid of you for the rest of his life."

Grazia's face drooped as she realized the distinguished man must have left town, since Mrs. Zordi was going to write to him. She was tempted to ask Mrs. Zordi where he lived, but couldn't muster the courage to do so.

Grazia's eyes shone with tears. *He's a closed chapter in my life, and I'll never see him again.*

As soon as Grazia got home, she showed her bag to her mother. "I brought the head and feet of a chicken that Mrs. Zordi wanted me to throw out and a whole kilogram of pastina."

Norina beamed.

Humming a song, Norina cooked chicken parts with pastina. When she was done preparing the soup, she stepped outside and looked for her children, who were playing on the street.

"Come and eat, the chicken soup is ready," Norina shouted.

The children ran into the house.

Titina the Alligator and Lina the Warm House exchanged looks.

"How can Norina afford meat? She has a lover for sure," Titina said.

Lina raised an eyebrow. "Did you notice that she's always dressed up when she goes out? She just wore her church dress and it wasn't even Sunday."

"She wears expensive clothes. I wonder who gives her the money."

"Colombina the Farmer's Wife complained that Norina smiles at her husband."

"Once, I saw Giovanni the Farmer go into Norina's house with a whole case of eggplant."

"She also does work for him in the fields." Titina narrowed her eyes. "God knows what people do to afford meat."

The Voltinis ate the chicken soup with delight. When they finished, Grazia confronted her mother and told her she felt guilty for stealing the pastina.

"Don't worry, you can go to the priest and confess your sin," Norina said. "He's going to wipe it clean for sure. He can't refuse to do his job."

Grazia's eyes became gloomy as she surmised that it wasn't so simple to wipe a sin from one's conscience.

XIV

A crowd had gathered by Laura the White Flower's house. Four men in traditional black carried the coffin and placed it on a hearse, which was elegantly adorned with white flowers.

Albina hurled herself onto the hearse, desperately clinging to the last physical reminder of her daughter. "No," she shouted. "Don't go. I don't want you to go to the cemetery." Her two sons took her by the arms and dragged her away.

It was a dramatic scene. Most people were so moved that they had tears rolling down their faces. Many people followed the hearse while the town band played the funeral march. As the procession lumbered down the streets, the passersby stopped to observe, and to express their sympathy. Men took off their hats and women joined their hands in prayer. It was the last interaction they would have with the deceased. As she led the mourners escorted by her two sons, Laura's mother felt comforted by the people's respect.

Laura never got so much attention when she was alive, Grazia thought. *She was an abused woman, condemned to endless cycle of unwanted pregnancy and childbirth.*

"She was such a nice person," Bellina the Good Deed said.

"Laura was a saint," Candida the Rosy Cheeks said.

The dead become saints. People always say good things about them, no matter what they have done during their lives, Norina thought.

Among the people following the procession, Grazia saw Saveria the Midwife. Grazia noticed the midwife had a somber expression on her face. *She's probably thinking that Laura's death could have been avoided.*

Contessa Fiorella watched the funeral procession from the shutters of her window. Her eyes gleamed with tears. *It's so hard to be a woman in a small town. Laura was treated like an incubator. She had the right to have a life.*

When the procession arrived at the cemetery, the pallbearers took the casket out of the hearse and placed it by the grave. Albina attempted to jump into the grave. Her two sons grasped her arms and pulled her away.

"I should have died instead of my daughter," Albina yelled. "I'm old! I'm worthless. Laura was too young to die."

Saveria the Midwife gave Albina a hug. "Calm down. You can't afford to get sick. You have to be strong for the sake of your grandchildren."

Laura's children gathered around her coffin and cried silently.

They're the real victims, Grazia thought. *They'll be motherless for the rest of their lives. No one can ever replace their mother. Laura's husband can always replace his wife.*

"The midwife refused to give Laura's husband the condolences," Titina the Alligator whispered.

"Why?" Grazia asked.

"If she won't give the widower condolences, she must have a good reason," Candida said. "Saveria the Midwife is one of the smartest women in town."

"She probably has a personal reason not to give him her condolences," Bellina said. "Fabrizio is so devastated by Laura's death that he can't stop crying. I heard that he wanted to jump off the balcony."

"*But he didn't jump,*" Grazia wanted to say. Instead, she decided to remain silent. *They're so taken by people's performances that they can't distinguish between fiction and reality.*

Fabrizio embraced the casket. "Laura, can you hear me? Laura, please talk to me. Say something."

Many of the onlookers were impressed. Their eyes were filled with pity.

"He thinks that she's still alive," Bellina said.

"Laura, I don't want to live without you," Fabrizio cried out. "I want to be with you."

"I hope he doesn't kill himself," Bellina said.

Two men dragged the grieving husband away. The Margassi Sisters walked towards Fabrizio and held his hands.

"Calm down," Gina Margassi said. "Laura is in Heaven."

"I want to die," Fabrizio yelled. "I want to be with Laura."

Giovanna Margassi patted Fabrizio's shoulder. "Calm down, Fabrizio. You'll end up getting sick."

"They shouldn't be so nice to him." Lina the Warm House rolled her eyes. "He's a widower. He may get some ideas…"

"He's going to have some fun with them later," Titina said.

"He would never marry one of the Margassi Sisters," Candida said. "They're not even considered women. They're just a couple of whores."

Grazia felt heartbroken to hear the Margassi Sisters were considered whores. The sisters approached Grazia and greeted her with a hug.

Giovanna Margassi indicated an elegant, attractive woman in her forties wearing a purple suit and a black hat. "The Lucky Widow is here. She's paying her respects to Laura's mother. They're distant cousins."

"I heard all about the Lucky Widow," Bellina said. "She became famous in town when she got married."

"Why?" Grazia asked.

"After her wedding reception, she was kidnapped and raped. Her husband was so ashamed that he sent her back to her mother because she was no longer a virgin."

Grazia's eyes became gloomy. "I feel sorry for her."

Candida revealed a hint of a smile. "She became rich after her husband dumped her. She became the lover of a very rich doctor."

Grazia grinned. "She found true love."

"She was only his lover," Candida said. "The rich doctor couldn't marry her while her husband was still alive. She didn't get any respect from people because she was nothing but a *commara*."

"She got lucky the day she became a widow," Titina said. "Her husband fell off his horse and died, so she got to marry the rich doctor. That's why people call her the Lucky Widow."

Giovanna Margassi's eyes sparkled. "She was lucky to find someone who loved her."

"My mother used to say that luck comes when you least expect it." Gina Margassi bounced up. "I hope my sister and I get lucky."

Candida and Titina exchanged looks.

They think the Margassi Sisters will never get lucky, Grazia thought.

The Lucky Widow didn't greet Laura's husband. She gave her attention to Laura's children. She hugged and kissed them one by one and whispered something in their ears. The children felt comforted by her affection.

She's going to be good to those children, Grazia thought.

The Dumb Brothers appeared at the cemetery. Intrigued, many of the people walked over to them, eager to hear what they had to say.

The two brothers had an unusual way of expressing their condolences: "We wish you many happy days," they said to the relatives of the deceased.

Many in the crowd made their best efforts to refrain from laughing.

Anna the Heavyweight slapped each of the Dumb Brothers in the face. "You don't wish happy days at a funeral."

"We wished them happy days because we felt sorry for them, since they've been crying for the past three days," the elder brother said.

"You should give condolences when someone passes away," Candida said. "You should say: I'm so sorry for your loss."

"Laura is the one that has lost her life," the younger brother said.

"Laura deserves our sympathy more than her relatives," the elder brother said, leading his younger brother by Laura's coffin.

"Laura, we are so sorry for your loss," the younger brother said. "You have lost your life."

"They say that you are in Heaven with the angels," the elder brother said. "I'd like to pay you a visit."

The younger brother widened his eyes. "You'll have to die to pay her a visit."

The elder brother contorted his lips. "Laura, I'll pay you a visit when I die, but I hope it won't be soon."

People began to break off from the crowd, now barely able to conceal their laughter. The Dumb Brothers always generated laughter, and were always in high demand. Since they had a weakness for sweets, people would display candies and cookies on their windows to attract them to their houses. The brothers couldn't resist the temptation to visit people who would offer them sweets. They thought people were generous to them. It never occurred to them that the joke was on them.

Fabrizio invited all the funeral attendees over to his house. He provided a buffet in honor of his deceased wife. Norina filled her stomach with: three sandwiches, a glass of *aranciata*, a handful of cookies, and a cup of *caffè latte*. In contrast, Grazia behaved like a *signora*. She only took one sandwich and a cookie, and then left to go to work. Norina was disappointed she didn't get a chance to place food in her purse because two women dressed in gray were watching her and whispering among themselves.

They keep looking at me, Norina thought. *They're talking about me for sure. I hope they don't know that I stopped talking to Laura many years ago, and that I came to the funeral for the food.*

The women were talking about other matters. They thought Norina had come to the funeral to get noticed by the widower.

"He has ten children. He would never marry a widow with six children. There would be an army of children," Norina heard one of the women say.

Norina had no intention of being noticed by the widower. It would have been a futile hope anyway.

He has no use for me, Norina thought. *He's going to marry a young woman with no children for sure.*

A group of old women, eager to begin their prayers, congregated in the bedroom.

Those old women can pray forever. Norina decided to go home. It felt good to have a full stomach, even when somebody had to die to provide it.

XV

Norina and Grazia welcomed Angela the Crazy Head into their house with heartfelt cheer.

"I hope a lot of people come for the reading," Grazia said.

Norina was on the verge of tears. "I'm having nothing but bad luck lately. I'm not getting any work, and Pasquina has refused to give me credit. She said that in America no one gives credit. Just because her sister married an American, she wants to do things the American way."

"Pasquina refused to give me credit too," Angela said. "She's a petty woman who enjoys having a little power."

Lina the Warm House and Giacomino the Blind Man walked into the house. To Norina's relief, Lina brought a plate filled with green olives.

"You didn't have to bring anything," Norina said.

Lina grinned. "A reading by Angela the Crazy Head is worth every olive."

Grazia guided Giacomino into a chair.

The blind man tapped his feet. "I can't wait to hear the next chapter."

"I invited Baronessa Rosa, but she refused to come," Lina said. "She's very upset. Her pigeon Bianchina has disappeared."

Norina bit the inside of her lip. Baronessa Rosa usually brought a whole box of mint candies. The children were looking forward to those candies.

"Carmine the Shepherd isn't coming either," Giacomino said.

"Why?" Angela asked.

"His wife has forbidden him to come." Giacomino exhaled. "These days women have their say in the household. In my day, things were different."

"Even Colombina the Farmer's Wife won't let her husband and son come," Lina said.

"I don't understand why," Angela said. "They loved the novel."

Grazia's face blushed. *Colombina didn't allow Giorgio to come because of me. She doesn't want her son to associate with me.*

"What a foolish reason to miss a great story," Lina said.

"Giovanni and Carmine asked me to give them a summary when the reading is over," Giacomino said.

Angela scrunched her forehead. "I forbid you to give them any information about the story."

"They have no right to know if they refuse to come," Lina said.

Old Veronica entered the house. The old woman presented a plate heaping with dried figs as if she had brought some sort of treasure. "The children love my figs."

"Angela, when are we going to begin the reading?" Giacomino asked.

"Let's wait for more people to arrive," Angela replied.

Minutes later Titina the Alligator, Anna the Heavyweight, and Margherita walked into the house. Anna brought a jar of dried sunflower seeds.

"You didn't have to bring anything," Norina said. To her disappointment, Titina came empty-handed.

"I hope Angela didn't start the novel yet," Margherita said.

Angela winked. "I would never start a reading without you and your mother."

Anna took Grazia aside and whispered, "I took care of Antonio the Devil this morning. I punched him in the face, and threatened to strangle him if he does it again."

Grazia leaped as she flashed a smile. "What did he say?"

"He swore on his dead mother that he's never going to laugh at you again."

Grazia gave Anna a hug. Even though Grazia was grateful, she would have preferred Antonio the Devil to have promised never to victimize another woman.

The children are going to love the leftover snacks, Norina thought as she displayed the olives, sunflower seeds, and dried figs on the table. She entertained the hope that her guests would eat as little as possible.

"I know you won't mind, but I loved the novel so much that I took the liberty of inviting Mrs. Fatti to the reading," Margherita said.

Mrs. Fatti's attendance meant lots of American chocolates and candies. Norina beamed. "I don't mind at all. I'm glad that she's coming."

"Angela, when are you going to begin?" Giacomino asked.

"Soon," Angela responded. "Did anyone invite Carmela the Daughter of the Umbrella Repair Man? Last time she enjoyed the reading."

"I don't think she's going to come," Titina said. "She's hiding."

Grazia's mouth fell open. "Hiding?"

"She's pregnant, and she's so ashamed of it that she doesn't want anybody to see her," Titina whispered.

Lina narrowed her eyes. "He doesn't want to marry her."

"He said that the baby is not his," Titina said.

"Who is he?" Angela asked.

"Umberto, the son of Rinaldo the Lawyer." Titina contorted her face. "Carmela can't expect the son of a lawyer to marry her."

"Carmela's brothers are so disgraced by her pregnancy that they're forcing her to hide," Lina said. "I heard that they send her to work in the fields early in the morning."

No wonder Carmela was dressed as a man, she was disguising herself, Grazia thought.

"Last week I went to borrow a pot from Carmela's mother, and I saw Carmela," Titina said.

"Did she look pregnant?" Norina asked.

"She didn't look pregnant. Her dress was so tight." Titina pressed her hands around her belly. "That's what they do. When they're ashamed of a pregnancy, they wrap up their belly tight, so tight..."

"*Mamma mia*," Norina said. "She could suffocate the baby."

"We have more people coming," Grazia said.

The women stopped gossiping and turned their attention to Maddalena walking into the room. Maddalena brought a plate filled with cookies and a chair. She placed the plate on the table and seated herself on her chair.

Giacomino turned to Angela. "When are you going to start reading the novel?"

Angela patted his shoulder. "When Mrs. Fatti comes."

"She's on her way," Maddalena said. "I saw her coming out of her house."

A deep silence pervaded the room as they waited for the American Wife. She was the guest of honor. They were all looking forward to American goodies. When Mrs. Matilde Fatti appeared clad in a flashy orange outfit, the scent of her hairspray permeated the air. A delicious aroma emanated from a brown bag she carried with her. They all guessed what was in the bag.

"Good to see you, *Signora* Matilde," Angela said.

The American Wife waved her hand. "It's a pleasure seeing you all."

Grazia noticed everyone except Giacomino had their eyes glued on the brown bag.

Finally, Mrs. Fatti handed the bag to Norina and said the magic words, "I brought some American chocolates and candies."

Many of the attendees could not contain their smiles. Norina opened the bag, feeling everyone's eyes on her. She arranged the goodies on a plate and placed it reverently at the center of the table.

Norina scrutinized the many guests as they grabbed the American chocolates and candies. Her eyes became gloomy. *I hope they leave some for my children.*

As if reading Norina's mind, Angela said, "I'm ready to start."

She began the reading of the third chapter of the novel entitled, *Going to America* and immediately had the undivided attention of the listeners. The story about the two lovers who dreamed of going to America was so appealing to them that they didn't take any more American goodies. Soon after it began, shouts coming from the street disturbed the reading.

"Who wants thread! The best thread in town. Come and see my colorful thread," Lillino the Vendor kept repeating over and over.

Anna the Heavyweight leaped out of her chair and headed outside. "I'm going to fix him. I'm going to make him disappear in no time."

Most of the listeners got up from their chairs, eager to follow Anna.

"There's no need to go outside," Angela said. "Let's just hear what goes on out there. It'll be a short scene. Lillino will vanish once Anna tells him to go away. Let's pretend it's a radio play."

They all sat still, straining to hear the voices through the front door.

"Hey Lillino, go and sell your threads someplace else. We don't want to be disturbed right now. Angela the Crazy Head is reading a novel to us," they heard Anna's voice say.

"I didn't know that you were interested in books," they heard Lillino say.

Many listeners figured the fortress of a woman would not appreciate that remark.

Anna grabbed the diminutive vendor by his waist and lifted him up. "Who do you think we are... a bunch of ignorant peasants? Shut your idiot mouth before I slam you against the wall."

"Lillino the Vendor is so small that he shouldn't dare contradict someone like Anna the Heavyweight," Giacomino said.

Many listeners nodded.

Lillino's voice came promptly. "Please put me down, I'm afraid of heights."

Giacomino exposed a trace of a smile as he pictured the scene in his mind. "She's holding him up in the air."

"I'll put you down, but you'd better get the hell out of here," Anna's voice said.

"I'll go," the vendor's voice said.

Anna's voice got louder. "You have to disappear now."

Giacomino giggled. "Lillino is running away."

The listeners laughed hysterically. When Anna returned to the house, they all clapped their hands.

"*Brava* Anna," many listeners shouted.

Angela shook Anna's hand. "Your performance was great."

Anna didn't know what Angela meant by "performance," but refrained from asking so as not to reveal her ignorance. She figured it must be something good, since everyone was applauding.

Angela went on with the reading. The novel was fascinating and full of twists. Nardo arranged a fake marriage with his cousin Raimonda in order to reside in America legally, but he didn't have the courage to tell Vincenza. He still vowed to Vincenza that he would marry her. Vincenza believed his pledge, and refused all her other suitors. At the end of the chapter, Angela took a break and allowed her listeners to make their comments.

Titina shook her head. "I don't think that Nardo is going to keep his promise."

"He's a romantic man," Margherita said. "He's definitely going to keep his word. He'll never give up on the woman he loves. I wouldn't give up the love of my life for the world."

"A woman should never believe in a man's promise," Maddalena said."

"What about Melina the Fairy Tale's boyfriend? He didn't keep his promise," Lina said. "After being engaged to Melina for eight years, he got a chance to go to America and married an American woman to get his green card."

Titina nodded. "That's why they nicknamed her the Fairy Tale, because Melina believed in fairy tales."

"When her fiancé dumped her, Melina was so devastated that she wanted to kill herself," Old Veronica said.

"What happened to her?" Norina asked. "Did she ever get married?"

"Melina had to settle for an old man," Lina responded. "No one else would ever have married her. A woman is no longer considered pure after eight years of engagement."

"How can Nardo marry Vincenza if he's already married?" Old Veronica asked.

"Nardo can always divorce his wife and marry Vincenza," Mrs. Fatti said. "In America, people can get divorced and get married again."

Maddalena's eyes lit up. It sounded like the best idea she had ever heard. *America would be a great country to live in.*

The Voltini children entered the house. As soon as they saw the American goodies, they attacked the plate.

Norina manufactured a stern look. "It's not nice to take the candies and the chocolates. They're for the guests. Where did you learn such bad manners?"

"Let them enjoy the goodies," Old Veronica said. "They're kids."

The children grabbed more American goodies.

"That's enough." Norina indicated the door. "Go outside and play."

The children skipped out the door, each chewing on a treat.

Giacomino stamped his feet. "Angela, read the next chapter. I want to know what happens."

As Angela continued the reading of the novel, the listeners were enthralled. Margherita's eyes gleamed with tears when she learned Vincenza, who was stuck in Italy, kept waiting for Nardo even after she found out he had married Raimonda.

"That's true love," Margherita said.

"That's not love," Anna said. "That's stupidity."

In the meantime, Pasquale and Olimpia sneaked into the house and took more American goodies.

Norina slapped Pasquale on his arm. "Get out, and don't you dare come back in."

It was all an act. In her heart, Norina was happy her children were having the American goodies.

Mrs. Fatti turned to Norina. "I'm worried they'll get sick. My son always gets a stomachache when he eats too many sweets."

"Maybe it's better if I take the American treats to the back room," Norina said.

To Norina's relief, Mrs. Fatti said, "Good idea, take the dish away. I don't think the guests will want anymore chocolates and candies, they're too fattening."

Though everyone wanted more American goodies, everyone was too captivated by the novel to protest. Norina took the plate furtively off the table and secreted it in the back room. She was glad her children would be able to have American goodies for dessert.

Angela began the next chapter. It was filled with surprises. Nardo discovered the cousin he had wed didn't want to dissolve their marriage.

"She married Nardo and promised she would grant him a divorce once he became an American permanent resident. But now that she's married, she has no intention of breaking up. She doesn't want to let him go," Angela said to Titina, who didn't clearly comprehend the plot.

"A woman lucky enough to get married should never let her husband get away," Titina said. "She should fight for him, tooth and nail."

"She has no right to fight for him," Margherita said. "That marriage doesn't count because it wasn't made out of love. The judge should give him an automatic divorce."

"A divorce is a terrible thing," Old Veronica said. "When people get married, the priest makes them promise to be together forever."

"A divorce can be a good thing if the husband abuses the wife," Grazia said.

Maddalena bobbed her head in agreement.

Margherita shut her eyes and flashed a light grin. "I hope the two lovers are reunited."

"I wonder what happens next," Lina said.

Giacomino tapped his feet. "Be silent. We can only find out if Angela reads us the next chapter."

Angela consulted her watch. "I can't continue. I have to go."

"Are they going to get together at the end?" Lina asked.

Angela placed the manuscript in her bag. "I can't tell you what will happen."

Angela loved to leave the listeners in suspense. She waved goodbye and dashed out of the house.

That evening, after everyone had departed, the Voltini children had American chocolates and candies for dessert. They were always thrilled to get a taste of America.

XVI

"Get out of my house," Marta said, indicating the front door to her nieces and nephews.

The Voltini children ran out of the house.

Marta followed them outside, screaming, "I don't have any food to give you. Your mother takes the luxury of having your portrait taken by the most expensive photographer in town, and then she sends you to ask for food."

Grazia contorted her face as if she was about to cry. *Those damned photographs! We should have used the money for a rainy day.*

Many neighbors and passersby gathered by Marta's home. Mario hid his face with his hands.

Grazia froze when she spotted Colombina the Farmer's Wife. *Giorgio is going to find out my family begs for food.* She felt so humiliated that she wished she could disappear.

Marta turned to the neighbors and passersby. "Their mother feeds them veal and chicken for dinner and then she sends them to ask for onions. I barely have pasta, bread, and vegetables for dinner. I never grant myself the luxury of having meat."

Many of the people nodded. Marta was pleased to have some witnesses who sympathized with her.

The Voltini children didn't defend themselves by explaining that they had only eaten veal once in their lives, or that their chicken dinner had only consisted of a thin soup made from the head and feet. Letting their aunt advertise they had meat for dinner was preferable to admitting the truth. It was always better to be envied by one's neighbors than pitied.

Pasquale pointed his index finger to his temple. "My aunt is out of her mind. She thinks we want her onions. Who needs onions? We usually have meat for dinner."

"Onions… don't make me laugh," Caterina said. "We have plenty of meat at my house. We don't need her lousy onions."

To their satisfaction, some people believed them and empathized with them. Pasquale and Caterina were proud to have saved face in public, but they would have both traded the moral victory for some of the very onions they had scoffed at. Onions were better than nothing.

Marta glared at the Voltini children and yelled, "If you want food from me, you should stop your uncle from spending his money on whores. They eat better than I do."

"They call her the Screamer of Horseshoe Street," a wiry teenage boy said. "She screams all day long just because her husband runs around with whores."

Pasquale narrowed his eyes. "My uncle has a good reason to visit whores. Who would want to live with a crazy witch like her?"

"The whores that I know are good-looking and reasonable. They live near the castle, in a house with a red light in the window."

Pasquale winked. "I've been there. The house is beautiful, and so are the women."

"*I remember the signora whore who lived in the house with the red light,*" Mario wanted to say, but remained silent. Pasquale had introduced him to a beautiful whore once. She wore a bright red dress, and spoke in a gentle tone. *No wonder Uncle Vituccio goes to visit those signore whores,* Mario thought.

Mario would have loved to be surrounded by these lovely *signore* who sported colorful dresses. They were cheerful and kind. His mother and aunts looked dull in their dark dresses, and were always mad about something.

The following day, the children looked forward to Grazia's arrival from work. They were utterly disappointed that she didn't bring any food.

"What's the matter with you?" Pasquale asked. "You don't know how to take food?"

"I didn't get the chance," Grazia responded. "Mrs. Zordi didn't buy any food. She goes out to dinner most nights."

Pasquale gave Grazia a harsh look. "You don't bother to take any food because your belly is full. Don't tell me you didn't eat."

"I eat whatever the other maids eat," Grazia said.

Pasquale stamped his foot. "If there's food for the maids, there should be food for us."

"You can't expect me to take food when people are around."

"Tomorrow I'm going to go to Aunt Clotilde's house and I'm going to get some food," Norina said.

"But Aunt Clotilde is out of town," Caterina shouted.

Norina forced a smile, but she couldn't control the tears that shone in her eyes.

As soon as she was out of the children's sight, Norina confined herself to the bedroom, threw herself on the bed, and cried uncontrollably. She was relieved to be able to unleash her sobs, and she cried until her tears ran dry. The painting of *Jesus and the Children* hanging on top of her bed caught her eye. Jesus had a blissful expression and was surrounded by many children in a spring garden illuminated by a bright sky that seemed to emanate straight from Heaven. The children looked happy and well nourished. Her children didn't even know what it was like to have enough food to satisfy their hunger.

"Why is my sky so dark?" Norina kept mumbling.

Clotilde was away on a pilgrimage. Vituccio was working out of town. Angela the Crazy Head was too busy to do another novel reading. Norina didn't know who to turn to. She was ashamed to admit to her neighbors that she was in dire need. Once, Baronessa Rosa had helped her in the past. Now Norina couldn't count on her since the Baronessa was in mourning. She was so depressed that she refused to talk to anyone. Her pigeon Bianchina had been killed by a wild cat. Norina gave it a lot of thought, and finally decided to ask Carolina the Good Life for food.

When Norina headed to Carolina's house, she noticed the front door was shut. "Carolina is out of town?" she asked the neighbors.

"Carolina is staying at the hospital with her baby boy," Lina the Warm House answered.

"He's very ill," Giacomino the Blind Man said.

"I hope the baby gets better," Norina said, walking away.

Filled with despair, Norina went home and passed the burden to Grazia.

"It's up to you to decide who we are going to ask for help," Norina said.

"I'll ask Maddalena," Grazia said. "She's a good person. She wouldn't tell a single soul."

Norina agreed. Grazia scrambled outside.

As soon as Grazia arrived at Maddalena's house, she rang the bell, but she got no response.

Titina the Alligator, who was seated by her front door, waved at Grazia and said, "Maddalena had a fight with her husband and took off. This time it's very serious."

Grazia approached Titina. "How serious can it be?"

"Maddalena said that she was going to throw herself into the river."

"I feel sorry for Maddalena. She's the victim of an abusive animal."

Titina got up from her chair. "Maddalena is the bad one. She deserves what she gets. She should be ashamed of what she does."

"You have no empathy for other women. How dare you say Maddalena deserves to be abused," Grazia wanted to say, but she decided to remain silent.

Grazia felt relieved when Titina walked away.

Old Veronica thrust her front door open. Grazia figured the elderly woman was listening to her conversation with Titina.

"Titina thinks the worst of everybody," Old Veronica said.

Grazia nodded. "Titina is horrible."

Grazia didn't have the heart to ask Old Veronica for food, knowing that the elderly woman could hardly support herself.

Caterina had found a way to fill her stomach. She visited Rocco, the son of Carmine the Shepherd, and tempted him into letting her taste some fresh cheese. Rocco charmingly kissed her every time he gave her a piece of cheese. Caterina enjoyed being kissed by him. As Caterina was eating a particularly generous piece of goat cheese, Carmine the Shepherd burst in. Utterly infuriated, he smacked his son and hauled Caterina out of his house.

"I'm going to tell your mother," the shepherd shouted. "She'd better pay me for that cheese."

"I only had a bite." Caterina's lips quivered. "I just tasted it. Please don't tell my mother."

Her mother finding out would have meant a whipping. Caterina squeezed her eyes. *Thank God I didn't get caught kissing Rocco.*

The shepherd gave Caterina a stern look. "Telling your mother is the least I should do. You're a thief. God knows how many times my fool of a son has given you free cheese."

The sight of Arturo emerging down the street with two men holding him by his arms captured Carmine's attention. The two men were Giovanni the Farmer and Ninuccio the Painter.

"What happened?" the shepherd asked, running towards them.

Arturo was soaking wet. A lot of curious neighbors gathered around him.

Caterina exhaled. *Rocco's father has more important things to think about for now,* she thought, joining the group of neighbors.

"What happened?" Old Veronica asked.

Arturo was wheezing, but no words came out of his mouth.

"What happened?" many neighbors kept asking.

Finally Arturo said, "I killed her."

Carmine widened his eyes. "Oh my God! Arturo, why did you do it?"

Giacomino the Blind Man's mouth fell open. "*Mamma mia*! Arturo, you killed Maddalena?"

Arturo's face blushed. "I did."

"How?" the blind man asked.

Arturo lowered his head. "She threw herself into the river because of me."

Carmine gave a sigh of relief. "You didn't kill her. She killed herself."

"She drowned?" Grazia asked.

"I went to look for her, but I couldn't find her." Arturo burst into tears. "She's dead!"

The neighbors congregated around Arturo. They stood still and remained speechless. Their silence was their way of paying their respects to Maddalena, who had often entertained them with scenes of drama that surpassed what they could have seen in a cinema.

Suddenly, a woman appeared down the street. All eyes were immediately fixed on the approaching figure.

Titina the Alligator pointed to the woman. "She looks like Maddalena."

Arturo placed his hands on his chest and felt his heart pounding heavily.

"Could it be her ghost?" Caterina asked.

"She's too tall to be Maddalena," Ninuccio responded, as the woman got closer.

It was Anna the Heavyweight. She was also soaking wet.

"Maddalena is out of the river," Anna shouted. "I went to look for her myself and I found her. I got her out."

"You found Maddalena's body?" Carmine asked.

"I found Maddalena," Anna waved her hands in the air. "She's alive."

"Are you sure she's alive?" Arturo asked.

"Yes." Anna winked. "I slapped her on both cheeks to make sure."

"How is she?" Grazia asked.

Anna flashed a glint of a grin. "She's fine."

"Where is she now?" Arturo asked.

"She's at the monastery," Anna replied. "The nuns are taking care of her."

Arturo got down on his knees in front of the strong woman. "Thank you for saving my wife. I'm going to be grateful to you for the rest of my life."

Anna contorted her face. "I like to help the weak women in town, the ones that don't know how to defend themselves."

Arturo covered his face with his hands. "I love my wife. She doesn't know how much I love her."

"You should tell her," Giacomino said. "You've probably never told her how much you love her."

"I wish I had the guts," Arturo mumbled. Overtaken by a fainting spell, he fell to the ground.

"Arturo," Old Veronica yelled.

"I think that he's dead." Titina gestured the sign of the cross. "That's how my husband died. He just dropped dead. The doctor told me that it was an attack on the heart."

Carmine the Shepherd turned to Caterina. "Go and call a doctor. Hurry up!"

"Do you promise not to tell my mother about the cheese Rocco gave me?" Caterina asked.

"I promise I won't tell her on the condition that you never come into my house ever again," the shepherd responded.

"I swear on my father's grave that I won't come to your house." Caterina dashed towards the doctor's house. Though she was relieved the shepherd had promised not to tell her mother, she was crushed that she had lost the opportunity to see Rocco and get free samples of cheese.

Caterina didn't share the cheese with her siblings. She is very selfish, Grazia thought, glaring at Arturo as he lay on the ground.

"He looks dead," Giovanni the Farmer said.

Margherita's eyes gleamed with tears.

"And the wife threw herself into the river, but didn't die," Titina said.

Contessa Fiorella had witnessed the whole scene through the shutters of her window. She was pleased something bad had finally happened to Arturo. *He finally got what he deserved, she* thought.

Twenty minutes later, a short bald man appeared on Saint Peter Street.

"He looks familiar," Titina said. "Who is he?"

"He's Doctor Polo, the best doctor in town," Lina the Warm House said. "They call him the Married Priest because he was going to become a priest, but then he fell in love with a woman and got married."

Doctor Polo got down on his knees and examined Arturo as he lay on the ground. After a short time, he stood up and said, "It's just a panic attack."

Carmine the Shepherd exhaled heavily. "Just a panic attack?"

"He got too excited by the news that his wife is alive," Giacomino the Blind Man said. "He wants to see her."

"I heard his wife threw herself in the river," the doctor said. "How's she doing?"

"She's fine." Anna the Heavyweight twisted her lips. "But she doesn't want to see him."

"He'll get better quickly if he makes up with his wife," Doctor Polo said. "I know Arturo. He gets sick every time he fights with her."

Giovanni the Farmer nodded. "If Arturo doesn't make up with his wife, he won't get better."

Arturo is so mentally sick that he feels physically sick when he loses his victim, Grazia thought. *His wife is his victim and he can't live without her.*

"I'll talk to Maddalena," Carmine said.

"In the meantime, Arturo could use some rest," the doctor said.

Giovanni and Carmine lifted Arturo up and carried him all the way to his house.

"I wonder if Maddalena will talk to Arturo," Giacomino said.

"She will if they tell her that he had a panic attack," Ninuccio the Painter said.

"She should know how much he loves her," the blind man said.

Arturo became so depressed that he refused to go out, and spent most of his time in bed. The neighbors were convinced Arturo would get better if Maddalena came back home.

"I spoke to Maddalena. There's no point in anyone trying to convince her. She has no intention of coming back," Carmine the Shepherd said to the neighbors.

"Maddalena doesn't appreciate what she has," Titina the Alligator said. "Arturo is a good husband. He puts food on the table and buys her nice things. He even took her to the opera. She has no heart. She doesn't even feel sorry for the poor man."

"That poor man didn't feel sorry for Maddalena when he gave her all those beatings," Grazia said.

Titina lifted her chin. "If your husband beats you up, there's always a reason."

"How can you sympathize with an animal like Arturo?" Grazia wanted to say, but decided not to retort to Titina *It's useless to talk to ignorant people. Their heads are harder than rocks.*

The neighbors noticed that Norina hadn't been cooking, since they didn't smell any food by the doorway during meal times. They figured the Voltinis must be desperately hungry. Unfortunately, Norina didn't get any sympathy from her neighbors.

"She's in need because she doesn't know how to save," Titina the Alligator said. "I heard that she buys her children bananas whenever she has the money."

Lina the Warm House bobbed her head in agreement. "What about the veal? Norina doesn't even settle for horse meat, which is much cheaper. She buys veal as if she were a White Fly."

"What about the portrait?"

"She took the luxury of taking her daughter to the best photographer in town."

"Norina got cursed by the sky," Colombina the Farmer's Wife said. "Don't spit into the sky, because it's going to fall right back on your face. She kept trying to spit into the sky by wasting her money, and now it's coming right back to her."

The only neighbor who took pity on Norina was Anna the Heavyweight.

"I don't care if Norina had bananas and veal yesterday," Anna shouted. "I don't smell any food coming from her house today. Her children deserve to be fed."

The neighbors remained silent. No one dared contradict the strong woman. Anna had just surprised the rest of the neighbors, showing a compassionate heart under her tough exterior.

That night, Anna the Heavyweight paid the Voltinis a visit.

"What brings you here?" Grazia asked.

The strong woman withdrew three bundles wrapped in a towel from her bag and placed them on the table. "I brought two kilograms of pasta, two kilograms of bread, and a little bottle of oil."

Norina's eyes sparkled. "You didn't have to."

"I had to do the right thing," Anna said.

"You should think about yourself," Grazia said. "You're not swimming in gold."

"I have my ways of getting things," Anna said. "Can you keep a secret?"

Grazia nodded. "Of course."

Norina crossed her hands on her chest. "I swear on my husband's grave that I'm not going to tell anybody."

Anna took a deep breath and whispered, "I steal from the bottega."

Grazia's mouth fell open. "You do?"

"I'm the enforcer there. Teresina has made a lot of money from her bad credit customers because of me. Every now and then, I take a few things to pay myself for my services." Anna narrowed her eyes. "Is that so wrong?"

"It is wrong," Grazia wanted to say, but remained silent.

"It's not wrong." Norina gave Anna a warm hug. "Thank you for thinking of us."

The Voltinis had pasta with garlic and oil for dinner, and bread soaked in water seasoned with oil for lunch, for two days in a row. On the third day, they were hungry again. The children waited impatiently for Grazia's arrival from work, hoping she would bring food from the Zordi residence, but to their disappointment, she was empty-handed once again.

"You're so stupid," Caterina shouted. "You don't know how to steal food."

Grazia's chin quivered. "Mrs. Zordi is on a diet. She doesn't buy any pasta and bread."

If I had a chance to work in Grazia's place, I'd get to eat a lot of food, Caterina thought. "If I were to go to work in your place, I'd bring home lots of food."

"What would we tell Mrs. Zordi?" Grazia asked.

"We'll tell her you're sick," Caterina responded.

Caterina is going to steal a lot of food and she's probably going to get caught, Grazia thought. "I don't think it's a good idea."

Caterina's face turned beet red. She banged her fists on the table and sobbed.

Norina turned to Grazia. "Let her work for a while."

Overruled, Grazia could only acquiesce. "Fine. Caterina can have my job for a short while."

Caterina jumped up and gave Grazia a hug.

Caterina's sky had brightened. At the Zordi residence, she ate a lot of delicious food. She was very talented at filching food from the household, but she would usually eat most of her booty on the way home. She barely brought any food home.

To alleviate her siblings' disappointment, Caterina would often use the same excuse: "Grazia was right. It's almost impossible to steal any food."

The first day Grazia went back to work, Mrs. Zordi welcomed her with a bright smile. "I'm so happy to have you back. I was worried when your sister told me you were very sick."

"I'm fine," Grazia said.

Grazia avoided talking about her illness. She knew Caterina loved to exaggerate, and couldn't imagine what sort of lies her sister had told Mrs. Zordi.

"Don't go out of your way," Mrs. Zordi said. "Take it easy. Have the other maids do the heavy work for today. I'm going to write to my friend and give him the good news that you are well."

Mrs. Zordi is writing to her friend because Caterina probably told her I was close to death, Grazia thought.

Grazia brought home pasta, a small jar of sugar, and a loaf of bread. Norina gave the children the pasta for dinner and saved the sugar and the bread for the following day. A chill swept over her as she realized she didn't have milk for Little Donato.

That evening, an unexpected visitor knocked at the Voltinis' door. When Norina opened the door, she was surprised to see Old Veronica.

The old woman gave Norina a cup wrapped in a towel. "I brought some milk for Little Donato. He told me that you had no milk. He needs milk to build up his bones."

"Please, don't tell the neighbors that I'm in need."

"I won't tell a soul."

Norina thanked Old Veronica with a warm hug and led her out of the house. She watched the old woman walk away until she disappeared into the obscurity. The sky had turned black and was bare of any stars. Norina's whole body trembled as she leaped inside the house and locked the door. She ran to the bedroom and got down on her knees in front of the statue of Our Lady of Sorrows.

"Please, throw some light into my dark sky."

XVII

"I need a better sky," Norina kept mumbling, as she paced the kitchen back and forth.

Norina's desperation had not abated. She needed a job and her nerves were shot. Sad thoughts consumed her mind. She was living under a dark sky. She was condemned to a miserable, wretched life. She was tired of struggling. Death increasingly seemed like a welcome relief from her despair. She shut her eyes and exhaled heavily. Her mind went blank. It was like not existing. It was such a peaceful feeling she wished it could last forever.

When Norina heard a series of *buongiornos* getting closer and closer, she opened her eyes and directed her gaze to the front entrance. She saw Clotilde's silhouette behind the fishnet curtain. Norina noticed Clotilde was not carrying a bag. An empty-handed Clotilde was the last person Norina wanted to see. She was not in the mood for her sister-in-law's preaching. Clotilde pulled the curtain aside and entered triumphantly into the house. As she closed the curtain, she drew a dark green bill from her pocket and waved it up in the air.

When Norina realized what it was, her eyes expanded. She had never seen a hundred-dollar bill in her life. "A hundred dollars?"

Clotilde flashed a smile. "Yes, a hundred dollars. It is worth sixty thousand lire. People work months to earn sixty thousand lire."

"Where did you get the money?"

"I'll tell you." Clotilde sank her heavy body onto a chair that groaned under her weight.

Norina shook Clotilde's shoulders. "Tell me. Tell me!"

"I had a hard time contacting my cousin Ignazio who lives in America, because I didn't have his address. Two months ago, I finally got his address. I wrote a letter to him to announce my brother's death." Clotilde breathed in deeply and let her breath out in a long sigh. "I finally received a response from him."

"Go on," Norina shouted.

"I forgot what I was talking about."

"You were talking about your cousin." It took all of Norina's willpower to curb the immediate urge to snatch the American bill from Clotilde's hand.

Clotilde drew a letter from her pocket. "My cousin sent me a letter of condolence with a hundred-dollar bill. Ignazio has always been a poet. You should listen to the words he wrote."

Clotilde reached for her eyeglasses, put them on and read:

Full of deep sorrow for the loss of a great man who lived according to his ideals and blazed a trail for his successors...

Though Norina didn't fully understand many of the words, she didn't ask for the meaning. Her eyes were still transfixed on the American bill. "Who is the money for?"

"Well, I guess it is for the *buon anima*, the deceased. My brother was such a good man."

"Dead people don't need money. Dead people don't need to eat." Norina ripped the bill out of her sister-in-law's fingers.

"You should at least buy a Mass for my brother's soul."

"Instead of paying a priest to celebrate a Mass for the deceased, I'm going to go to church and listen to a Mass, and make believe it's for the deceased, the *buon anima*. What difference does it make?"

Clotilde rubbed her chin. "It makes a big difference."

"I need the money. I have a lot of debts to pay. My children went to school today without breakfast. Do you want to know what we had for dinner yesterday?"

Clotilde shut her eyes. She didn't want to know.

"We had pasta that Grazia stole from Mrs. Zordi's house."

Clotilde's face blushed. "Grazia stole pasta? If people were to find out, I could never show my face to the Catholic League."

Norina raised her voice. "I told Grazia to steal anything that she can get her hands on because I don't have the money to buy food."

"Stop yelling, the neighbors may hear you. Ignazio requested a family picture in his letter."

Norina slapped her hand on the table. "I don't have a family picture."

"I know." Clotilde patted Norina's arm. "You can send him Grazia's photograph."

Norina's eyes lit up at the prospect of sending her daughter's portrait to America. It would have been a good opportunity for Grazia to be noticed by an American. She promptly reached for the photo and handed it to her sister-in-law. Clotilde placed the photo reverently in her bag and walked out of the house.

Norina examined the American bill carefully to assure herself that it was real. The number 100 was printed on the four corners on both sides of the bill. At the center of the bill there was the picture of an old man.

He looks like an important person who can be trusted. Norina turned the bill over and saw the picture of a huge building. *It must be the bank where the hundred-dollar bill came from.* She had never seen a building that big. She figured all American banks must be big since they stored so many dollars. *It's a real hundred-dollar bill!* Norina's face radiated as she spun around.

Norina tucked the American bill furtively in her brassiere and trotted back and forth, patting her breast. She beamed as Caterina and little Donato entered the house.

Norina promptly unlocked the credenza and pulled out the jar of sugar. "Caterina, you can have all the sugar that you like today, and you can put plenty of sugar in Little Donato's glass."

"I can take as much as I like?" Caterina asked.

Norina tapped her feet as if dancing. "I'm going to buy Little Donato a whole liter of milk."

Caterina's mouth fell open. "Are you sure?"

Norina winked. "I'm more than sure."

Caterina poured equal shares of sugar into two glasses and filled them with water. She gave one glass to Little Donato. The child gulped the sugared water quickly. Caterina drank her sugared water just as fast.

When Norina reached for the broom, Caterina stared at her mother with her eyes wide open. *She's going to hit me with the broom for wasting all the sugar.*

Norina swept the floor while humming a song.

As soon as Norina finished sweeping, she turned to Caterina. "Go outside and play with the baby. I want to wash the floor with soap."

"Is an important guest coming?" Caterina asked.

Norina flashed a smile. "No."

She must be going insane, Caterina thought. She took Little Donato in her arms and scrambled outside.

At the sight of the sugar pot lying on the table, Norina couldn't resist the impulse to treat herself. She grabbed the loaf of bread that was previously destined to be her children's dinner, cut a piece, and sprinkled it with water. She then poured sugar on top. The sugared bread tasted like a cake. She devoured it like a starving animal.

Norina drew the box of soap out of the credenza, took a handful of the soap powder, and scattered it on the whole kitchen floor, which was paved with the same white stones as the street. Once Norina brushed a wet rag on the floor, she marveled at the burgeoning foam. She played with the foam with childlike glee as she scrubbed the floor. When she dumped a bucket of water on the floor, to her disappointment, the foam disappeared.

Norina pulled the fishnet curtain open and shoveled the water outside with the broom. She threw another handful of soap powder on her sidewalk and brushed the wet rag, eager to create more foam. As soon as the Voltini children noticed the foam, they ran towards their mother.

"You can play with the bubbles," Norina said.

The children jumped up and down. Norina rested, sitting by her front door and watching her children's merriment. The Voltini children shrieked and giggled. They invited their friends to play. They all took off their shoes and had lots of fun playing with the foam. When they got tired of playing, they splashed buckets of water on their feet. The children were elated by the fragrance of the soap. The ground had never smelled so good, and neither had their feet.

"If everyone wasted soap on the street like that, no one's feet would smell," Titina the Alligator said.

Lina the Warm House laughed heartily.

Nearly intoxicated by the scent arising from the pavement, Norina drew her hand to her brassiere and felt the hundred-dollar bill, as if to make sure it was still real. She visualized all the things she could buy with the American dollars: shoes for her children, fabric to make new clothes, and plenty of food. Olimpia popping by the house distracted her from her reverie.

"*Mamma*, what are we having for dinner?" Olimpia asked.

"I'm going to buy a pizza pie for everyone," Norina said.

"We're having pizza for dinner," Olympia shouted, swinging her arms. She got the attention of her siblings. They rapidly congregated around her.

"Are we really having pizza?" Pasquale asked.

Norina's face radiated. "I'm going to send Grazia to buy the pies as soon as she comes home."

The children waited impatiently for their sister to come home. They ran towards Grazia as soon as she emerged down the street.

"*Mamma* is going to buy us a pizza pie each," Olimpia shouted.

Grazia quickened her pace, eager to confront her mother.

"*Mamma*, you're buying pizza?" Grazia asked.

Norina smiled as she nodded.

"With what money?" Grazia whispered in her mother's ear.

Norina drew the hundred-dollar bill from her brassiere and waved it up in the air.

Grazia's jaw dropped. "Where did you get it?"

"Ignazio, your father's cousin, sent it from America."

"We should go to the bank and exchange it for Italian money."

Norina handed the U.S. bill to Grazia. "We can pay our debts another day. Go to the pizzeria, order seven pizza pies, and show the pizza man the hundred-dollar bill. When he gives you the pies, tell him that you are going to pay him as soon as you get a chance to go to the bank and change the dollars for lire."

"What if the pizza man refuses to give me the pies?"

"No one in town refuses to give credit to people who have American bills. Tell the pizza man that we got the dollars from our cousin. And tell him that our cousin has a business and that he's going to send us many more dollars."

"I'll tell him." Grazia hid the American bill in her purse. She knew there was no way to make her mother see reason at a time like this.

Once Grazia arrived at the only pizzeria in town, she peered at her reflection in the window and smiled lightly. She looked good. She was glad she had worn her black Sunday dress to work. She pushed two rebellious curls towards the back of her voluminous hair and walked into the pizzeria.

The pizza man welcomed Grazia with a grin. "I saw your photograph on display in the photo studio. You look… *molto bella.*"

Grazia drew the hundred-dollar bill from her purse and said, "I want seven pizza pies."

The pizza man's eyes lit up. "They'll be ready in twenty minutes."

An American Wife turned to Grazia. "Who do you have in America?"

"My cousin, he owns a business," Grazia responded, relishing the feeling of importance it gave her.

The American Wife waved at Grazia as she headed out of the pizzeria. Grazia waved back at her. As she waited, Grazia's senses were overwhelmed by the aroma of the pizza pies. With delight, she watched the pizza man lifting the pies out of the oven with a trowel.

Those pies are as big as plates. No one will go to bed hungry tonight in our house. Grazia turned to the pizza man. "Do you have change for a hundred dollars?"

The pizza man giggled. "I wish!" He wrapped the pizzas in sheets of brown paper and handed them to Grazia.

Grazia placed the bundles in her fishnet bag. "I'll pay as soon as I get the chance to exchange the dollars for lire."

People with American bills pay their debts. They aren't night payers, the pizza man thought. "Don't forget to pay me once you change the hundred-dollar bill."

Grazia flashed her magical smile. "I won't forget."

The pizza man stared at Grazia as she sauntered out of the pizzeria. *She's one of the most stunning girls in town.*

Grazia quickened her pace, eager to get home and feed her family. She merrily waved hello to friends and acquaintances, enthralled by the delicious scent of the pizza pies she carried with her. It was like wearing an expensive perfume.

As soon as Grazia entered Saint Peter Street, her siblings eagerly congregated around her.

"Give me a pizza pie," Olimpia said.

Happily, Grazia opened up the fishnet bag. Pasquale and Olimpia immediately took a pie each and skipped cheerfully onto the street.

Caterina tapped her feet. "Give me three pies: one for me, one for *Mamma*, and one for Little Donato. I'll feed him."

As soon as Grazia handed her three pies, Caterina took off.

Mario didn't have the audacity to ask for his pizza. He was staring at his sister, with his mouth open.

"This is for you," Grazia said, as she gave him his pie.

Mario shut his eyes, enraptured as he placed the warm pie against his cheek. It gave him the sensation of being held by his mother. Norina used to hug him every time she put him to bed when he was the baby of the family.

Grazia patted Mario's shoulder. "Eat the pizza before it gets cold."

Mario promptly opened his eyes, freed the pie from the paper, and began to eat it.

Seated by the front door, Norina enjoyed her pizza. She noticed Pasquale and Olimpia were eating their pizza voraciously and Little Donato was ecstatically chewing on a tiny piece of pizza. Caterina sneaked into the back room with Little Donato with the intention of eating his leftovers. She didn't hesitate to eat the baby's portion as soon as he clasped his hand on his mouth to indicate to her he didn't want any more.

Grazia offered Mario half of her pie, but he refused. In the narrow street, illuminated by the moon and the pale lamps, Mario summoned his courage and said, "Every-every time-time we-we eat-eat some-thing good-good, we-we always-always run-run out of-of food. I'm af-afraid that-that we-we are-are going-going to-to run-run out-out of-of food again-again."

Grazia showed him the hundred-dollar bill. "You shouldn't be afraid. We are going to have a lot of food. We have American money now."

Mario beamed with joy.

XVIII

Rumors made the rounds in the town that the Voltinis had a millionaire cousin in America who had sent them money. Many people stopped Norina in the street and bombarded her with questions about their benefactor.

"My cousin is very old, and has no wife and no children," Norina would say. "He's so generous that he keeps sending me hundred dollar bills. I told him not to send me any more money, but the more I tell him not to send, the more he sends."

Numerous townsfolk believed Norina was about to inherit her cousin's fortune, since he was old and had no heirs.

When Father Camillo heard the gossip, he sermonized in church. "There are good people in America who have generous hearts and think about the orphans and the widows. These people are blessed by God. People who help others are blessed from the sky. One day, God is going to reward them by opening the Pearly Gates for them."

Norina began to give herself an air of prestige, as if she were a minor celebrity. When she passed by the old part of the town, poor people seated by their front doors moved their chairs away from the sidewalk to allow her to pass. In the past, only the Dumb Brothers had showed her such deference. Poor people showed Norina respect because they felt she had been blessed by the sky. Norina was no longer considered an unfortunate poor widow. Norina Voltini had been upgraded.

Norina now often avoided greeting poor people when she passed them on the street. She didn't value their reverence towards her. She valued the attention she got from the wealthier people in town. She was in Seventh Heaven every time she received acknowledgement from the White Flies. On those occasions, she felt like one of their peers.

Grazia, on the other hand, relished the respect she received from poor people. One day she bumped into Pino the Red Eye, who was wheeling his cart. Pino greeted her like a gentleman, bowing and taking off his hat.

"Is it-it true that-that you-you-you got one-one-one hun-dred dol-lars from a-a-a rich cousin-cousin in America?" Pino asked.

"Yes, it's true," Grazia replied.

"I'm very-very happy-happy for-for you-you. Poor-poor people deserve-deserve luck-luck more-more than-than rich-rich people."

Grazia flashed her magical smile.

"Buy some-some-some fish. I'm going-going to-to give-give you-you a-a-a good price, because-because you-you-you are *muy-muy-muy bonita*."

"I don't have any money with me. My mother has the hundred-dollar bill."

"You can-can-can pay-pay me-me later."

Grazia indicated the fish she liked. Pino wrapped the fish hastily in newspaper sheets and handed her the bundle.

"As soon as my mother gets a chance, she'll go to the bank and exchange the dollars for lire."

Pino had no doubt that Grazia would pay him back. He kept sneaking looks at her as she walked away. *She's a star in the sky,* he thought, flashing a smile.

The hundred-dollar bill was truly a blessing from the sky. It was like a magical credit card. By showing the American bill to the storeowners and vendors, the Voltinis could easily obtain credit. They always promised they would pay once they had a chance to go to the bank and convert the dollars into lire.

Teresina from the bottega had gained so much respect for Norina that she allowed her to stand in the line of the paying customers when she visited the bottega. Teresina gave Norina credit for anything she desired, confident Norina was going to pay her. People that had American dollars always paid her.

When Norina inherits the fortune from her old cousin, she'll become one of my best costumers, Teresina thought.

Norina felt like a White Fly. She lavished her family with lots of food: five kilograms of sugar, ten kilograms of pasta, a kilogram of Parmesan cheese, a quarter-kilogram of coffee, ten liters of olive oil, ten kilograms of flour, ten jars of homemade tomato sauce, a quarter-kilogram of *mortadella*, a quarter kilogram of salami, three kilograms of bread, twelve bottles of *aranciata* and a big candle. Norina lit the candle for Our Lady of Sorrows. The Madonna deserved it. After all, she had granted her the miracle of the American bill.

Now that she belonged among the well-to-do in town, Norina confidently entered the butcher's shop.

Norina flaunted her American bill. "What's the freshest meat you have today?"

Domenico the Butcher stared at the bill with his mouth wide open. "I recommend the flank steak."

"Give me ten slices."

The butcher looked at Norina intensely as he sliced the beef. *She's still a beautiful woman.* He wrapped the meat in white paper and smiled at Norina as he handed her the bundle.

Norina used the magic line she had now learned by heart: "I'm going to pay you when I get a chance to go to the bank and exchange the American bill for lire."

The butcher didn't complain. He was confident Norina would pay him. The American Wives were accustomed to doing the same and they, always reimbursed him. He had no doubt Norina would be just as honest. All the butchers in town gave Norina credit once they saw the American bill.

The Voltinis' house became the most aromatic house on Saint Peter Street. The neighbors guessed everything Norina cooked by the delicious scents that emanated from her doorway.

"They're having chicken soup for dinner," Ninuccio the Painter said. "Dollars make a big difference in the kitchen."

"Norina is so lucky to have a rich cousin in America," Lina the Warm House said.

"I heard that Norina's American cousin is going to provide a good dowry for her three daughters," Colombina the Farmer's Wife said.

"Norina will become a White Fly the day her cousin dies," Carmine the Shepherd said. "She's going to inherit all his money."

Titina the Alligator twisted her lips. "That could take years."

"Norina's cousin is very old," Lina said. "He could die any day."

Old Veronica faced upward. "We all live under the sky, anything can happen."

Braciole with ragú sauce was a delicacy the poor had only on holidays. Norina prepared each *braciola* by rolling each slice of beef and stuffing it with parsley, Parmesan cheese, and garlic. The Voltini family feasted on *braciole*. The overpowering aroma of the meat coming from the Voltini's doorway diffused throughout the street.

Grazia overheard Giacomino the Blind Man say: "I smell ragú. I haven't had ragú in a long time."

Grazia turned to Norina. "May I give Giacomino a *brasciola*?"

As soon as Norina agreed, Grazia prepared a plate with a *brasciola* and brought it outside.

Grazia saw Colombina the Farmer's Wife seated among the neighbors. *Colombina is not ashamed to sit by my front door now that my house is the most aromatic house on the street.*

Grazia was pleased to show off the delicacy to Colombina. *She* turned to Giacomino. "I want you to taste a *brasciola*," she said, handing him the plate.

"Are you sure you want to give me a whole *braciola*? the blind man asked. "You should give it to the children."

"The children had plenty of meat today."

Colombina smiled at Grazia. "Feel free to come to my house anytime you want. I have lots of fresh fruits and vegetables."

Grazia widened her eyes and remained speechless.

Giacomino ate the *braciola* with gusto. "We used to eat *braciole* on the holidays back when I was able to see and work."

"Those times are gone, and they're never going to come back," Lina the Warm House said. "We don't have generous cousins in America."

As soon as Grazia walked back into her house, the neighbors began their usual gossip session.

"The Voltinis must be getting a lot of dollars if they can give away a whole *braciola*," Titina the Alligator said.

"The Voltinis can have plenty of *braciole* in their future," Giacomino said. "Norina's cousin owns a business. He can make the papers for them to go to America."

Titina shut her eyes and revealed a wistful smile. She wished she had a cousin who would give her the opportunity to go to America.

Early in the morning, as soon as Olimpia woke up she turned to her mother and her sisters. "I dreamt that I had ricotta cheese for breakfast."

Norina gave Olimpia a hug. "Today your dream can come true."

Olimpia frowned as she tilted her head. "How?"

Norina turned to Caterina. "Go to Carmine the Shepherd and get a bowl of ricotta cheese."

Since Caterina had promised the shepherd she'd never set foot in his house again, she said, "I don't want the responsibility of handling a hundred-dollar bill. Someone could steal it from me. You should send Grazia. She's older."

"I'll go, but I'll only ask for the milk for Little Donato," Grazia said.

"Ask for a bowl of ricotta cheese too. The shepherd is going to give it to you for sure once he sees the dollars." Norina handed Grazia the American bill. "Try to get as much as you can."

Grazia's hand trembled as she placed the bill in her handbag. "*Mamma*, you should exchange the American bill for lire. I hate asking for credit."

"You're asking for credit showing cash. You're giving them a guarantee."

"I'm afraid the shepherd will yell at me."

"He's going to be nice to you for sure." Norina flashed a light grin. "No merchant refuses credit to customers who have American dollars."

Carmine the Shepherd treated Grazia with kindness once he saw the American bill. He even gave Grazia a taste of his fresh mozzarella.

"I just made the mozzarella. It's still warm," the shepherd said.

"It's delicious," Grazia said, savoring the fresh cheese. "When I exchange the dollars for lire I'll buy some."

"You can buy it now. I'll give you credit for anything you want. People who have American dollars are my best customers."

He had offered credit without her even asking. Grazia stared at the shepherd with her mouth open.

"You can come any time. I'll give you credit for a whole month's worth of milk. I don't want you to buy milk from another shepherd."

Grazia flashed a smile.

Carmine the Shepherd presumed that the Voltinis were receiving many American bills. He considered them preferred customers, and didn't want to lose them. He figured Caterina could also be an ideal match for his son since she was bound to get a dowry, and had become a candidate to go to America. He himself dreamt of going to America one day, just like everyone else in town who dreamt of becoming rich.

Grazia brought home a liter of milk, seven bowls of ricotta, an entire wheel of goat cheese, and three balls of mozzarella. The whole Voltini family feasted on a deluxe breakfast.

Olimpia swung her arms. "I never believed we would have fresh ricotta for breakfast."

To Caterina's surprise, Carmine the Shepherd greeted her kindly when he saw her in the street.

"You're welcome in my house, and you can have all the goat cheese you want," the shepherd said. "I'll give you credit."

"I'll come by soon," Caterina said. She jumped up and down. *The shepherd forgot all about the incident with the goat cheese.*

Caterina was also excited by the notion that she would get to see Rocco. His absence in her life had only intensified her crush on him.

When Caterina went home, she turned to her mother and her siblings and said, "Our creditors sure are nice to us."

Pasquale bobbed his head in agreement. "People show us respect now."

Norina's eyes coruscated. "I always told you that one day our sky was going to brighten."

"I'm so glad it's finally happened," Olimpia said, shutting her eyes in relief.

Mario's face radiated warmth. He loved this bright new sky.

The Voltini children were happy to live under a better sky. Caterina visited Carmine the Shepherd's house every day on the pretext of getting milk for Little Donato. She felt love from Rocco and respect from his family, who gave her plenty of ricotta and goat cheese. The Voltini children treasured the delicious food they had for breakfast, lunch, dinner, brunch, and even a snack here and there. Pasquale bragged to his friends that he gorged himself on mouth-watering cuisine, and derived gratification from their faces filled with amazement. He would often give his friends a sampling of the food to prove he was not lying. Mario, for his part, had freed himself from all worries. Grazia had been right. The family no longer had money problems, and didn't have to fret about finding food. He firmly believed the American bill was going to last forever.

It was a custom among the poor people to make lasagne only on holidays, but that didn't stop Norina from preparing a large tray on an ordinary weekday. Pasquale then brought the lasagne to the community oven to have it baked. Tonino the Baker knew all about the American money, and figured Norina was celebrating her bright sky. Like every merchant in town, he gave credit to the Voltinis. When the neighbors saw Pasquale carrying a tray of steaming lasagne, they surrounded him, attracted by the delicious aroma.

"It smells so good," Giacomino the Blind Man said, inhaling as deeply as he could.

Lina the Warm House and Titina the Alligator couldn't stop staring at the lasagne.

"The lasagne is thick, with plenty of mozzarella and tiny meatballs," Lina said, watching Pasquale carry the tray carefully into the house.

A few minutes later, Norina came out of the house with a small plate of lasagne. She handed the plate to Giacomino.

Norina must be doing extremely well. "Thank you," Giacomino said over and over.

The following day, Grazia saw a silhouette resembling Colombina the Farmer's Wife standing behind the fishnet curtain.

It can't possibly be her, Grazia thought, but as soon as she pulled the curtain aside she was faced with Colombina.

"I've got fresh fruits and vegetables," the farmer's wife said. "Come and get some."

"I don't have any money on me," Grazia said.

"You can pay me later. You can come and get the fruits and vegetables now."

Colombina escorted Grazia to her house. Grazia was so astonished that she wondered if she was dreaming. Colombina gave Grazia credit for five kilograms of fruits and vegetables, as well as a kilogram of almonds, two kilograms of dried figs, and three jars of marmalade. Grazia's heart skipped a beat when Giorgio appeared in the room.

"*Ciao* Grazia, I'm so happy to see you," Giorgio said.

Grazia was so excited Giorgio had greeted her in his mother's presence that she couldn't find the proper words to say. She skipped merrily out of the house, and forgot to take the goodies. Giorgio asked his mother for permission to deliver the goodies to the Voltinis' house. To Giorgio's relief, she agreed. Grazia was no longer just a peasant girl. She had a rich and generous cousin in America who was about to leave his fortune to her family.

Grazia was both astounded and exhilarated to see Giorgio standing behind the fishnet curtain. She couldn't resist the impulse to invite him into the house, though it was not in keeping with proper etiquette. An unwed woman should never allow a man into the house when she was alone.

"Where is everybody?" Giorgio asked, placing the basket on the table.

Grazia's face blushed. "The children are playing outside, and my mother went shopping."

Giorgio held Grazia by the arms, and couldn't fight the temptation to give her a passionate kiss. Grazia savored the kiss, despite her fear that someone would barge in at any moment.

Grazia nearly panicked when she saw an image moving quickly behind the fishnet curtains. She pushed Giorgio away. "You should go."

"Before I go, I want you to know that I love you," Giorgio said. He then stepped outside and closed the curtains.

Prancing around the room, Grazia repeated Giorgio's words to herself. "I want you to know that I love you."

The neighbors had counted the minutes that Giorgio had spent in the Voltinis' house.

"He barely had time to kiss her," Ninuccio the Painter said.

Titina the Alligator raised her chin. "They all start with a kiss. Look what happened to Carmela the Daughter of the Umbrella Repair Man... she ended up getting pregnant."

To Giorgio, that kiss had meant the world. The neighbors watched him saunter happily down the street.

Giorgio obtained his mother's permission to whistle whenever he passed by Grazia's house. Grazia was overjoyed every time she heard his whistle because it signified Giorgio's proclamation to all the neighbors he was courting her.

Norina felt that Giorgio's whistle, backed by the permission of his parents, deserved consideration. It meant he had serious intentions. Giorgio was the son of the most successful farmer on Saint Peter Street. Though Norina would have been thrilled if Giorgio were to marry her daughter, she knew it was impossible with no more hundred-dollar bills coming from America. A chill swept over Norina when she conceded to herself that she would have to convert the dollars into lire to pay her debts. She pushed the task away from her mind, wanting to enjoy the line of credit as much as possible. She didn't want to let go of the American bill.

Thanks to the hundred-dollar bill credit card, Norina was able to get two dozen fresh eggs from Tommasino the Donkey Ears. Norina sat by her front door and watched her children parading down the street sucking on the raw eggs. They finally knew what people were talking about when they said Tommasino's eggs were the best in town.

"We should have the rest of the eggs raw," Pasquale said.

"I have better uses for the eggs," Norina said. "I'm going to make almond cookies and a cake with custard cream, marmalade, and crushed almonds for Little Donato's birthday."

The children cheered. They couldn't remember the last time they had cake.

The following day, Pasquale and Mario were spotted on the street carrying big baking pans. The neighbors approached them, attracted by the delicious scent.

"Is there a special occasion?" Titina the Alligator asked.

"Yes, we're going to celebrate Little Donato's birthday," Pasquale responded.

"A big cake like that for a baby's birthday?"

"*Mamma* is going to fill the cake with marmalade, custard cream, and crushed almonds."

"Norina is making the royal cake, the traditional cake that people make for weddings," Lina the Warm House said as she watched the boys carry the big baking pans into the house.

"Norina's cousin must be sending her a lot of money," Titina said. "She keeps showing hundred-dollar bills every time she shops."

"God knows how many hundred dollar bills she's gotten from her millionaire cousin," Ninuccio the Painter said. "People who make it in America love to show off for their poor relatives in Italy."

The neighbors were not aware Norina had only one hundred-dollar bill.

The Voltinis had an extraordinary birthday party for Little Donato. They sang and danced happily, and everyone enjoyed the yummy dessert.

"The cake is delicious," the neighbors heard the children say.

Giacomino the Blind Man licked his lips. "Mmm, I wish I could have a taste of that cake."

"They gave you a taste of the lasagne and the *braciole*," Lina the Warm House said. "I'm sure Norina or Grazia is going to let you taste the cake."

They waited three long hours, anxious to taste the cake. Once the darkness descended from the sky, their hopes faded.

"Norina and Grazia forgot all about us," Giacomino said.

"We'd better go to sleep." Lina yawned. "I wish I had a rich relative in America."

The blind man exhaled. "I wish I had a generous relative in America. It's not a matter of being rich. It's a matter of having a big heart."

The Voltini children gorged themselves on the cake, and didn't even give Norina or Grazia a chance to put a piece aside for the neighbors.

The following day, Grazia apologized to Giacomino for not giving him a piece of cake, and compensated him with a plate filled with almond cookies.

The neighbors paid the Voltinis lots of visits and kept them up to date with the latest gossip, always entertaining the secret hope of getting a taste of whatever delicacy was on hand. Norina was generous to her neighbors because she wanted everyone to believe she had plenty of money. She felt it was a strategic way to extend her line of credit.

Norina and Grazia welcomed Titina the Alligator and Lina the Warm House into their home and promptly offered them sweet coffee and cookies. Titina and Lina enjoyed the treat.

"Carmela the Daughter of the Umbrella Repair Man had the baby," Titina mumbled.

"Carmela's parents are so ashamed that they're keeping it a secret," Lina said. "Carmela went to her brother's house to give birth. She had a boy."

"The baby was so big that he looked like a three-month-old." Titina lowered her voice. "But the baby died ten minutes after he was born."

Grazia's eyes became gloomy. "I feel sorry for Carmela."

"How did she expect a baby to survive with those tight clothes she wore?" Lina asked.

Titina narrowed her eyes. "It's worse than that…"

"What's worse?" Norina asked.

"I heard that they got rid of the baby's body by tossing it into the sewer."

Grazia widened her eyes.

"Don't tell anyone," Titina whispered.

Norina crossed her hands on her chest. "I'm not going to tell a soul."

Ercole the Rag Man's yells interrupted their gossip. "Trade in old rags for new pots and pans. Rags are valuable. They're better than my whore wife."

"We can use some new pots and pans," Norina said.

Norina reached for a bag filled with rags and scrambled out of the house to which they all followed.

"Ercole, I want a nice pot," Norina said, handing him a bundle of threadbare cloths.

Norina was pleased when the rag man gave her a brand-new pot. The pot was indispensable, since she was doing a lot of cooking.

As soon as the rag man walked away, Titina resumed her gossip. "Carmela's lover was happy that the baby was born dead."

Grazia twisted her face. "How can someone be so cruel?"

"It's all Carmela's fault," Titina said. "A *signorina* should never allow a man in her house when nobody else is around."

She's trying to tell me I made a mistake allowing Giorgio to be alone with me, Grazia thought. *Titina doesn't have a life of her own, so she's a spectator of other people's lives.*

Lillino the Vendor appeared in the street wheeling his cart.

"Who wants thread?" he kept shouting out.

Grazia and Norina ran towards the vendor and bought lots of thread. Lina and Titina noticed that Norina showed the vendor an American bill when it was time to pay him. They both wished they had American bills. They would have granted themselves a lot of luxuries.

Norina couldn't resist the temptation to use her hundred-dollar bill credit card to obtain fabric from Silvestro, the owner of the best fabric store in town. Norina utilized the material to make herself and her daughters brand new black outfits. Grazia insisted on using the leftover fabric to sew a pair of pants for Mario. He was the one who had the fewest clothes.

Though Grazia was very conservative, she bought a flower print fabric from Modesto, a store that had mediocre fabrics. She got a good deal. She gave a small deposit up front and showed the hundred-dollar bill as a guarantee of payment. At the Sewing school, she created a beautiful pleated bottom dress with the flower print fabric. Grazia didn't show the dress to her mother since she wasn't allowed to wear colorful clothes.

Thanks to the hundred-dollar bill credit card, the entire Voltini family got new shoes, and new slippers, from Orfino, the owner of the best shoe store in town.

"All the Americans that come to town buy shoes in my store," Orfino said. "Americans could never make shoes like the Italians do."

From Chiarello the Shoe Maker, Norina was able to obtain school-bags for Mario, Olimpia and Pasquale and handbags for herself and her daughters, Grazia and Caterina. Norina was even able to get new furniture. She got two night tables from Ippolito the Artisan.

Chiarello, Ippolito and Orfino, like everyone in town, were certain Norina was going to pay them because people who received plenty of dollars always paid them.

Even Clotilde used the hundred-dollar bill credit card. She visited Father Camillo and ordered a Mass for her deceased brother. She vowed to the priest she would pay him once her sister-in-law exchanged the dollars for lire. Father Camillo promptly agreed to celebrate the Mass.

Clotilde invited all her friends of the Catholic League to the service in honor of her deceased brother. The Voltinis sported their best attire in church. Norina donned her brand-new outfit for the occasion. In her new clothes, she felt like a White Fly. She even sensed looks of admiration from a few men. She was greeted warmly by many *signore* of the Catholic League, who spoke erudite Italian. Aware of being illiterate,

Norina tried her best not to expose her ignorance of the Italian language and spoke as little as possible. The *signore* of the Catholic League didn't associate with indigent and uneducated people, but they made an exception for Norina, who seemed to be a White Fly in the hatching.

The Mass was well attended. Vituccio and Marta were granted the honor of sitting in the first row among the immediate family. The Margassi Sisters and the neighbors of Saint Peter Street were seated in the back rows. Norina was happy to be seen by her neighbors, socializing with the *signore* of the Catholic League. In her nice clothes and her new shoes, she looked like one of them. The Margassi Sisters waved at Norina. Norina acknowledged them with a grin, but didn't dare wave back. She knew it was not appropriate to wave in church. She had to behave like a *signora*.

Baronessa Rosa sang a hymn during the Mass. The *signore* of the Catholic League were held rapt. They were abuzz with rave reviews of the performance.

"I didn't know your sister-in-law had such brilliant friends," a *signora* of the Catholic League whispered to Clotilde.

"Baronessa Rosa is also my friend. I've known her for years," Clotilde whispered back.

Grazia's heart pumped faster as soon as she spotted Giorgio among the neighbors. He was seated next to his mother, who kept smiling at her. His father also smiled at her. Grazia felt like the happiest girl on earth. Giorgio's parents had finally accepted her, and even acknowledged her in public.

Clotilde recited a poem in Latin. The poem was dedicated to her late brother. As usual, her Latin impressed the White Flies. Clotilde's eyes filled with tears when she used her best erudite Italian locution to speak about her late brother. She concluded her speech on the note that her beloved Gino lived in the celestial skies and was looking after his family. Norina didn't understand the difficult words Clotilde used, but knew that it was time to cry, and managed to produce some tears.

After the Mass, Norina invited everyone to Clotilde's house for refreshments. Caterina served coffee, dried figs, and almond cookies. She gave a double portion to Anna the Heavyweight and the Margassi Sisters. They thanked her with bright grins. They felt highly respected.

"The almond cookies are delicious," a *signora* of the Catholic League said.

"I made them myself," Norina said.

"You're very talented."

Norina beamed, even though she didn't quite understand what the word "talented" meant.

Clotilde took Norina aside and whispered, "There was no need to invite your neighbors and the Margassi Sisters. They're a bunch of lowlifes."

"They're not all lowlifes." Norina indicated Giovanni and Colombina. "The farmers are well off." She realized Giorgio was seated next to Grazia. "I think Giorgio wants to marry Grazia. He whistles when he passes by the house."

Clotilde flashed a half-smile. She knew the farmers would never accept a Voltini girl without a dowry.

Giorgio and Grazia were so happy to be together in public that they couldn't find the proper words to say to each other. They kept looking into one another's eyes.

The neighbors of Saint Peter Street and the Margassi Sisters relished the treats with a mixture of gratitude and admiration. Sweet coffee, almond cookies and dried figs were luxuries some of these people hadn't enjoyed in months.

"Norina gave us a royal treatment," Giovanna Margassi whispered to her sister.

Gina Margassi beamed as she bobbed her head in agreement.

XIX

Norina thought her new life would last forever, but eventually she found that the hundred-dollar bill's line of credit had been maxed out. Storeowners and vendors refused to give the Voltinis any more credit. Creditors no longer believed them when they promised they would go to the bank and convert the American bill into Italian lire. They grew impatient, and they all justifiably wanted to get paid. Eager to repay the priest, Clotilde kept begging Norina to go to the bank. Norina kept postponing the occasion. She didn't want to let go of her prestigious credit card, even if it had expired. She was once again without money, and had creditors knocking at her door daily. Norina often locked herself in the house and hid in the bedroom. Consequently, the entire Voltini family became the laughingstock of the town. Worse than that, they had acquired the reputation of being night payers. People pointed at them whenever they saw them on the street.

One morning Pasquina from the bottega knocked at the Voltinis' front door, but received no answer. Clenching her fists, Pasquina stepped back, looked up at the window and yelled, "Norina, I gave you a lot of costly goods: sugar, Parmesan cheese, coffee… and you didn't pay me. You shouldn't live in luxury at my expense."

Pasquina attracted several curious neighbors, who gathered quickly outside of Norina's house. To Pasquina's relief, she was able to win their sympathy. Many neighbors nodded, but to her disappointment, no one actively backed her up. A concert was always better than a solo player. Pasquina would have felt much more confident if the neighbors had joined her in rebuking Norina.

Norina was seated on a chair in the bedroom, staring at the wall. She didn't pay attention to Pasquina. Grazia's whole body trembled as she watched the scene, peering through the shutters of the window.

"Norina, you told the whole town your cousin in America is old, unmarried, and childless, and that he's going to leave you his fortune. It's a big lie. I found out that he has a wife, children, and a *commara* on top of it. There's no way he's going to leave you his money. He's not going to file the papers to let your family go to America. He doesn't even have a business! Norina, you are a liar. People who don't pay their debts are night payers. They're thieves! You should be ashamed of yourself." Pasquina turned to the neighbors of Saint Peter Street. "You should yell at Norina for being a fraud. Tell her to pay her debts!"

The neighbors remained silent. They didn't have the heart to scold Norina, since they had also benefited from the hundred-dollar bill. They were disappointed that Norina's line of credit had been exhausted. They missed having a taste of her exquisite home cooking.

Pasquina commanded Anna the Heavyweight to go after Norina for the overdue sum.

"I've threatened Norina many times," the strong woman said. "If I hurt her, I'm going to end up in jail. I just got out two days ago for giving Gisella Maori a black eye. I have to let some time go by."

Anna didn't want to give Norina a beating. She didn't even pressure Norina to reimburse the bottega. She felt a kinship with another poor single mother, and didn't blame her for incurring debts. Norina had the right to feed her children. Moreover, Norina paid her a lot of respect. Norina always invited her over when Angela the Crazy Head did a novel reading, and Anna couldn't wait to hear the next chapter.

Pasquina rubbed her hands together. "Norina, I'm going to call the marshal."

Ninuccio the Painter raised his eyebrows. "What is the marshal going to take, her crappy furniture? A chamber pot filled with shit?"

"Pasquina should be nice to Norina if she wants to get paid," Baronessa Rosa said. "Pasquina has everything to lose and nothing to gain."

Laughing under their breath, many neighbors of Saint Peter Street agreed. They entertained the secret thrill of watching the drama unfold.

Pasquina stamped her feet. "I want satisfaction! I want to speak to the eldest daughter. She should talk on her mother's behalf. Grazia, show your face."

Confined in the bedroom, Grazia's eyes filled with tears. She wished she could disappear.

The following morning, Colombina the Farmer's Wife knocked at the Voltinis' front door, and received no answer.

"Grazia, you're a lowlife," Colombina shouted. "You're nothing but a night payer. You should be ashamed of yourself. You should cover your face in mud! I can't believe that I trusted you. I gave you the best fruits and vegetables, a whole kilogram of almonds, two kilograms of dried figs, and two jars of marmalade and you didn't pay me. Your mother didn't even pay me a lira. If I get a hold of your mother I'm going to pull her hair out."

Colombina got the attention of neighbors and passersby, who congregated around her.

A passerby turned to Colombina. "I don't think she's ever going to pay you."

Colombina placed her hands on her hips. "I know that, but at least I'm getting the satisfaction of telling everybody."

Grazia burst into tears as she listened to Colombina's performance from her bedroom window. *I'll never get to see Giorgio again.*

Colombina forbade her son to whistle when he passed by Grazia's house. Grazia was brokenhearted. She missed his whistle. It had been a declaration of respect for all to hear.

He's abandoning me because his parents no longer approve of me. I'm not getting any more hundred-dollar bills from America, Grazia thought as tears dripped down her face.

Three days later, Grazia received a letter from Giorgio.

The letter read:

Dear Grazia,

I still love you. I don't care if you have the reputation of being a night payer. I miss you dearly. To me, you are the most beautiful girl in town. I believe in fate, and I know that someday we'll be together. I hope that day comes soon. No matter what happens, you'll be in my heart always.

Loving you forever,

Giorgio

Grazia shut her eyes and daydreamed, lost in the promise of "someday." As she opened her eyes, the vision suddenly faded and she burst out sobbing. It was an impossible dream!

The next day, Grazia sneaked out of the house when it was time to go to work. She walked the streets with her head down. She was afraid to be seen by her creditors. To her disappointment, she bumped into Giorgio and his mother. Grazia was mortified.

"A night payer like you shouldn't go out of the house," Colombina the Farmer's Wife yelled. "You should be ashamed to show your face in public."

Colombina attracted the attention of many curious passersby who nodded. She indicated Grazia. "She's a night payer. She should put mud on her face."

Grazia's eyes filled with tears. She ran away as quickly as she could to hide her tears. Once Giorgio and Colombina were out of sight, Grazia sobbed uncontrollably. She was devastated that Giorgio didn't say a word against his mother's insults. Grazia was so demoralized that she wanted to do just what Colombina had said: sequester herself in the house to avoid facing the creditors. Unfortunately, she still had to go to work.

On her way to the train station, Grazia ran into Silvestro, the owner of the best fabric store in town.

"You should put some sense into your mother's head and convince her to pay her debts," Silvestro yelled.

"I'll try to convince her." Grazia scampered away, weeping hysterically.

Grazia didn't tell her mother about her harrowing encounters. Norina refused to even hear stories about her creditors, and didn't care that she had acquired a bad reputation. Norina was mourning the loss of her new furniture. She was devastated by the thought that she had to give back the two night tables to Ippolito the Artisan. Grazia, on the other hand, was so wounded by the downfall of her family's respectability that she wished she weren't a Voltini.

Caterina was punished for being a Voltini. Carmine the Shepherd glared at her and spat on the floor when he saw her on the street.

"You had the nerve to take my milk for a whole month with the promise that you were about to exchange the hundred-dollar bill," the shepherd shouted. "You made a fool out of me... and your sister, Grazia? She's worse than you are! She took goat cheese, ricotta, and even mozzarella. Your whole family should be arrested. The Voltinis are nothing but a bunch of scoundrels, a bunch of thieves, a bunch of liars, and a bunch of night payers. Don't ever come to my house again. And stay away from my son, Rocco. He'll never marry a lowlife like you."

Caterina ran away. Once she arrived home, she confined herself to the bedroom and sobbed desperately. She didn't care about the insults addressed to her and her family, but she was utterly inconsolable that she had lost the opportunity to see Rocco. He was the love of her life.

Even Mario could not escape the consequences of being a Voltini. One afternoon he came home barefoot.

"What happened to your new shoes?" Grazia asked.

Mario remained silent. He hung his head low to hide his watery eyes.

It took Grazia a long time to convince her brother to talk, and it took Mario a longer time to explain to Grazia that Orfino, the owner of the shoe store, had taken the shoes away from him on the way to school. Many of the schoolchildren made fun of him when they noticed he walked barefoot. Grazia bit her lower lip to fight back tears as she pictured the degradation her brother had to endure.

Grazia gave Mario a bear hug. "Don't worry. 'It's never going to happen again."

The Voltinis went back to wearing their old shoes, for fear their new shoes would be taken away.

The following day a tall, muscular young man approached Pasquale on the street. Pasquale recognized him. He was Sebastiano, Domenico the Butcher's son.

"You should tell your mother to stick to horse when she gets a craving for meat," Sebastiano said, punching Pasquale in the mouth. "My father only sells beef, pork, and veal. His customers are all White Flies. My father is such a gentleman that he wouldn't even tell me that your mother never paid him. I had to hear the story from other people."

Pasquale contorted his face. "You're a real tough guy, starting a fight with someone half your size."

Sebastiano retorted with a kick to Pasquale's stomach. Pasquale struggled to stand up, but staggered and fell.

Sebastiano showed his fists. "Tell your mother to pay her debts if you don't want another beating."

Pasquale lowered his head. He could think of nothing to say.

When Pasquale got home, Caterina inquired about his bruises. Pasquale said he fell while he was playing soccer.

"There's no way you got all those bruises from one fall," Caterina said. "Someone has beaten you up."

"No one in town can knock me out." Pasquale forced a smile. "My friends call me Voltini the tough guy."

Many creditors brought their complaints to Clotilde. The poor woman was utterly mortified.

"I didn't know what Norina was doing," Clotilde kept telling the creditors.

"I gave credit to your sister-in-law out of respect for you," Pasquina from the bottega said. "You should pay her debt to save your family's reputation."

"I wish I could." Clotilde's eyes shone with tears. "I'll just have to convince Norina to exchange the American dollars and pay her debt."

Clotilde had told her sister-in-law many times to convert the damned dollars into lire, but Norina didn't listen. Norina just couldn't let go of the American bill. Clotilde's last resort was to steal the bill from Norina, by any means necessary.

When Clotilde arrived on Saint Peter Street, she noticed the Voltinis' front door was fastened shut. People barred their front doors whenever something disgraceful happened. Under those circumstances, they didn't want to face the neighbors. More than mere humiliation, Norina feared the increasingly real prospect that more of her creditors resorting to violence. Clotilde knocked on the door, but to her disappointment, no one answered.

"Norina, Grazia, Caterina," Clotilde called out, rapping repeatedly at the door. Still, there was no answer.

Clotilde attracted the attention of the neighbors, who promptly popped out of their houses.

Finally, the door sprang open and Grazia appeared. Her face was as white as a ghost.

"Grazia opened the door," Titina the Alligator whispered.

"Norina is hiding upstairs for sure," Lina the Warm House whispered back.

Clotilde walked stealthily into the house and closed the door behind her. The neighbors swiftly tiptoed towards the entrance, careful not to make any sort of noise. They were excited to listen.

It'll be better than a radio play, Giacomino the Blind Man thought.

Once inside the house, Clotilde was faced with Grazia.

Clotilde flared her nostrils. "Where's your mother?"

Grazia indicated the back room.

"Norina, I know where you are. You'd better come out before I come and get you," Clotilde shouted.

Norina emerged from the back room and lowered her head.

Clotilde narrowed her eyes. "You're hiding from your creditors."

Norina remained silent. She turned around and headed to the stairs.

"Stay where you are." Clotilde banged her fist on the table. "You're not going anywhere."

Norina froze.

Clotilde took a deep breath and said, "You've been branded a night payer. If you don't fix this, you'll ruin the whole family's reputation without any hope of repair, and nobody will marry your daughters."

Norina gazed at the wall. She was numb. She didn't show any emotion.

"Where is the hundred-dollar bill?" Clotilde asked.

"I don't know where it is," Norina responded in a feeble voice.

"Yes you do. You keep it in your brassiere."

Norina drew the American bill from her brassiere, but held it tightly in her hand.

"I'm stronger than you think." Clotilde laid her hands on Norina's shoulders and pushed her against the wall.

"It's mine," Norina cried out. "No one can take it away from me."

"It's not yours." Clotilde's eyes flashed. "It belongs to your creditors."

Norina turned to Grazia. "Help me."

Grazia stood still. "Paying your debts is the least you should do."

Norina launched a stern look at her daughter. "I'm going to whip you with your father's belt."

Grazia raised her chin. "I'd rather get whipped than be a night payer." She gave a sigh of relief. It felt good to be true to herself. She was standing up for what she believed in.

Clotilde grabbed Norina's hand. She used all her strength to pry open Norina's fist. When she finally succeeded, Clotilde extricated the American bill from Norina's fingers. Grazia remained speechless and motionless. She watched the scene as if it were being projected on a big screen.

Norina had lost the battle. Her eyes filled with tears. "You have no right to take my money. I need the money."

"You have no right to keep something that doesn't belong to you," Clotilde said.

Norina abandoned the notion of giving Grazia a whipping. She didn't have the strength. She was mourning the loss of her prestigious credit card. That credit card had been her ticket to respectability, and now it was gone forever.

As soon as Clotilde exited Norina's house, she saw the neighbors dispersing. She figured they had been listening to her conversation with Norina.

Clotilde sneered. *I can't believe I gave these lowlifes the satisfaction of knowing my business.*

Clotilde ignored their stares. She held her head up high and scurried down the street. Clotilde went straight to the bank and exchanged the American bill for Italian currency, once and for all.

Clotilde paid approximately one third of the debt to the creditors who knew her personally, to save face. The creditors asked her when she was going to pay them the balance.

"My cousin Ignazio has promised me he's going to send the rest of the money to pay Norina's debts," became her new mantra.

The creditors believed Clotilde, since she had the reputation of being a pious an honorable woman.

If I don't pay the creditors, my reputation will be blemished forever, Clotilde thought. She was haunted by that thought. Keeping her word of honor meant the world to her.

Clotilde wrote to her cousin Ignazio and her Aunt Elvira and implored them to send her the money to pay Norina's debts. She emphasized in the letter that she wanted to save the family's reputation. Clotilde managed to pay the priest for her late brother's Mass out of her own pocket.

It was a difficult time for the Voltinis. Their name had been tarnished. Norina couldn't get any work because of her reputation. The dole Norina received from the government was barely enough to pay her rent. Grazia's earnings were needed to provide food for the family. Grazia had to buy groceries in the city because the merchants in town wouldn't give her any more food even if she was willing to pay up front. They demanded that old debts first be paid in full. Grazia's monthly wage was barely enough to provide food for two weeks. For the third and fourth week of the month, the only hope for food rested on whatever Grazia was able to bring from the Zordi household. The children walked in and out of the house like starving pigeons, waiting for Grazia to come home. The food their sister brought was never enough to satisfy their hunger. To fill her stomach, Caterina wanted to fill in for Grazia at the Zordi residence again.

"I'll bring a lot of food home," Caterina said.

Pasquale glared at Caterina. "You managed to fill only your stomach when you worked for Mrs. Zordi. You forgot all about us. At least Grazia doesn't eat what she takes on the way home."

Caterina's face blushed. "I've never eaten anything on the train."

"You have, and my friends saw you do it. I have witnesses. You can't deny it." Pasquale drummed his fingers on the table. "It's time to receive your sentence."

Caterina grabbed her cheeks. "My sentence?"

Pasquale pointed at Caterina. "You'll never work for Mrs. Zordi again."

Caterina turned to her mother. "But I want to work. I have the right to fill my stomach."

Norina shook her head. She felt Caterina deserved the penalty. She trusted Grazia more than Caterina. Caterina remained silent even though her stomach was churning with anger, and hunger.

Desperation prevailed in the Voltini household because of the latest famine. A sinister melancholy overtook Grazia. She regretted having squandered her money on the flower print fabric. Ten kilograms of flour would have been much more beneficial for the family. Her portrait always returned to her mind. The money Norina wasted on the portrait haunted her. Her mother should have used the money to buy groceries. Grazia increasingly felt that the duty to provide food to nourish her family fell to her. She couldn't rely on her Uncle Vituccio, who was out of town. Aunt Clotilde had made it clear to her that she didn't have any food or money to spare, since she was paying some of Norina's debts out of her own pocket. Grazia's last resort was Angela the Crazy Head. Grazia implored Angela to do another reading of the novel. Still a loyal friend, Angela agreed to help her out.

Colombina the Farmer's Wife was so furious when she found out her neighbors were going to Norina's house that she stopped them on the street.

"You should be ashamed to go to a night payer's house," Colombina said.

"Norina doesn't have any debts with me," Titina the Alligator said.

How could anyone have debts with Titina? She's so poor that she doesn't even have the eyes to cry, Colombina thought. "Norina has debts with many people in town."

Giacomino the Blind Man shrugged. "It's none of my business. I don't care about other people's business."

Colombina giggled. "You live to gossip about other people's business."

The blind man didn't bother to retaliate. He had other things on his mind. He was excited to hear the ending of the novel.

The reading wasn't as successful this time, because many people to whom Norina owed money didn't attend. To everyone's disappointment, Mrs. Fatti couldn't make it because she had to go to a party. Consequently, the Voltinis didn't get any American goodies. They only got dried sunflower seeds from Carmela the Daughter of the Umbrella Repair Man, a loaf of bread from Anna the Heavyweight and Margherita, dried figs from Old Veronica, and olives from Lina the Warm House and Giacomino the Blind Man. Titina the Alligator again came empty-handed.

The listeners enjoyed the happy ending of the novel. Nardo divorced his cousin and went to Italy to find Vincenza, the love of his life. The lovers were finally reunited and had a fairy tale wedding. The newlyweds then went to America, where they became rich and were able to help their underprivileged relatives in Italy.

Norina's eyes gleamed with tears. She wished her American cousin would send her more dollar bills.

"The novel was great," Margherita said. "It was romantic."

Carmela revealed a somber look. *These wonderful endings only happen in novels.*

Grazia read the sadness in Carmela's eyes. *Poor girls like us can't count on romance. Carmela paid a high prize for falling in love.*

"I'm glad Nardo ended up in America with the woman he loved," Giacomino said.

Margherita shut her eyes and revealed a glint of a grin. "It would be so wonderful to go to America with the person you love."

Carmela exhaled heavily. "It would be nice to go to America even on your own."

In Carmela's situation, only America could save her, Titina thought. *There isn't a single man in town that is going to marry her after what she did.*

Angela turned to the listeners. "Don't tell the people who didn't come about the ending of the novel."

"I won't say a word," Giacomino said.

"I love novels," Margherita said. "I can't wait to attend another reading."

Norina patted Margherita's shoulder. "You are going to be the first one invited."

Margherita placed her palm on her forehead. "Oh, I forgot to tell you: I passed by Ubaldo the Photographer's studio the other day, and a man was looking at Grazia's portrait. He asked me if I knew her."

Norina tapped her feet. "Do you know this man?"

Margherita shook her head. "I don't know him. He's probably from out of town. I gave him Grazia's name and address."

With the Voltinis' reputation, only a man from another town can be interested in Grazia, Titina thought.

Old Veronica flashed a smile. "I think that Grazia is going to get a marriage proposal."

For the first time in weeks, Norina beamed.

When the guests left the Voltinis' house, the neighbors of Saint Peter Street approached them, eager to hear about the events of the last chapter of the novel. Titina told the curious neighbors all about the happy ending. She enjoyed the undivided attention she got from people, when she had exclusive information to reveal.

The Voltini children ate what leftovers remained from the treats the guests had brought. The meager pickings were a tease to their stomachs.

"We didn't do so well," Angela said. "We didn't get the American Wife."

"The American Wife will definitely come next time," Grazia said. "If you would come and do another reading sometime soon, it would be a great help."

"I won't be able to do another reading for a while. I'm going to be busy working for the notary. It's only a temporary job." Angela's eyes became gloomy. "I keep dreaming of getting a permanent job, but so far it's never happened. Sometimes I think I should just give up hope."

"You should never give up on your dreams," Grazia said.

Norina smiled in agreement. "Everything else costs money, but at least dreams are free."

That night, Norina dreamed about a rich man proposing marriage to Grazia.

XX

The Voltini boys were resourceful. To warm themselves from the cold, they gathered at the entrance of the community oven, where they enjoyed the delicious aromas of the baked goodies for the upcoming Christmas festivities. Tonino the Baker didn't mind having the children around during the busy season since they came in handy when he ran short of delivery boys.

The community oven was in an enormous room. Over the years, every surface had turned almost black from the smoke emanating from the large wood oven. A huge table and two chairs stood in close proximity to the oven. Around the walls, there were many shelves on which Tonino would place pans of *focaccia* bread, cookies, lamb, chicken, and all sorts of other culinary delights.

When the shelf space was not sufficient, the baker resorted to placing the pans on the floor. Especially around the holidays, when the oven was in high demand, people could barely walk into the room since most of the ground space was filled with pans.

Due to the heat, the dough of the *focaccia* bread would continue to rise. The baker instructed the kids to cut the overflowing dough from the big pans and place it into smaller pans. Thus would Tonino obtain several small *focaccie* out of the extra dough. Pasquale had mastered the skill of cutting the overflowing dough, and was often compensated with a small *focaccia*. Moreover, Tonino sometimes gave the other children small slices of *focaccia*.

Whenever there was a pan of succulent lamb with potatoes, the baker would always treat himself by taking a rib. He would then cover up the missing rib by placing a potato over the empty spot. He figured none of the customers would notice a missing rib, since the lamb had many. To his disappointment, he had never managed to find a similar technique to steal a cookie. There was no way he could camouflage an absent cookie, since the shape would be imprinted on the pan once it was baked.

Mario and Pasquale considered themselves lucky when Tonino used them as delivery boys because they often got little tips. Like Tonino, Pasquale always treated himself to a rib when he delivered a lamb with potatoes. Mario never dared to do so. He was afraid of getting caught. The Voltini boys wished they could work at the community oven on a full-time basis, but the baker already had plenty of regular delivery boys. He even had three sons who worked for him.

Norina wanted a job even more than her sons did, but with her reputation tarnished, most people shunned her. Norina stopped leaving the house. She couldn't take the chance that she might bump into one of her creditors. She had even heard Colombina the Farmer's Wife wanted to pull her hair out in full view of everybody. Norina was so depressed that she felt physically weak. She didn't have the courage or the strength to defend herself in case one of her creditors accosted her. Her only consolation was praying to Our Lady of Sorrows, constantly begging her for a job.

When Mrs. Matilde Fatti paid Norina a visit and asked her to make almond cookies, Norina thought that Our Lady of Sorrows had performed a miracle. Mrs. Fatti gave Norina a basket filled with two kilograms of almonds, a dozen eggs, and a kilogram of sugar. Norina looked at the goodies as if they were treasures.

Perhaps because her soul had grown tired of dishonesty, Norina said, "I only need the whites of the eggs to make the cookies. If you want, I can give you the yolks."

"I don't need the yolks. You can throw them out," Mrs. Fatti said as she walked out of the house.

I can use part of the sugar that the American Wife gave me and beat it with the egg yolks, Norina thought. She flashed a glint of a grin as she pictured her children feasting on the sweet egg yolks.

When the children got home from school, Norina gave them egg yolks beaten with sugar. The children devoured the confection.

Norina started her work with zeal. She boiled the almonds, drained them, and patiently peeled the rinds off one by one. She minced the peeled almonds in the coffee mill by turning the crank repeatedly. She then mixed the crushed almonds with the egg whites and sugar and made little balls out of the mixture. Humming a song, she arranged the little balls carefully in a pan. When she finally completed her task, she summoned Grazia and instructed her to take the pan filled with cookies to the baker.

Grazia carried the pan all the way to the community oven. Pasquale and Mario were among the children seated by the entrance. They waved cheerfully at Grazia.

"That's my sister," Pasquale said to his friends.

The children moved aside to allow Grazia to pass by. Tonino the Baker smiled at Grazia.

"These cookies are for Mrs. Matilde Fatti," Grazia said.

"If all my customers were as generous as her, I'd be a rich man," the baker said as he took the pan and placed it in the big oven.

In the meantime, Zina the Silk Stockings, a tall, attractive brunette with prominent breasts, walked into the room.

Zina glared at the baker. "My lamb had a missing leg."

Tonino's mouth fell open. "A missing leg?"

"Someone ate the leg. It must have been the delivery boy."

"I've been so busy today that I don't even remember who delivered your lamb. I'll fire the boy. Tell me his name."

Zina shrugged. "I don't know his name."

The baker led Zina outside and lined up his boys. "Take a look at them. Can you recognize the one who delivered the lamb?"

While Zina looked at the boys, Pasquale managed to sneak a bite of a big piece of *focaccia*. The *focaccia* covered most of his face. Luckily, since Pasquale was eating, Zina assumed he was a customer and didn't look closely at him.

"I don't see the boy that delivered the lamb," Zina said.

Pasquale gave a sigh of relief.

My son must have eaten the lamb's leg. Thank God he's not here, Tonino thought. "I fired a delivery boy earlier today. He must have been the one who ate the leg. Sorry for the inconvenience. I'm going to make it up to you. I'm not going to charge you for your next baking."

"We have a deal," Zina said, shuffling away.

The baker sighed heavily as he walked back into the room.

Grazia turned to the baker. "When will the cookies be delivered to the American Wife?"

"I'll deliver them in about an hour."

The baker looked intensely at Grazia as she walked out of the room. She reminded him of Norina. Years ago, he had been one of Norina's suitors.

Later in the day, Norina received a visit from Mr. Fatti. He was sporting a gray coat, a black hat, and a white scarf.

"I want to thank you for the delicious cookies," Mr. Fatti said, handing her a crisp dollar bill. "You make the best cookies in town. They remind me of the cookies my mother used to make."

Norina remained silent with her mouth open. She stared at him as he walked away. He looked like one of the powerful gangsters she had seen in movies. Norina placed the American bill in her brassiere and skipped happily around the kitchen.

Norina was forbidden to buy food from the bottega due to her outstanding debt. She gave Clotilde the dollar bill, and asked her to buy groceries on her behalf. Clotilde immediately exchanged the American bill for lire and bought pasta, dried beans, bread, fruits, vegetables, garlic, oil, five jars of homemade tomato sauce, and a sack of charcoal. Norina considered the dollar bill a blessing from the sky. She had plenty of food and coal for the warming pan, and this time it was all paid for in full.

It was a tradition to have *anguilla,* or eel, on Christmas Eve. People in town would trade their jewelry to be able to afford the expensive fish. Most of the neighbors on Saint Peter Street had fried eel as an appetizer and eel with spaghetti and tomato sauce for the main course. The aroma of the fried fish spread all over the narrow street. Unfortunately, Norina couldn't afford the costly eel.

"We're having pasta with tomato sauce and oranges with sugar," Norina said to her children.

Grazia read the disappointment on her siblings' faces. "Let's play *tombola,*" she said, attempting to cheer them up.

Tombola was a game similar to bingo that was often played during the holidays.

Olimpia swung her arms. "I love *tombola.*"

"We have no money." Pasquale stamped his foot. "We need money to play *tombola.*"

Grazia reached for the tombola set and a box filled with buttons. "We can use buttons instead of money."

Norina heated up the warming pan and placed it under the table. Olimpia decorated the pan with orange peels. They enjoyed the warmth on their feet and the aroma of oranges diffusing into the room while they competed.

When Grazia called the numbers out, her siblings correlated every number with animals or people. Number seventy-seven was associated with Aunt Clotilde's legs. Number one was Father Camillo. Sixteen was the jackass. Forty-seven: the speaking dead, fourteen: the betrayed lovers…

"*Tombola!*" Pasquale shouted.

Pasquale claimed to have won, but when Grazia checked the numbers, she realized he had been cheating, so they had to start the game over again.

A knock startled everyone. Norina promptly opened the front door. Vituccio bounded into the house, carrying a little cage containing two live chickens and a bucket filled with live eels.

Vituccio placed the cage and the bucket on the floor. "I drove a White Fly to Naples, and I got the fish and the chickens for free," he whispered to Norina.

Norina grinned. "Our Lady of Sorrows helps you because she knows that you help me."

Little Donato opened the cage and freed the chickens. "I play chicken."

Norina turned to the children. "What do you say to your Uncle Vituccio?"

"Thank you," the children replied in unison.

Olimpia hugged Vituccio with affection. "Uncle Vituccio is the best uncle in the world."

Little Donato grabbed his uncle's legs. Vituccio was the happiest man alive when he was embraced by his nephews and nieces. He walked outside, followed by the joyful chatter of the children.

Humming a song, Norina cooked the eel with tomato sauce. The aroma of the delicious *anguilla* permeated the house. When she was done cooking, she opened the front door to allow the scent to drift into the street. She wanted to proclaim to everyone she was also having eel on Christmas Eve.

"I smell eel," Clotilde said when she walked into the house.

"Vituccio brought it," Norina said.

Vituccio may be a womanizer but he has a good heart, Clotilde thought as she drew a plate wrapped in a towel from her bag and placed it on the mantle of the fireplace. "I brought dried figs. We'll have them for dessert."

As soon as Norina drained the spaghetti, the children gathered around the steam to warm their hands.

"Get away," Norina yelled.

Norina arranged the spaghetti, the tomato sauce, and the eels onto a platter. She then positioned the platter ceremoniously on the table. They all took a seat around the table, and Clotilde forced the Voltinis to repeat a prayer. As soon as they were done praying, the children armed themselves with forks. Before they attacked the platter, Clotilde rationed some spaghetti onto a small plate she had brought from home. They all relished the spaghetti with eels and tomato sauce. The children didn't bother with Clotilde's dessert. They weren't fond of dried figs after such a great meal. Dried figs were only exciting when there was nothing better to eat.

At the sound of church bells, Caterina jumped up. "It's time to put on our costumes. The procession is about to start."

Norina dressed up Little Donato in a white tunic and a red mantle. He looked like a wealthy little shepherd. Since Pasquale and Mario wore all sorts of rags on top of their coats, they resembled poor shepherds. Grazia, Caterina, and Olimpia masqueraded as poor Madonnas by donning old capes on top of their coats. The Voltini children scrambled outside, with Clotilde pursuing with a bunch of candles. Since Norina wasn't in the mood to see her creditors, she remained inside and watched the procession through the window.

Maddalena and Arturo were leading the procession. They took on the roles of the Virgin Mary and Saint Joseph. Since they kept smiling they gave the impression of being a happy couple.

"When did Maddalena come back?" Grazia asked.

"She came back this morning for the sake of the baby Jesus," Old Veronica responded.

"Father Camillo helped sort everything out," Lina the Warm House said.

Titina the Alligator revealed a trace of a smile. "We have the perfect Virgin Mary and the ideal Saint Joseph."

"They're the only ones who have the costumes," Anna the Heavyweight said.

Old Veronica moved towards Little Donato. "He looks adorable. He looks like a little shepherd."

The old woman escorted Little Donato to the first row of the procession and handed him a statuette of the baby Jesus with great care. She then covered the statue with a white cloth.

"Why did you cover the baby Jesus?" a child asked.

"Because the baby Jesus hasn't been born yet," Old Veronica replied. "We're going to uncover him at midnight."

Clotilde lit the candles and handed them to her nieces and nephews. Many of the people following the procession carried lit candles. Though Contessa Fiorella could only watch the procession through the shutters of her window, she was delighted. The candles looked like little stars illuminating the dark street.

Without warning, two chickens popped out of the Voltinis' house and followed the procession as well.

"Shoo, shoo," Lina shouted, attempting to scare the chickens away.

"Let them stay," Old Veronica said. "When Jesus was born, there was a mule and a lamb. Who knows? Maybe there were also a couple of chickens."

The neighbors couldn't help but laugh at her remark.

Grazia saw Carmela the Daughter of the Umbrella Repair Man among the people following the procession. She had donned a black mantle and a miserable countenance.

She's probably thinking about her baby, Grazia thought. She twisted her lips when she spotted Carmela's lover among the men dressed as kings. *He picked the appropriate* costume. *That man is so full of himself that he probably thinks he is a king.*

Grazia's face blushed when she noticed Giorgio was also dressed as a king. *He's a king and I'm a poor Madonna. I'm not worthy of royalty,* she thought, turning her eyes away from him.

"We should start singing," Giacomino the Blind Man yelled as he played his violin.

They all sang in a chorus:

The king of the sky is descending from the stars…

At the sound of the church bells announcing midnight, they all exchanged jolly looks.

"Baby Jesus is born," Giacomino shouted.

Old Veronica stealthily uncovered the statue of newborn Jesus. She indicated Maddalena, dressed as the Virgin Mary, to Little Donato. "Now you have to give the baby to the mother."

Obediently, Little Donato gave the statuette of baby Jesus to Maddalena, who embraced it as if it were a real child.

"What Maddalena and Arturo need is a child," Old Veronica said. "Maybe then they would stop fighting."

Lina nodded.

"Baronessa Rosa is going to sing 'A Day in Paradise,'" Giacomino bellowed.

A deep silence descended upon the narrow street. White pigeons danced in the starry dark blue sky as Baronessa Rosa sang,

In Paradise, people beam with joy thanks to Jesus,
whose heart is filled with fraternal love and compassion.
Jesus forgives our sins…

Contessa Fiorella's eyes filled with tears as she listened to the song. Her husband had not forgiven her for her indiscretion.

XXI

Norina calculated that none of her creditors would be so heartless as to publicly embarrass her on Christmas Day, and decided she would take her children to church.

"*Mamma*, do we have to wear our new shoes?" Olimpia asked. "I'm afraid the owner of the shoe store will take them away from us."

"Not today," Norina responded. "He's never going to be disrespectful on baby Jesus' birthday. Go ahead, you can wear your new shoes."

Unfortunately, Mario could only wear his old shoes since his new shoes had been taken away by the owner of the shoe store. Mario donned his First Communion suit, though it was far too small for him.

Norina attached a black mourning button on the collar of Mario's jacket. "Put your hands in your pockets so the sleeves are not going to look too short. Don't shake when we go outside. I don't want people to think that you're cold."

Mario nodded. It was cold outside, and he would have liked to have worn his old coat to keep warm, but he didn't dare ask his mother.

Pasquale had nothing decent to wear. His jacket had ripped, and though Grazia mended it well, the patches were all too visible.

"I'll stay home," Pasquale said.

"Aunt Clotilde is going to be very upset if you miss Mass on Christmas Day," Norina said.

"I'll tell Aunt Clotilde I'm sick."

"Fine," Norina said.

Little Donato looked like an American child clad in a blue velvet coat that Grazia had made from Mrs. Zordi's jacket. Norina sported a black coat, also formerly Mrs. Zordi's. Grazia, Caterina, and Olimpia wore old dresses of Mrs. Zordi's that Norina had altered to fit them. They resembled three distinguished *signorine*. Since they didn't have decent coats, they were cloaked in light jackets, and struggled not to shiver on their way to Saint Maria's Church.

When the Voltinis entered the church, many men looked intently at Grazia, whose beauty made her stand out among her sisters. Clotilde had a row of seats reserved for her relatives. The Voltinis sat proudly among the *signore* of the Catholic League.

Norina saw her sister Ada, who was seated next to her husband Rodolfo and her daughters Catia and Mariella. They were all well dressed. As Rodolfo turned his head, Norina made eye contact with Ada. Their faces showed their affection for each other.

Norina eyed Teresina from the bottega with her daughter Costanza and Costanza's fiancé, Ottavio. She noticed that Ottavio was a handsome man. *Candidates to go to America get to marry the best-looking men in town*, she thought. Her eyes scanned the whole of the church in search of her brother Vituccio, but to her disappointment, he wasn't there. She furrowed her brow. *It's strange. Vituccio never misses a Christmas Mass.*

Giorgio was seated with his parents. He fixed his gaze on Grazia throughout the entire Mass, while Grazia avoided his eyes. She wanted to cross Giorgio out of her mind now that his family didn't consider her worthy of him.

That evening, the Voltinis had a poor Christmas meal. They ate spaghetti with plain tomato sauce, with dried figs for dessert.

Pasquale invented a game to entertain his siblings. He dressed up as a bandit and chased his siblings around the house with a piece of wood shaped like a gun.

"I'll shoot anyone who doesn't run fast enough," Pasquale said.

The chickens seemed to participate in the game as well. They ran ahead of the children.

Little Donato named the chickens after his sisters, Grazia and Caterina. The children had a merry time playing. Even Chicken Grazia and Chicken Caterina looked like they were having a good time.

Wealthy and poor people alike would traditionally celebrate the arrival of the New Year. From windows, balconies, and front doors, the neighbors of Saint Peter Street would dispose of all sorts of old things, tossing them onto the deserted street. Baronessa Rosa defenestrated a brand-new terracotta pot, which was reduced to pieces once it landed. Anna the Heavyweight smashed many empty bottles on the ground.

"Go away 1952, we can all use a better year," Anna's voice boomed. "1953 is going to be a better year."

Poking his head out of his house, Ninuccio the Painter saw a hand sticking out of Count Torre's window. "It's Contessa Fiorella's hand," he shouted.

People watched the contessa's hand fling a crystal glass, which shattered into thousands of pieces when it hit the ground.

They all took great satisfaction in destroying things that belonged to the old year. It was their way of getting rid of the past. At midnight, they all stopped throwing old things out and welcomed the New Year with loud whistles and cheers.

Anna waved at the Voltinis from her balcony. "Come to my house."

Standing on their balcony, the Voltinis promptly waved back at her. They felt so honored to be invited that they dashed into Anna's house. Anna and Margherita welcomed them with sincere joy.

Anna indicated the Dumb Brothers and winked. "I have special guests."

The Dumb Brothers's faces radiated joy. No one had ever referred to them as special guests.

"Anna is very generous," the elder Dumb Brother said. "She gave us so many cookies that we couldn't eat them all. We stuffed our pockets with the rest of the cookies."

"We're saving them for a rainy day," the younger Dumb Brother said.

"I gave you all those cookies because I didn't know that I'd have more guests," Anna said. "Take them out of your pockets and give them to the new guests."

Obediently, the Dumb Brothers shared their cookies with the Voltinis.

Anna reached for a bottle of *spumante,* a sparkling white wine. "I have many bottles of *spumante.* Teresina from the bottega gave them to me." Anna stumbled as she turned to the Dumb Brothers. "If you drink lots of *spumante,* you are going to get smart."

The Dumb Brothers smiled, eager to have a drink that would finally make them smart.

They all drank the *spumante* with delight. Norina allowed the children to have some *spumante.* Even Little Donato got a taste of it.

"*Spumante* brings good luck for the New Year," Margherita said.

Anna drew a bottle of homemade wine from her bag and placed it on the table. "I like wine better than *spumante.* Wine makes you stronger."

They all sang and danced in a circle to welcome the New Year. Anna and Margherita avidly drank the wine as they danced. They both got so drunk that they could barely stand up.

Norina patted Anna's arm. "You look tired. You could use some sleep."

"You read my mind," Anna mumbled.

"I can't wait to go to sleep and dream about my Franchino," Margherita whispered.

The Voltinis and the Dumb Brothers thanked Anna and Margherita for the hospitality and walked out of the house. They were happy to have celebrated the New Year with *spumante.*

"*Spumante* makes you smart and brings you good luck," the elder Dumb Brother said.

"We drank a lot of *spumante*," the younger Dumb Brother said. "We're going to be really smart and lucky."

The Voltinis stifled their laughter.

On January 6th, the day of the Epiphany, the people of Vocevero celebrated Little Christmas. It was a celebration of the Three Kings who brought the baby Jesus presents. The Epiphany was considered a night of magic, because anything could happen. On the night of the Epiphany *la Befana*, an imaginary old woman dressed in rags, was said to fly on a broom delivering presents to children. Vituccio never failed to give the children gifts he claimed had been delivered by *la Befana*. Mario, Olimpia, and Little Donato were so anxious to receive toys from Uncle Vituccio that they waited for him on the street. Caterina and Pasquale stood outside by the front door. They were also eager to see their uncle, even though they were too old for toys. They were entertaining the hope that he would give them some money.

"When is Uncle Vituccio coming?" Olimpia asked.

"You've been a bad girl this year," Caterina responded. "You're going to get a bag full of coal."

It was a tradition for unruly children to receive bags of coal instead of toys.

Olimpia twisted her face as if she was about to cry. "I've been a good girl. I deserve a beautiful doll."

Olimpia lost hope as the sunset descended on the narrow street. Pasquale noticed she had tears rolling down her cheeks.

"You're behaving like a baby," Pasquale shouted. "You're too old to cry."

Mrs. Fatti's son had received a toy fire truck. Since he wasn't allowed to play on the street, he showed off his toy from his balcony. It had real lights, and it made the sound of a siren. The poor children were mesmerized by the toy truck. Pasquale avoided looking at the truck. He did not want to give the rich boy the satisfaction of admiring his toy. Mario, on the other hand, kept staring at it with his mouth agape. He couldn't figure out how a toy truck could have real lights.

"You look like a fool, staring at the toy like that," Pasquale yelled.

Mario lowered his head. "I l-like to-to lo-ook at-at the toy-toys."

"At your age, you should be looking at girls." Pasquale took Mario by the arm and dragged him into the house.

"Mario behaves like a kid. He stares at toys," Pasquale said to his mother as he entered the house with Mario.

Mario's face blushed as he remained speechless.

Olimpia and Little Donato popped into the house.

Olimpia stamped her foot. "We're the only kids who didn't get anything from *la Befana*."

"Maybe *la Befana* didn't bring any gifts to Uncle Vituccio," Norina said.

"*La Befana* never forgets to bring toys to Uncle Vituccio," Olimpia shouted. "You should go to his house and get them."

"I want toy," Little Donato cried out.

"I'll go to Uncle Vituccio's house," Grazia said.

"You can't go walking the street alone in the evening," Norina said. "Pasquale has to go with you."

"I'll escort Grazia," Pasquale said.

Olimpia skipped around the kitchen, swinging her arms.

When Grazia and Pasquale reached their uncle's house, they saw a feeble light filtering through the window, but to their disappointment, the front door was shut. It was a bad sign. They knew it meant something dramatic had happened.

Grazia knocked on the door, but received no answer. "Uncle Vituccio," she called out.

Pasquale and Grazia waited in front of the house for ten minutes.

Finally the door opened and Marta appeared. She contorted her lips. "Your uncle had an affair with Loretta the Madman's Wife, and he got a beating from her husband."

Loretta is a beautiful woman, Pasquale thought. *My uncle isn't stupid.*

"How is he?" Grazia asked.

"He's in bed with a broken leg." Marta bit her finger. "What's worse is that he won't be able to work for at least two months."

Marta led Grazia and Pasquale to the bedroom. Vituccio had bruises all over his face and a cast on his leg.

"I'm so sorry you got hurt." Grazia gave Vituccio a warm hug. "Why didn't you tell us?"

"He was too ashamed to tell you," Marta said.

Vituccio's eyes dimmed. *My wife dishonors me in front of my niece and my nephew. She doesn't even spare innocent kids.* "I never touched that woman. The husband is insanely jealous. He's crazy. That's why he's nicknamed the Madman. He thought I was having an affair with his wife just because I drove her to her lawyer's office."

He's a real man, Pasquale thought. *A man who has an affair should always deny it.*

Grazia remained silent. She wanted to avoid the subject, sensing her uncle's embarrassment.

Marta turned to Grazia. "Your uncle's lover, Loretta, had the guts to come to my house after all the trouble she's caused. Loretta is a whore and a half."

Vituccio shut his eyes tightly. "I refused to see Loretta. I didn't want to get another beating from her crazy husband."

"I believe you're innocent," Grazia whispered in Vituccio's ear.

Vituccio smiled, but his smile quickly faded. "I'm sorry. I couldn't buy the kids any toys."

"Don't worry about that," Grazia said.

Pasquale patted Vituccio's shoulder. "I hope you recover soon."

Marta escorted Pasquale and Grazia to the front door. "Do you see what I have to go through? I'm ashamed to go out because of your uncle."

Grazia and Pasquale didn't respond. As much as they wanted to defend their uncle, they didn't dare contradict their aunt.

Once they exited the house, Pasquale said, "Olimpia and Little Donato are going to have a fit when they find out they aren't getting anything from *la Befana*."

Grazia was reluctant to go home empty-handed. She bit her lower lip as she imagined the children's faces filled with disappointment.

As they meandered back to their house, Grazia and Pasquale bumped into Olga the Scared Cat, who was wheeling her cart filled with fruits and vegetables.

Olga turned to Pasquale. "What did you get from *la Befana*?"

"I'm too old to get toys from *la Befana*," Pasquale said. "I'm upset my younger siblings didn't get anything."

"I'm going to talk to *la Befana*, and I'm going to put in a good word for them." Olga scrunched her forehead. She had run out of toys and candies, and was wondering what she could give the children.

Steering her cart, Olga the Scared Cat followed Pasquale and Grazia to Saint Peter Street. Grazia noticed her siblings wandering on the street.

Olimpia waved her hands in the air as soon as she saw the vendor. "It's Olga the Scared Cat."

Olimpia, Mario, and Little Donato ran towards the vendor.

Olga flashed a wide smile that revealed her lack of front teeth. She sank her hands into her pockets and said, "*La Befana* told me that she didn't have the time to buy you presents, so she left some money for you."

The children were enchanted as Olga pulled out all her pocket money and gave it to them.

"We have a lot of money," Olimpia shouted. "We can buy our own toys."

Mario smiled as he nodded.

Olimpia and Mario were unaware they needed more than pocket change to buy toys.

Olga the Scared Cat walked away with her cart. She amused herself with the idea she might bump into a friend willing to buy her a drink. She was in desperate need of a drink.

"Is it true that Olga the Scared Cat is related to *la Befana*?" Olimpia asked.

Pasquale nodded. "I heard *la Befana* is also Santa Claus' poor cousin."

"Who's Santa Claus?" Olimpia asked.

"He's an American saint," Grazia responded.

"Santa Claus is rich," Pasquale said. "He delivers the most beautiful gifts to all the children in America."

Olimpia looked up at the sky. "I wish I lived in America."

XXII

"I don't have enough money to pay my debt," Norina said as if by rote when Giovanni the Farmer bounded into her house.

"I didn't come to collect money," the farmer said. "I came to ask if you're willing to work in the artichoke fields tomorrow."

Norina grinned. "You know that I'm always willing to work."

"Meet me on the street around five o'clock."

Norina nodded. She didn't ask him to allow her boys to accompany her because she didn't want to expose them to the cold weather. As soon as the farmer stepped out of the house Norina climbed up the stairs, eager to tell the good news to her daughters.

"Giovanni the Farmer hired me to work in the fields tomorrow," she shouted, walking into the bedroom.

"You shouldn't go," Caterina said. "It's too chilly."

"You have a cold already and you could always get worse," Grazia said.

"If I don't go, the farmer is not going to give me another chance to work for him." Norina exhaled. "We need the money. I want to buy lots of food and coal for the warming pan."

When Norina woke up the following morning, she felt weak. She summoned her strength and got up from the bed. She donned her housedress and a heavy jacket, reached for a blanket, and went down the stairs taking pains not to make any noise that would wake up her children. She staggered out of the house, eager to earn a day's wage.

The headlights of the farmer's three-wheeler vehicle glittered in the dark. As Norina walked forward onto the street, she noticed Anna the Heavyweight seated in the vehicle. She let out a sigh of relief. She didn't want to be seen in a vehicle alone with Giovanni the Farmer. It would have generated gossip in town.

Anna welcomed Norina with a smile. "I'm glad you came."

"I'm always happy to work with you," Norina said, getting into the vehicle.

As soon as Giovanni revved the engine, the vehicle picked up speed. Norina had the sensation that the houses were running, one after another. She felt nauseated, but she refrained from saying anything, fearing Giovanni would bring her back home. Norina felt a bit better when the vehicle came to a halt by the artichoke field.

Anna pursed her lips. "Too bad the ride is over."

They saw the Dumb Brothers already laboring.

Anna hastily took Norina's blanket and placed it on her head. "I'm going to pretend to be Sister Felicia, the mother superior of the orphanage where the Dumb Brothers grew up. I know how to mimic her voice."

Norina played along, waving at the Dumb Brothers. "Look, Sister Felicia is here."

The Dumb Brothers widened their eyes as they turned their gaze towards Norina.

"We haven't done anything bad," the elder Dumb Brother said.

"We've been good boys," the younger Dumb Brother said.

Anna tapped Giovanni's arm and said, "Put the lights on."

As soon as Anna jumped onto the hood of the vehicle, Giovanni turned on the high beams. As the light reflected on Anna's figure, from a distance she could pass for a particularly burly nun.

"I heard that you have been bad boys. You have sinned," Anna said, imitating Sister Felicia's voice.

"We cursed," the older brother said.

"To whom?" Anna asked.

"To our relatives and to our friends," the younger brother responded.

Anna stamped her foot. "That's a sin."

The older brother bowed his head. "We've also cursed the saints."

Anna raised her voice. "That's a very grave sin. You've got to say three Hail Mary's each."

The Dumb Brothers got down on their knees and recited the prayers.

"You have to pray every day to Our Lady of Sorrows, otherwise you are going to get bad luck," Anna bellowed.

In the meantime, the farmer turned off the high beams.

The elder brother gave a sigh of relief. "Sister Felicia has disappeared."

"She seemed to be very upset with us," the younger brother said. "We better stop cursing."

The Dumb Brothers went back to work.

Anna jumped out of the vehicle, laughing it up. Norina also chortled heartily.

Giovanni chuckled and hooted. "Anna, you are a devil."

"They are going to stop cursing for sure." Anna winked. "I did a good deed."

"Now it's time to get to work," the farmer said.

The strong woman smiled as she looked at the artichoke field. "If it were up to me, I'd work day and night in the countryside."

The pink light of daybreak emerged from the sky. Anna and Norina began removing tiny artichoke offshoots from the sides of the main plant. Doing so, allowed the main plant to grow healthier and stronger. The Dumb Brothers hummed a song as they labored. They were slow workers, but they were always willing to do the job, and never complained about being paid less than other employees.

Giovanni got into his three-wheeler vehicle and started the engine again. "I'm going to check out my other fields. I'll be back soon."

The vehicle made a screeching noise and vanished into the distance.

Anna drew a bottle of wine from her bag. "When I drink wine, I don't feel cold." She sipped the wine and spun around. "Want some?"

"No, I can't drink wine. It gives me a headache." Overtaken with a dizzy spell, Norina fell to the ground.

Anna immediately placed the bottle on the ground and lifted Norina up. "What's wrong?"

Norina drew her hand on her forehead. "I felt my head spinning."

"You're not strong enough to work in the fields. Get some rest. I'm going to continue the work for you."

Norina thanked her with a tiny grin. She wrapped herself with the blanket and lay down on the ground, and soon felt some relief from the cold.

Norina noticed grayish clouds emerging in the sky. *It's a bad sign. It's going to rain soon.* Minutes later, she felt drops on her face. *The sky is crying.* The drops got thicker and thicker.

"It's pouring," Anna yelled, jumping up and down.

The Dumb Brothers continued their work despite the heavy rain.

Anna danced under the downpour. "You take the best showers when it rains."

Norina's whole body began to tremble. "I hope the farmer comes soon."

By the time Giovanni the Farmer came to pick them up, the poor workers were all drenched.

When Norina got home, she showed her children the money she had earned. "I'm going to give Grazia the money to buy sugar from the city."

"We are getting sugar," Olimpia sang.

"*Mamma*, you should change your clothes," Grazia said. "You're soaking wet."

"I'm going to…" Overtaken with another dizzy spell, Norina's words were interrupted, and she fainted.

The children surrounded her. "*Mamma!*"

Grazia felt her mother's head with her palm. "She has a high fever." She patted Norina's face. "*Mamma*, talk to me. *Mamma*, please say something."

Norina was breathing heavily. She kept gasping for air. "I felt... my head spinning... all of a sudden."

Grazia helped her mother get up from the floor. "You should be in bed."

Caterina and Grazia took their mother by the arms and led her up the stairs. Once into the bedroom, they helped Norina change into her nightgown and get into the bed.

Grazia covered her mother with a blanket. "You need a lot of rest."

"But the children didn't get any dinner," Norina mumbled.

"I'll take care of dinner," Grazia said. "I brought home the feet and the head of a chicken, and some pasta."

Norina gave a sigh of relief.

Norina didn't have the strength to get up for days. She spent most of her time in bed. She suffered severe congestion, and coughed frequently. One night, Norina's cough got so loud that it woke up her children. Pasquale and Mario bounded into the bedroom. They stood petrified as Norina was wracked by another coughing fit. Mario sensed there was something seriously wrong with his mother when he noticed her eyes were fixed to the ceiling. His father had his eyes fixed to the ceiling as well, on the day he died.

"*Mamma* will be fine," Grazia said. "Go back to sleep."

Pasquale and Mario returned to their room. They were so preoccupied that they couldn't get any sleep. Grazia stayed up all night by her mother's bed. She panicked every time her mother coughed. Grazia's eyes shone with tears when she noticed Little Donato was also coughing.

As soon as the morning approached, Grazia shook Caterina's shoulder vehemently. Caterina woke up from her sleep.

"Go to Aunt Clotilde's house and tell her *Mamma* and Little Donato coughed all night long. I need her advice. I don't know what to do," Grazia whispered.

Caterina promptly got up from the bed. She changed into her day clothes, grabbed her coat, and ran out of the room.

Twenty minutes later, Clotilde walked into the bedroom.

Clotilde drew a cup wrapped in a towel out of her bag. "This is the best cough syrup. I mixed mallow with figs juice."

"My sky is so dark," Norina mumbled.

Grazia remained speechless. She couldn't find the proper words to console her mother.

"The sky can't be always dark." Clotilde forced a smile. "It will shine soon."

"The sky…" Norina's words were muffled by her gasps for air.

Norina hacked so much that it seemed she was about to choke. Grazia and Clotilde promptly helped Norina sit up on the bed and patted her on the back.

When Norina finally stopped wheezing, Clotilde handed Norina the cup of syrup and said, "Drink it. It's going to make you feel better."

Streams of tears fell on Norina's cheeks as she drank the syrup.

Vituccio was bedbound with his broken leg, and couldn't help his sister. Marta paid Norina and Little Donato visits in his stead, and even brought them soup. Clotilde and Grazia did everything in their power to nurse Norina and Little Donato back to health. They continued to administer them the homemade cough syrup. They took them for a walk by the train station and allowed them to inhale the steam of the locomotive. Clotilde bought extra coal for the warming pan to keep them toasty. Despite these efforts, Norina and Little Donato were still coughing their lungs out. Little Donato lost so much weight that he now looked emaciated. Norina did not fear her own death, but she was terrified at the prospect of losing her little son. At night, she pictured her coffin next to a little coffin for Little Donato and wept desperately.

One night, Norina's high fever reached the point where she was not longer coherent.

"I want to go to work, my children…" Norina's words were broken up by a severe coughing fit.

Grazia's eyes filled with tears as Norina collapsed on the bed. She patted Norina's face. "*Mamma*, talk to me."

Finally, Norina stopped coughing. She fixed her eyes on Grazia, but no words came out of her mouth. Grazia widened her eyes as she felt her mother's head. She urgently called out for Pasquale. Minutes later, Pasquale ran into the room.

Grazia gave him a grave look. "*Mamma* has high fever. Go to Aunt Clotilde and tell her to come as soon as possible."

As Pasquale dashed out of the room, Little Donato began to cough. Grazia took the baby from the crib and rocked him in her arms, hoping to provide some relief. But the poor baby kept hacking so forcefully that Grazia feared he would choke to death. Caterina and Olimpia woke up. They looked at their little brother, petrified.

"My baby," Norina mumbled.

When the baby's hacking ultimately halted, they were relieved.

Clotilde finally arrived. She stared at Grazia with wide eyes as she noticed Norina's breathing was labored. "We have no time to waste."

"Little Donato was coughing so hard that I thought he was going to choke," Grazia said.

"We should go to Doctor Polo," Clotilde said. "He sees patients at night."

Caterina and Olimpia quickly changed into their dresses and slipped on their coats. Grazia didn't even bother to change. She wore her coat on top of her nightgown. She bundled up the baby with a blanket and carried him downstairs. Caterina and Olimpia helped Norina get out of bed. They threw a coat on her and escorted her down the stairs.

They were followed immediately by Clotilde. Once into the kitchen, they bumped into Pasquale and Mario.

"Where are you going?" Pasquale asked.

"We're taking *Mamma* to the doctor," Olimpia responded.

"I want to come too." Pasquale looked at Aunt Clotilde to seek her approval.

"You can all come along." Clotilde drew her index finger to her lips. "You shouldn't tell anybody your mother is going to the doctor."

"Why?" Pasquale asked.

"People may think she'll be sick forever and they won't give her any work," Clotilde replied.

The boys put on their coats over their pajamas. They all scrambled out of the house.

To Clotilde's relief, Norina and Little Donato didn't have any coughing fits as they walked down the street. More importantly, no one saw them since the streets were deserted. The sky was dark and barren of stars. Only the full moon was shining.

"Save Norina and Little Donato," Clotilde said under her breath.

"Are you talking to yourself?" Olimpia asked.

"No, I'm talking to God."

Olimpia's eyed gleamed. *God is a good friend of Aunt Clotilde. She always visits him in Church. God is going to listen to her.* Olimpia bounced. She was filled with hope.

Just the opposite, Grazia felt hopeless. She wanted to cry and scream about all the pain she was feeling inside, but she decided to remain silent. She had to give courage to her siblings. Little Donato hugged her neck, and Mario held her hand tightly.

Once they reached the *piazza*, they saw a bright light glittering in the dark.

Clotilde pointed at the light. "It's Doctor Polo's house."

Since Doctor Polo was the best doctor in town, people were willing to wait around all night to be examined by him.

When Norina entered the waiting room with her children and Clotilde, they were all greeted warmly by the patients seated there.

"She's very pale. What's wrong with Norina?" Bellina the Good Deed whispered to Clotilde.

"She has a high fever, and the baby is also unwell." Clotilde abstained from saying they both had a bad cough.

People were afraid of anyone who had coughing fits. They immediately assumed it was tuberculosis. Given that many in town had lost loved ones to the highly contagious disease, people stayed away from anyone who had any symptoms. Clotilde prayed Little Donato and Norina wouldn't have a coughing fit. A fright swept over her at the thought that they could have contracted tuberculosis.

"We should let them go ahead of us," Bellina said. "We can't let a sick mother with a sick child wait all night."

As soon as the others nodded, Bellina turned to Clotilde. "They can go ahead of us."

"Thank you," Clotilde said, helping Norina onto a chair.

Little Donato was breathing heavily in Grazia's arms. Bellina twisted her face as she looked at him.

"I don't want to lose my baby," Norina whispered.

"Contessa Gilda has been in the doctor's office for over an hour..." a blond woman said.

"...and she didn't even look ill to me," a brunette woman said.

"Rich people go to the doctor just because they have nothing better to do."

The door that led to the doctor's office finally swung open and Contessa Gilda fluttered out of the room, sporting a white fur coat and lots of jewelry. She stopped for a moment and waved hello to Clotilde. "One of these days I'm going to invite you over to my house to recite a poem in Latin."

Clotilde forced a smile. "I'll be glad to come."

Contessa Gilda didn't even bother to look at the Voltinis. She hurriedly sashayed outside.

Little Donato's cough thundered fiercely, and the patients seated in the waiting room exchanged looks. Rocking the baby in her arms, Grazia rushed into the doctor's office. Clotilde and Norina followed right behind her.

"The baby's got tuberculosis. He's not going to make it," the brunette woman whispered to the blond woman.

The blond woman crossed her hands on her chest. "Thank God we didn't touch him."

Once inside the office, Clotilde indicated Norina and Little Donato to Doctor Polo. "My sister-in-law and my little nephew are very sick."

"Come with me." Doctor Polo picked up Little Donato in his arms and led Norina into the examination room.

As they waited, Clotilde and Grazia paced back and forth across the room. Ten minutes later Norina, Little Donato, and Doctor Polo emerged from the examination room. Grazia took the baby from the doctor's arms. Clotilde's lips trembled as she looked at the doctor.

"They both have pneumonia. If they don't take the medication, they'll only get worse." Doctor Polo turned to Norina. "Your son needs calcium. His legs are malformed due to a lack of calcium in his body. Are you giving him enough milk?"

Norina bit her lower lip and remained silent. Many times she had given Little Donato sugar and water instead of milk.

"How much do I owe you for the visit?" Clotilde asked.

"Nothing, if you're willing to buy milk for the little boy," the doctor said.

Clotilde patted her chest. "I'll buy the milk for my nephew."

Doctor Polo scribbled on a piece of paper and handed the prescription to Clotilde.

"Thank you." Clotilde flashed a light grin. "God is going to compensate you for the goodness of your heart."

As they departed the doctor's office, Clotilde gave a sigh of relief.

"Doctor Polo is like a priest," Clotilde said. "No wonder they call him the Married Priest."

Grazia bobbed her head in agreement.

Doctor Polo was filled with love and compassion. He hardly ever charged the poor of the town. The poor compensated his benevolence by paying him a lot of respect. The farmers gave him their finest fruits and vegetables, and the fishermen gave him the best fish. When he was able to do something major for them, like saving a life, they would take up a collection and send him a basket filled with meat. He was a White Fly, after all!

The purple and gray shades of the dawn bathed the sky as the Voltinis, led by Clotilde, walked the deserted streets.

Clotilde covered little Donato's head with the blanket. "Put your heads down. I don't want people to recognize us."

They all walked with their heads bowed. Mario tightly gripped Grazia's hand. When they reached Saint Peter Street, Clotilde relaxed a bit. Through the blinds of a window, a neighbor watched them. She figured there was something wrong with Norina, since Pasquale and Caterina held her by the arms.

As she watched the Voltini family enter the house, Titina the Alligator wondered why Clotilde was with them at the crack of dawn. After some thought, Titina came to her conclusion: *Norina is seriously ill!*

Norina's hacking resonated throughout the whole house as she staggered into the bedroom. Olimpia and Caterina patted her back, and when Norina finally stopped, they helped her get into bed.

"Thank God she didn't cough in public," Clotilde said.

Mario confined himself into the back room and wept. *Mamma is going to die. Papa died the day after he went to the doctor.*

Pasquale walked into the room and noticed that Mario was in tears.

"When are you going to learn to behave like a man? You should never cry," Pasquale shouted. He grabbed Mario by the arm and shoved him onto the bed. "I can't stand the sight of a sissy like you."

As Pasquale stormed out of the room, Mario buried his head in the pillow. He was unable to quell his tears.

Little Donato had another coughing fit. Norina looked at him, terrified. Grazia picked up the baby and patted him on the back until he stopped coughing.

Norina burst into tears. "Where am I going to get the money for the medicine?"

"Don't worry. I'll find a way." Clotilde indicated the statue of Our Lady of Sorrows. "The Madonna is going to help you find the money. She'll never let you down. Besides, I'll also ask Saint Joseph to assist you."

Norina didn't show any emotion. It seemed as if she had lost hope.

Clotilde turned to Grazia. "Keep an eye on your mother and Little Donato. I have to go."

Grazia nodded as Clotilde exited the room.

Minutes later, Norina struggled with her worst coughing fit yet. Caterina and Olimpia were dismayed. Mario and Pasquale ran upstairs, overtaken by panic.

"Go back downstairs," Grazia said.

As the boys left, Norina finally stopped coughing.

Norina dropped her head on the pillow. "Where is Clotilde going to get the money for the medicine?"

The light of daybreak was brightening the purple and gray in the sky. The streets filled with farmers riding motorcycles, bicycles, tractors, and wagons pulled by their mules.

"I'll find a way," Clotilde kept mumbling to herself as she marched down the street.

When Clotilde saw the photo studio from a distance, her thoughts shifted to the money she had received from her Aunt Elvira. She regretted having used the five-dollar bill to pay for Grazia's portrait. The cash could have been better used to pay for the medicine, if she had only been wise enough to save it.

What's going to happen to Norina and Little Donato if I can't find the money for the medicine? Clotilde kept asking herself.

It was unusual to see a respectable woman ambling on the road so early in the morning. As Clotilde sensed the eyes of people on her, she quickened her pace and held her head down to avoid looking at them. She wasn't in the mood to greet people. Her mind was filled with worries. She had to find a way to come up with the money for the medicine. Clotilde gave it a lot of thought and concluded that Ada was the only person that could help her.

The sound of church bells startled Clotilde. She counted the rings in her mind. It was seven o'clock. It was the right time to visit Ada. Her husband, Rodolfo the Great Shoulders, would usually leave for work at six o'clock in the morning. She pictured his broad figure with his muscled shoulders standing by the church, surrounded by many farmers. The landowner was entitled to pick the fieldhands he wanted to hire to work for the day. Rodolfo was very harsh with his employees. He would often bark at them, calling them all sorts of names. Nobody liked Rodolfo the Great Shoulders, though everybody respected him. He felt proud of all the worship he got from people. He was not aware that the respect people showed him was driven by fear. Even his wife and daughters were afraid of him. They would cringe whenever they heard his heavy footsteps.

Clotilde stopped by a yellow house and rang the bell. Minutes later, the door opened and Ada appeared.

"I'm here because of Norina and Little Donato," Clotilde said.

Ada closed the door behind Clotilde and led her into the house. "What happened?"

Clotilde sank into a chair. "I took Norina and Little Donato to the doctor. They're both sick. They're coughing their lungs out."

Ada's lips trembled. "Is it tuberculosis?"

"Don't worry. It's not tuberculosis."

"Thank God!" Ada gave a small sigh of relief. "I wish I could see them."

"If you visit them, a neighbor will see you and your husband will find out."

Ada wrung her hands together. "You're right. I can't take that risk."

"They both need medicine."

"I have no money on me. My husband has refused to give me any money ever since I paid for Norina's husband's funeral."

Clotilde contorted her face as if she was about to cry. Ada slid a ring off her finger and handed it to Clotilde. "Take this ring, sell it, and buy the medicine."

"I appreciate your generosity, but I don't want you to get into trouble. What if your husband finds out?"

"I'll tell him I lost the ring." Ada held Clotilde's hands. "I don't want to lose another sister."

Clotilde placed the ring into her purse. She then got up from the chair and hugged Ada with affection. Clotilde knew that Ada's eldest sister had died from tuberculosis when she was a teenager.

On her way to the jewelry store, Clotilde felt fine drops of rain on her head. As she noticed a gray cloud in the sky, she quickened her pace. She ran into many of her friends, but simply nodded hello. She refrained from stopping and talking to them.

Once Clotilde reached the jewelry store, she was reluctant to walk in, and stood in front of the window. She had donated a ring and two bracelets to the saints. She had never sold a piece of jewelry in her life. She considered it a shameful thing to do.

Clotilde finally entered the jewelry store, since the drizzle had become a light shower. She was greeted warmly by Donna Lucia, a well-dressed woman with an extravagant hairdo.

"I'd like to sell a ring," Clotilde said as she withdrew the ring from her purse. "It was given to me by a person I no longer speak to, and it brings back bad memories."

Donna Lucia scrutinized the ring. "I can offer you two thousand lire for this ring."

Clotilde's face blushed. "Is that the best you can do?"

Donna Lucia looked straight into Clotilde's eyes. "I wouldn't take advantage of you. We've been friends forever."

"Fine, I'll sell it, but, please, let's keep it between us," Clotilde whispered. "I don't want anyone to know."

"I won't tell a single soul," Donna Lucia whispered back, handing Clotilde the money.

Clotilde rushed out of the store. To her relief, it had stopped raining.

Clotilde headed to the only pharmacy in Vocevero. The owner, Don Lorenzo, was one of the wisest men in town, and was universally well-regarded. The poor consulted him for all sorts of advice. They even used to summon him when members of their families were feuding. Don Lorenzo always found a peaceful solution. He was truly a man of justice and peace. In return for his services, he received nothing more than respect and admiration.

Don Lorenzo didn't have any children of his own, but he had been godfather to many of the poor children in town. The identical twin brothers who worked in the pharmacy were Don Lorenzo's godsons. They were short young men with small heads. People nicknamed them Primo and Secondo. No one knew their real names, so everyone called them by their nicknames. Primo and Secondo bragged about working in the medical profession as if they themselves were pharmacists. They were grateful to Don Lorenzo for giving them such a prestigious job.

"What can I do for you?" Primo asked in a mellow voice as soon as Clotilde walked into the pharmacy.

"I need medicine," Clotilde responded, handing him the prescription.

Primo read the prescription carefully and reached for the pills. He then showed the prescription and the pills to Secondo, his twin brother. "We're very precise. We always double check everything." As soon as Secondo nodded, Primo handed the medicine to Clotilde. "The price is two thousand and two hundred lire."

Clotilde stroked her chin. She didn't have enough money to pay for the medicine. "Can I get a discount? I'm the president of the Catholic League of Saint Maria's Church."

"You don't have to tell me who you are. I know everyone in town. I'll ask Don Lorenzo if I can give you a reduction."

Primo headed to the back room. Clotilde used the moment to murmur a prayer.

Primo returned, flashing a smile. "Don Lorenzo said that he can offer you the medicine for one thousand and nine hundred lire."

Clotilde handed him the money. "Thank Don Lorenzo for me."

"I will."

The twin brothers waved at Clotilde as she rushed out of the pharmacy.

Lying on the bed with Little Donato in her arms, Norina's eyes were set on the grays and violets of the sky, framed by the decrepit window.

"My sky is very dark," Norina whispered to herself. "Our Lady of Sorrows has abandoned me. She didn't protect me from getting sick, and she didn't even send a marriage proposal for Grazia."

Grazia walked into the room. She handed Norina a cup of hot tea. "It's good for you."

As Norina drank the tea, tears fell to her cheeks. She was immersed in despair. She had nothing to look forward to. No shining sky waited in her future. Clotilde was never going to come up with the money to buy the medicine, and therefore she had no way out. A chill swept over her at the thought she was going to end up dead like her eldest sister, Dina. But at least her sister didn't leave any children. As she gave it more thought, Norina realized she was of no use to her children. She was too ill to work and too poor to take care of them.

Norina's eyes came to rest on the painting of Jesus surrounded by children in the Garden of Paradise, and she wished she could be in a place so filled with beauty. She would only have to die in order to go there, and death would be a release for her. All her worries would die with her. Even her poverty would die with her.

As she gazed at Little Donato, who was breathing heavily, she widened her eyes. *He's too young to die.* "Why did God give me six children if I can't even afford medicine when they get sick? He should have given them to an American Wife."

Grazia remained silent. She couldn't find any words to console her mother.

Norina was unable to suppress her sobs. "My children deserve to live well. They deserve to have all the things that wealthy children have."

Loud yells coming from outside, startled them.

"Margherita," Anna the Heavyweight kept calling out.

Grazia peered through the window and saw two medics carrying Margherita on a stretcher. Four men were holding Anna by the arms to stop her from assaulting the medics. Margherita had contracted tuberculosis, and they were taking her away to the hospital.

"Give me back my daughter. No one can take her away from me," Anna shouted, kicking the men.

"Poor woman," Norina said. "Are they taking Margherita away?"

Grazia twisted her lips as she nodded.

At the sound of the doorknob turning, they both watched as the door swung open. It was Clotilde.

Clotilde spread her arms wide open. "I got the medicine."

Norina remained silent. She stared at Clotilde for a long minute. Norina finally asked, "Where did you get the money to buy the medicine?"

Clotilde pointed at the statue. "Our Lady of Sorrows never lets you down."

"Who gave you the money?" Grazia asked.

"Your Aunt Ada gave me a ring to sell," Clotilde responded.

Norina beamed as she stood up from her bed. "I have a sister who loves me."

XXIII

I n the span of two weeks, Norina's and little Donato's health had improved considerably, but Margherita's health had deteriorated. Father Camillo informed Anna the Heavyweight that her daughter was not likely to survive.

Anna locked herself in her house and cried all day long, calling out, "Margherita, Margherita, Margherita…"

Angela the Crazy Head paid Anna a visit and suggested that Margherita might be better off back home, and could potentially be cured with penicillin smuggled from America. At the first opportunity, Anna visited the hospital and absconded with her daughter.

Anna was shocked when she heard the price of penicillin. She realized she couldn't afford to buy the medicine. She was so devastated she lost all her strength. She crumbled, often succumbing to crying spells. It was a remarkable sight to see the strong woman cry. People would often pass by her house just to see her weeping by her front door.

"I'm damned," Anna would tell the townspeople. I'm going to lose my daughter."

"Margherita is going to get better," Grazia said, attempting to give her comfort, but Anna responded with the somber look of a person who had lost hope.

Many neighbors took pity on Anna the Heavyweight.

Even Serafina the Maid paid Anna a visit and said, "I went to a gypsy and she told me that your daughter is going to be fine."

Anna burst into tears. "There's no way out."

To Anna's astonishment, it was Franchino the Bird's Nest who found a way out. He sold his cart and used the proceeds to buy Margherita penicillin. The antibiotic worked wonders. Margherita came back to life in a matter of days. Franchino celebrated her recovery by whistling whenever he passed by her house. Margherita poked her head out of the window when she heard Franchino's whistle. Many of the neighbors, who had believed Margherita was certain to die, were astounded every time she appeared at the window. Franchino's loud whistle heralded to everyone that Margherita lived on. All the girls on Saint Peter Street were impressed by Franchino's whistle. They thought it was a resounding proclamation of love.

Anna was so exhilarated by her daughter's recovery that she regained all her strength. When she bumped into a nurse who hadn't treated Margherita properly at the hospital, she slapped her on both cheeks and shouted, "You should learn how to respect poor sick people."

The strong woman was especially grateful to Franchino the Bird's Nest. "Franchino has a big heart," she said to the neighbors. "It doesn't matter that he's married and has eleven children. What matters is that he loves my daughter so much that he gave up everything to save her life."

"That's true love," Baronessa Rosa said.

"Franchino and Margherita deserve to be called the Lovers of Saint Peter Street," Maddalena said. "They truly love each other."

Grazia admired the Lovers of Saint Peter Street. She wished deep in her heart for someone to love her the way Franchino loved Margherita.

"Franchino is stupid," Carmine the Shepherd said. "He sold the most valuable thing he owned. How can he work without a cart?"

"Franchino is going to lose his business," Titina the Alligator said.

Apparently, Franchino's business didn't suffer from the absence of the cart, as he continued to work. He was so strong that he simply carried bottles of seawater, oil, and wine to his customers by hand. More than his strength, what saved his business was more customers bought his merchandise out of respect.

"We have to give him the opportunity to buy a new cart," Ninuccio the Painter said. "Franchino deserves it."

Carmela the Daughter of the Umbrella Repair Man bobbed her head in agreement. "He's a good man."

Titina the Alligator narrowed her eyes. "A good man doesn't have a *commara*."

"But Franchino and Margherita's relationship is strictly platonic," Baronessa Rosa said.

Carmine the Shepherd raised an eyebrow. "No man would ever sell his cart for a platonic relationship."

"He sold the most valuable thing he had for the sake of love," Maddalena said. "I think it's very romantic."

Grazia couldn't help but smile at Maddalena's idealism.

Franchino soon had enough extra money to send flowers to the woman he loved. When she received them, Margherita was so jubilant that she bundled up with a blanket and stood on her balcony, holding the bouquet of roses. She wanted the whole neighborhood to know she had received flowers from the man she loved.

Old Veronica crossed her hands on her chest. "She looks like the statue of a saint."

Colombina the Farmer's Wife pursed her lips. "Saints don't have lovers."

"Franchino and Margherita are not lovers," Old Veronica said. "I've never seen them going out on a date."

"They don't tell you when they get together," Titina the Alligator said, tapping the sides of her index fingers together.

Titina is so spiteful, Old Veronica thought.

"Franchino is a gentleman," Maddalena said. "He behaves just like a White Fly."

Titina and Colombina widened their eyes as they exchanged looks. They thought no one would have ever dreamt of associating Franchino the Bird's Nest with a White Fly.

There were numerous cases of tuberculosis in town. Many people died from the terrible disease. Carolina the Good Life lost her pride and joy, her baby boy, Little Gianni. During the wake, Carolina kept wailing like a maniac. The whole neighborhood heard Carolina's cries. From the shutters of her window, Contessa Fiorella saw people gather in front of Carolina's house, eager to listen to the drama unfold.

"When a baby dies, it's like an angel flying to Heaven," Grazia heard Old Veronica' voice say as she walked into Carolina's house.

"If God wanted to take one of my children, he should have taken one of my girls instead of the only boy," Carolina yelled.

"Don't say that," Old Veronica shouted. "It's sacrilegious!"

Carolina bit her finger. "God had no right to take away my baby boy."

Baronessa Rosa patted Carolina's shoulder. "Calm down. You can always have another baby."

"I can't have any more children. I'll never get another chance to have a baby boy." Carolina slapped herself in the face. "My husband didn't even get a chance to see little Gianni. How can I tell him that his baby boy is dead when he comes back from Venezuela? He was so thrilled to have finally gotten a boy after four girls."

Baronessa Rosa turned to Old Veronica. "She needs more tranquilizers."

Old Veronica agreed. She grabbed the mourning mother by the arms and dragged her away.

Grazia noticed that Serafina the Maid was attentive to the drama. *Serafina never misses a wake.*

The Margassi Sisters were serving refreshments to the mourners. They walked by Grazia and gave her a sweet cup of coffee and cookies. Grazia thanked them with a hint of a smile.

"We washed little Gianni and dressed him up as soon as he died," Gina Margassi said.

"Carolina begged us to do it," Giovanna Margassi said. "She was afraid to touch her dead son."

The poor women feel useful doing things other people are scared to do, Grazia thought. *They'll do anything to feel accepted.*

Grazia then spotted Lina the Warm House, Maddalena, and Titina the Alligator. She walked over to them and nodded hello. They didn't pay attention to her, since they were having an intense conversation. Intrigued, Grazia listened in.

"Carolina's husband is going to get very upset when he finds out that he has lost his only boy," Lina said.

Titina nodded. "He's going to abandon Carolina and find a *commara* in Venezuela for sure."

"There's a solution for every problem," Lina said.

"What solution?" Maddalena asked.

"Carolina can go to the orphanage and adopt a baby boy."

"My aunt had seven boys and wanted a girl to take care of her in her old age," Titina said. "She went to the orphanage and picked the most beautiful baby girl."

Maddalena raised her eyebrows. "Carolina's husband may refuse to adopt a baby."

"He doesn't know that the baby died. Carolina didn't write to her husband about the baby's death."

"Carolina can pick a baby that looks just like her late little boy," Lina said. "Carolina's husband is not going to be able to tell the difference. He has never seen his son. When he comes back from Venezuela, Carolina doesn't have to tell him right away. She can tell him later on."

"What if he refuses to accept the boy when he finds out?" Maddalena asked.

"He's not going to get mad. Once you get attached to a son, you can't help loving him."

Grazia's jaw dropped.

Grazia wore her black Sunday frock to attend Little Gianni's funeral. Olimpia instead donned her First Communion dress. As soon as they arrived at the cemetery, Olimpia joined the Little Virgins, a group of girls clad in white dresses, standing by the petite casket.

Carolina stared at her departed baby boy. "Look how many Little Virgins you have around you."

"They look like angels," old Veronica said.

"You're taking my Little Gianni away from me," Carolina yelled as soon as two men picked up the tiny coffin.

Overwhelmed with intense emotion, Carolina lost her senses and fell to the floor. The Margassi Sisters fanned Carolina with their purses until she regained consciousness. Once on her feet, Carolina invited the funeral attendees over to her house for refreshments. The Margassi Sisters served sandwiches and *aranciata* to the guests. They gave extra treats to the Little Virgins. They gave Grazia two sandwiches wrapped in a cloth for Norina. Grazia thanked them and hugged them with affection.

Norina and Little Donato soon fully recovered from their bout with pneumonia. No sooner was Norina on her feet than she was eager to get a job. When she heard Giovanni the Farmer was hiring people to work in the fields, she begged Caterina to ask for work on her behalf.

Obediently, Caterina went to the farmers' house. As soon as she rang the bell, the door opened and Colombina the Farmer's Wife appeared.

Caterina forced a smile. "Do you have any work for my mother?"

Colombina lifted her chin. "We have no need for your mother. We need a strong woman who doesn't have a contagious disease."

"My mother doesn't have a contagious disease."

Colombina wrinkled her nose. "She looked very sick to me when I last saw her."

Caterina showed her index her finger to Colombina. "You can't hide yourself behind a finger. You could get a deadly disease anytime.

You should not spit into the sky. You may end up catching your own spit on your face."

"You're putting a curse on me. You're giving me the *malocchio*." Colombina gave Olimpia the sign of the horns by showing her index finger and her pinky finger.

Caterina curved her lips and walked away.

Colombina repeated the horn sign, to ward off the *malocchio*.

When Caterina went home, she simply told her mother the farmer didn't need anyone to work in the fields.

Margherita had lost so much weight that looked undernourished. Most of the neighbors on Saint Peter Street didn't believe she had really recovered.

"Margherita looks like she's ready to die," Colombina the Farmer's Wife said to the neighbors.

Titina the Alligator nodded. "'Tuberculaisi' is very contagious. We have to stay away from Margherita. All the people that I know that got that disease died."

Most of the locals were so afraid to contract the fatal disease that they stayed far away from Margherita. Whenever Margherita went to fetch water from the main fountain, she struggled to carry the heavy bucket, but none of the townsfolk dared to help her out. Only the Dumb Brothers assisted her when they bumped into her on the street.

The elder Dumb Brother took the bucket out of Margherita's hands. "We cannot allow a *signorina* to carry a heavy bucket of water."

"Next time, I want to have the honor to carry your bucket," the younger Dumb Brother said.

"I saw the Dumb Brothers walking with Margherita. They're so dumb that they're not afraid to die," Titina said to her neighbors.

Though Norina and Little Donato had completely recovered from pneumonia, rumors had spread they had tuberculosis. Many of the townspeople stayed far away from them for fear of being infected.

Norina felt isolated from her friends and her acquaintances. The poor woman thought it was due to her dishonest reputation. She wasn't aware that Clotilde had finally managed to pay off all of her debts with the money she had received from her American relatives.

Grazia did everything in her power to convince the neighbors that her mother and her brother were well again. The neighbors gave her looks of disbelief.

Ignorant people are worse than mules, Grazia thought with dismay.

The only friends willing to set foot into the Voltinis' house were Angela the Crazy Head, Old Veronica, and the Margassi Sisters. Anna the Heavyweight would have paid a visit, but she was too busy doting on her daughter.

When Titina the Alligator saw people near the Voltinis' house, she approached them immediately and whispered, "You could get the mortal disease."

Angela giggled. "I'm not stupid. I know how to distinguish pneumonia from tuberculosis."

"I'm old," Old Veronica said. "It doesn't matter. If I get the mortal disease, I'll only die a little bit sooner."

"I cannot abandon Norina," Giovanna Margassi said. "We have been pals since we were children."

Titina contorted her face. "Do you want to die?"

Gina Margassi shrugged. "I believe in destiny. When it is your time, you die."

Old Veronica turned her face up. "Everything is written in the sky."

"You're crazy to visit Norina," Titina said. "I better stay away from you. If you get 'tuberculaisi', you could give it to me."

They chuckled as they watched Titina hurry away.

The children in town had been instructed by their parents to stay away from Little Donato. The poor child was brokenhearted when his friends refused to hold his hands, and would not include him in their games.

"I want play," Little Donato kept saying.

"You are very sick," an older boy said. "You have a bad disease. We don't want to get your disease."

Little Donato wandered forlornly in the street, until Old Veronica took his hand and escorted him back to his house.

"No baby play with me," Little Donato said. "Baby say I am sick."

"I'm going to tell all the kids that you are no longer sick," Old Veronica said.

"I want play with baby." Little Donato burst into tears.

It's not going to be easy to convince people that my son and I aren't contagious, Norina thought as she hugged her baby and wiped his tears.

Norina missed her friendships desperately. She felt so isolated that she even missed her enemies. She was grateful to see the few people who did drop by. She always implored them to visit her more often. Norina even begged Angela the Crazy Head to do another reading of a novel at her house, just to get people to come over. Norina felt it would entice her neighbors. To her relief, Angela agreed to do the reading.

"Invite everyone," Norina mumbled. "I don't care if they don't bring anything, as long as they keep me company."

Norina has lost most of her friends and she's willing to do anything to get them back, Angela thought. She didn't have the heart to tell Norina that most of the people were not going to show up.

The following day, Angela the Crazy Head strolled along Saint Peter Street carrying a folder with her. She was hoping to attract the attention of the neighbors, but they ignored her completely.

Grazia did everything in her power to spread the news about the reading of a new novel. She even paid the neighbors visits to invite them personally.

"I can't come," Lina the Warm House said.

"I'm going to get a headache," Titina the Alligator said. "I get a headache every afternoon."

"Arturo doesn't want me to come," Maddalena said. "He thinks that I come to the readings to fool around with men."

All the neighbors refused Grazia's invitation, with the exception of the Voltinis' most loyal supporters: Anna the Heavyweight, Margherita, and Old Veronica. Angela suggested to Grazia to invite the Dumb Brothers and the Margassi Sisters as well. The Dumb Brothers were elated to be included even though they didn't know what a novel was. Grazia told them a novel was like a long story. The Margassi Sisters were also thrilled at the prospect of hearing a love story since they had always loved to dream about romance.

Later that day, Anna the Heavyweight and Margherita arrived at the Voltinis' house, eager to listen to the new novel. Grazia, Norina, Angela the Crazy Head, Old Veronica, the Margassi Sisters, and the Dumb Brothers greeted them warmly. Anna had brought a small plate filled with dried sunflower seeds, and placed it on the table. Norina thanked her with a hug.

"I want to start," Angela said.

"Nobody else is coming?" Anna asked.

Norina revealed a somber look. "Most of the neighbors didn't come because they're afraid to get 'tubercalosi.'"

Margherita nodded. "They're terrified. I heard Titina the Alligator telling a neighbor that I'm still contagious."

The Dumb Brothers couldn't figure out what the words "tuber-calosi" and "contagious" meant, but they didn't dare to ask. They were intimidated by Anna the Heavyweight's muscle as well as Angela the Crazy Head's intellect.

Margherita's eyes filled with tears. "A lot of people avoid me."

The strong woman's face turned red like a burning coal as she stormed out of the house.

They all followed her outside and stood by the front door to watch the scene.

Anna ran towards Titina like an infuriated animal. She pushed Titina against a wall. "You said that my daughter still has 'tubercalosi.'

You stupid whore. You better shut your mouth, or I'm going to pull your goddamn tongue out."

"I never said that," Titina crossed her trembling hands on her chest. "I swear on my husband's grave that I never said that."

Anna grabbed Titina's head and pulled her hair. "I have witnesses. You told everybody. I'm surprised you didn't tell the people that work for the radio."

"Help," Titina screamed, shutting her eyes.

Many of the neighbors scrambled out of their houses to get a better view of the scene.

"Titina the Alligator is fighting with Anna the Heavyweight," Lina the Warm House shouted. "We need some strong men to pull them apart."

Anna glared at Titina. "You also had the nerve to call my daughter a whore."

"I never said such a thing. You're the one that always says it."

"I'm her mother, and I can say anything I want about my daughter. You've got to wash your mouth with turpentine before you talk about my daughter."

The Dumb Brothers and the Margassi Sisters kept giggling as they watched the scene. Titina was furious that they were laughing at her. She considered them lesser creatures. Titina widened her eyes when Anna grasped her by the neck.

"You need to be taught a lesson," Anna yelled.

Titina felt relieved when she saw Giovanni the Farmer and Ninuccio the Painter walking forward.

"Anna, that's enough," Giovanni said.

"Anna, let her go," Ninuccio said. "She's a midget compared to you."

Finally, Anna released Titina.

Titina immediately approached Ninuccio and Giovanni. She felt protected by their presence.

"I'm going to call the *carabinieri*," Titina said, placing her hands on her hips.

Anna lifted her chin. "Call them. I get special treatment when I go to jail."

Angela the Crazy Head turned to Titina. "It wouldn't be wise to call the *carabinieri*. Margherita could sue you for slander."

Titina scrunched her forehead. "Slander?"

"Margherita could hire a lawyer and sue you for defamation of character and for ruining her reputation."

Titina didn't want to have anything to do with lawyers. She speedily scuttled away.

Angela led the audience for the novel back into the Voltinis' house. When Anna bounded into the house, they all gave her congratulations.

Angela patted Anna's shoulder. "You were great."

"Anna, you taught Titina a lesson," Grazia said.

Anna smiled. "Titina deserved it."

Angela began to read a novel entitled *True Love*. As usual, the listeners gave her their undivided attention. The plot was intriguing and filled with surprises. The protagonists were Minerva and Davide. They were madly in love with each other. Unfortunately, the couple was separated under mysterious circumstances. Davide sold his car to pay for a private investigator to look for Minerva, the love of his life.

Margherita was so touched by the story that she burst out crying. "It's very romantic. The main character is just like my Franchino."

The Margassi Sisters were enchanted by the love story, while the Dumb Brothers couldn't keep up with the narrative. They thought it was confusing, but they didn't dare ask any questions. Angela took a small break after reading the first chapter.

"A man like Franchino deserves to be in a novel," Anna the Heavyweight said.

"Writers put real people in books?" the elder Dumb Brother asked.

"Writers get inspired by real people," Angela responded.

"It would be a great honor to be in a book," the younger Dumb Brother said.

"You become important once you are in a book," Old Veronica said.

Giovanna Margassi shut her eyes and flashed a glint of a grin. "I wish a writer would put me in a novel."

Gina Margassi spread her arms wide open and spun around. "You can live forever once you're in a novel."

After reading three chapters, Angela closed the folder. "I'll do another reading soon." *I'll do another if I get a lot of listeners. A plate of sunflower seeds, a cup of rice, a cup of olives, and eight figs won't satisfy the Voltini children's appetites.*

Norina desperately needed a job. She entertained the hope that some-one would hire her to jar vegetables or make cookies. Regrettably, as time went by, no one gave her any work because of the prevailing rumors regarding her health and reputation.

"People don't want anything to do with me," Norina said to Our Lady of Sorrows. "My friends stay away from me. They all think that I have a contagious disease. I don't want to feel isolated. I want to be among people. Please, tell my neighbors that I'm not contagious. I can't live without talking to my friends, without hearing their stories. I don't feel alive."

Grazia overheard her mother talking to the Madonna. *Isolating my mother from people is like taking her life away.*

Clotilde made enormous sacrifices to provide milk for Little Donato. The poor woman couldn't have done more. Her means of support was a small pension, and she could barely afford to buy food for herself.

The children always eagerly awaited Grazia's return from work, whishing she would bring home some of the Zordi's leftovers. As soon as she was within their sight, they would run to her. When her siblings searched for food in her empty bags, she felt mortified. She was under so much pressure to provide for her family that she now regularly stole food from the Zordi residence. One day, Mrs. Zordi caught Grazia red handed as she was placing a whole kilogram of pasta into her bag.

"I suspected you were stealing," Mrs. Zordi said. "Now I know the truth."

Grazia's eyes welled with tears. "Please, forgive me. I stole to feed my little brothers and sisters. My mother can't get any work since she got sick."

Mrs. Zordi sighed. "I understand. I know the way things are in your house. Next time, however, I want you to ask when you need food."

"You are a real *signora*," Grazia mumbled. Tears streamed down her face. *I'll never forget this day. It's been the most humiliating day of my life.*

The following day, when Grazia went to work at the Zordi residence, she noticed a picture of the distinguished man on the desk. She froze at the thought he could have been in the house. She didn't have the heart to see him. She was nothing but a thief. He was a special man, a noteworthy man, a respectable man, an honorable man… a distinguished man!

When Grazia opened the refrigerator, she saw a lot of leftover food. She didn't dare take any food even though Mrs. Zordi would have been glad to part with the leftovers. Unable to overcome her own guilt and shame, Grazia went home empty-handed. Her mother and her siblings were utterly disappointed. That night, they only had hard bread for dinner.

XXIV

The neighbors of Saint Peter Street exchanged amazed looks as they stared at a sky they had never seen before.

Olimpia turned her face up. "Little white crystals are falling from the sky."

"It's a holy blessing," Old Veronica said. "It's a gift from God. It's *manna* falling down from Heaven."

"It's snow," Baronessa Rosa said. "When I lived in Switzerland, it would snow all the time."

The children enjoyed grabbing at the snowflakes even though they dissolved in their hands.

"I've heard about snow, but I never got to see it," Giacomino the Blind Man said. "What does it look like?"

"It's made of tiny, white, soft, icy flakes," Baronessa Rosa responded.

Giacomino scrunched his forehead.

"Come with me." The baronessa took him by the arm and escorted him to the middle of the street.

The blind man lifted his head and faced the sky. He instantly licked his lips as a snowflake fell on it. "It's like a velvety cold kiss that melts on you."

The curious neighbors gathered on the street to feel the white flakes. Contessa Fiorella watched the snow with delight through the shutters of her window. She couldn't resist the impulse to extend her arm out of the window to feel the white flakes.

"There's Contessa Torre's arm poking out of the window," Lina the Warm House said to the neighbors, who immediately turned their gaze towards Count Torre's *palazzo*.

Ninuccio the Painter exhaled heavily. "I'm dying to see what she looks like."

"I saw the contessa when she got married," Giacomino said. "She was one of the most magnificent women in town. I wish I had my eyesight back for a minute just to see her again."

"Do you think we're going to get to see her?" Carmine the Shepherd asked.

"She's not going to poke her head out of the window," Grazia replied.

The blind man beamed as the snowflakes brushed his face. "Even though this snow comes with cold weather, it feels like a good omen. What are the benefits of snow?"

"The only good thing about snow is that it kills all the germs," Baronessa Rosa said, then walked away.

"You mean it cures diseases?" Titina the Alligator asked.

"It does," Ninuccio responded. "It's common sense. Many diseases are caused by germs, and the snow kills them."

Titina had a revelation. "That means that Norina, Margherita, and Little Donato are not contagious anymore."

As soon as Lina the Warm House nodded, Grazia gave a sigh of relief. It was what she had been hoping to hear ever since Norina and Little Donato got sick.

Grazia paid a visit to Angela the Crazy Head and informed her that Titina the Alligator believed the snow killed germs and contagious diseases.

Angela laughed heartily. "Titina is so ignorant."

"The good thing is that my mother won't have to be so isolated if her friends believe she's no longer contagious. My mother is miserable without her friends."

Angela winked. "I'm going to tell Titina she's absolutely right, that snow does kill transmittable diseases. I want your mother to be accepted again."

Grazia winked back. "We should tell Titina before someone makes her change her mind."

Titina the Alligator was standing by her front door when Grazia and Angela passed by.

"Are you enjoying the snow?" Grazia asked.

"I had never seen snow in my life." Titina said. "I must say that the snow is nice."

"And it's also very useful," Angela said. "It kills all the germs and contagious diseases. My best friend, the doctor, told me."

Titina nodded. "I know. A lot of people with contagious diseases are going to get cured thanks to the snow."

Grazia and Angela agreed and scurried away to laugh it off.

"How can a person be so ignorant?" Grazia asked.

"Titina doesn't even know how ignorant she is," Angela responded.

"We've done a good deed."

"I have a feeling your mother is about to gain back her friends."

As Angela dashed away, Grazia cheerfully ran inside her house to give her mother the good news.

"*Mamma*, people won't think you're contagious anymore, thanks to the snow."

Norina tilted her head and stared at Grazia.

"Baronessa Rosa and Angela the Crazy Head said the snow kills germs, and Titina the Alligator believed them. Titina will spread the word in no time."

Norina beamed. She was going to be accepted by her friends and neighbors again thanks to those white flakes falling from the sky. "Snow is a blessing sent by the sky. Of course, Our Lady of Sorrows has arranged this to help me out."

As the night descended, the neighbors of Saint Peter Street retreated into their houses and gathered by their warming pans. From time to time, they peered from their windows and glass doors to take one more look at the white puffs falling from the sky. Serafina the Maid stood by her window, mesmerized. She couldn't comprehend what they were. They looked like tiny cottonballs.

"How can cotton fall from the sky?" she kept asking herself.

The street lamps illuminated the snow on the ground. The street seemed to be covered by a gleaming white carpet. Serafina thought the street had never looked so magical.

Giacomino the Blind Man was so captivated by the snow that he sat outside and played his flute. Enthralled by his music, Maddalena and Arturo came out of their house and danced on the white carpet. He was dressed in a black coat and a white scarf, while she wore a red jacket and a yellow hat. They looked like a pair of movie stars straight out of a television box. As they danced, their footsteps were imprinted on the snow, creating beautiful designs like one of the works of Matisse.

Due to the weather, the schools closed, and the poor children had the privilege of playing in the street all day long. They came up with all sorts of games. A group of them enjoyed lying on the snow and making impressions in it. They called the impressions snow ghosts. Another group of children used sticks to draw designs. People were delighted by the sight of the images on the snow carpet. The children of the wealthy couldn't partake, since they were not allowed to play in the street. With bitter disappointment, they watched the poor children having fun.

The Voltini children and their friends enjoyed throwing little snowballs at the passersby. Pino the Red Eye and the Dumb Brothers participated in the game, challenging the children to score a hit. People watched the scene with amusement. It was like watching a live movie.

Serafina the Maid was so captivated by the one-sided snowball fight that she rushed outside to get a better view.

Pino smiled when he got hit by a snowball. "I-I-I like-like the-the balls-balls that-that melt on-on my-my face."

The Dumb Brothers always managed to cover their faces with their hands when they saw a snowball coming.

"If it snowed more often, people wouldn't need to buy ice," the elder Dumb Brother said.

"It would be nice if it snowed in the summer too," the younger Dumb Brother said. "People could cool off."

As Serafina giggled, hiding her mouth with her hands, the children laughed heartily.

As the temperature dropped, the white carpet on the streets turned into ice. Many of the townspeople slipped and fell on the ground as they attempted to walk, and some got hurt. Most of the people didn't go out, fearing they would topple and break a limb. The only people seen on the streets were the White Flies, who were equipped with warm fur coats and tracked rubber boots.

"I'm not afraid to walk on that nasty ice," Anna the Heavyweight said, but as soon as she stepped out of her house, she lost her balance and crashed to the ground.

Anna was so heavy that she needed the help of three White Flies equipped with snow boots to get up from the icy carpet. The neighbors stifled their chortles. No one dared to make fun of the strong woman.

"I should build a wagon that slides on the ice like Anna the Heavyweight," Pasquale said. "It would be fun to take a ride on something like that."

"Good idea," Grazia said.

Grazia helped Pasquale convert an old night stand into a sled. She even lined the interior with fabric and placed two pillows in it.

"Can I be the first one to take a ride?" Olimpia asked.

"Of course," Pasquale responded. "We have to test it to make sure it works."

While Olimpia sat comfortably in the sled, Pasquale and Mario pushed it. Olimpia enjoyed the ride, but her brothers glided off course and crashed.

Grazia helped her brothers get up. "You need snow boots."

"I'm going to make some," Pasquale said.

Pasquale was inventive. He made boots for himself and for Mario with rubber scavenged from an old tire his Uncle Vituccio gave him.

Olimpia took another ride on the sled pushed by Mario and Pasquale, who were delighted to show off their new vehicle and their rubber-soled boots. Little Donato also took a ride on the sled with his young pals. His friends' parents had allowed them to play with him again, since word had spread he was cured. Little Donato was ecstatic to have gained his friends back.

The Voltini boys attracted the envy of the wealthy families' children, who kept watching the sleigh in amazement.

"Come and take a ride on the magical ice," Pasquale shouted, encouraging the privileged kids to travel on his invention.

The children begged their parents to allow them to take a ride. Robertino, Matilde Fatti's son, was especially impatient to try out Pasquale's contraption.

"This is the only chance I'll get," Robertino said to his mother. "It may never snow again."

The American Wife reluctantly gave her son permission to take a ride on the sled, and compensated the Voltini children with a generous tip. Afterwards, most of the well-off parents made an exception to their usual overprotectiveness, allowing their children to play on the street for as long as the snow persisted. The sled came to be in high demand. Pasquale and Mario gave free rides to their poor friends, but charged wealthy children a small fee. At the end of the day, they handed their mother a considerable sum of money.

"Snow is a blessing from the sky," Norina said.

The farmers, in contrast to the rest of the townsfolk, considered the snowfall a curse from the sky. They called it the Evil Ice. To their dismay, most of the fruits and vegetables they had cultivated had been damaged by the frost.

Colombina the Farmer's Wife was outraged when she realized her husband had lost out on the profit of the whole year's work. She told everyone that someone had given her the *malocchio*. Titina the Alligator paid Colombina a visit, eager to hear more details about the alleged incident.

"Someone has put a curse on me," Colombina said. "Someone gave me the *malocchio*, and I know who did it."

"Who did it?" Titina asked.

"I know for sure that Caterina, the Voltini girl, gave me the *malocchio*."

"She's just a girl. I don't think that peasant girls have the power of giving the *malocchio*."

Colombina narrowed her eyes. "There are witches of all ages."

"You should talk to Olga the Scared Cat."

"But Olga gives the *malocchio* too."

Titina flashed a trace of a grin. "People that give it know how to take it away."

Olga the Scared Cat refused to remove the *malocchio* from Colombina the Farmer's Wife.

The spooky vendor glared at Colombina. "You deserved it, for sure from whoever gave it to you."

Colombina remained speechless. She didn't dare to retort. She could end up with another *malocchio* from Olga. Colombina hired Old Veronica to pray to have the *malocchio* removed.

"Heavy snowfall is creating a state of emergency," a radio announcer said. "If it continues to snow, food shortages are expected. The climate has paralyzed the roads, and grocery stores are not receiving any deliveries."

Fearing it would snow for a long time, the townspeople hoarded provisions. The merchants in town were quickly sold out of all foodstuffs. Once Teresina ran out of goods, she closed the bottega, but the customers kept banging on her door.

"There's no use keeping the bottega open if we don't have any food," Pasquina kept saying to the customers.

"When are you going to get more food?" a customer asked.

"I don't know. People are afraid to travel in the snow."

Norina found herself in an unusual situation. She had money, but there was nowhere to buy food. The poor mother yet again had nothing to feed her children. Her last resources were the live chickens Vituccio had given her for Christmas. Norina chased the chickens until she caught one of them. As she grasped the chicken by the neck, Little Donato flapped his hands.

"Let her go," Grazia said. "The chicken is too young. We're not going to get much meat out of her now, so why not wait until she fattens up? I'll buy some food from the bottega in the city where Mrs. Zordi shops."

"Chicken Grazia," Little Donato cried out.

As Norina released the chicken, Little Donato sighed happily. "I want Chicken Grazia and Chicken Caterina go to *Nonna* Veronica. *Nonna* Veronica is nice to chicken."

Grazia brought the chickens to safety at Old Veronica's house.

"Those chickens are going to keep me company," the old woman said.

The following day, Grazia went to the city and bought lots of food.

"*Mamma*, we have food for a whole week," Grazia said when she came home with the groceries.

Norina beamed.

The Evil Ice caused many problems in town. When an old balcony collapsed due to the weight of the snow, the mayor hired Franchino the Bird's Nest to take care of the problem. His job consisted of removing the ice from the roofs and balconies of old houses and buildings. Furthermore, since many people were still slipping on the Evil Ice and getting injured, the mayor had Franchino spread salt on the streets and sidewalks. He gave Franchino a truck filled with buckets of salt. Franchino the Bird's Nest got the promotion of his life: he became the official salt man of the town. In turn, Franchino hired the Dumb Brothers and a team of poor children as his assistants. Of course, the children were better workers than the Dumb Brothers, but Franchino didn't complain. The Dumb Brothers were funny, and entertained their co-workers. The Dumb Brothers felt they had gotten the promotion of their lives too.

Mario also got the promotion of his life: his first real job. He loved being able to earn money without doing any talking, and he was elated to be a highly respected colleague of the Dumb Brothers. They made him feel like he was as bright as any other boy!

People cheered whenever Franchino and his assistants dumped salt on the ice. When Franchino passed by Margherita's house, he whistled loudly. Margherita appeared at her window to get a full view of him.

Franchino threw a whole bucket of salt on the sidewalk by her house and said, "The salt makes it safe to walk on the ice. I don't want you to fall in case you go out, my *signorina*."

Margherita's eyes coruscated as she blew him a kiss.

Anna the Heavyweight, standing by her front door, thanked Franchino with a radiant smile. "Not even the White Flies have so much salt in front of their houses."

Many White Flies hired Franchino the Bird's Nest and his crew to spread extra salt by their sidewalks. They tipped him and his crew generously. The snow was a blessing in the sky for Franchino the Bird's Nest. He made so much money that he was able to afford his own three-wheeler vehicle.

As the days went by, the Evil Ice began to melt, and eventually it completely vanished. The schools re-opened, the bottega got food delivered, and the neighbors of Saint Peter Street went back to their normal lives. The children were devastated by the disappearance of the show.

"Where did the snow go?" Olimpia asked.

"The sun melted the snow," Ninuccio the Painter responded.

"The sun doesn't like the snow?

Ninuccio nodded.

"I'd rather have the snow than the sun." Olimpia tapped her feet. "When is it going to snow again?"

Ninuccio exhaled heavily. "It could take a whole lifetime to see the snow again in this little town. My grandfather told me that it snowed once when he was young, but I've never seen it before."

The farmers were grateful to the sun for killing off the Evil Ice. They discarded all the fruits and vegetables that had been damaged and raked the soil. Soon it seemed as if the snow had never happened.

XXV

A short, fat, and bald man stopped by Ubaldo the Photographer's studio. As he looked at the window, he couldn't help but notice the portrait of a youthful woman. He was so mesmerized by her that he walked into the photo studio to see if the photographer could give him information about her.

"Good to see you, Carlo," Ubaldo the Photographer said.

Carlo the Broken Neck gave Ubaldo a friendly nod. "Who is that lovely young woman in the window in the lavender dress? Her face looks familiar."

"Her name is Grazia Voltini."

"Is she related to Norina, the widow who lives on Saint Peter Street?"

"Yes, she's her daughter."

"I can't believe Norina has such a beautiful daughter."

The photographer revealed a trace of a smile. "Grazia is one of the most beautiful women I have ever photographed."

Carlo the Broken Neck was one of the richest landowners in town. He was nicknamed the Broken Neck due to his ability to effortlessly break chickens' necks with his bare hands, which he loved to do. It made him feel strong and powerful. He was supremely confident due to his wealth, and was fond of everything he owned. Carlo wanted to own Grazia. He divulged a lascivious smirk as he surmised he would have the opportunity to be with Grazia if he hired her to work in his fields.

He knew the Voltinis needed money, he was sure Grazia wouldn't turn down a job offer.

Later in the day, Norina had an unexpected visitor: Carlo the Broken Neck. Norina was overjoyed that a White Fly had personally come to her house.

"I could use your daughter Grazia to work in the fields," Carlo said.

Norina's lips quivered. "Grazia works as a secretary in the city, but I can work in the fields along with my boys."

Carlo forced a smile to conceal his disappointment. "Aren't your boys too young to work?"

"They're not too young. They work in the fields all the time."

Carlo figured it couldn't hurt to be charming towards Grazia's mother. "You can bring the boys. I'll meet you and your sons tomorrow at six o'clock by the church."

Norina twisted her lips as she watched Carlo walk out of the house. *I'd rather starve than allow my girls to work in the fields.*

Many unmarried women who had worked in the fields had lost their reputations. In many cases, the owners of the fields took advantage of isolated girls and raped them. Once a girl lost her virginity, she was deemed ruined for life.

The following morning, Norina and her boys met Carlo the Broken Neck by Saint Maria's Church. There were many men waiting in line to be picked for work. There was only one woman among them, and it was Anna the Heavyweight.

"What a surprise," Anna said, giving Norina a hug. "I didn't know you were coming."

"I never refuse work," Norina said.

Anna indicated the Dumb Brothers. "They're hoping to get hired. They're so thick that they don't even realize that they are slow workers and the field owners don't want to hire them."

"I want to say hello to them."

"Have fun." Anna scurried away.

Norina walked towards the Dumb Brothers. The somber expressions on their faces revealed their mood.

"Things are bad," the elder Dumb Brother said. "We haven't worked for the past two weeks."

"We come here every day, but we only get picked once in a while." The younger Dumb Brother shrugged. "I don't know why they don't pick us."

"You need a lot of luck to find work these days," Norina said.

"Sister Felicia the Mother Superior told us to pray to Our Lady of Sorrows," the elder brother said. "We keep praying to the Madonna and we keep asking her to find us work, but she doesn't answer our prayers."

"Have you seen Sister Felicia again?" the younger brother asked.

"No," Norina replied.

A tall worker knew Sister Felicia, and he also knew she had passed away years ago. "You saw Sister Felicia?"

The Dumb Brothers widened their eyes as they nodded.

Norina winked at the tall worker. "I was there when they saw Sister Felicia."

"We told Sister Felicia that we cursed a lot," the elder brother said. "She told us to pray for forgiveness, because cursing is a bad sin."

"Since that day, we stopped cursing and we started praying instead," the younger brother said.

"We didn't even curse once in the last two weeks, but we still can't get any work, and we're down to our last heel of bread," the elder brother said. "We deserve a reward from Our Lady of Sorrows since we prayed a lot."

Norina felt sorry for the Dumb Brothers. She wished she had the power to help them. Her eyes lit up when an idea came to her mind. She approached Carlo the Broken Neck and whispered in his ear.

Carlo turned to the Dumb Brothers. "You can work for me today."

Invigorated with joy, the brothers hastily took their bikes. Norina, her sons, and Anna got into Carlo's truck. As Carlo revved the engine, all the men who were picked to work in the field for the day followed the truck with their bikes.

Once they arrived at Carlo's fields, the workers began to till the soil. As they toiled, Anna the Heavyweight created some entertainment by teasing the Dumb Brothers.

"Tell them about the time when you got paid to eat six kilograms of cherries," Anna said to the brothers.

"Giovanni the Farmer told us that he was going to give us eight hundred lire if we were capable of eating six kilograms of cherries," the elder brother said.

"I ate three kilograms of cherries, and my brother ate the other three kilograms," the younger brother said.

"And he gave you the money?" the tall worker asked.

"He gave four hundred lire to me and four hundred lire to my brother," the elder brother responded.

"It took me so long to count the money," the younger brother said.

The tall worker's mouth fell open. "He gave you a lot of money."

Anna smiled. Her smile faded as she leveled her gaze at the Dumb Brothers. "Tell them what happened next."

"On our way home, we got robbed by a group of bandits wearing masks." The elder brother's eyes became gloomy. "They took the money from us."

"One of the bandits seemed to be a woman," the younger brother said. "She was fat and tall and had big breasts."

The workers figured the big woman was Anna the Heavyweight. They did their best to stifle their laughter.

"Next time it happens, call me." Anna showed her fists. "I'm going to fix the bandits with a good beating. You're my friends, and you deserve respect and protection."

The elder brother beamed. "I'm honored to be under your protection."

"You're stronger than any man," the younger brother said.

Many workers scurried away laughing.

The tall worker took Anna aside. "You robbed the Dumb Brothers."

"I had to give the money back to Giovanni the Farmer." Anna giggled. "No one gets paid eight hundred lire to eat six kilograms of cherries."

"Were you also Sister Felicia the Mother Superior?"

Anna winked.

The tall worked laughed uncontrollably.

Carlo the Broken Neck generously compensated Norina and her boys.

"I can't believe we got paid so much money," Pasquale said. "We got paid as much as the men."

Mario flashed a smile. No one had ever paid him as much as a man.

"Carlo the Broken Neck is a generous man," Norina said

"He's a great man," Pasquale said.

Mario bobbed his head in agreement.

Carlo the Broken Neck felt he had wasted his money, since he didn't get the opportunity to meet Grazia. The following day, he walked by the Voltinis' house many times, eager to see her.

Carlo grinned when he finally saw Grazia leaving the house. *People are right when they say that Grazia is the beauty of Saint Peter Street.*

Carlo followed her from a distance and noticed she joined a group of people entering Carolina's house. As he walked away, he wondered why Grazia would visit Carolina the Good Life.

Many neighbors of Saint Peter Street were paying Carolina a visit to welcome her new baby boy. She named him Gianni, like her late son.

"How is the baby?" Giacomino the Blind Man asked.

"He's the cutest baby I have ever seen," Grazia responded.

"May I hold him?" Carmela the Daughter of the Umbrella Repair Man asked.

Carolina nodded.

Grazia noticed Carmela's eyes gleaming with tears as she held the baby in her arms. *Little Gianni reminds her of the child she lost.*

"The baby looks just like Carolina's late son," Lina the Warm House said.

Lina turned to Carolina. "Your husband is not going to notice the difference when he sees the little boy. When are you going to tell him that you have adopted the baby?"

"I'm going to tell him when the right time comes." Carolina folded her hands. "Thank God my mother-in-law and her family promised never to tell my husband about the death of my Little Gianni. I hope no one tells my husband."

Titina crossed her hands on her chest. "You can trust me. I know how to keep a secret."

Lina widened her eyes. *Titina is the last person in town who can keep a secret.*

Norina was overcome with happiness when Lina the Warm House and Titina the Alligator paid her a visit. Norina promptly offered them each a cup of sweet coffee.

"Norina, I'm so glad you've recovered from that terrible disease," Lina said.

Titina drank her coffee all in one shot. "We were so worried about you. We thought you were going to die."

"Old Veronica said that the snow was sent from God. I believe that God wanted to save your life." Lina sipped her coffee. "The snow was a blessing from the sky, even for Margherita."

"Margherita has gained some weight," Titina said. "She looks good."

"You made peace with Anna the Heavyweight?" Norina asked.

"I swore on my mother's grave that I'm never going to say anything bad about Margherita. I don't care if Margherita has ten lovers. I mind my own business."

Norina agreed, even though she was perfectly aware that Titina minded everybody's business.

Lina turned to Norina. "I heard that your brother-in-law Rodolfo bought the two houses next door to his house."

"His house is going to be so big that people are going to call it a *palazzo*," Titina said.

"He must be doing well with money," Norina said.

"He still doesn't talk to you?" Lina asked.

Norina shrugged. "He doesn't want to talk to me. I didn't do anything to him."

"You never said anything bad about him," Titina said. "You're like me. You mind your own business."

As Norina watched her friends walking out of her house, her thoughts shifted to Ada. She missed her sister. She wished she could have a chance to see her.

Norina had no clue that Rodolfo had seen the ring Ada had given to Clotilde on display in the jewelry store's window. It looked exactly like his mother's ring. He promptly dashed into the store and asked Donna Lucia to show the ring to him. Once he noticed his mother's birthday engraved inside the ring, he gritted his teeth and flared his nostrils. He purchased the ring and rushed out of the store, impatient to interrogate his wife.

Rodolfo stormed into the house and immediately confronted Ada. "You sold my mother's ring."

Ada's face blushed. "I never sold a ring."

Rodolfo punched Ada in the face. "Then how did it get to the jewelry store."

"I don't know. I lost it." Ada's eyes filled with tears as her whole body trembled.

"How can you lose such a precious thing? You don't deserve to be my wife," he bellowed, landing another blow under her eye. "You don't know how to behave like Rodolfo the Great Shoulder's wife. You act like a lowlife. You are scum just like your sister. The pear doesn't fall far from the tree."

Ada cried silently, and didn't even attempt to defend herself. She felt she had done something wrong and deserved the punishment. Ada was horrified when she looked at herself in the mirror. Her face was filled with bruises. She felt so ashamed to show herself that she refused to go out for weeks.

XXVI

"**O**n the day of *Carnevale*, anything goes," a plump clown yelled out as he led a rainbow of people sporting all sorts of costumes in a festive parade. Their masks disguised them all, and the neighbors on Saint Peter Street wondered who each reveler could be.

No one recognized Margherita, the Lover of Saint Peter Street, who was wearing a mask along with her princess costume. Margherita bounced up as she saw a hulking gladiator carrying a bunch of white roses.

It has to be my Franchino, Margherita thought. *He said that he had flowers for me.*

Carmela the Daughter of the Umbrella Repair Man was clad in a butterfly costume. She floated as soon as she identified her lover by the dragon costume she had sewn for him.

Margherita and Carmela approached their men. *Carnevale* was a special day for them, since it gave them the opportunity to walk in public with the men they loved.

Annibale the Announcer drew the megaphone to his lips. "Tonight, at seven o'clock, the funeral of *Carnevale* is going to take place in the *piazza*. Everyone is invited to come after the parade."

Annibale was employed as the town crier. He was often hired privately to announce births and deaths. There was also a clown juggling balls, attracting the children's attention. Many children shrieked with excitement as they joined the parade. Amused, Contessa Fiorella watched the parade from the shutters of her window.

Carnevale, the Italian version of Halloween, was the only time of year the Voltini children had the opportunity to pay a visit to their Aunt Ada. Disguised by their masks and costumes, none of Ada's neighbors could truly identify them as the Voltinis.

The Voltini children improvised their own costumes. Caterina made herself a gypsy costume by draping a black, tattered shawl on her shoulders and tying a purple scarf around her head. Pasquale paraded into the kitchen in his late father's striped pajamas.

"What's that supposed to be?" Caterina asked.

"I'm a prisoner," Pasquale responded.

Caterina scrunched her nose. "That's not a costume."

"Prisoners wear pajamas at night in jail."

Olimpia dressed up as a bride. She was actually wearing her First Communion dress, which had previously belonged to Grazia and Caterina. Grazia made a paper costume for Little Donato, which resembled a red tulip. The baby pranced cheerfully in his costume.

Norina smiled. "He looks like a real flower."

Mario, looking sad, had confined himself to a corner. He was the only one without a costume. Grazia figured it was because he didn't have the courage to ask for one. Grazia created a clown costume by patching some rags on an old sweater. When she was done, she proudly showed it to Mario.

"Do you like it?" Grazia asked.

Mario nodded and slipped on his costume. Grazia burned a cork and drew thick eyebrows on Mario's forehead. She then drew huge lips on his face with lipstick.

"Mario looks like a real clown," Norina said.

Mario covered his face with his hands as he grinned.

Grazia withdrew to the bedroom and returned five minutes later dressed as a nun.

"Where did you get that dress?" Caterina asked.

"It's Aunt Clotilde's old dress from when she was much thinner," Grazia responded. "All her dresses look like nuns' habits. I only had to add a collar and a head piece."

Norina turned to her children. "When you go to Aunt Ada's house, ask if Uncle Rodolfo is home. If he's home, run away. If he's not home, ask Aunt Ada for food. He usually gets home around seven o'clock."

The children agreed. They wore their masks and dashed out of the house.

Sporting their costumes, cheering, and throwing confetti into the air, children and adults alike were parading on the streets.

Olimpia was enchanted by the streets, which were filled with colorful confetti. "They should keep confetti around all the time."

"They can't," Pasquale said. "The wind would blow them away."

Little Donato twisted his face as he pointed at a short, fat person in a devil costume who was staring at Grazia. "Me scare."

Grazia caressed the baby's cheeks. "Don't be afraid."

"Let's go to the American Wife's house," Olimpia said, leading her sibling to Mrs. Fatti's house.

Pasquale pursed his lips when he saw Serafina the Maid standing by the door distributing American goodies. "She's so cheap that we'll hardly get anything."

The old maid gave them one American candy each.

"Where's Mrs. Fatti?" Olimpia asked.

Serafina gave her a stern look. "It's none of your business."

The Voltini children walked away.

"Let's go to the woman whose husband works in Venezuela," Pasquale said.

Michele, Carolina the Good Life's husband, was seated by the front door with Little Gianni in his arms. It was obvious that the baby boy was his pride and joy. He was playing with Little Gianni and cooing at him, calling him all sorts of pet names. Carolina came out of the house with a plate filled with dried figs. Reluctantly, the children took a fig each and walked away. They were utterly disappointed.

"People who work in Venezuela are not as rich as the ones who work in America," Caterina said.

"Does he know that his wife got the baby from the orphanage?" Olimpia asked.

"You should not tell anyone Carolina adopted the baby," Grazia said. "It's supposed to be a secret. Her husband doesn't know. Carolina is planning to tell him later on."

"I'll keep it a secret," Olimpia whispered.

People stood at their front doors, at their windows, and on their balconies watching the masquerades go by. The spectators marveled at the children of the American Wives. They distinguished themselves with the most elaborate costumes. Mario was amazed when he saw Mrs. Fatti's son, who was dressed as a Roman soldier and had a helmet and a sword that looked real. The child was clad in the same uniform as a soldier Mario had seen on television. Grazia noticed the girls from the Sewing School. They looked stunning in colorful turn-of-the-century gowns they had made for themselves. A storm of white pigeons flying distracted Little Donato. Baronessa Rosa roamed the street, proudly sporting her Madame Butterfly violet kimono.

"She looks like a real opera singer," Caterina said.

Grazia smiled in agreement.

Little Donato pointed at a man dressed as a wolf, who was walking around barking. He hugged Grazia. "Me scare."

"Don't be afraid," Grazia said. "He's not a real wolf."

Children cheered joyfully when they saw Olga the Scared Cat wheeling her cart filled with fruits, vegetables, and candies.

"She's coming," they yelled in unison.

Olga's face was so dirty that it seemed to be painted black. She was dressed in black rags and carried a broom made of wicker.

"Why is she carrying a broom?" Olimpia asked.

"She's carrying a broom because she's impersonating *la Befana*," Pasquale responded.

The children made a big fuss over *la Befana*. They gathered hastily around her cart. Olga merrily distributed the candies to the children. Pasquale, Little Donato, Caterina, and Olimpia grabbed as many candies as they could and stuffed them in their pockets. Mario only took two candies. They all waved at Olga as she tottered away.

"I think that Olga is the real *Befana*," Olimpia said.

Mario nodded.

"Let's go over to Aunt Clotilde's house," Grazia said.

Pasquale huffed. "I'm not in the mood for chickpeas. Can we skip her?"

"No, *Mamma* will be very upset," Grazia said." We have to pay Aunt Clotilde respect."

Once they arrived at Clotilde's house, Grazia knocked at the front door.

"Aunt Clotilde, it's us," Pasquale shouted.

Clotilde opened the door for them and led them into the home.

"How do I look?" Pasquale asked.

"Are you supposed to be a sick man?" Clotilde asked.

Caterina giggled. "Yeah, sick in the head."

"I'm a prisoner," Pasquale said.

"Little Donato is a flower," Grazia said.

"I like his costume." Clotilde gave the baby a kiss on his forehead. *If his costume wasn't made of paper, I would show him off to my friends at the Catholic League.*

Clotilde turned her gaze to Olimpia. "You could pass for a little bride." *I can't show her off in her First Communion dress. It's not a real costume.*

Caterina showed off her costume. "I'm a gypsy."

"I'm a nun and Mario is a clown," Grazia said.

Clotilde was ashamed of their shabby costumes. "Make sure you wear your masks in the streets." She indicated a plate filled with roasted chickpeas. "Have some."

The children didn't show any enthusiasm. They each took only a few chickpeas. They'd rather have gotten candies.

Sensing their disappointment, Clotilde forced a smile as she escorted them out of the house. "Go to Mrs. Gisella Maori's house. She's an American Wife. She lives down the street in the pink house. I'm sure she'll give you chocolates and candies. Her husband just arrived from America."

Olimpia swung her arms. "Let's go."

Grazia led her siblings to the pink house. They saw many children standing in line.

"The American Wife must be giving out something good," Pasquale said.

A delicious smell of chocolate emanated from the doorway. They went to the back of the line and waited impatiently.

Pasquale beamed when he saw youngsters coming out of the house with both hands full. "They give two chocolate bars to each kid. It's worth waiting a whole day."

A short, fat devil dropped a bar of chocolate on the ground and walked away. He didn't even bother to pick it up.

He must be an American kid who has tons of chocolates, Pasquale thought.

Pasquale tried to reach for the chocolate bar. To his disappointment, another boy grabbed it first. Pasquale grimaced as the boy placed the chocolate bar furtively in his pocket.

The Voltini children gave a sigh of relief when their turn finally came. Mr. Maori, a wiry middle-aged man sporting a thick gold necklace, led them inside. The kitchen was spectacular! The walls were paneled with sparkling blue ceramic tiles. A tall, shimmering white box stood up against the wall. Caterina wondered what the box was. With a wide smile that showed his perfectly white false teeth, Mr. Maori rolled open the white box. A draft of cold air emanated from within. To the children's astonishment, the white box was filled with food and chocolates. Caterina realized what it was. She had heard rich people owned cold boxes called refrigerators. Mr. Maori pulled big chocolate bars out of the white box and gave two bars to each child. As soon as they walked out of the house, the Voltini children ripped open the silver aluminum foil wrappers and gorged themselves.

Olimpia took the aluminum foil from her siblings. "I'm going to make jewelry out of the silver paper."

Pasquale giggled at two boys disguised as women. *They got dressed as women to get a chance to mingle with the girls and kiss them on the cheeks.*

"We have to go to Uncle Vituccio's house," Grazia said.

As they headed to their uncle's house, Little Donato waved at a devil. "Me no scare."

"I'm glad you're not afraid of devils anymore," Grazia said.

Once they reached Vituccio's house, a scarecrow approached them and said, "Don't go in there. The woman is a cheap, crazy bitch. She doesn't give you anything, and she yells at you on top of it."

"That woman happens to be my aunt," Pasquale bellowed. "I'll break your neck if you disrespect her again."

The scarecrow ran away as fast as he could.

Pasquale giggled. "He's probably some stupid kid who's already tasted one of my beatings."

Grazia knocked at the front door.

"Get away," they heard their aunt's voice scream.

"Aunt Marta, it's us," Grazia shouted.

Marta promptly opened the door. "I'm sorry. I thought it was one of those crazy masked delinquents."

"How's Uncle Vituccio doing?" Grazia asked.

Marta twisted her face. "He still has the cast on his leg." She led them inside the house and pointed at Vituccio seated on a chair. "There he is."

Vituccio reached out his arms at Little Donato. "Let me hold my little boy."

Caterina set Little Donato down on Vituccio's lap. The baby stared at the white cast on Vituccio's leg.

"He likes your cast," Grazia said.

Marta curled her lips. "He wouldn't like it if he knew how he got it."

Vituccio's face blushed. "Marta, please don't start in front of the kids."

For once, Marta relented. She turned to Olimpia. "You look beautiful."

Olimpia spun around to give a better view of her dress. "I'm dressed as a bride."

"I created the pattern for your dress, and I also did the embroidery," Marta said.

"*Mamma* always says you're the best seamstress in the family," Grazia said.

Marta folded her hands and looked up. "Thank God I can sew; otherwise we'd end up in the poor-house. Your uncle hasn't worked for the past two months."

"Marta, get some figs for the kids," Vituccio said.

Reluctantly, Marta withdrew into the back room. She returned a minute later with a plate filled with dried figs and offered them to the children. To Marta's surprise, they only took one fig each.

"Take more figs. Fill up your pockets," Vituccio said, ignoring his wife, who was giving him harsh looks while chewing on her lower lip.

His nieces and nephews declined to take more figs. They preferred American chocolates.

"They have enough," Grazia said.

Marta gave a sigh of relief.

"It's getting late. We have to go," Grazia said, escorting her siblings outside.

Marta stepped out of the house and watched them trotting down the street. *They're beautiful children. It's too bad they're so poor.*

She wasn't doing well herself. The money she was making sewing was barely enough to buy pasta and bread. If Vituccio didn't recover by next month, they would end up just like the Voltinis, who hardly had any food to fill their stomachs.

The Voltini children passed through a narrow lane nicknamed Ghost Street. The houses were all painted white with the exception of one dark gray house, whose windows were broken.

"That house is abandoned. It's haunted by a ghost," Caterina said. "The owner, Delfino the Big Knife, was a butcher. He was killed with his own knife by his lover's husband. His ghost has been there since the day he got killed."

"I don't believe in ghosts," Pasquale said.

All of a sudden, they heard noises coming from within the gray house. Olimpia and Mario walked stealthily away.

"I want to hear. I'm curious." Caterina stepped towards the gray house.

They heard the bleating of a lamb.

"I think there are animals in there," Grazia said.

Pasquale shrugged. "The house is abandoned. There can't be any animals."

"I heard that the ghosts of the animals the butcher killed are in there," Caterina said.

Pasquale shook his hands in front of him. "Don't make me laugh."

Caterina widened her eyes as a group of ghosts dashed out of the gray house. The ghosts were all equipped with long sticks.

A short ghost waved his stick up in the air. "We're real ghosts. We live in the haunted house."

"Oh my God," Olimpia screamed.

Mario remained speechless as his lips trembled.

As the ghosts began to giggle, Pasquale mocked their giggling.

"You should be afraid of us," the short ghost said.

Pasquale lifted his chin and crossed his arms. "I'm not impressed by stupid little kids dressed as ghosts."

The short ghost pointed his stick at Pasquale.

"I'm not afraid of your stick," Pasquale hollered, showing his fists.

Grazia stepped in front of her brother and held him tightly by the arms. "I don't want you to fight. There are too many of them. You'll get hurt."

The short ghost took ahold of Mario and struck him on the head with his stick. Mario's face twisted as his whole body quivered. He thought a real ghost had struck him.

"Leave my brother alone," Grazia yelled.

"No one hits my brother," Pasquale shouted, releasing himself from Grazia's grip.

Pasquale leaped, ready to attack the short ghost, but two overweight ghosts restrained him by holding his arms.

"Help," Olimpia and Caterina screamed in unison.

To the girls' relief, a group of people dressed as pirates emerged down the street.

"Come and help us," Grazia yelled, waving her hands up in the air.

The pirates ran towards them. A tall pirate drew his sword and hacked the short ghost's stick in half. The overweight ghosts promptly released Pasquale.

"If you don't leave them alone, you'll have to deal with my real sword," the tall pirate said in a severe timbre.

The ghosts ran away as quickly as they could. The girls exhaled heavily. Mario was still trembling.

Grazia gave Mario a hug. "It's over. They're gone."

The tall pirate took his mask off and revealed his face. Grazia couldn't believe her eyes. It was Giorgio!

Giorgio bowed and smiled at her. "Sorry for the inconvenience, *signorina*."

Grazia removed her mask and presented her magical smile. "Thank you for helping us."

Giorgio beamed. "I helped the person I wanted to help the most. I knew it was you. I recognized your voice. You didn't make out my voice because I disguised it. I had to disguise my voice to scare off the ghosts."

The Voltini children felt safe under Giorgio's protection as they walked away from Ghost Street.

"No one is going to mess with us now," Olimpia said.

Caterina nodded. Mario showed a half-smile.

"I'm so grateful you rescued my brothers and sisters," Grazia wanted to say to Giorgio, but no words came out of her mouth. She put her mask back on, fearing people would identify her. She didn't want to risk being seen walking by Giorgio's side.

"I'm so happy to be with you," Giorgio wanted to say, but he didn't have the courage. He donned his mask and smiled as he pictured Grazia's angelic face underneath her mask.

When they finally reached the *piazza,* where the funeral of *Carnevale* was taking place, they joined the people standing on the sidewalks watching the spectacular procession. The children were ecstatic. The personification of *Carnevale* was a madman, who pretended to be dead. A carriage pulled by four white horses transported the open coffin of *Carnevale.* Six men wearing silk stockings on their faces walked aside the carriage and carried huge candles. A tall, heavy woman dressed in black with a veil draped over her face posed as the mourning widow. Two men, dressed as vampires, were holding her as she walked. The mourning widow fainted and regained consciousness from time to time.

Caterina indicated the widow. "It's Anna the Heavyweight."

"Anna has the guts to do anything," Grazia said.

"My husband is dead," the widow bellowed. "I'm never going to find another man as crazy as him."

The man playing the role of *Carnevale* laughed hysterically and sprang out of the coffin every now and then. As he did so, the vampires and the men wearing silk stockings on their faces acted as if they were terrified.

"You're better off dead," the widow shouted every time she helped *Carnevale* get back in the casket.

Olimpia pointed out the man impersonating *Carnevale*. "Look, it's Arturo, Maddalena's husband."

"Arturo does all the crazy things," Pasquale said.

Lots of people parading in their costumes followed the procession. A band played the funeral march at the rear. The most respectable people in town walked in the first row of the procession. Don Lorenzo the Pharmacist was dressed as the Pope. His two godsons, Primo and Secondo, walked at his sides wearing their altar boys' tunics.

"Don Lorenzo is so good to the poor that they gave him the costume of the Pope out of respect," a woman impersonating a Madonna said.

A girl disguised as an angel bobbed her head in agreement. "Don Lorenzo is the Pope of the town."

Doctor Polo, the Married Priest was dressed as a priest. His wife, clad in a nurse uniform, walked at his side.

Doctor Polo is more kindhearted than a real priest, Grazia thought. *His wife is more merciful than a real nurse. She's a volunteer nurse at the hospital.*

The Four Seasons Contessas were sporting their black lace Spanish dancer outfits. A tall, muscular man dressed as Prince Charming was escorting Saveria the Midwife, who was impersonating a queen.

She's the queen of the town, Grazia thought.

The midwife's husband, camouflaged as a pharaoh, also followed the procession wheeling his wheelchair.

A woman portraying a maid indicated the Dumb Brothers dressed as clowns. "They couldn't have picked better costumes. They're the biggest clowns in town."

The Dumb Brothers were marching with the musicians of the band. They enjoyed playing the drums, even though they weren't producing any sound. The ends of their drumsticks were covered with a cloth.

Lisetta was the only one in the procession who didn't wear a costume. She was exhibiting an ostentatious red outfit and a matching hat. Pino the Red Eye, clad in a musketeer costume, merrily held her hand.

"Lisetta and Pino the Red Eye are still together," a man masquerading as a gangster said.

"Pino the Red Eye is not ashamed to walk with her," a short man disguised as a devil said. "She's not even wearing a costume. She should have worn at least a mask to conceal herself." The devil had been one of Lisetta's best customers.

"He's so stupid that he even shows her off," a man camouflaged as a pig said. He had also been one of Lisetta's most frequent clients.

The Margassi Sisters joined the procession dressed up as brides, and were escorted by two older men disguised as knights.

"Those whore sisters even have the audacity to wear wedding gowns. No one will ever marry them," Grazia heard a woman impersonating a witch say.

Giorgio was happy to have Grazia at his side. She was the most stunning nun he had ever seen in his life. He wished *Carnevale* would last forever. He felt like he was living a dream, and was afraid to wake up.

Grazia felt like she was someone else. It felt good not being a Voltini for a day. Grazia was unaware that the devil man was staring at her, and knew who she was. He had been following her since she had left her house.

Grazia leaped at the sound of the church bells. She counted the chimes in her mind. It was six o'clock. "We have to go now."

Pasquale compressed his lips. "Now comes the best part. The procession is going to the cemetery. They're going to bury *Carnevale*."

"We can't go to the cemetery," Grazia whispered in Pasquale's ear. "We have to go to Aunt Ada's house and ask her for food before Uncle Rodolfo goes back home."

Pasquale's face radiated as he pictured the food they were sure get from his aunt.

Grazia turned to Giorgio. "We have to leave. I'll see you some other time." She expanded her eyes, surprised by her own words.

Giorgio's eyes sparkled. He waved enthusiastically. He couldn't get over his shock at the fact that Grazia had promised to see him some other time. It meant the world to him. He trotted away, driven by the hope that he might not have to give Grazia up just because his mother despised her. He could have a secret relationship with her.

Grazia escorted her siblings to Ada's house. They stopped in front of the yellow house. Grazia rang the bell. Seconds later, the door opened a crack and Ada revealed her face. She looked like she was wearing a mask herself, since she had bruises all over her face. Mario thought she had put make-up on to look like a clown.

Grazia gritted her teeth. *Her husband must have given her one of his trademark beatings.* "Aunt Ada, it's us."

Ada smiled as she recognized Grazia's voice. "My husband is not home. You can come in."

The Voltini children scrambled into the house and removed their masks.

Ada looked at Little Donato. "You're a little pale but you're fine." She exhaled heavily. "Thank God!"

The baby stared at her.

"Aunt Ada, we could use some food," Caterina said.

Ada ran into the back room and returned a few minutes later with a basket filled with all sorts of goodies: flour, eggs, sugar, and oil. Pasquale filled his pockets with eggs. Olimpia was able to fit a little sack of flour into the puffy skirt of her First Communion dress. Caterina covered a bag of sugar with her shawl. Grazia removed her nun's headpiece and used it as a cloth to cover the bottle of oil.

Ada scrunched her forehead as she looked at her watch. "My husband may come home in a little while. If he sees you here, he'll have a fit."

Grazia wore her mask and turned to her siblings. "Put your masks on."

As soon as they applied their masks, Grazia led them out of the house. Grazia froze when she noticed a devil standing by the corner. *Could it be Uncle Rodolfo?* As she took a better look at him, she crossed that thought from her mind. She realized her uncle was much taller.

The devil took off his mask when he paid Colombina the Farmer's Wife a visit.

"Good to see you, Carlo," Colombina said. "I can't believe you still dress up for *Carnevale*."

"Did your son Giorgio wear my pirate costume with the real sword today?"

Colombina nodded. "It's such a nice costume, and it still looks brand new."

"I saw him at the procession with Grazia, the Voltini girl. I recognized the costume."

Colombina bit down on her fist. "I have told my son many times not to hang out with the Voltini girl."

"My mother is right when she says kids don't listen to their parents these days."

"A Voltini girl would be a curse on my family."

"Please, don't tell Giorgio I told you."

"I won't say a word."

"I have to go."

"Give my regards to your mother."

"I will." Carlo the Broken Neck walked out of the house.

Norina was jubilant when her children returned home loaded down with food. She used the flour to make *frittelle*, or Italian fritters. Everyone loved the delicious aroma. Pasquale and Olimpia scrambled out of the house, eager to show off their *frittelle* to their friends.

Norina took a *frittella* and went to sit outside by her front door. Savoring it, she smiled at her children who were eating with delight. She didn't lose her smile when Colombina the Farmer's Wife passed by. Colombina took that as an insult.

"You even have the nerve to smile at me," Colombina shouted.

Norina contorted her face. "What's wrong with smiling?"

"You shouldn't smile at me because I don't want anything to do with you. And tell that daughter of yours to stay away from my son."

At the sound of the altercation, several neighbors gathered around Norina's house.

Norina lifted her chin. "Grazia has nothing to do with your son."

"Your daughter and my Giorgio were together at the procession. I have witnesses. People saw them."

Norina leaped out of her chair. "It's impossible. My daughter has no interest in your son. She's beautiful, and she could do much better."

Colombina giggled. "She could do better? Who the hell is going to marry her? She's just a lousy maid."

Norina placed her hands on her hips. "Who the hell do you think you are? No one has forgotten that your father used to collect chamber pots full of everybody's shit."

"At least my father had a job, and paid his debts. He wasn't a night payer like you."

"Your father had the shittiest job in town."

Colombina showed her fists. "I'm going to pull your hair out."

Anna the Heavyweight grabbed Colombina by the arm. "If you touch my friend, I'm going to crush you."

"Take her away," Norina screamed. "I don't want lowlifes around my house."

"She has some nerve calling me a lowlife," Colombina screamed back as the strong woman dragged her away.

Norina stormed into the house and confronted Grazia. "I told you not to mess around with boys."

"I didn't mess around with anybody," Grazia said.

"People saw you with Giorgio, the son of that bitch, Colombina." Norina reached for her late husband's belt.

"*Mamma*, Giorgio was with us to protect us from a bunch of boys dressed as ghosts and armed with clubs. One of them hit Mario in the head. Pasquale tried to fight them off, but there were too many. If you don't believe me, ask Caterina."

"Grazia is telling the truth," Caterina said.

Norina turned to Grazia. "It better not happen again. If people see you with boys, you are going to ruin your reputation." Norina slapped the belt on the table. "Once you ruin your reputation, no one is ever going to marry you."

Grazia's eyes became gloomy. "No one will marry me anyway because I don't have a dowry."

"I'm devoted to Our Lady of Sorrows. The Madonna works miracles." Norina flashed a hint of a smile. "Why do you think Little Donato and I recovered? It was because of the Madonna. Miracles do happen."

Grazia's eyes shone with tears. She didn't believe in miracles.

XXVII

On Saint Joseph's Day, it was the tradition of the people of Vocevero to light a bonfire and have Saint Joseph's pasta and *zeppole*. It was their way of honoring the saint on his namesake day. Saint Joseph's pasta consisted of broad noodles topped with anchovies, sautéed in hot olive oil, and sprinkled with fried bread crumbs. *Zeppole* were large, soft pastries filled with custard cream. Though the Voltinis had Saint Joseph's pasta for lunch, they didn't have *zeppole*. Norina would have loved to make the delicious pastries, but she couldn't afford the ingredients. The Voltini children wandered the street, taken by the scent of the pastries wafting from the doorways of their neighbors.

When the neighbors lit the bonfire, the Voltini children forgot all about the *zeppole* and jumped ecstatically around the quivering flame, which seemed to imitate their movements. Baronessa Rosa brought little cups filled with salt and gave them to the children. As they threw salt into the blaze, they shrieked with delight at the loud crackling, popping sounds and the sight of the sparks that leaped off the flames.

The misty grays and purples of the sunset were descending onto Saint Peter Street. Norina and Grazia joined the neighbors seated by the bonfire. The glistening flame was burning the wood into ashes. It captivated the old women surrounded by the smoke that fogged the air. Hypnotized, they saw their lives consumed in those embers. Their days had shriveled up in their struggle to survive and provide for their children. Having reached the twilight of their existence, the white-haired women appeared serene. All the worries and difficulties of their time on earth had dissipated. The only thing they looked forward to was their encounter with the tranquility of mortality.

A sinister melancholy swept over Norina as she stared at the bonfire. She had no money, and was running out of food. She was losing the hope that Grazia's picture exhibited in the photo studio would ever produce a rich husband who could help the family. She was destined to be poor forever. She was tired of struggling to survive. She closed her eyes and abandoned herself to a deep dream of death. She felt relief at the thought that she would be in peace one day. Titina the Alligator's voice distracted Norina from her thoughts.

"Maddalena had another fight with her husband this morning," Titina said.

Norina was so consumed with her troubles that she didn't show any interest, and immediately returned to her reverie.

"Arturo threw garbage at Maddalena from the balcony, and called her all sorts of names." Titina shook her hands in amusement. "What a scene!"

Grazia curled her lips. "Arturo is nothing but garbage."

Titina got up from her chair. "He has a good reason to throw garbage at her. Maddalena should be ashamed of what she does."

"You should be ashamed for being so malicious," Grazia wanted to say, but she restrained herself. She wasn't in the mood to fight with Titina. She gave a sigh of relief when Titina walked away. Then Grazia bounced up as she noticed the Margassi Sisters emerging from the street. She shook her mother's arm. "Your friends are coming."

The Margassi Sisters waved at Norina as they came towards her. Norina welcomed them with a tiny smile.

"I don't have a fiancé anymore," Giovanna Margassi said.

"What happened?" Grazia asked.

Giovanna revealed a somber look. "His wife came to my door and told me to leave her husband alone. I was shocked. I didn't know that Giuliano was married. He swore on his mother's grave that he was single."

"You should not believe what men say, even when they swear," Norina said.

"My boyfriend swore to me that he was going to give me an engagement ring on my birthday, but he hasn't shown up since." Gina Margassi lowered her head. "I thought he loved me."

"It wasn't meant to be," Norina said. "Everything is written in the sky."

Giovanna flashed a hint of a smile. "My mother used to say that luck comes when you least expect it."

Gina nodded. "I'm devoted to Saint Joseph. I believe he's going to help me find true love."

Thank God they have faith. I'd hate for them to lose their hope of finding true love, Grazia thought.

"I'm going to play a *Tarantella*," Giacomino the Blind Man shouted. "The young people want to dance."

As soon as Giacomino maneuvered his accordion, people began to dance. Caterina and the Margassi Sisters joined the revelers dancing in a circle around the bonfire.

As soon as Giorgio saw Grazia, he waved at her to get her attention.

His parents must not be around, Grazia assumed, greeting him with her eyes.

Giorgio couldn't resist the impulse to invite Grazia to dance. Grazia was reluctant to accept.

"You should dance with him, it's not nice to refuse," Margherita said, pushing Grazia into Giorgio's arms. She wished Franchino could dance with her, but unfortunately, he had to spend time with his family.

Grazia and Giorgio looked like a happy couple as they danced the *Tarantella*.

Caterina had her eyes fixed on Rocco, the shepherd's son. When he finally invited her to dance, she accepted with a skip.

"I like to watch young couples dance," Old Veronica said. "It reminds me of the good old days when I used to dance."

Enchanted, Serafina the Maid stared at all the couples. She had never had the audacity to dance on the street when she was young and pretty.

Seated on the farmer's balcony, Carlo the Broken Neck watched the merry scene. He paid Colombina a visit to keep an eye on Grazia.

Carlo wasn't worried about Giorgio conquering Grazia. *Giorgio is stupid. He doesn't know how to seduce a woman. He should consider himself lucky if he even gets a kiss from her.* He turned to Colombina. "Who is Giorgio dancing with by the bonfire?"

Colombina searched among the people for her son. "*Mamma mia!* Giorgio is with the Voltini girl. I'm going to fix him," she screamed, running to the stairs.

From the balcony, Carlo looked at Colombina as she walked hastily down the street. *She's furious,* Carlo thought with a glint of a smile.

Lina the Warm House waved at Colombina. "Come and dance the *Tarantella.*"

"I'm not in the mood," Colombina said. She gave her son a stern look.

But Giorgio didn't notice her presence. He kept dancing with Grazia, enjoying every step of the popular peasant dance. Grazia was in high spirits, amazed her mother was allowing her to dance.

Colombina's face turned crimson and was ready to explode at her son, but she held back. It was Saint Joseph's day, and it would have been a sacrilege to the saint to make a scene that would have darkened his name day.

Norina wrinkled her nose when she saw Colombina. "I don't want my girls to dance with boys."

Colombina glared at Norina. *She has some nerve. I should be the one forbidding my son to associate with her daughter.*

"Let the young people have their fun," Lina said.

"I better get my girls," Norina said. "I never gave my girls permission to dance."

"I remember how you used to dance on the street on Saint Joseph's day," Old Veronica said.

Norina remained silent.

"There's nothing wrong," Lina said. "They're out on the street. They're not somewhere you can't keep an eye on them." She turned her gaze to Carmela the Daughter of the Umbrella Repair Man who had Carolina's baby in her arms. "Look at her. She let her lover into her house when nobody was there to keep an eye on her. She got pregnant and has ruined her life."

"I feel bad that Carmela's boyfriend refused to marry her," Norina said.

Norina noticed Carmela had a sad look as Carolina took the baby from her arms. She wondered what had happened to Carmela's baby. Babies that were born out of wedlock were usually abandoned in orphanages, even though the family would often spread rumors of the child's death.

"He was never going to marry her," Titina said. "A White Fly doesn't marry a peasant girl."

To their surprise Umberto, Carmela's lover, approached Carmela and invited her to dance. She accepted, but avoided meeting his eyes as Giacomino sang a romantic song entitled "Remember my Love."

"People are right," Lina said. "They are still lovers."

"Carmela has no choice," Titina said. "She has to keep him as a lover. There isn't a single man in town that is going to marry her after what she did."

When the song was over, Umberto withdrew. Carmela's eyes gleamed with tears as she watched the love of her life disappear into the distance.

"Giacomino, I want to sing 'My Shining Sun,'" Carolina's husband Michele shouted. "I want to dedicate the song to my son, because he's the sunshine of my life."

As Giacomino played his accordion, Michele began the verse:

You are a shining sun in my life
You make me smile even if I want to cry
You bring me joy even when I'm sad…

People enjoyed Michele's singing even though he was off key. The ballad was so popular that many people knew the lyrics by heart and sang along. When Michele finished, he blew a kiss at his little boy.

Lina and Titina exchanged looks.

I wonder how Michele is going to react when he finds out that the baby is adopted, Lina thought.

Michele is going to bring the baby back to the orphanage for sure when he finds out, Titina mentally answered back.

Giorgio, who was not aware of his mother's presence, had another dance with Grazia. But before the dance was over, Colombina took him by the arm and dragged him away without a word. Giorgio didn't dare protest. It was like a scene from a silent film. Most of the neighbors didn't even notice it. The ones that caught sight of it figured that Colombina had restrained herself from shouting for the sake of Saint Joseph. If Colombina had yelled, Norina would probably have yelled back. They would have created an exciting dramatic scene for all the neighbors to watch.

Contessa Fiorella saw the scene from the shutters of her window. To her relief, Grazia didn't show any emotion. It seemed to everyone that Grazia barely even noticed being abandoned by her suitor.

Carlo the Broken Neck, who had watched the scene from the farmer's balcony, revealed a half-smile. *Giorgio wouldn't have a chance with Grazia even if he did have good intentions. Colombina would never give him permission to court her. Giorgio is too afraid of his mother.*

Carlo looked down the street and waved at Giorgio and Colombina as they reached the house. "Giorgio, you got tired? At your age, I used to dance all night long."

Colombina looked up at the balcony. "He was dancing with the wrong girl."

Giacomino shouted, "Here comes Baronessa Rosa."

The neighbors applauded when the opera singer appeared, fluttering in a yellow Madame Butterfly costume.

As if she were on stage, she bowed. "I'm going to sing 'One Fine Day,' an aria from the opera *Madame Butterfly.*"

The glittering red and orange bonfire reflected on the opera singer. A deep silence overcame the street. As soon as Giacomino maneuvered his hands on the violin, the sound of music blasted into the air. Baronessa Rosa looked up in the sky and began to sing. At the sound of her voice, many wealthy people appeared on their balconies to listen. A flock of white pigeons flew up into the starry navy blue sky. They seemed to dip and dart in harmony with the soprano's singing. Illuminated by the street lamps, the poor and the wealthy spectators lifted their heads up to the sky.

The sky is universal. It covers everyone, the wealthy and the poor, Grazia thought.

"The pigeons are so beautiful dancing in the sky," Margherita said.

Giacomino the Blind Man smiled, enchanted with the image in his mind of the white pigeons dancing.

People were entranced by Baronessa Rosa's singing. Her voice was powerful. When she was done, she faced the listeners and bowed. The audience gave the singer a thundering ovation.

"*Brava,*" Anna the Heavyweight shouted.

The Margassi Sisters were so mesmerized that they couldn't find the proper words to express their compliments. Overtaken by intense emotion, Baronessa Rosa's eyes sparkled. The ovation had brought back many memories. She used to be a famous opera singer in her hometown in Greece. She had entertained large crowds, and had always received enthusiastic appreciation from her audience. The spectators watched the Baronessa as she glided away and disappeared into her doorway. Contessa Fiorella noticed from the shutters of her window that the pigeons had also vanished into the sky.

"I want to serenade my wife," Arturo said.

Many people looked at him, stunned, while he whispered the name of the song to Giacomino. Arturo took the musician by his arm and escorted him to the front of his house. Many neighbors followed them, eager to witness Maddalena's reaction. Looking up at his balcony, Arturo sang his favorite song:

Maddalena, Maddalena, why do you keep on ignoring my love?
You don't know how much you hurt my feelings.
You don't even know you've stolen my heart.
You shouldn't forget how much I've loved you.
You should tell me why you don't respond to my love.
You don't even realize how ungrateful you are.

Arturo's eyes filled with tears as he sang. He sounded sincere. The Margassi Sisters were fascinated by Arturo's singing.

Serafina the Maid's face radiated as she listened to the song. *Arturo looks like such a good husband when he sings.*

"It's very romantic," Margherita said.

A passerby joined the listeners, enthralled by Arturo's presentation. "He sings with passion."

"He dedicated the song to his wife," Lina said.

"He's a very generous husband," Titina said. "He buys his wife a lot of jewelry."

"He even takes her to the Opera," Lina said.

"He must be in love with his wife," the passerby said.

Arturo has no shame, Grazia thought. *After all the beatings he's given his wife, he has the nerve to serenade her. Who does he think he's fooling?*

Driven by the secret hope of witnessing Maddalena's appearance, the spectators' eyes were fixed on her balcony. Many spectators exchanged glances when a faint iridescent light filtered through the glass door that led to the balcony. Alas, to their disappointment, Maddalena didn't appear.

When Arturo finished singing, the opalescent light disappeared into the darkness. Arturo trudged down the street, beating on his thighs with his fists.

"Where is he going?" Titina asked.

"He's probably going to the bar to drink it off," Ninuccio the Painter responded.

"I'm a good friend of Arturo," Carmine the Shepherd said. "I know him well. He feels miserable when he fights with his wife. Serenading her is his way of asking her for forgiveness."

"Maddalena is still upset at her husband for throwing garbage at her," Lina said.

"When Maddalena was single, she was so poor that she didn't even have the eyes to cry." Titina said. "She should be grateful to Arturo. He gives her the best food and the best jewelry."

"*He treats her like an animal. He abuses her,*" Grazia wanted to say, but decided to remain silent. *It's useless to argue with ignorant people.*

Contessa Fiorella was delighted that Maddalena had refused to come out onto the balcony. *It's the least she can do. I hope the abused woman has had a revelation.*

"Maddalena should forgive him," Lina said. "He sang such a nice song for her."

"Maddalena is playing with fire." Titina narrowed her eyes. "If she loses him, she's going to end up in a whorehouse, just like her sister Lisetta."

"I heard that Lisetta is no longer a whore," Margherita said.

"That cannot be," Titina said. "The wolf loses his fur, but not his habits. Her mother was also a whore. Lisetta comes from generations of whores."

Lina nodded. "The pear can't fall too far away from the tree."

"It's a disease that's in the blood," Titina said.

"Lisetta comes to church every morning," Old Veronica said. "She's engaged to Pino the Red Eye."

Titina giggled. "Pino the Red Eye is the only man in town who could have gotten engaged to Lisetta."

"There's someone for everyone," Gina Margassi said.

"No fruit is left unsold at the market," Giovanna Margassi said.

"They're two fools. They still think that someone is going to marry them," Titina whispered to Lina.

"They like to dream," Lina whispered back.

One by one, the spectators returned to their houses. The bonfire had diminished into glittering embers until it faded out completely and disappeared, just like the spectators under that dark twinkling sky.

XXVIII

Enchanted, the wealthy and the poor alike admired the white pigeons flying carefree in the pale, azure sky as Baronessa Rosa sang,

We are having beautiful sunny days.
There are flowers blooming everywhere.
Our lives have been renewed for another year.
Our hearts are filled with hope for better years,

"Spring is in the air." Giacomino the Blind Man pictured the fields filled with blossoming trees and wildflowers. Those fields were more vibrant than ever in his imagination. He smiled as he visualized people carrying branches of peach and almond trees, inebriated with the scent of flowers. "This is the most beautiful season of the year. Everything is renewed with the coming of spring."

Vituccio felt revitalized with the arrival of spring since he had finally recovered completely from his leg injury. He also rekindled his love for the Voltinis by paying them a visit.

Norina perked up the first time she saw him on his feet. "Vituccio! You can walk again!"

Vituccio handed her a basket filled with dried fava beans and a bunch of dandelions.

"Uncle Vituccio," the children shouted.

He smiled. He felt like the most important man on earth.

"Did you bring us any pastries?" Olimpia asked.

He held his head down to avoid looking at them as he realized he had no real treats to give to them. "This is the best I can do."

"I can make dandelions with fava bean purée for dinner. It's delicious," Norina said.

"Uncle Vituccio, did you come by car?" Pasquale asked.

"I have the car parked by the corner on the main street."

"Can you take us for a ride?" Olympia asked.

Norina gave Olimpia a stern look. "You don't ask your uncle for a ride. The car is not a toy. Uncle Vituccio uses his car for work."

"Never mind, Norina… they're kids." Vituccio turned to the children. "I'll take you all for a ride to the fields."

Olimpia clapped her hands. "Uncle Vituccio is the best uncle in the world."

"Promise you won't say anything to Aunt Marta." Vituccio drew his index finger to his lips.

The children nodded and scurried outside.

Vituccio looked at Grazia and raised his eyebrows. *"Should I trust the children?"* he was about to ask her.

Grazia read his mind. "You can trust them. They won't say a word."

Vituccio gave a sigh of relief.

"Vituccio, can you get me some flowers for Our Lady of Sorrows?" Norina asked.

"Sure. I'll pick the most beautiful flowers."

Vituccio exited the house. Grazia followed him carrying Little Donato in her arms. They all got into the car. The Voltini children waved at friends, acquaintances and passersby. They were always exhilarated to ride in a vehicle. When Vituccio revved the engine, the children sang,

Hold my hand and come with me
I'll take you dancing on the moon
The sun will smile and follow us
And all the stars will dance with us…

The car came to a halt in front of a field filled with blooming flowers and fennel plants. The children leapt out rapidly. Vituccio admired the way the sunrays reflected on their faces. They looked like figures in a painting he had seen in church of Jesus feeding some children seated around him in a green meadow.

"Uncle Vituccio, may we get some fennel?" Olimpia asked.

"Go ahead," Vituccio replied. "The owner of the field is a friend of mine. I gave him a free ride."

The children each picked some fennel and stuffed their pockets.

Vituccio's face drooped. *They're hungry.* He wished his business would pick up. He felt he was a miserably and desperately poor man, a Poor Jesus, and couldn't possibly provide for his nieces and nephews to their satisfaction.

Vituccio jumped out of the car as he recalled he had promised Norina he would get some flowers for Our Lady of Sorrows. He searched the fields and picked the most beautiful wild daisies. When he was done he turned to the children and whistled.

"The circus has come to town," Olimpia said. "Can you please take us to see the tent and the caged animals?"

Vituccio didn't have the heart to say no. "Fine, we'll pass by." He would have loved to take them to the actual show, but unfortunately he was broke. Once again, he felt like a Poor Jesus.

They all piled into the car. Pasquale's eyes lit up as soon as Vituccio revved the engine. "Uncle Vituccio, go faster."

As soon as Vituccio accelerated, the children applauded with exhilaration.

"This is fun," Olimpia said. "We're flying under the sky."

Vituccio reduced his speed once they reached the *piazza*. There were a lot of stands topped with colorful umbrellas. The children fixed their eyes on a vendor selling crushed ice topped with red syrup.

Little Donato pointed at the stall. "Ice."

Vituccio felt heartbroken. Unfortunately, he didn't have the money to buy goodies. In better times, he had always bought the children *gelato*. He loved to see their blissful expressions whenever he was able to treat them.

"Let's go. I'm going to show you the caged wild animals of the circus," Vituccio said, hoping to distract them from their craving of the crushed ice with syrup.

"The circus!" the children cheered in unison.

Vituccio stopped his car in the old section of the town where an enormous flag-bearing marquee had been installed. Only wealthy and middle-class children attended the performances. Poor children derived what entertainment they could by looking at the tent, the trailers, and the caged wild animals, parked on the street.

Once they were all out of the car, Little Donato stared at a lion. "Big, bad dog."

"It's a lion. He's locked up so he won't hurt you," Grazia said.

Olimpia's eyes expanded when she saw a tiger. "It looks like a big cat with stripes."

They bumped into Pino the Red Eye.

Vituccio patted Pino's shoulder. "Good to see you."

"I'm always-always happy-happy to-to see-see you." Pino directed his gaze at Grazia. "You-you look-look *muy-muy bonita*."

Grazia gave him her trademark magical smile.

Pino turned to Vituccio. "Are you-you-you taking the-the-the kids-kids to-to-to see the-the-the circus?"

"I'd love to…" Vituccio lowered his voice. "…but I can't."

Pino winked his red eye. "I-I-I can-can get-get-get them-them in."

Vituccio scrunched his forehead. "You can get them in to see the show?"

"Yes-yes. I'm-I'm-I'm going-going to-to be–be part-part of-of the-the show and-and-and the-the-the kids-kids could say-say-say that-that they are my-my-my nephews and-and nieces."

Vituccio's mouth fell open. "You're going to be an entertainer?"

"Yes, yester-day I-I-I went to-to see the-the-the owner of-of the-the circus with-with-with Lisetta and he-he-he picked me. I don't know-know what-what-what I did, but I-I-I made every-every-body laugh. They are-are paying me."

"That's wonderful!" Vituccio whistled to get the children's attention.

They avoided looking at him, thinking it was time to go.

"You can go to the circus," Vituccio shouted.

The children ran towards their uncle.

"We can go inside and see the show?" Olimpia asked.

"Yes. Say-say-say that you-you-you are related-related to-to-to me: Pino-Pino Pioventri."

Pasquale tilted his head and stared at his uncle.

Vituccio smiled in affirmation. "They'll let you in. He's one of the performers."

Pasquale's face radiated. Mario smiled.

Olimpia jumped up and down. "Can my mother come?"

"Of course-course-course, she-she can-can-can say-say that-that-that she-she is my-my-my sister."

Olimpia clapped her hands.

"Thank you, Pino," Grazia said.

Pino beamed.

"It's time to go." Vituccio turned to Pino. "Would you like a ride?"

"Yes-yes. Take-take-take me to-to Lisetta's house-house-house."

They all got into the car. Pino felt important sitting in the front seat. The children all managed to sit in the back seat, one on top of the other. The children and Pino cheered with joy as they rode in the vehicle. They waved mirthfully at the passersby.

As they passed by Saint Maria's church, Vituccio saw his wife and froze. Marta waved her hands in the air. She lambasted him with a harsh look, and gestured to stop. Vituccio blushed as the car screeched to a grinding halt.

The screamer is ready to perform, Grazia thought.

"Where are you going?" Marta asked.

"I took the children for a ride," Vituccio replied.

"You waste your gasoline on them when we hardly have money to buy food," Marta shouted. She instantly attracted the attention of the passersby, who gathered around the car. They anticipated a drama.

"It was a very short ride," Pasquale said.

Marta looked at the wild daisies and twisted her face. "You went to pick daisies from your friend's field. I know where it is. It's very far."

Vituccio lowered his head. "I won't do it again."

"You better not do it again." Marta bit her tongue. "Don't make me curse in front of the church." She indicated Pino the Red Eye. "What is he doing in your car?"

Pino pointed at Vituccio. "He-he offered me-me-me a ride-ride. He's taking-taking me-me-me over to-to Lisetta's house."

Marta flared her nostrils as she clenched her teeth. Lisetta was the best-known whore in town. She was worse than the devil. Marta couldn't bear the thought that her husband was still associating with prostitutes. She was about to explode. To avoid the explosion, Vituccio revved up the engine and pulled away.

Grazia sauntered into the house carrying a big bundle of wild daises in one arm and Little Donato in the other. Norina took the flowers and placed them in a vase. She then filled the vase with water.

"Circus," the baby said, flapping his hands.

"We're going to the circus for free," Grazia said. "All we have to do is say we're related to Pino the Red Eye."

Norina was confused. It took Grazia a long time to explain to her mother that Pino the Red Eye was going to be a performer at the circus and they were entitled to complimentary tickets if they pretended to be his relatives. Norina was ashamed to be associated with Pino the Red Eye.

"Don't tell anybody else that we're related to Pino. People may believe it... better yet, don't even tell anyone about free tickets." Norina winked. "I want people to think that we bought tickets."

Grazia nodded.

Norina reached for the vase filled with wild daises, eager to offer them to Our Lady of Sorrows. *The Madonna has put in a good word for the circus.*

Going to the circus was a special occasion for the Voltinis. Norina wanted her family to look their best, since they would be surrounded by White Flies. She checked her children's spring clothes to see if they needed any mending or alterations. To her relief, most of their best spring clothes were in good condition. Caterina's dress was the only one that was too worn out and couldn't be restored or refashioned.

When they were having dinner, Norina looked at Caterina and said, "You can't come to the circus. You don't have a decent dress to wear. If you come, you are going to make the whole family look bad."

Caterina threw her spoon onto the table. She had bragged to all her friends about the circus, and she didn't want to look like a fool. "I want to come. I don't care about the dress. I have just as much right to go to the circus as anyone in the family. It may never come to our town again. It's once in a lifetime."

Norina said nothing.

Caterina began to cry. She was so upset she refused to eat, though she was famished.

"I can alter a dress Mrs. Zordi has given me to fit Caterina," Grazia said.

"You don't have much time," Norina said.

Grazia patted Caterina's shoulder. "Trust me. I can do it."

Caterina exposed a hint of a grin as she dried her tears with her sleeve.

Two hours later, Grazia had remodeled Mrs. Zordi's dress to fit Caterina's measurements. She proudly showed the dress to her sister. Caterina's eyes sparkled. She embraced Grazia and gave her a big kiss on the cheek.

The Voltinis put on their best attire for the circus. Grazia, Caterina, and Olimpia were happy to be allowed to wear black and gray instead of solid black. When women wore black mixed with gray, their garb was known as *il mezzo lutto*, and indicated a state of half mourning. On special occasions even during full morning, it was permissible for girls to wear *il mezzo lutto*.

Norina dressed up in a damask black outfit that had belonged to Mrs. Zordi. Unfortunately, the skirt had a small but visible patch. Having no alternative, Norina decided to conceal the patch by carrying her purse close to it. Grazia wore a gray and black silk dress that she had refashioned for herself out of one of her employer's discarded dresses. Caterina looked great in the gray dress with black trimming that Grazia had remodeled. Olimpia was in a gray dress with black ruffles Grazia had created out of Caterina's old dress. Norina took the time to curl Olimpia's hair with the hot iron, and then adorned the curls with a gray bow. Olimpia looked charming. Pasquale sported a white shirt Grazia had made out of Norina's old housedress. He pinned a black mourning button on the collar of the shirt. Mario donned his First Communion suit with the black mourning button attached on the collar. Norina reminded Mario to keep his hands in his pockets to hide the sleeves, which were too short on him. The only one who didn't have to wear a sign of mourning was Little Donato, since he was a baby. He looked like a little prince in a blue satin suit that Grazia had fashioned for him out of a jacket Pasquale's had outgrown.

The Voltinis looked like a White Fly family as they walked down the street. It was a special occasion for all of them. Norina felt a great deal of satisfaction as she sensed her neighbors' admiration.

A lot of rich men are going to be at the circus. They are going to notice Grazia for sure. Norina thought, smiling with anticipation.

She had great pride and delight as the children waved at the neighbors.

"Go to circus," Little Donato kept saying, flapping his hands.

"We're going to the circus," Olimpia shouted, swinging her arms.

Her girlfriends congregated around her. Olimpia spun around to give a better view of her dress.

Titina the Alligator and Lina the Warm House exchanged looks filled with amazement as they watched the Voltinis trotting down the street.

Titina raised an eyebrow. "Where did they get the money to go to the circus?"

"Where does Norina get the money for those beautiful clothes?" Lina asked.

"I think Norina has a lover on the side that lends her a hand."

"Once I saw Carlo the Broken Neck going into her house."

Titina narrowed her eyes. "He must be the one. He's a womanizer."

Carlo the Broken Neck was seated by Colombina the Farmer's Wife's front door, having a conversation with her. He couldn't believe his ears when he heard the Voltini children proclaiming they were going to the circus.

How can the Voltinis afford tickets? Is it possible that Grazia has a rich lover? I'd better check it out. Carlo turned to Colombina. "Would you and your family like to go to the circus?"

"My husband can't come because he's busy working in the fields." Colombina said. "I'm sure Giorgio is going to want to come, he likes the circus. But I want to pay for the tickets. You have been too generous to us."

Carlo shook his head. "Don't even think about it. I'm paying for the tickets. After all, I invited you and your family."

Carlo is a real gentleman, Colombina thought. *He's such a bighearted man.*

As soon as the Voltinis arrived at the circus, Norina approached the ticket booth. Hiding her embarrassment with a fake smile, she quietly told the ticket attendant she was Pino Pioventri's sister.

"Pino the new *torero*?" the attendant asked.

Norina didn't know if Pino the Red Eye was playing the part of a *torero*. She quickly understood that as his sister she was supposed to know.

"Yes," Norina responded.

If the *torero* was another Pino, Norina concluded she would be glad to be taken for his sister instead. Any brother named Pino was better than Pino the Red Eye.

The box office attendant found Norina very attractive. He exposed a charming smile. "Are you here alone?"

"No, I'm here with my children." Norina pointed at them.

The box office attendant raised his eyebrows as he counted six children. He took a deep breath. "Lisetta, Pino's fiancé, is seated in the first row. You can sit next to her."

Norina bit the inside of her lip. The last thing she wanted to be seen doing was fraternizing with a prostitute. Her daughters' reputations would be soiled instantly. "We can't sit next to Lisetta. We don't talk to her because she never paid her respects at my late uncle's funeral. But please, don't say anything."

"I won't tell a soul." The box office attendant sighed. "I understand. All families have problems. You can all sit in another section."

The Voltinis sat in the second row of the pavilion, on the opposite side of where Lisetta was. In their best attire, they blended in with the crowd, which was filled with many White Flies. A White Fly *signora* greeted Norina with a smile. Norina returned the smile and glowed with pride. Norina felt she deserved the White Flies' respect. After all, she was well dressed and was seated in the second row. As Norina turned to look at the people in the back rows, she spotted Colombina the Farmer's Wife. Norina quickly snorted and turned her head. She didn't even notice Colombina was seated between Carlo the Broken Neck and Giorgio.

Colombina indicated Norina to Carlo. "The night payer puts on airs. I wonder where she got the money to buy tickets for the circus."

"Her daughter probably has a rich boyfriend," Carlo said.

Colombina twisted her lips. "Girls like her can only get a rich lover who will take advantage of them."

Giorgio's eyes flashed with jealousy as he thought Grazia could have a lover. Carlo was equally curious as to whether Grazia had a rich lover. He wanted to be her lover. Ever since he first laid eyes on her portrait, he hadn't been able to stop thinking of her.

"Ladies and gentlemen, welcome to Paradise Circus," a clown shouted, hitting his drum.

The audience cheered. As the sound of the drum got louder, the spectators grew quiet and stared at the center of the arena.

The show was spectacular! The audience saw lions, elephants, tigers, monkeys, and even snakes. The animals were great entertainers.

Olimpia was eager to see Pino the Red Eye's performance. "When is Pino coming out?"

"He'll come out sooner or later," Grazia whispered. "He's part of the show."

Mario's eyes expanded as a clown swallowed fire. "I hope-hope-hope he-he-he doesn't burn-burn his-his mouth."

"He won't burn his mouth," Pasquale said. "That's some sort of trick."

Mario stared with his mouth agape at a ballerina who walked on a high wire. She looked like a princess he had seen in a fairy tale book. He feared she would fall, and prayed for her well-being.

Pasquale was impressed by the ballerina's curves. *She's a woman and a half. I wish I could get to know her but soon she'll vanish with the circus. Well, I don't really have to talk to her. I can always tell my friends I got to talk to her.*

The Voltini children got up from their seats and applauded when Pino the Red Eye appeared in the arena. Clad in a *torero* costume, he was riding a donkey. When he dismounted and waved a red cloth, the donkey chased him. Pino ran away calling the donkey all sorts of names. Unexpectedly, a spotlight illuminated a fabulous Spanish dancer in a revealing, costume that sparkled. The woman waved at Pino. Pino jumped on the donkey and attempted to reach her, but he kept falling off. The crowd went berserk with laughter.

"Pino," many spectators shouted.

Pino beamed as he waved to his fans.

Pino loves any sort of attention, Grazia thought.

All of a sudden, several kids began to boo Pino. Three rascals seated in the back row threw tomatoes at him. Pino responded with a smile, and avidly ate all the tomatoes he was able to catch. He didn't realize the rascals were also throwing rocks at him. Pino's smile quickly disappeared when a rock hit him just above his left eye. Lisetta clenched her fists as she got up from her seat. She ran towards Pino.

"It-it-it do-do-doesn't ma-ma-matter. That's my-my-my bad-bad eye-eye-eye anyway."

Pino's eye was bleeding, but he didn't complain. He didn't want to lose his job. He wanted to put money aside to marry Lisetta. Rocks were still flying in the air.

Grazia compressed her lips as she bounced from her seat. She was ready to explode.

Norina held Grazia by the arm and whispered, "We're in a public place. You have to behave like a *signora*."

To Grazia's relief, Lisetta grabbed the microphone and turned to the audience. "Whoever is throwing rocks at Pino, if you don't stop, you're going to have to deal with me and the people I know."

The rascals stopped immediately. They knew what sort of people Lisetta knew. Over the years, she had slept with half the criminals in town. A deep silence descended upon the audience.

The circus announcer took the microphone from Lisetta's hands and faced the public. "Ladies and gentlemen, Pino the *Torero* will now perform a dance."

Lisetta quickly wiped the blood out of Pino's eye with a handkerchief and went back to her seat. The spectators applauded to encourage Pino. Overcome with joy, Pino the Red Eye flashed a bright smile and forgot all about his wounded eye. Pino danced a passionate tango with the Spanish dancer. He kept stumbling as he attempted to dip her down and generated so much laughter that some of the people were in tears.

"Bravo Pino," many spectators shouted, clapping their hands.

"More than a few people come just to see Pino," the box office attendant said.

Many spectators smiled in agreement.

At the end of the performance, Norina felt obligated to go backstage and check on Pino's eye. Since she was pretending to be his sister, Norina knew she had to act like one. Grazia insisted on escorting her mother on the pretext she was playing the role of Pino's eldest niece.

Lisetta was standing by Pino's side, pressing gauze on his wounded eye.

Grazia turned to Pino. "How do you feel?"

Pino appreciated her concern. His face radiated contentment. "I'm fine-fine-fine."

"Let me see." Grazia took a closer look at the wound and realized the cut was on Pino's eyebrow. She gave a sigh of relief. "Thank God the eye is fine."

"I don't know the name of the person who did this," Lisetta said. "If I find out who it was, he's going to have to deal with me. I'll make sure he gets a thrashing he'll never forget."

"He-he-he won't do-do-do it-it again. He's afraid of-of-of you-you-you."

Lisetta kissed Pino's wound. "Are you happy to have a woman who's able to protect you?"

Pino beamed as he nodded.

Norina curved her lips. *How gross! She's in love with him. Only a prostitute could fall in love with Pino the Red Eye.*

Grazia revealed a glint of a grin. *She's truly in love with him. It's so wonderful!*

The misty purples and dark grays of the sunset were descending on the streets when the Voltinis left the arena. Norina quickened her pace, eager to see her neighbors. She figured they would be waiting to hear all about the show, and she couldn't wait to give them a detailed description of Pino the Red Eye's performance. When Norina arrived at Saint Peter Street, she saw Colombina the Farmer's Wife surrounded by many neighbors. Norina gritted her teeth. Colombina had stolen her opportunity to be the news reporter of the day.

Pasquale delivered the big story to the local boys. As Pasquale spoke, he had their undivided attention. Pasquale loved to exaggerate. As he told it, the show featured a donkey that blew fire from its mouth and ears.

Pasquale also spoke glowingly about the stunning woman in a short puffy skirt who had walked on the high wire. "I got to talk to her. She was very friendly with me. She looked like a movie star. What am I saying? She looked just like Contessa Fiorella Torre."

"What did she say to you?" his friend Biagino asked.

Pasquale winked. "She said she likes younger men."

Biagino's mouth fell open. "Are you going to ask her out?"

"If I do, I'm not going to tell you." Pasquale flashed a half-smile. "A real man doesn't kiss and tell."

At dinnertime there was barely any food on the table, but the Voltini children didn't complain. They were so happy to have gone to the circus that they didn't even realize they were hungry when they went to bed.

XXIX

On Holy Thursday, it was a tradition for people to visit all the churches in town. The three local churches were overcrowded with people from all walks of life.

On their way to Saint Giovanni's Church, Norina and Grazia heard loud yells coming from a street nearby.

"Let's go and see what's going on," Norina said, eager to witness the live drama.

As they entered the street, they saw a group of people standing in front of a blue house. Norina noticed Bellina the Good Deed among the spectators.

"Come out, you slut," a large-breasted woman shouted, waving her hands at the balcony. "You had the nerve to sleep with my husband. If you want a lover, you should find a single man, not a man who has six children. Show your whore face."

Norina and Grazia approached Bellina.

"What happened?" Norina asked.

"Zina the Silk Stockings is having an affair with a married man," Bellina said. "Zina sleeps with men for money and gifts. The butcher told me that Zina's lover bought her a whole lamb."

That sounds like the lamb that Zina brought to the baker, but it wasn't a whole lamb. It had missing a leg, Grazia recalled, but refrained from butting in.

Norina turned to Bellina. "You know me. I'm a widow with six children. I've never laid my eyes on another man. I have three daughters, and I'm never going to have an affair and ruin the family's reputation."

Bellina nodded. Norina grinned. It felt good to have her respectability affirmed.

When Norina and Grazia entered Saint Giovanni's Church, they saw Marta and sat next to her. After reciting some prayers, they ushered Marta out.

"I could use your company to visit Saint Maria's Church and Saint Gennaro's Church," Marta said.

Norina was not in the mood for her sister-in-law's company. "We've visited all the churches in town."

"I wouldn't mind visiting the churches again," Grazia said.

"I have to go home," Norina said. "The children are waiting for me."

When Grazia and Marta entered Saint Maria's Church the seats were all taken, so they had to stand.

Carlo the Broken Neck flashed a smile as he noticed Grazia. He occupied almost two seats since he was so fat. He moved out of his seat, and thus allowed both women to sit down.

"Thank you," Marta whispered.

Grazia thanked him by revealing her magical smile. Again, he was enchanted by her. Pretending to pray, he kept staring at her until she left the church, escorted by her aunt.

Once they were out on the street, Marta and Grazia headed to Saint Gennaro's Church.

"I'm surprised that a man like Carlo the Broken Neck gave us his seat. He behaved like a gentleman, and was staring at you the whole time. I think he likes you." Marta exposed a trace of a grin. "You never know. He may send you a marriage proposal."

Grazia froze. The last thing she wanted to do was marry Carlo the Broken Neck. "He's old enough to be my father."

"He's one of the richest landowners in the town. Many rich men have married younger women."

Grazia remained silent.

As they entered Saint Gennaro's Church, Marta looked at the statue of the Virgin Mary, made the sign of the cross, and wished with all her heart that Carlo the Broken Neck would ask for Grazia's hand in marriage.

He would lift up the entire family. They would have plenty of fruits and vegetables. Since it was unlikely that a powerful man like Carlo would marry a poor peasant girl, Marta begged the Madonna to perform a miracle.

Later that day, Carlo the Broken Neck stopped by Ubaldo the Photographer's studio to take another look at Grazia's portrait. He noticed two men staring at the pictures exhibited in the window.

One of the men pointed at Grazia's portrait. "She's the most beautiful girl in the window. She's the kind of woman I would love to marry."

Carlo took note that the man spoke with a foreign accent. *He's probably an American. He may propose marriage to Grazia.*

The Broken Neck made up his mind. There was no doubt. He had to have Grazia at any price!

It was the custom for all Catholics to fast on Good Friday, to honor the suffering of Christ on the anniversary of his death. Whoever couldn't resist the temptation to eat during the fasting hours, committed a sin. The fasting ended in the late afternoon, but even then, people didn't have a large supper. The traditional meal was a pie called *calzone*, which consisted of two layers of dough stuffed with sautéed scallions, olives, tomatoes, and anchovies. Clotilde brought the Voltinis a large *calzone* pie.

"It's delicious," Olimpia mumbled with her mouth full.

Clotilde gave her a stern look. "You should never talk with your mouth full." She then turned to Norina. "Did you go to confession?"

"I did," Norina exposed a tiny smile. "The priest has a fun job. He must know so much hot gossip. It's too bad he can't tell anyone."

Clotilde's eyes flashed. *She shouldn't say such a thing about a priest.* Clotilde was ready to explode, but decided to contain herself. She refused to start an argument with her sister-in-law. *It's useless. When you try to wash a donkey's head, you end up wasting the time and the soap.*

The Good Friday procession was well attended. Clotilde, being the president of the Catholic League, led the holy procession with many members of the League. Norina and Grazia were privileged to walk in the third row. Most of the women were dressed in black, and wore lace veils over their heads. Two teams of men in black suits carried the life-size statue of Our Lady of Sorrows and a glass coffin containing the life-size statue of Jesus. Among the men, Grazia saw Franchino the Bird's Nest, Arturo, Ninuccio the Painter, and Giovanni the Farmer. It was considered so prestigious to carry a divinity on Good Friday that men fought amongst themselves for the honor. Margherita appeared as if she were in mourning in her black dress and black veil. She was sneaking smiles at her Franchino, but he couldn't return the gesture because he was carrying Jesus in the coffin, and was required to maintain a solemn expression. Saveria the Midwife, escorted by her new lover, joined the procession among the honored participants in the first row. Her new lover attracted a lot of attention. He was breathtaking.

"The midwife picks the best," Melina the Fairy Tale said.

"I wonder if she's going to have a child with him," Candida the Rosy Cheeks whispered.

"I don't think so," Melina said. "She's too busy. I heard that she's studying to become a doctor."

"We'll have the first woman doctor in town," Grazia said.

They directed their attention towards Carolina the Good Life, escorted by her husband Michele, who proudly held his baby boy in his arms.

"He's crazy about that baby." Candida lowered her voice. "Did she ever tell him that she got the baby from the orphanage?"

"She's waiting for him to get more attached to the baby," Norina whispered.

Candida turned her gaze to Carmela the Daughter of the Umbrella Repair Man, escorted by her brothers. "I heard that Carmela didn't give her baby to the orphanage. What could she have done with him?"

"I don't know." Norina didn't feel like gossiping about Carmela's offspring. She didn't trust Candida.

Pino the Red Eye was parading pompously with his fiancé Lisetta, clad in a red spring coat. They were holding each others' hands. Pino and Lisetta waved at Norina and Grazia. Norina pretended not to see them, but Grazia waved back at them.

"Do you know them?" Candida asked.

Grazia nodded.

"We know him. We buy a lot of fish from him." Norina forced a smile. "Who doesn't know Pino the Red Eye? He's become famous since he started working in the circus."

Candida scrunched her nose. "Lisetta has some nerve to attend a procession. She has no shame."

Norina nodded. "I heard that Lisetta even goes to church."

"Jesus has to accept all sinners. No one can kick Lisetta out of the house of God," a voice behind them said.

As Candida and Norina turned their heads, they were faced with Old Veronica.

"I hope Lisetta has no intention of seducing the priest," Candida whispered.

Old Veronica widened her eyes. "That could never happen. Father Camillo is a servant of God."

Grazia spotted the Margassi Sisters and waved at them. The sisters waved back at her.

"You know them?" Candida asked.

"I know them," Grazia responded.

Norina didn't have the heart to say she didn't know them. They had been good to her. "They took care of my mother when she was sick."

Candida curled her lips. "With the sort of reputation they have, the only thing they can do is take care of sick people."

"The last time I saw them, they were in the company of their boy-friends, Melina said. "Now they're alone again.""

Candida giggled. "They're like chamber pots: they get dumped over and over again."

Grazia furrowed her brow. "It's not their fault that men have been cruel to them. Those poor women were raped in the fields."

Candida stamped her foot. "They had no business working in the fields."

"They worked in the fields because they needed money to survive. I blame the man that raped them. I would put him in jail. The Margassi Sisters didn't have the courage to report him to the *carabinieri*. They were ashamed to say they were raped. No victim should ever be ashamed for sins committed by others."

"The Margassi Sisters sure aren't ashamed to behave like whores. They've slept with half the men in this town."

"It's not their fault if their boyfriends use them. They're romantic. They dream about true love."

Candida glared at Grazia. "I've never seen a woman defending whores."

At the sound of Baronessa Rosa's powerful voice, everybody stopped talking and directed their attention to her. The song was dedicated to the Virgin Mary:

Look at your People, beautiful Lady.
They are all honoring you with intense joy...

Most of the people who followed the procession knew the words by heart, and sang along with the opera singer. As the procession passed Saint Peter Street, people appeared at their front doors, on their balconies, and at their windows. Some people got down on their knees in honor of Jesus and Our Lady of Sorrows. Contessa Fiorella watched the parade of people through the shutters of her window. She noticed that numerous women became emotional as they sang. She witnessed Maddalena and the Margassi Sisters wiping their tears with their hands.

Those women need faith to accept all the injustices life serves them, the contessa thought.

Norina spotted Fabrizio, Laura the White Flower's widower, holding hands with a young woman. "Who's that woman walking with Fabrizio?"

"She's his new wife," Candida said. "He couldn't be alone after his wife died. Who was going to take care of him and his children?"

"She's so young," Norina said.

"She's twenty years younger than he is. To tell you the truth, she didn't have a good reputation, so they married her off to a widower. I heard that they were lovers when Laura was still alive. She has to consider herself lucky that he married her."

Grazia noticed that Melina's face drooped. Grazia recalled that Melina the Fairy Tale had been in love with a man who had dumped her after many years of engagement. Melina had to settle for an old man because her reputation had been ruined. A woman wasn't considered pure after being engaged to a man for many years.

I don't think Melina feels lucky to be married, Grazia thought.

As the procession turned back to the church, the statue of Our Lady of Sorrows was brought closer to the statue of Jesus in the glass coffin. The expression of mourning sculpted on the Madonna's face was appropriate for the scene. It conveyed deep sorrow for the death of her son.

"It's heartbreaking," Melina the Fairy Tale said.

It was the most emotional moment of the procession. The scene repeated itself three times in a row. Many women's eyes welled up with tears.

Melina dried her tears with a handkerchief. "Our Lady of Sorrows is devastated to see her dead son."

The spectators genuflected as they watched Our Lady of Sorrows and Jesus enter the church.

Norina's lips trembled as she prayed to Our Lady of Sorrows. "Please, find a rich man for Grazia," she whispered after she had recited her prayers.

Before long, Norina saw Colombina the Farmer's Wife and her son entering the church.

She noticed that Giorgio smiled at Grazia, though his mother scowled. Norina couldn't resist the impulse to walk by them.

"I get a headache when I'm around low class people," Norina said.

Colombina flared her nostrils, but she restrained herself from an outburst. *The night payer is lucky that today is Good Friday and I don't want to make a scene.* It would have been a sacrilege to blacken Good Friday.

When times were good, Vituccio would bring the Voltinis lamb for Easter. On Holy Saturday, Norina waited the whole day for her brother to pay her a visit, but to her disappointment, he didn't show up. Norina decided to have a chicken meal for Easter. She paid a visit to Old Veronica and asked for one of her chickens.

"It's a waste to kill the chicken," the old woman said. "You should wait until she grows and gives you some eggs. Having the chicken today, means losing the eggs tomorrow."

"I have no choice. It's the only food I can give to my children for Easter lunch."

Old Veronica's eyes dimmed. "Little Donato is going to be devastated if he finds out that you killed one of his chickens."

"Don't tell him. Just tell him that the chicken ran away." Norina grabbed one of the chickens. The powerless animal made screeching noises, as if she were aware of her destiny.

Old Veronica placed her hands on her cheeks. *Norina is about to kill Chicken Grazia. Little Donato is going to cry when he is going to find out that his favorite chicken has disappeared.*

Norina brought the chicken to Anna the Heavyweight's house. Anna was the only woman on Saint Peter Street who had the guts to kill chickens. She was able to strangle a chicken with one hand. She would then pull the feathers out while it was still warm. As a reward for her services, she kept the chicken's head, feet, and feathers. She made soup out of the chicken parts and used the feathers to stuff a little pillow.

On Easter Sunday, the Voltinis attended Mass. Saint Maria's Church was crowded. Many White Flies sported new outfits with matching hats. Norina was surprised to see Ada with her husband and daughters, seated in the pew in front of her. Ada didn't turn her head to look at her sister, fearing Rodolfo would notice. When Lisetta entered the church wearing a red outfit with a complementary hat, everyone's eyes were on her.

"The priest should not allow someone like her in here," Rodolfo whispered.

"The priest welcomes everybody in the house of God," a *signora* from the Catholic League whispered back.

Rodolfo compressed his lips. He didn't respond, knowing he couldn't start an argument in church.

Among the crowd, Grazia spotted her uncle Vituccio seated next to his wife. She noticed he had a bandage on his forehead.

Grazia bit her tongue. *Aunt Marta probably threw something at him. She belongs in a madhouse.*

As soon as the Mass was over, the Voltinis exited and waited for Vituccio and Marta. The children were eager to see Uncle Vituccio, who would always give them chocolate eggs on Easter. When Vituccio and Marta walked out of the church, the children were disappointed their uncle was empty-handed.

"Coco egg," Little Donato kept saying.

Pasquale and Mario dragged the baby away.

"Vituccio, what happened to your forehead?" Norina asked.

"I fell," he replied as his wife dragged him away.

Norina figured Marta had caused the injury. *My poor brother is the victim of that crazy woman.*

On their way home, the Voltini women ran into Carlo the Broken Neck.

"Signora Norina, I want to wish you a Happy Easter." Carlo bowed and kissed her hand.

"Thank you… and Happy Easter to you too," Norina replied.

Carlo exposed a light smile. "I can see that you're in the company of your lovely daughters."

"Yes, these are my three daughters: Grazia, Caterina, and Olimpia."

"It's a pleasure meeting all your girls." He shook their hands. He stared intensely at Grazia. "Is your portrait on display in the window of Ubaldo's studio?"

Grazia nodded.

"Ubaldo the Photographer insisted so much on putting Grazia's picture in the window" Norina said. "I didn't want him to do it."

"Your daughter's beauty deserves to be exhibited," Carlo said. "She's a lovely girl." He then bowed and walked away.

Can it be that Carlo the Broken Neck wants to marry Grazia? He likes her for sure. He looked at her in a special way. Norina's eyes lit up. She was filled with hope. *Our Lady of Sorrows has answered my prayers! The money I spent on Grazia's portrait was well worth it.*

Wealthy children were parading in the streets showing off their large chocolate Easter eggs wrapped in colorful paper.

"Coco egg," Little Donato kept saying.

Mario gazed at the chocolate eggs with his mouth open.

Pasquale gave him a slap on the head. "Stop staring. You look like you've never seen a chocolate egg in your life."

Mario managed to avert his eyes, but he couldn't help picturing the chocolate eggs in his mind.

The Voltinis had chicken breast and chicken thighs for lunch. Little Donato savored the meat, unaware he was eating his favorite playmate. For dessert, Grazia gave a piece of sugared bread to each of her siblings. They devoured the delicacy in no time.

Olimpia contorted her face as if she was about to cry. "I thought that Uncle Vituccio was going to bring us chocolate Easter eggs, but he forgot about us."

"Leave him in peace," Norina said. "He has too many problems of his own. When I was a little girl, there was no such thing as a chocolate Easter egg."

"You had the *gurrugulo*," Pasquale said. "A *gurrugulo* is better than nothing."

Poor children had a large pastry in the shape of a round braid with a whole egg embedded in it. In town, it was known as the *gurrugulo*.

"We're going to have the *gurrugulo* in better times." Norina flashed a light smile. "Better times are going to come. The sky can't always be dark for us." *Our sky is going to change for sure if Carlo the Broken Neck marries Grazia. He's going to help the whole family for sure. He's the richest landowner in town.*

Little Donato pointed at the door. "Me go to *Nonna* Veronica to get coco egg."

If Old Veronica had a chocolate Easter egg, she would have given it to him already, Grazia thought, leading the baby outside.

Grazia saw several children playing down the street. "Let's go and play with the children," she said. *If Little Donato gets wrapped up in playing, he'll forget all about the chocolate egg.*

Old Veronica's chickens running on the street captured the baby's attention. "Me play with chicken."

Grazia gave a sigh of relief. *I'm glad he forgot all about the chocolate egg.*

The child ran into Old Veronica's house looking for his chickens. Grazia followed him inside.

Little Donato flapped his hands and stamped his feet as he realized one of his chickens was missing. "Where Chicken Grazia go?"

"She ran away," Old Veronica said.

Little Donato searched all over the house for his chicken. "Why Chicken Grazia go away?" he kept asking.

"She's going to come back," Old Veronica said. That's what chickens do. They run away, but they always find their way back."

Little Donato wept hysterically.

Old Veronica picked up the baby and rocked him in her arms. "I'm going to sing a *Ninna Nanna*."

She softly sang a lullaby to calm him down. She was relieved when Little Donato finally fell asleep.

"Chicken Grazia," Little Donato kept murmuring in his sleep.

"I had no idea he loved those chickens so much," Grazia said.

"Chicken Grazia was his favorite chicken," Old Veronica said. "He named the chicken after you, because you're his favorite sister."

If I go away, I guess he'll miss me as much as his chicken, Grazia thought, picking the baby up from the old woman's lap.

Grazia returned home with Little Donato sleeping in her arms. She turned to her mother. "*We*'d better not kill the other chicken."

"Why?" Norina asked.

"Little Donato would be devastated. He cried desperately when he realized one of them was missing."

"Who cares what a little kid thinks?" Norina giggled. "I can't believe that he was crying so much for a stupid chicken." *If I run low on of food, we can always have the other chicken.*

That chicken was almost as important to Norina as it was to Donato. It gave them both a sense of security.

XXX

Desperation once again prevailed in the Voltinis household. Norina wanted to kill Chicken Caterina, but Grazia convinced her to spare the innocent animal's life.

"We need more than a chicken to feed the children," Grazia said. "We can get more food by hosting another novel reading."

Later in the day, Norina and Grazia paid a visit to Angela the Crazy Head and asked her to do another reading.

"I can't," Angela responded. "I'm busy working for Contessa Fiorella."

"What kind of work?" Grazia asked.

"I can't tell you. The contessa made me promise not to talk about it. You know me. When someone tells me to keep a secret, I don't squeal."

"Angela, can you put in a good word with Count Torre and remind him that I'm looking for work?" Norina asked. "He usually lets me jar vegetables."

Angela huffed. "I hate Count Torre. Talking to him is the last thing I want to do."

Norina exposed a somber look, and remained speechless.

Angela's whole face lit up as an idea popped into her mind. "I may have a good solution to your problems."

"What's the solution?" Norina asked.

"You could put the boys to work," Angela said.

Norina scrunched her forehead. "Who is going to give work to my boys? Do you know how many boys are looking for work?"

"Do you have any debts with Paolino the Gas Man?" Angela asked.

"No, I paid him in full."

"I heard Paolino is bedridden due to a pinched nerve in his back. You could ask him if he would hire your boys to deliver the tanks."

"That's a very good idea," Norina said.

Grazia agreed.

The following day, Norina woke Grazia early in the morning.

"We have to go over to Paolino's house," Norina said.

Grazia's eyes were still heavy with sleep. She was reluctant to get up. "You're not even dressed."

"I'm dressed."

"You have your house-dress on."

"There's no need to dress up when we have to beg for a favor. Paolino is not going to feel sorry for me if he sees me in my best clothes."

She wants to attract pity, Grazia thought. *Pity is what I hate the most in life.*

Ninetta the Gas Man's Wife bit her lower lip when she saw the Voltini women.

"Ninetta, I heard that Paolino is not feeling well," Norina said. "I'm paying you a visit out of respect, to see how he's doing. He's such a good man."

Ninetta forced a smile. "Thank you for thinking of us." Her smile faded. "My husband is bedridden with back pain."

"Back pains are the worst thing a person can get."

"It may be the *malocchio* that causes the pain. Do you know how to remove it by reciting the special prayer?"

Norina sighed. "I wish I knew how to do that."

Ninetta's face drooped.

Norina patted Ninetta's shoulder. "Since Paolino is not feeling well, my boys can deliver the gas tanks in his place."

"In the last two days, I've had about ten mothers begging me to hire their boys."

"I'm not just any mother. I'm a poor widow with six children."

Ninetta shrugged. "Many widows came to ask for jobs for their sons."

Norina produced some tears. "All the other widows are not in need like I am."

Ninetta didn't show any emotion.

"I'm a poor and honest widow. I gave you my word of honor that I was going to pay you for the gas tank, and I did."

Ninetta didn't respond. *I had to beg to get paid for that gas tank,* she thought, gritting her teeth.

Norina joined the palms of her hands. "Please give my boys the job. Do it for the *buon anima* of my husband. Do it for Our Lady of Sorrows."

Ninetta remained silent.

Norina got down on her knees. "I'm desperate. You're the only one who can help me."

"All the mothers said they're desperate as well."

Norina realized she had to be more dramatic. She widened her eyes. "If you don't help me, I'm going to do something crazy."

"What are you going to do?"

Norina sprang off her knees. "I'm going to throw myself off the roof," she shouted, pulling her hair. She then turned and started a forceful jog up the stairs.

Grazia remained still, knowing her mother wouldn't throw herself off the roof.

Ninetta moved quickly towards Norina and held her arms. "Please don't do that. I'm going to hire the boys. Tell them to come after school tomorrow. But remember, I'm not paying them. The only money they get is going to be whatever tips the customers give them… is that clear?"

Norina exhaled. "Very clear."

My mother's acting is superb, Grazia thought. *She'll go to any lengths to get what she wants.*

The Voltini boys were happy to have work, especially Mario. It was a job he could do well, since it didn't require any talking. Pasquale mastered the skill of installing the gas tanks, and Mario helped his brother lift the tanks on and off the dolly. The boys loved to wheel the dolly. It gave them the sensation of driving a car. Sometimes they used the dolly to give rides to their friends. When pretty girls asked for a ride, Pasquale refused any help from his brother. He wanted to be alone with the *signorine*. On those occasions, Mario stood on a corner to allow his brother to socialize with them. Mario didn't even dream of talking to girls, knowing there wasn't a girl in town besides his sisters who would talk to him.

Pasquale was in charge of the gratuities they collected, but he didn't hand over all of the earnings to his mother. Pasquale kept some pocket money for himself, eager to show off to his friends. He bragged that he was making a fortune. His friends, Albertino, Luigino, and Biagino, believed him because he always had lira coins in his pockets, and often bought them candies. Once, Pasquale even bought his friends and his brother each a *gelato*.

Luigino thanked Pasquale with a hug. "You must be making lots of money."

Biagino patted Pasquale's shoulder. "You're so lucky."

Albertino exhaled heavily. "I wish I had a good job."

Pasquale beamed. His friends' admiration gave him a feeling of importance. "One day I'm going to take you all to the cinema."

His brother and his friends jumped up and down.

"I've only been to the cinema two times in my life," Albertino said.

Mario wanted to say he had been to the cinema three times, but he decided to remain silent.

"I've never been to the cinema," Luigino said.

Pasquale lowered his voice. "I'll take you to the cinema if you promise not to tell my mother."

"I won't tell her," Luigino said. "You can trust me."

Biagino crossed his arms on his chest. "I swear on my grandmother's grave, I won't tell your mother."

"I promise I won't even tell my friends," Albertino said.

Pasquale didn't want the trip to the cinema to be so secret that he missed out on the admiration of the neighborhood kids. "You can tell your friends as long as they don't tell my mother."

When the Voltini boys received a particularly generous tip from Mrs. Fatti one day, Pasquale delivered on his promise to take Mario and his friends to the cinema. Mario was scared someone would recognize him and report back to Norina, so, he wore a hat and hid his lower face with his hands throughout the entire movie. The boys had the time of their lives. They got to see the most glamorous American stars on the big screen. During the intermission, Pasquale boasted that he had dated girls just as attractive as the movie stars. His friends were so grateful for the tickets that they even pretended to believe him. Pasquale was the big shot, so he deserved respect. At the end of the film, Biagino, Luigino, and Albertino thanked Pasquale repeatedly.

"If it weren't for you, we would never have been able to go to the cinema," Biagino said.

"I'm glad you're sharing your good luck with us," Albertino said.

"You are the best pal in the world," Luigino said.

Pasquale smiled. "What good is it to have money if you don't share it with your friends?"

Luigino, Albertino, and Biagino smiled in agreement.

Pasquale's generosity aside, the Voltini boys barely earned a modest income. Most of the poor didn't give them any tips when they delivered the gas tanks. Some people offered dried figs. The only ones that tipped them with cash were the White Flies. The American Wives were the most generous, giving money and American goodies. Unfortunately, the boys didn't get to serve the American Wives often, but Paolino was a generous employer and managed to give them a loaf of bread twice a week. That bread was highly appreciated by Norina.

The Voltini boys' modest employment lasted only two months. One day, Norina received an unexpected visit from Ninetta the Gas Man's Wife.

"What brings you to my house?" Norina asked.

"There's a big problem," Ninetta shouted.

"What big problem?"

"Do you know Filomena the Grave Heart?"

"Yes, she's so mean that people say that she has a stone instead of a heart. She has no compassion for Bellina the Good Deed, the poor crippled cousin that lives with her. She treats Bellina like a slave."

"Filomena claims to have given the money for her gas tank to your sons. But they never gave me the money."

"That's impossible. The customers aren't even supposed to give my boys the money for the gas tanks. My boys didn't get any money."

"Your boys went to the cinema with their friends the other day. Pasquale paid for all the tickets." Ninetta raised an eyebrow. "How can a boy afford that sort of luxury?"

"Let me ask my sons." Norina poked her head out of the front entrance. "Mario! Pasquale! Come here right now," she called out.

The boys ran immediately into the house. Norina turned to Pasquale. "Is it true that Filomena the Grave Heart gave you the money for a gas tank and you used that money to go to the cinema with Mario and your friends?"

"No, Filomena the Grave Heart didn't give me anything. She didn't even give me a tip." Pasquale crossed his arms on his chest. "I swear on my *Papa*'s grave."

Ninetta glared at Pasquale. "I have witnesses. People saw you and your brother at the cinema with your friends. They also saw you pay for the tickets."

Pasquale's face blushed. "I did pay for the tickets."

Norina narrowed her eyes. "Where did you get the money to buy the tickets?"

"I got the money from Mrs. Fatti. Mario and I delivered a gas tank to her and she gave us a generous tip. She also gave us two chocolate bars each."

Norina's eyes flashed with anger as she held Pasquale by his ear. "You got a good tip and you wasted it on the cinema?"

"I only did it once." Pasquale contorted his face. "Please let go of my ear."

Mario burst into tears.

Norina gave Mario a harsh look. "Keep quiet. You're too dumb to have come up with such an idea. I can't blame it on you."

Ninetta stamped her foot. "I have to fire your sons."

Norina released Pasquale's ear. Her mouth fell open. "Why?"

"Because people who don't want to pay us could say that they gave the money to your sons." Ninetta marched out of the house.

Norina reached for her late husband's belt and gave Pasquale a whipping.

"For God's sake, I'm innocent," Pasquale yelled.

Mario cried silently with his head bent down.

Grazia ran down the stairs and bounded into the kitchen. "Leave him alone. He's only a kid."

Norina directed the whipping to her daughter.

Grazia didn't protest. *I'd rather get the beating than my brother.*

When Norina got tired swinging her late husband's belt, she went upstairs into the bedroom. Grazia burst out crying. Her brothers cried with her. Mario and Pasquale had a more important reason to cry: They had lost their only opportunity to make money.

Just as Ninetta the Gas Man's Wife had predicted, once rumors spread in town that Filomena the Grave Heart had accused Mario and Pasquale of stealing the gas tank money, a lot of customers swiftly claimed that they too had paid the boys. Soon the Voltini boys became the two most infamous thieves in town. When the scandal reached the ears of the Catholic League, Clotilde was utterly mortified.

Clotilde stormed into the Voltinis' house and shouted, "You want to drag my face through the mud again?"

Norina's eyes welled up with tears.

"Filomena the Grave Heart made the story up because she doesn't want to pay for the gas tank," Grazia said.

Mario sank into a chair and hugged his knees to stop them from trembling.

"They can't accuse us without evidence," Pasquale said. "We're innocent, and we can prove it."

"How are you going to prove it?" Clotilde asked.

"It's my word against theirs."

"Your word doesn't count." Clotilde banged her fist on the table. "You are a kid."

"We'll make it count." Pasquale flashed a bit of a smile. "I have witnesses. Mrs. Fatti will say she gave me the money as a tip. She'll also say she has never given me the fee for the gas tank. I wasn't allowed to collect payments for the tanks. Like you said, I'm just a kid."

He makes a lot of sense, Clotilde thought. *He talks like a lawyer.*

"We should consult Angela the Crazy Head," Grazia said. "She'll be able to give us advice."

Clotilde nodded. "Angela is smarter than a lawyer."

Later in the day, Clotilde, Norina, and Grazia paid Angela the Crazy Head a visit. Grazia told Angela about the accusations against her brothers and asked her to come up with a way out of the predicament. Angela agreed to find a solution.

"You know we can't afford a lawyer," Grazia said. "I hope we can count on your help."

"We can have a trial in the rectory of the church to clear the boys' names," Angela said. "I'll be their lawyer, and I'll convince Don Lorenzo to be the judge."

"That's a great idea," Clotilde said.

Norina and Grazia smiled in agreement.

When Filomena the Grave Heart was informed by Don Lorenzo that Angela the Crazy Head was having a mini-trial in the rectory of the church, she hired Mr. Claudio Querone, the most famous attorney in the region. Since Mr. Querone was a White Fly, he usually refused to represent poor people, who barely had the funds to pay him. He made an exception for Filomena the Grave Heart, enticed by the opportunity to match wits with Angela the Crazy Head. He resented the fact that Angela was highly praised for her learning and her cleverness. He felt that only men deserved recognition for such qualities.

Filomena the Grave Heart was confident she was going to win the case. *I have a real lawyer and so many witnesses. I convinced lots of people in town that the boys stole the gas tank money. Plus, all the people who don't want to pay for their gas tanks are going to testify in my favor. It's going to be the customers' word against the word of two boys. Who's going to believe the Voltini boys? I know for sure that one of them is retarded.*

In the rectory of the church Angela had arranged chairs, a table, and a witness stand the same way they were positioned in a real courtroom. She even placed a Bible on the witness stand. The trial was well attended. People were eager to see Angela the Crazy Head compete against a legitimate attorney, Mr. Claudio Querone.

The Voltini family wore their best attire for the occasion.

Grazia smiled at her friends in the audience. *They all came to give us moral support.*

The Margassi Sisters and the Dumb Brothers waved at Grazia. It was a special event for them. They were excited to be spectators at a trial. Grazia waved back. She was honored by their courtesy. Grazia froze when she spotted Colombina the Farmer's Wife and Giorgio. Colombina was there to witness the Voltinis' failure and humiliation, while Giorgio wanted to get another chance to see Grazia.

Grazia's secret admirer, Carlo the Broken Neck, was also in the audience. He wasn't interested in the trial. He wanted an opportunity to talk to Grazia. He just kept staring at her. He was so captivated by Grazia that he didn't notice the Margassi Sisters seated in the audience. The Margassi Sisters flinched when they spotted Carlo the Broken Neck.

Don Lorenzo took his seat on the bench reserved for the judge. Angela the Crazy Head looked great clad in a black suit she had borrowed from an American Wife. Mr. Querone wore a high-end tailored gray suit and a burgundy silk tie.

"I call Mrs. Crescenza Atoni to the witness stand," Mr. Querone shouted.

People in the audience wondered who the woman was. When a tall brunette woman got up from her seat, they realized Crescenza Atoni was Zina the Silk Stockings.

"How come he didn't call her by her nickname?" a farmer whispered to a White Fly.

"They don't use nicknames in court," the White Fly whispered back.

Mr. Querone turned to the witness. "Mrs. Crescenza Atoni, place your hand on the Bible and repeat after me: I swear to tell the truth, the whole truth, and nothing but the truth, so help me God."

Zina revealed a half-smile when she swore on the Bible, repeating the attorney's words.

The use of the Bible impressed many people in the audience.

"This is serious stuff," Lina the Warm House said.

"Keep quiet," said a voice behind her.

The audience was transfixed on Mr. Querone. Everybody was waiting for the attorney to pose the first question. After a lengthy pause he asked, "Mrs. Atoni, did you pay for your gas tank?"

Zina nodded. "Of course I paid. I don't have any debts. I pay up front for everything I buy."

"To who did you give the fee for the gas tank?"

"To the boys."

"Mrs. Atoni, you have to be more specific."

"To the Voltini boys." Zina indicated Pasquale and Mario, seated in the first row.

Pasquale beat his thighs with his fists while Mario hid his face with his hands.

"No further questions," the attorney said.

Angela the Crazy Head approached Zina and asked, "Mrs. Atoni, did you give the alleged payment to Mr. Pasquale Voltini and Mr. Mario Voltini personally? Remember, you are under oath."

"I did."

"No further questions."

Zina walked back to her seat.

"I call Mrs. Filomena Bavordi to the witness stand," Mr. Querone said.

People in the audience whispered among themselves.

"Who is Filomena Bavordi?" Margherita asked.

"Filomena the Grave Heart, the bitch that accused the boys of stealing," Anna the Heavyweight whispered.

"Silence," Don Lorenzo yelled.

A deep silence dominated the room. Filomena Bavordi, also known as Filomena the Grave Heart walked to the witness stand and swore on the bible.

The attorney asked, "Mrs. Bavordi, did you give the cash to pay for your gas tank to Mr. Pasquale Voltini and Mr. Mario Voltini?"

"I did, and I also gave them a tip," Filomena responded.

Pasquale jumped up from his chair. "What a liar!"

Grazia grabbed Pasquale's arm and forced him to sit down.

Pasquale twisted his face as if he was about to cry. "If all these people keep telling lies, we're going to lose the case."

Grazia placed her hand over Pasquale's mouth. "Keep quiet."

People in the audience turned their attention to Angela the Crazy Head, who was about to cross-examine Filomena the Grave Heart.

"Mrs. Bavordi, are you certain you gave the money personally to Mr. Pasquale Voltini and Mr. Mario Voltini?" Angela asked.

"I'm certain," Filomena replied.

"When did you give them the money?"

"A month ago."

"No further questions."

As Filomena the Grave Heart walked back to her seat, she sensed people's eyes on her.

Filomena felt like a movie star. "How did I do?"

Zina the Silk Stockings patted Filomena's arm and whispered, "You were great."

Grazia clasped her hands together hard, to keep them from shaking. *Things don't look good. We may lose the case.*

Don Lorenzo asked, "Mr. Querone, do you have anyone else you would like to call forth?"

"Not at this time," Mr. Querone replied.

Don Lorenzo turned to Angela, "Then you may proceed."

"I call to the witness stand Mrs. Anna Ventuni, also known as Anna the Heavyweight," Angela said.

Anna the Heavyweight strutted towards the stand. She placed her hand on the Bible and said, "I swear to tell the very truth, all the very truth, and nothing else but the very truth, so please help me God."

"Mrs. Ventuni, are you a good friend of Mr. Paolo Orvei?" Angela asked.

"Paolino the Gas Man is more than a friend. He's my godson," Anna replied. "He pays me a lot of respect. He always invites me to his house and gives me wine."

"Do you spend a lot of time in Mr. Orvei's house?"

"Yes."

Mr. Querone looked at Don Lorenzo. "Objection. The question is irrelevant."

"We don't know yet if it's relevant or not," Don Lorenzo said.

Angela continued the interrogation: "Mrs. Ventuni, do you know Mrs. Crescenza Atoni, nicknamed Zina the Silk Stockings?"

"I know her very well, and I also know for sure that she never paid for her last gas tank that she got."

"Explain how you can determine Mrs. Crescenza Atoni never paid for the gas tank."

"A month ago, Paolino came to my house and begged me to ask Zina to pay for her gas tank. So I went to Zina's house and I asked her for the money."

"Did Mrs. Crescenza Atoni give you the money?"

"She didn't give me the money. She told me that she had a rich cousin named Colino who was going to pay the debt for her."

"And what happened?"

"I asked Colino to pay for the tank, but he didn't give me the money."

"Can you explain why?"

"Colino said that he wasn't Zina's cousin. He also said that his wife had a bad fight with Zina and didn't want him to talk to Zina. Colino also said that he treated Zina like a princess. He paid a lot of Zina's debts. He gave her a lot of presents, and once he even bought her a whole lamb."

The spectators instantly deduced that Zina's supposed cousin was indeed her lover. Zina's face turned beet red from embarrassment.

Angela faced the audience. "Mrs. Crescenza Atoni couldn't possibly have given the money to pay for the gas tank to Mr. Pasquale Voltini and Mr. Mario Voltini if she promised Mrs. Anna Ventuni that her imaginary cousin, Colino, was going to settle the bill. I can also prove that Mrs. Crescenza Atoni has committed perjury, by claiming to have no debts. She asserted that she pays for everything she buys. According to Mrs. Anna Ventuni, Mrs. Crescenza Atoni had plenty of debts, and doesn't settle her debts personally. She relies on her imaginary cousin Colino to provide for her."

Angela's statement created an escalating buzz in the audience.

"Silence," Don Lorenzo shouted.

Overawed by the judge, the people in the audience kept quiet.

"I have no further questions," Angela said.

Anna the Heavyweight flashed a light smile, even though she didn't understand half of what Angela had said.

Mr. Querone took the floor. "Mrs. Anna Ventuni, you mentioned that Mr. Paolo Orvei pays you a lot of respect, and offers you wine when you visit him."

"He gives me homemade wine," Anna said. "He makes the best homemade wine in town."

"Do you like to drink wine?"

"Yes, I like wine very much."

"How many glasses of wine do you usually drink?"

"I can drink a whole bottle of wine."

"So it's possible you were drunk when Mrs. Crescenza Atoni allegedly told you about her rich cousin."

Anna shook her head. "I was not drunk."

"How can you be certain?"

"Because when I get drunk, I don't remember anything."

Many people in the audience giggled. Mr. Querone gave them a harsh look. He turned to Anna. "No further questions."

Anna scrunched her forehead. She remained still. Don Lorenzo noticed her perplexity and said, "You may leave the stand."

Waving vivaciously, Anna the Heavyweight headed to her seat. Many of the spectators shook her hand. She felt like a celebrity.

Angela the Crazy Head said, "I call Mrs. Veronica Guardoni, also known as Old Veronica, to the witness stand."

Old Veronica walked up to the witness stand and swore on the bible.

"Mrs. Guardoni, do you know Mrs. Filomena Bavordi, also known as Filomena the Grave Heart?" Angela asked.

"I know Filomena Bavordi very well," Old Veronica responded. "I worked for her."

"What sort of work do you do?"

"I pray for people who are sick or dead."

"When was the last time you were employed by Mrs. Bavordi?"

"Two months ago. Filomena hired me to pray for her mother, who was very sick. Many people in town say that Filomena doesn't talk to her mother. I want them to know that she made peace with her mother."

"Mrs. Bavordi's mother lives in town?"

"No, she lives out of town."

"How long were you out of town with Mrs. Bavordi?"

"For five weeks. We got back three weeks ago."

"So Mrs. Filomena Bavordi was out of town a month ago."

"Yes."

"I have no further questions." Angela shifted her attention to the audience. "Ladies and gentlemen, I can prove Mrs. Filomena Bavordi's testimony is false. She claimed she gave the money for the gas tank personally to Mr. Pasquale Voltini and Mr. Mario Voltini a month ago, but she couldn't possibly have done so if she was out of town."

Angela shifted her attention to the lawyer. "Mr. Querone, you can cross-examine the witness if you please."

Mr. Querone turned to the witness. "Mrs. Guardoni, how old are you?"

"I'm eighty-one years old."

"Do you have a tendency to forget things?"

Old Veronica shook her head. "No, I have a good memory. I remember all the prayers."

"Are you sure Mrs. Filomena Bavordi was out of town a month ago?"

"I'm more than sure. I have a letter here that I wrote for a friend, telling her that I was away with Filomena. You can look at the date." Old Veronica produced a postmarked envelope.

"No further questions."

Old Veronica returned to her seat.

Angela stared at the audience. "Ladies and gentlemen, there is no proof that Mr. Pasquale Voltini and Mr. Mario Voltini misappropriated the money for the gas tanks."

"There is one question that has not been answered," Mr. Querone said. "Where did the defendants get the money to go to the cinema?"

"I have an answer," Angela said. "I call Mrs. Matilde Fatti to the witness stand."

The American Wife looked distinguished in a conservative black outfit. She enjoyed the attention she got from people as she swore on the Bible. She was eager to be interviewed.

Angela said, "Mrs. Fatti, you're well known for your generosity. It's said that you give the best gratuities in town. I would like to know the amount of the gratuity you gave to Mr. Pasquale Voltini and Mr. Mario Voltini when they delivered the gas tank to your home."

"Two hundred and fifty lire," the American Wife said.

It was an outrageous tip. The spectators murmured among themselves.

"Silence," Don Lorenzo shouted.

A deep silence descended in the audience.

Angela continued her line of questioning. "Mrs. Fatti, I would also like to know if you ever paid Mr. Pasquale Voltini and Mr. Mario Voltini for the gas tank."

"I never paid the Voltini boys. I was instructed by Mr. Paolino Orvei never to give the boys payment for the gas tank itself."

Angela beamed. "Thank you for the information. I have no further questions."

Mr. Querone turned to the American Wife. "Mrs. Fatti, please explain why you gave Mr. Pasquale Voltini and Mr. Mario Voltini a gratuity of two hundred and fifty lire? Not even a millionaire would be so generous."

"The real millionaires are those who are generous to the less fortunate," the American Wife said.

The poor people in the audience stood up and clapped their hands. Mrs. Fatti felt like a superstar. Don Lorenzo enjoyed the scene so much that he didn't even bother to tell the spectators to keep quiet.

Mr. Querone's face flushed as he said, "No further questions."

The next witness to take the stand was Ciriaco the Tower, the tallest man in town. He swore confidently on the Bible without even being asked to do so.

Angela interrogated him promptly: "Mr. Ciriaco Corri, your job consists of selling tickets at the cinema box office."

Ciriaco bobbed his head in agreement even though he didn't quite understand the meaning of the word "consists."

"You have the reputation of having a brilliant memory. It's said that you remember the plot of every movie."

Ciriaco flashed a light smile. "I remember everything."

"Do you know Mr. Pasquale Voltini and Mr. Mario Voltini?"

Ciriaco raised his eyebrows.

Angela pointed at the Voltini boys seated in the first row.

Ciriaco nodded. "Yes, I know them."

"How many times have you seen Mr. Pasquale Voltini and Mr. Mario Voltini in the cinema over the last two months?"

Ciriaco held up his index finger. "One time."

"Did they come in company of their friends?"

"Yes."

"How many friends did they take with them?"

Ciriaco displayed three fingers.

"Three friends?"

"Three."

"Mr. Pasquale Voltini and Mr. Mario Voltini came to the cinema with three friends, Mr. Biagio Tormi, Mr. Luigi Felini, and Mr. Alberto Zerri. Is that correct?" Angela indicated the boys sitting in the first row.

The boys got up from their seats and bowed, overwhelmed to be addressed formally. Mario wondered why he was called Mr. Mario Voltini. No one had ever called him that before today.

"Yes," Ciriaco said. "The boys all came together to the cinema."

"How much is a movie ticket?"

"Fifty lire."

"How many tickets did Mr. Pasquale Voltini purchase?"

"Five tickets."

Angela raised her voice. "How much is five times fifty?"

"Two hundred and fifty." Ciriaco stood still. He felt like he was being interrogated by a teacher.

"No further questions." Angela turned to Mr. Querone. "You can cross-examine the witness."

Mr. Querone twisted and rubbed his hands together. "I have to go. I have a real court hearing to attend."

The spectators chatted among themselves as Mr. Querone rushed out of the room. Angela the Crazy Head had defeated a legitimate practicing attorney.

"I can't believe that a woman won the case against a real lawyer," Ciriaco said, walking back to his seat.

"Angela is brilliant," a White Fly whispered.

"She's better than the lawyer," a farmer whispered back.

Don Lorenzo banged his fist on the table. "Silence."

Angela got the immediate attention of the audience. "Ladies and gentlemen, the evidence proves Mr. Pasquale Voltini and Mr. Mario Voltini are innocent. Mrs. Fatti tipped them with two hundred and fifty lire. The boys went to the cinema once and spent two hundred and fifty lire on their tickets, since they brought three friends with them. Five times fifty is two hundred and fifty." Angela narrowed her eyes. "There's no proof Mr. Pasquale Voltini and Mr. Mario Voltini stole the money for the gas tanks to pay for the movie tickets."

Pasquale and Mario got up from their seats and waved their hands up in the air.

"Whoever spread these rumors and accusations... lied," Angela shouted.

A deep silence descended on the audience. People turned their stares to Filomena the Grave Heart and Zina the Silk Stockings. Their faces turned beet red as they experienced the most humiliating moment of their lives.

"Judge Don Lorenzo is ready to pronounce his judgment," Angela said.

Many in the audience instantly got up from their chairs, eager to listen to the judge.

"There's no evidence to incriminate the Voltini boys," Don Lorenzo said. "They are victims of false accusations. Mr. Mario Voltini and Mr. Pasquale Voltini are declared not guilty. Their names and reputations are hereby cleared."

Angela the Crazy Head faced the public. "Henceforth, anyone who persists in accusing Mr. Pasquale Voltini and Mr. Mario Voltini of misappropriating gas tank payments is at risk of being sued for slander."

The word "slander" scared off a lot of people. People that were accused of slander couldn't leave the country unless the accusation was withdrawn. Many of the unemployed people in town were hoping to find work in Switzerland and Germany. The spectators murmured amongst themselves.

"Silence," Don Lorenzo shouted.

The spectators again stopped chattering and shifted their attention to Angela.

"I have a list of all individuals who claim to have paid Mr. Pasquale Voltini and Mr. Mario Voltini for the gas tanks and have refused to pay Mr. Paolo Orvei." Angela raised her voice. "These individuals should pay their debt to Mr. Paolo Orvei today. Mr. Paolo Orvei, also known as Paolino the Gas Man will take legal action against anyone who refuses to do so."

Many people got in line to give Paolino the Gas Man the cash they had handy. Paolino received a considerable amount of money. It was an interesting scene. People were filled with shame and embarrassment as they paid their debts. Filomena the Grave Heart and Zina the Silk Stockings felt the weight of the town's scrutiny on them when they handed their lira coins to Paolino.

Paolino gave Angela a handshake. "You're smarter than a lawyer."

"If it weren't for you, we'd be out of business," Ninetta said, giving Angela a hug.

Grazia was glad that Angela had saved her family's reputation. Having a pair of thieves for brothers was worse than being poor.

"You are a great woman," Grazia said as she embraced Angela.

Norina's thoughts shifted to Grazia's portrait on display in the photo studio. The trial had generated good publicity for the whole family. Perhaps now the portrait would have a better chance of being noticed.

The Dumb Brothers bowed and kissed Angela's hand.

"You're smarter than any man," the elder Dumb Brother said.

"If someone ruins our reputations, are you going to defend us?" the younger Dumb Brother asked.

Angela smiled. "Of course."

Anna the Heavyweight pushed the Dumb Brothers away, impatient to talk to Angela.

"How did I do?" Anna asked.

"You were wonderful," Angela replied.

Ninetta and Norina thanked Anna for being the key witness for the trial.

"I really loved the trial." Anna's face radiated. "It was like being part of a novel."

The Margassi Sisters were so honored to have witnessed a trial they thanked Grazia for including them. Carlo the Broken Neck was eager to approach Grazia, but he hurriedly turned his head and pretended to look elsewhere as soon as he noticed the Margassi Sisters talking to her.

I'd rather meet Grazia on another occasion, Carlo thought, quickening his pace as he exited the room.

"Angela, you are indeed the smartest *signora* in town, and Don Lorenzo is the wisest man in town," Clotilde said.

Norina and Ninetta thanked Old Veronica for testifying as well.

Ninetta patted Old Veronica's shoulder. "I also have to thank you for praying for my husband. Paolino is feeling better now. His back pains are gone, and he can carry the gas tanks by himself again."

Norina clenched her teeth. *Paolino has no more use for my boys since he no longer has back pains.*

Though the Voltini boys had their names and reputations cleared, they had lost their jobs.

What good is a good name if you have no money? Norina thought.

Norina wished her boys were smart enough to have actually stolen some of the money of the gas tanks. At least then they would have had some cash. After all, Angela the Crazy Head was so smart that she probably could have cleared their names even if they had been guilty.

XXXI

One by one, the doors on Horseshoe Street began to open. It seemed as if they were yawning, like people who had gotten up from their afternoon naps. Marta was the only person on the block who usually stayed awake during the siesta. She was sewing seated in a chair by her front door. Marta gritted her teeth when she saw Norina emerging down the street.

"What brings you here?" Marta asked as Norina stepped forward.

"I came to see my brother," Norina said. "How is he doing?"

She came to check if her brother has any food to give her. "He's doing badly. He can hardly get any work." Marta huffed. "I'm working like a mule. I've been sewing since six o'clock this morning. I want to take advantage of the daylight. I don't want to sew at night, when I have to turn on the lights. The electricity is expensive."

"Is Vituccio home?"

"Vituccio isn't home. He went to look for work."

Marta dispensed those lies for fear that her husband would give Norina food again. A farmer had just given Vituccio a whole basket of vegetables, and she didn't want to share it with anyone.

Norina's face drooped. "I'm going to come back another time."

"Come another time, but let's make things clear: I have no food to give you." Marta got up from the chair. "My sky is as dark as black velvet."

"I don't need food," Norina mumbled, moseying away.

On the contrary, Norina was in dire need of groceries. A familiar desperation swept over her. She resisted sniveling on the street, and forced a smile to Concetta the Holy Water, who was seated knitting a shawl at her post by her front door.

Concetta put her work aside. "Your brother and his wife haven't fought in a week. You know that I always have holy water in my house. I threw some holy water on their front door. When I get a chance I'm going to throw holy water on your brother, maybe he's going to stop seeing his whores. But he needs more than holy water. He has to go to confession otherwise; he's going to go back to them for sure."

Norina didn't have the strength to speak in her brother's defense. She ambled away. The farmers had their fruits and vegetables on display on the chairs by their front doors. Norina inspected them hungrily. As she noticed a little basket filled with cherries, she recalled it was the time of year when Count Torre usually had sour cherries jarred.

When Norina got home, her somber expression revealed her mood.

"What happened?" Grazia asked.

"Marta has no food to give me. She said that Vituccio is having trouble finding work." Norina breathed out heavily. "No one gives me any jobs. Count Torre usually lets me jar the sour cherries at this time of year, but he hasn't sent for me."

Grazia patted Norina's shoulder. "Don't worry, *Mamma*. The cherry season isn't over yet."

"I think that Count Torre forgot all about the cherries. Rich people have a lot of things on their minds. I wanted to go and ask him, but I'm ashamed to talk to him because I don't speak good Italian. He uses difficult words when he talks. Sometimes I don't understand him." Norina produced some tears. "You have to go and talk to him."

"Let's wait. Why beg him to give you the job? He's going to call you sooner or later anyway."

Norina banged her fist on the table. "Our sky is as dark as black velvet."

"I'll pay him a visit, and I'll convince him to hire you." Grazia widened her eyes, surprised by her own words.

Norina tapped her feet. "Go right now. If I don't get any work, I'm going to go crazy."

"I'll go… but please calm down."

"Don't tell anybody. It doesn't look right when a young woman goes to a married man's house."

"I won't tell anybody." Grazia bit her tongue. *I would be too ashamed to tell anybody. I'm not allowed to go dancing with my friends for the sake of my reputation, but I'm allowed to visit a man at his house and beg him to employ my mother. My mother doesn't understand how humiliating this is. Count Torre is a horrible man. He keeps his wife a prisoner in her own house.*

As soon as Grazia walked out of the house, she noticed Carlo the Broken Neck. She wondered why he was standing across the street from her home, and concluded that he must be waiting for someone. Grazia was not aware Carlo was waiting for her. His eyes were fixed on her. He was filled with the burning desire to possess her.

I'm going to find a way to get ahold of Grazia, Carlo fantasized while following her from a distance.

When Grazia arrived at Count Torre's sprawling *palazzo*, she reluctantly rang the bell. The door swung open and the tall maid appeared.

"I need to talk to Count Torre," Grazia said.

She probably has an appointment with him. She's the youngest and prettiest one yet, the maid thought. "He's busy."

"I'll wait."

The maid led Grazia into the living room and withdrew. Grazia sat on a red sofa. A deep silence engulfed the room. After waiting for almost an hour, Grazia grew restless.

At the sound of footsteps, Grazia couldn't resist the impulse to walk out of the room. *That must be the maid. I'll tell her I'd rather leave than wait any longer.*

In the hallway, she bumped into a stunning lady wearing a black cape. The lady resembled Our Lady of Sorrows. She looked like a vision to Grazia.

"Can I help you?" the lady asked.

"I'm Grazia, Norina's daughter. I live down the street."

The lady revealed a diminutive smile. "I know who you are. I see everybody through the shutters of my window, even though nobody sees me."

Grazia bounced. "You're Contessa Fiorella, Count Torre's wife."

"Yes, I'm his unfaithful wife."

Grazia beamed as she extended her hand. "I'm so pleased to meet you."

The contessa shook Grazia's hand. "I'm pleased to meet you too. You're such a kind girl. You work hard to help your family."

"I'm here to help my mother out. Your husband has always given my mother the job of jarring fruits and vegetables. He hasn't called her in a while, and my mother asked me to remind him. I'm so embarrassed. Believe me, I don't want to impose."

"I understand. You wish you could be true to yourself and do only what you believe is right."

"Of course. I have to act like I'm someone else to ask your husband to give my mother a job."

"At the moment, my husband is busy. He's in bed with his mistress."

Grazia's mouth fell open. "He has a mistress?"

"He has always cheated on me. He believes he's entitled to cheat. I only cheated on him once, because I fell in love." The contessa's eyes became gloomy. "I was severely punished for that."

"You should leave him."

The contessa bit her lip so as not to cry. "There's no escape for women in a town like this."

"No escape?"

"Women are trapped. They are imprisoned. I'm not the only one who's locked up here. Other women are imprisoned in different ways.

Most of the women in the town can't be themselves, or who they want to be. They're imprisoned. They're trapped."

Grazia remained silent.

"Come back tomorrow. You're a stunning young woman. My husband looks at beautiful women with lust. He'll definitely ask you to become his lover. He'll never give your mother a job if you don't let him think he has a chance."

"You want me to do that?"

"He deserves to have someone make a fool out of him. He's always making a fool out of women."

"You're right."

"Your mother made a big mistake by allowing you to talk to him."

"I didn't want to talk to him."

"I know that. You have dignity and pride. I empathize with you. You're too honest to sell your soul."

"You're the only person in this town who understands me." Grazia's eyes lit up. "You know who I truly am."

"I know everything that goes on in our little town. I'm writing a book about Vocevero. Writing saves me from insanity. I am the author of the novels that Angela the Crazy Head has been reading in your house." The contessa revealed a smile. "Angela told me all about the reactions of the listeners."

"You're an extraordinary author. I loved your novels."

"You're the heroine of my latest manuscript. You are a great character. You deserve to be in my novel."

Grazia's face radiated. "I'm honored to be included in your new novel."

"It has been a pleasure meeting you." The contessa suddenly left, and disappeared down the hallway.

Grazia felt like she had just woken up from a dream. She attempted to say something, but no words came out of her mouth. She then recalled that she had actually shaken the contessa's hand, and concluded it must have been a real experience. She was thrilled by the news that Contessa Fiorella was the author of the novels Angela the Crazy Head had read.

Grazia's eyes gleamed with excitement. *I have the honor of being the heroine of the contessa's new manuscript,* she thought as she dashed out of the *palazzo.* She didn't notice Carlo the Broken Neck standing on the street corner.

She's definitely Count Torre's mistress. He likes young women. He's very generous to them. I can be as generous as he is. I'm willing to pay any price for her, Carlo thought, wearing a sinister grin.

When Grazia arrived home, Norina was waiting in the doorway. Grazia immediately let her mother know she would need to go back the next day to see Count Torre. Caterina and Pasquale wanted to know if Grazia had seen Contessa Fiorella. Grazia proclaimed to her siblings she had indeed seen the contessa.

Caterina raised an eyebrow. "Everybody says that. Even Pasquale said that he saw her."

"I did see her," Pasquale said.

Caterina giggled. "Liars should have a good memory."

"What do you mean?"

"Once you said that the contessa had brown eyes. Another time, you said that she had green eyes."

Pasquale remained speechless.

"She has the most beautiful blue eyes," Grazia said.

Caterina narrowed her eyes. "I still don't believe that you saw her."

Grazia shrugged. "You are free to believe what you want to believe."

Grazia didn't tell her siblings she was the leading character of a manuscript Contessa Fiorella was writing. She knew they would never believe that.

Grazia had a hard time sleeping that night. She kept thinking about Contessa Fiorella's words. Those words were ingrained in her mind.

"There's no escape for women in a little town. Women are trapped. They are imprisoned. I'm not the only one who's locked up here. Other women are imprisoned in different ways."

As Grazia gave it more thought, she realized women indeed were imprisoned. Maddalena stayed with her insanely jealous husband, and suffered endless abuse from him because of his money. Even her Aunt Ada stayed with her vicious, controlling husband because of his wealth. Women needed their husbands' resources to survive. They didn't have the freedom to be themselves because they couldn't be economically independent. They were like marionettes, and their husbands held the strings.

Many women who married rich men to escape the trap of poverty found themselves incarcerated in an even more insidious trap. They didn't have the freedom to be themselves. People in town blamed Contessa Fiorella for her own imprisonment. They believed she could have led a good life if she had been faithful to her husband. The contessa had refused to be a marionette, and had chosen to be herself. She was fully herself when she had fallen in love.

Love was an indulgence women who were not economically independent couldn't grant themselves. Only successful women like Saveria the Midwife were free to choose who they would love. Saveria had the luxury of being herself, or whoever she wanted to be. She had the same freedom as a man, and she behaved like one because she made her own money. Grazia realized happiness was freedom: freedom to love, freedom to speak your mind, and freedom to be yourself.

Marriage for many poor women had nothing to do with love. They married to survive. For many indigent women, marriage was a more dangerous trap than poverty. Transported by her reverie, for a moment Grazia dreamt of being an independent woman just like Saveria the Midwife, and marrying a man who allowed her to be herself. It was peculiar that the man she envisioned didn't look like Giorgio. It was a man with values and principles. A man filled with compassion and sensitivity. A gentleman who truly loved her.

Grazia wanted a real man who would recognize her freedom to leave whenever she felt trapped, imprisoned and unhappy. The distinguished man she had met at Mrs. Zordi's house came to her mind. She had been so flummoxed that she didn't even comprehend his name when he had introduced himself. She wondered what his name was, and where he came from. Her whole face coruscated when she recalled that Mrs. Francesca Zordi had mentioned her friend was soon going to be spending a few days at her house.

Everybody was asleep when Grazia woke up the following morning. She wanted to sneak out of the house before anybody got up. Grazia knew her mother would presume she had gone to visit Count Torre. She slid into her black dress and then proceeded to reach for her lipstick, her comb, and her flower print dress. She placed them in her bag and rushed out of the house. On the street, she walked swiftly with her head down to avoid greeting people.

When Grazia arrived at the train station, she promptly went into the bathroom and changed into her flower print dress. She checked herself in the mirror, combed her hair neatly, and applied lipstick on her lips. She perked up as she flashed a smile. She looked great! She resembled the person she wanted to be. She hoped the distinguished man would see her when she looked her best. She recalled that she had looked her worst the first time he met her. She was sad then, and her mourning dress had made her look even sadder.

Even when Grazia got on the train, she couldn't stop thinking about the distinguished man. He was fascinating, intelligent, and sensitive. She yearned to see him again. She had to think of a reason to visit Mrs. Francesca Zordi. Though she went over it in her head many times, she couldn't come up with a good excuse. Maybe she didn't need an excuse. She could simply tell Mrs. Zordi she wanted to see the distinguished man. She promptly abandoned that idea. She wouldn't ever have the courage to admit her feelings for him. Her eyes lit up at the idea of saying she had a party to go to, and had decided to stop by since she was in the area. But what party? She would have to make up a specific party… like a friend's birthday party. It sounded believable. When she got off the train, she quickened her pace and headed to the Zordi residence.

Once she reached the house, Grazia rang the bell. The door opened and Mrs. Francesca Zordi appeared.

"I'm on my way to my friend Patrizia's birthday party… and since she lives nearby, I decided to pass by to show you the dress, because I made the dress myself," Grazia said.

"You look wonderful. The dress is lovely. You're very talented. I've never seen you in such a colorful dress. It's too bad that my friend didn't come. I would have loved to show you off in your vibrant outfit. Last time he saw you, you looked so gloomy in your black dress. He couldn't understand why a young woman like you would dress all in black. I had to explain that you'd been wearing mourning clothes since your father passed away."

Grazia then blushed as she mustered the courage to inquire about the distinguished man. Her lips trembled as she asked, "Your friend was supposed to come?"

"He was supposed to come, but he cancelled at the last minute. I'm planning a trip to Paris. I'm going to ask him to visit me there."

Grazia forced a smile.

"Would you like a cup of coffee?"

"No, thank you. I have to go to the party." Grazia lowered her head as she left the house.

Tears rolled down Grazia's face as she walked down the street. When she arrived back at the train station, she went into the bathroom and changed into her mourning dress.

I'm never going to see the distinguished man again. The mirror reflected Grazia's heartbroken face.

As she exited the bathroom, she recalled that she still had to pay a visit to Count Torre.

Later in the day, the tall maid greeted Grazia at the *palazzo* with a half-grin. "You're back."

Grazia followed the maid up the stairs. In the hallway, the maid indicated the library to Grazia. When Grazia entered the room, she saw Count Torre. He was standing by the window smoking a cigar. He was a tall man in his late fifties with gray hair, a big moustache, and silver eyeglasses. He looked at her from head to toe. Grazia blushed as she realized his eyes were inspecting her.

"You're early, but I'll make an exception for you. I'll discuss business with you right now." Count Torre narrowed his eyes. "Your face looks familiar. I've seen you somewhere."

"I'm Grazia, Norina's daughter."

Count Torre took a drag of his cigar. "Norina, I think I know her. That name sounds familiar."

"Norina jarred some eggplants for you not long ago."

He took another drag of his cigar. "Oh, yes. I remember her."

"My mother jarred the sour cherries last year. She was wondering if she could jar the cherries for you this year as well."

"I'm glad you reminded me… I'll send Giovanni the Farmer to your house first thing in the morning with a whole case of cherries." Count Torre winked, pointing the cigar at her. "Whenever your mother needs more work, feel free to come and ask. I'll be glad to see you again."

"If you give my mother more work, you're definitely going to see me again." Grazia widened her eyes, surprised by her own words.

"Come on your mother's behalf when the cherry jars are ready." Puffing smoke into the air, he brushed his hand across her breasts. "I may have a generous gift for you."

Grazia summoned all her strength to force a smile.

He held her hand tightly and drew it to his crotch and pressed it on his penis. "I can teach you a lot of things."

When he finally let go of her hand, Grazia walked hastily out of the room. She wrinkled her nose. *What a beastly man! If my mother didn't need the job, I would have spat in his face. He forces his wife to be a prisoner in the house because she cheated on him, and meanwhile he sleeps with every girl he sees. I'd rather starve than come back to this house. I can't believe I was nice to him.* She dashed out of the *palazzo* not looking back.

As soon as Grazia arrived at her house, she informed her mother that Count Torre was going to send Giovanni the Farmer with the cherries to be jarred.

Norina stamped a kiss on her daughter's forehead. "Count Torre must have just forgotten to ask me to jar the cherries. Rich people forget things because they have a lot on their minds."

Grazia's eyes dimmed. *Rich men have young women on their minds.*

She couldn't stop thinking of how crude Count Torre was.

The following morning, Giovanni the Farmer delivered three cases of sour cherries, a kilogram of sugar, three bottles of rum, and two cases of jars to the Voltinis' house. Norina started the assignment immediately. She washed the cherries and placed them in a bucket filled with sugar and rum. She was dismayed by the realization that she had to marinate the sour cherries in the rum for two days before she could jar them. She wanted to complete her task as soon as possible. She was in great need of money.

Two days later, Norina finished jarring the sour cherries. She was glad she had finally concluded her work. She summoned Pasquale and Mario and instructed them to deliver the cases of the jarred cherries. The boys lifted the cases and followed her to Count Torre's *palazzo*, entertaining the hope that they would get to meet Contessa Fiorella.

At the *palazzo*, the tall maid greeted them with a nod. "Come with me," she said, leading them up the stairs into the hallway. She turned to the boys. "Wait here."

Pasquale nodded.

The maid escorted Norina to the library and walked away.

The boys' eyes bulged at the sight of a lady coming down the hallway. It was Contessa Fiorella. She looked like a vision to them.

"She's divine," Pasquale whispered.

Mario remained speechless. He kept staring at the contessa with his mouth wide open.

"You finally get to see me," Contessa Fiorella said, gliding forward. "I'm just as happy to see you. I hardly ever see anybody."

I'm going to tell all my friends she was happy to see me. In the moment, Pasquale couldn't find suitable words to say. He somehow mumbled, "I'm very pleased to meet you."

Mario remained silent.

Contessa Fiorella flashed a light smile. "I hope to see you again. You are great characters."

The boys watched her as she sashayed into her bedroom and disappeared behind the door.

Pasquale wondered what the contessa meant by "great characters." *How can a person be a character?*

Mario didn't know the meaning of the word "character" and didn't even bother to ask his brother. He was so thrilled to have seen the contessa that it didn't matter to him what she had said.

As soon as Norina bounded into the library, Count Torre clenched his teeth. He had flirted with the hope of seeing Grazia instead. He produced a fake smile and asked, "How is your lovely daughter?"

"She's fine," Norina replied.

"I'm happy to hear that." Count Torre handed Norina an envelope. He had another envelope in his pocket just in case Grazia had collected the money herself.

Norina flashed a light grin. "I can jar more fruits and vegetables."

Count Torre narrowed his eyes. "I'll think about it and I'll let you know. Today I have a lot of matters to address."

Norina's face brightened at the prospect that Count Torre would give her more work. She didn't have the slightest idea that he had already decided not to give her any jobs unless Grazia paid him another visit.

Pasquale and Mario joined their friends Biagino and Luigino, who were playing ball in the street.

"I spoke to Contessa Fiorella," Pasquale shouted.

Mario jumped up and down. "I-I saw-saw her-her too."

Biagino and Luigino promptly stopped playing and gave them their undivided attention.

Mario summoned his courage and said, "She-she was-was nice to-to us-us-us."

It must be true. Mario is too dumb to lie, Biagino thought. "What did she say?"

"Contessa Fiorella told me she's very lonely and wants to see me again," Pasquale said. "She also said I'm a great young man."

Luigino turned to Mario. "She said he's a great young man?"

Mario nodded. He didn't understand the difficult word "character" the contessa had used. He presumed it meant great young man.

"Please take me along when you go to the *palazzo* next time," Luigino said.

"Can I come too?" Biagino asked.

Pasquale winked. "I'll see what I can do."

Later in the day, Count Torre received an unexpected visitor: Carlo the Broken Neck.

"Do you have a hot lover that you can recommend to me?" Carlo asked.

Count Torre shook his head. "I don't have anyone good in bed at the moment."

"I've always been generous to you. I even handed you the Margassi Sisters when they were young and ripe."

The count took a drag of his cigar and blew the smoke into the air. "Those two sisters were not bad at all."

"You can pay me back by handing me your latest conquest. I really like her."

"Which one?"

"Grazia, the Voltini girl."

Count Torre expanded his eyes. "Her?"

"Yes. Have you slept with her?"

"Not yet, but I think she's a hard case."

Carlo broke into a wide smile. "I like hard cases."

"She's an inexperienced young woman."

"You can trap her with money. When the Margassi Sisters worked in my field, I overpaid them to encourage them to work for me again."

Count Torre inhaled his cigar and blew more smoke. "Grazia is so naïve that she doesn't even understand she has the prospect of making money. Plus, she probably doesn't have a clue of what to do with a man. She has no experience whatsoever."

"She's probably a virgin." Carlo's eyes lit up. "I love the ones who have no experience. I can mold them the way I want."

Count Torre crushed his cigar into the ashtray. "Give it a try. You know how to get women. You have your strategies. If you succeed, let me know… I like her as well."

Carlo winked. "I'll let you know."

XXXII

Little Donato cried uncontrollably when he realized that Chicken
Caterina was wounded. He saw Anna the Heavyweight pulling her
feathers out.

"Chicken Caterina break," the baby said. "Chicken Caterina no
move."

"Chicken Caterina is not going to move anymore because she
got killed by a bad wolf," Grazia said, hugging her little brother. "But
Chicken Grazia is fine and is going to come back soon.

Grazia sang a lullaby to calm him down. She was relieved when
Little Donato finally fell asleep.

"Chicken Grazia come back," Little Donato kept murmuring in
his sleep.

That evening, the Voltinis enjoyed a chicken meal. When they finished eating Norina's eyes shone with tears. She was on edge, knowing
the safety net of another chicken to kill was gone.

A sinister melancholy swept over Norina. Things had gotten so bad
that her children were constantly fighting over food. Their hunger bred
anger. Pasquale and Caterina were upset with Grazia because she had
again failed to bring food from the Zordi residence.

Pasquale shook Grazia's shoulder. "You don't think of us."

"You only think about yourself," Caterina yelled.

"I got caught stealing once," Grazia yelled back. "If I get caught a
second time, I'll lose my job."

Little Donato began to whimper.

"Go and fight outside," Norina shouted.

Pasquale ran out of the house. Even though Caterina picked up Little Donato and rocked him in her arms to quiet him down, the baby kept bawling.

Norina covered her ears with her hands. "I don't want to hear the baby cry."

Caterina escorted the baby out of the house.

"*Mamma*, you have to calm down," Grazia said.

Norina grabbed her hair. "I want to be alone."

As Grazia scrambled outside, Norina sank into a chair. A stream of worries invaded her mind. Carlo the Broken Neck had not made any attempt to propose marriage to Grazia. Norina figured his mother probably didn't want to give him the permission to marry a Voltini girl. Norina burst into tears as she thought that her sky was as dark as ever and was never going to change. She wept until her tears ran dry. The sound of footsteps coming from the street startled Norina. As she gazed at the front entrance, she saw the silhouette of a woman standing behind the fishnet curtain. It was Clotilde. Norina huffed when she noticed Clotilde wasn't carrying a bag. An empty-handed Clotilde was the last person she wanted to see.

Clotilde pulled the fishnet curtain aside and entered the house with a bright smile. "I have good news," she said, closing the curtain.

Norina flashed a hint of a smile. "You got another hundred-dollar bill?"

"No, I got a letter."

Norina's face drooped. "Just a letter?"

Clotilde drew a letter from her pocket. "This letter is worth more than a hundred-dollar bill."

Norina tilted her head and twisted her lips. "How can a letter be worth more than a hundred-dollar bill?"

Clotilde dumped her heavy body onto a chair that groaned under her weight. "My cousin Ignazio is such an angel. He's always helped me in difficult situations." She clutched the letter to her chest. "What a letter he's sent me!"

Norina shook Clotilde's arm. "Get to the point. I want to know how a letter can be worth more than a hundred-dollar bill."

Clotilde's face glowed, and she delivered the news slowly as if to savor it. "My dear cousin Ignazio showed Grazia's portrait to a friend… and… this charming young man wants to marry Grazia."

Norina's mouth opened but no words came out.

Clotilde raised her voice. "Do you understand? There's an American who wants to marry Grazia."

Norina trotted around the room. "Oh my God! Grazia is going to marry an American? Is it true? Can I see the letter?"

"It's true." Clotilde showed Norina the letter.

Norina attempted to puzzle out the composition of letters, which appeared to her as incomprehensible scribbles.

Clotilde wore her eyeglasses and pointed out the word "marry."

Norina beamed as she bounced up.

"The American who wants to marry Grazia is quite a handsome man. My cousin Ignazio also sent a picture of the suitor." Clotilde drew a tiny photograph from her pocket and pointed to the man next to Ignazio in the picture. "Ignazio looks very young. He took the picture many years ago. What do you think about the American?"

Norina stared at the picture. "But, you can hardly see the man who wants to marry Grazia."

"You can't see him well because you need eyeglasses. I can guarantee you he's a good-looking man. He has a refined look."

Norina's mind filled quickly with a deluge of questions. Among the questions, she picked the most important one. "Is he rich?"

"Everybody is rich in America."

Norina's face radiated. "You are right."

"Ignazio mentioned the suitor is related to the owner of the factory where he works. It's possible that he is the owner's son. Oh yes, he must be. Once, Ignazio wrote that he worked with the son of the industrialist."

"I don't understand. What's an 'industralist'?"

"An industrialist is an owner of a factory."

"What kind of factory? Where does Ignazio work?"

"He works in a factory that manufactures chandeliers."

Norina pictured a row of chandeliers like the ones she had seen at Mrs. Fatti's house, all lit up at the same time. She blinked her eyes as she visualized the light sparkling from them.

Clotilde took off her eyeglasses and gazed at Norina. "Let's talk about serious matters. Ignazio wants an answer as soon as possible. You've got to ask Grazia if she's willing to marry him."

Norina shrugged. "How can Grazia refuse such good fortune?"

"You have to make your daughter understand that this is a blessing from the sky." Clotilde waved the letter up in the air. "It's up to you to convince her to marry Sal…"

"What's his name?"

"His name is Sal."

"I've never heard such a name. What kind of name is it?"

"His real name is probably Salvatore."

"Salvatore is the perfect name for the savior of the family." Norina exhaled. "I can't wait to tell my relatives that Grazia is going to marry an American."

"You shouldn't tell anyone until Grazia accepts the marriage proposal."

"Can I tell people that an American wants to marry Grazia?"

Clotilde got up from the chair. "Why not?"

"People are not going to believe it."

"They have to believe it." Clotilde handed the letter to Norina. "You have a written letter. A letter is a document; it's black and white proof. You should show the letter to whoever doesn't believe you."

Norina stood still until Clotilde disappeared behind the fishnet curtain. She then placed the letter in her brassiere and danced around the kitchen. As she drew her hand to her chest, she felt her heart beating so fast that she almost lost her balance. Her sky was finally shining. Our Lady of Sorrows had finally answered her prayer, bringing happiness for both her and her daughter at the same time.

"My daughter is marrying an American," Norina kept repeating to herself.

The words were like a mirage looming in the distance, an illusion that was about to become reality.

"*He's not even a common American. He's a very rich man, the son of a factory owner*," Norina pictured herself telling people. Immersed in her reveries, Norina didn't even hear Grazia entering the house. As soon as she became aware of her daughter's presence, she sprang back to reality. "Grazia, we have to talk about an important matter."

"What matter?" Grazia asked.

"Grazia, do you remember when I had Maria the Purple Rose read your fortune and she said that your sky was going to change?"

Grazia nodded. "I remember, but it hasn't happened as far as I know."

"Luck is behind the door, and it knocks when you least expect it." Norina took a deep breath. "You got a marriage proposal. An American wants to marry you."

"How can that be possible? I don't think I've ever met a single man from America."

Norina flashed a light smile. "He saw you."

"When did he see me?"

"Clotilde sent one of your portraits to her cousin Ignazio, and he showed the portrait to him."

Grazia's mouth fell open. "An American asked to marry me? Just because he saw my portrait? He doesn't even know me."

"He's not a common American. He's a very, very rich man."

"Who is he?"

"He's Ignazio's friend."

"*Mamma*, I don't even know the man."

"You don't know how lucky you are to get this chance."

Grazia sank into her chair. "You expect me to marry a person I've never even seen? Are you out of your mind?"

"You can see him right now." Norina reached for Sal's photograph and showed it to Grazia. "He's the man next to Ignazio. What do you think? Do you like him?"

Grazia took a glance at the picture. "I don't know what to think. The photograph is so small and blurry."

Norina raised her voice. "How can you not like him? Aunt Clotilde said that he's a good-looking man."

"The face is so small in the picture that I can barely see it."

"But he's a good-looking man. He's tall and skinny. He's not an ordinary man. He's an important man. He's an American."

"I want to get to know him before I decide to marry him."

"You want to get to know him? You've seen what he looks like." Norina twisted her face as if she was about to cry. "Isn't it enough to meet him through the picture?"

Grazia shook her head. "It's not enough. I want to make sure I can get along with him before I decide to marry him."

"You must be out of your mind." Norina slammed her hands on the table. "You expect a man to spend the money for a trip all the way to Italy just to get to know a woman? He's not going to come to Italy if you don't guarantee that you are going to marry him."

Grazia stared at the wall. "I can't guarantee I'll marry him if I don't get to know him first."

Norina tapped her index finger on her temple. "You're crazy. You think you have the luxury of being picky. Don't you see that we barely have money for food? We're so poor that we don't even have the eyes to cry. Poor people don't have choices."

Grazia remained silent.

"This is a blessing from the sky. If this sort of luck had come to any other girl in town, she'd have married him for sure. Do you know what it means to marry an American? You're going to become a White Fly. Do you understand what it means to be a White Fly? You no longer have to behave like a Voltini."

Grazia didn't respond. *I may end up behaving like someone else. God knows if I'll ever be able to be myself.*

"You're going to have the best food, and all sorts of dresses made of silk. You're also going to get all the luxuries that Mrs. Zordi and Mrs. Fatti have: a television, a sink with running water, a 'refrigidade,' an electric iron, and many more…"

Grazia was impassive. No words came out of her mouth.

"What future do you have in this little town?" Norina produced some tears. "The best you can hope for is to get married to a farmer who gets hired to work in other people's fields as a day laborer once in a while, and gets you pregnant every year."

Grazia widened her eyes.

"Poor women are nothing but victims in this town. Men are more valuable than us. They have all the power." Norina folded her hands in prayer. "I'm sick and tired of living in poverty. Just because I'm poor, I can't do what I want to do. I can't be a good mother. I can't even provide enough food to feed my children. Don't you feel bad for Little Donato? His legs are still crooked because I can't give him enough milk. Our sky is dark. You're the only one who can change it."

Grazia remained speechless.

"You have the chance to change the sky and make it shine on us." Norina produced more tears. "You can live under a shining American sky, and you can share that sky with all of us."

Grazia was indifferent to Norina's tears. She knew her mother was able to produce tears whenever she wanted to manipulate someone.

"It's all up to you." Norina got down on her knees. "Our future is in your hands. You're the only one who can save us from poverty. Please, save us!"

Grazia got up from the chair. "I need some time to think about it."

Norina sprang off her knees. "I'm sure you are going to accept the American. Only a crazy person refuses such a blessing in life. There isn't a girl in town that is going to refuse to marry an American."

Grazia turned her back on her mother and went up the stairs.

The following day, when Norina strolled down the street, she noticed that many acquaintances that had fallen out with her over the Voltinis' various troubles now greeted her courteously. Some even smiled at her. Norina was stunned. Once Norina reached the *piazza*, she saw Domenico the Butcher talking to a White Fly. He was the last person she wanted to see. She had taken plenty of meat from him on credit, and had never paid him.

Norina's lips began to tremble. *I hope he doesn't yell at me in front of the White Fly.* Her jaw dropped when he grinned at her.

"Good to see you Norina," the butcher said.

"*Buongiorno*," Norina replied, hastening away.

Minutes later, when Norina bumped into Pasquina from the bottega, she quickened her pace in an attempt to avoid her.

Pasquina waved at Norina. "I haven't seen you at the bottega in a long time."

Encouraged by Pasquina's kindness, Norina headed to the bottega. *Pasquina and Domenico the Butcher must already know that Grazia got a marriage proposal from the American. Clotilde didn't waste any time. She told them for sure,* Norina thought. She was not aware Clotilde had paid her debts in full with money she had received from her American relatives.

As soon as Norina walked into the bottega, Teresina raised her hand in greeting.

Norina nodded hello. "Have you heard the news?"

"What news?" Teresina asked.

"An American wants to marry my daughter Grazia."

Teresina tilted her head and stared at Norina. Norina drew the letter from her brassiere and handed it to her.

Teresina read the letter speedily. "This is a marriage proposal from an American."

The news astounded all the customers in the store. They all gave Norina their congratulations.

"This is a blessing from the sky," a short credit customer said.

Teresina turned to Norina. "I'll give you all the credit you want. Take whatever you need."

The letter has more value than a hundred-dollar bill, Norina thought.

The letter was also a prestigious credit card. Norina took three kilograms of pasta, a liter of olive oil, half a kilogram of sugar, a kilogram of flour, and a kilogram of lentils. Norina's eyes sparkled when she dumped the groceries into her fishnet bag. The credit customers looked at Norina as if she had won the lottery.

Three credit customers followed her outside the bottega.

"Children can change your future," a chubby credit customer said.

"I wish my daughters were as lucky as your daughter," the short credit customer said.

"How did your daughter meet the American?" a tall credit customer asked.

"Through the portrait," Norina responded.

"The portrait?"

Norina winked. "My daughter's portrait was sent to my cousin in America and he showed it to his friend."

"I have a cousin in America too," the chubby credit customer said. "I'll send him my daughter's portrait. Maybe she'll have the same luck."

On her way home, Norina showed the letter to everyone she encountered. She enjoyed the amazement on their faces. People believed her.

Clotilde was right, Norina thought. *A letter is a document; it's black and white proof.*

Norina headed to Vituccio's house, eager to give him the good news. When she turned onto Horseshoe Street, she saw Marta seated by her front door and waved at her. Marta gritted her teeth. She didn't bother to wave back.

She thinks I came to ask for food, Norina thought as she walked forward. "I have good news."

"What's the good news?" Marta asked.

Norina handed the letter to Marta. "Grazia got a marriage proposal from an American."

After a quick read, Marta leaped from her chair. "Vituccio, come outside. Your niece is marrying an American."

In a fraction of a second, Vituccio emerged from the house.

Norina passed him the letter.

Vituccio read the letter and broke into a jubilant smile. "My niece deserves to marry an American. She's the prettiest girl in town."

Norina drew a kilogram of pasta wrapped in paper from her fishnet bag and handed it to her brother. "Take it. You didn't work for a long time. You can use it."

Vituccio shook his head. "I can't accept it."

Marta grabbed the bundle and held it to her bosom. "Well I can accept it."

"I want you to have it with all my heart." Norina said. "My sky has changed. I'm going to be able to help you now."

Vituccio stared at Norina with his mouth open.

Marta flashed a smile. "When the farmer prospers, so do his chickens."

As soon as Norina returned home, she went into the bedroom and kneeled in front of the statue of Our Lady of Sorrows and recited her prayers.

When she finished praying, Norina blew a kiss at the Madonna. "Thank you, my Lady, for sending me an American. I just need one more favor: Make sure that my daughter comes to her sense and accepts the marriage proposal."

Norina cooked a special meal: pasta and lentils for the main course and *frittelle* coated with sugar for dessert.

As everyone sat down to have dinner, Norina waved the letter up in the air. "We have something to celebrate. Grazia got a marriage proposal from an American."

The children jumped up and down. It seemed like Grazia had received a marriage proposal from a prince.

"Once Grazia marries the American, we can all go to America," Pasquale said.

Norina nodded. Grazia's face immediately flushed. She had no intention of marrying the American suitor.

XXXIII

In small towns, good news and bad news alike spreads faster than the wind. In less than a day, the entire municipality was aware that Grazia was marrying an American. Whenever a poor girl was betrothed to an American, she would become the envy of the town. Grazia was like the leading lady of a romantic movie. Norina, however, was more focused on the effect of the marriage proposal on her own life than Grazia's. She had again been upgraded, perhaps permanently this time. Norina felt like a small-scale celebrity.

Every time she encountered an acquaintance, Norina said the same lines she had learned by heart: "My daughter got a marriage proposal from an American. He's no ordinary American. He's an 'industralist' who owns a huge factory where they make chandeliers."

Norina used those lines to make an impression on all the people she knew. People greeted her reverently. She was no longer the pitiable, widowed night payer struggling to feed her children. She was the future mother-in-law of a rich American. Moreover, she was a candidate to go to America.

Norina used the letter containing the marriage proposal as a credit card just like the hundred-dollar bill. The letter was more valuable than the American bill, because it had a higher credit line and a longer expiration date. Just by showing the letter, Norina was able to go on shopping sprees and buy anything she needed.

From the best shoe store, Norina was able to get new shoes for herself and for her children. When Norina went to the flea market, she couldn't resist the temptation to purchase lingerie for Grazia, a new fishnet curtain for the front door, a tablecloth, and a flower print curtain for the back room.

Norina was proud to be seen coming home with all her goods in hand. She smiled triumphantly at her neighbors, who looked at her in dumbstruck jealousy. Her neighbors were convinced that she must be receiving plenty of hundred-dollar bills.

"The American must be very rich," Lina the Warm House said.

"Norina has luck falling from the sky," Titina the Alligator said.

Norina felt like the luckiest person in the world when she saw her sister Ada standing behind the fishnet curtain at her front door. Norina pulled the curtain.

Ada smiled. "I got my husband's permission to visit you."

Norina gave her sister a warm embrace. "I always prayed for this day to come."

"I've done a lot of praying myself."

"I'm surprised your husband gave you permission to come to my house. What made him change his mind?"

"He feels the American is upgrading the family. Your children are welcome in my house now. I have lots of string beans and cherries that Rodolfo brought from the fields. Send the boys to pick them up."

The two sisters attracted the attention of the neighbors, who watched them disappear behind the fishnet curtain into the house. It was a moving scene: two sisters who hadn't spoken for years were finally reunited.

"I wonder what they're talking about," Titina the Alligator said.

"They're talking about the American for sure," Lina the Warm House said.

The two sisters were indeed talking about Grazia's suitor. Grazia overheard their conversation from her bedroom.

"His name is Sal and he's very rich and good-looking," her mother said.

"Let me know when Sal arrives," Aunt Ada said.

"Of course, you're going to be the first one to know."

Grazia's eyes filled with tears. She didn't have the courage to tell her mother she had no intention of marrying Sal.

Norina stood by her front door and watched her sister walk away. She spotted her son playing on the street. "Pasquale," she called out.

Pasquale ran towards his mother. "What is it, *Mamma*?"

"Go over to Aunt Ada's house. She has string beans and cherries for us."

"We're having lasagne for dinner." Pasquale shook his hands in front of him. "I'm not in the mood for string beans and cherries."

"We can always use the cherries to make marmalade."

"Alright, I'll go." Pasquale skipped and caught up with Ada down the street.

Lina and Titina exchanged looks. As soon as Norina walked into her house, they began to gossip.

"It's unbelievable," Lina said. "Pasquale doesn't want string beans and cherries because they're having lasagne for dinner."

"Norina is going to have plenty of fruits and vegetables from her sister," Titina said.

Lina flashed a bit of a smile. "When the farmer prospers, so do his chickens."

Rodolfo smiled charmingly as he welcomed Pasquale into his house. Pasquale flashed a light grin.

"Let me look at you." Rodolfo patted Pasquale's head. "You've grown into a fine young man. I heard you're doing well in school."

"I'm the smartest kid in the class," Pasquale said.

"I'm proud of you."

Pasquale was stunned to be treated with respect by his uncle. Rodolfo had never acknowledged him in the past.

Ada reached for a basket filled with string beans and cherries and handed it to Pasquale. "Come whenever you want. I always have plenty of fruits and vegetables."

Pasquale thanked her and his uncle and scrambled out of the house carrying the heavy basket.

As Pasquale headed home, he ran into his friend Biagino.

Biagino raised his eyebrows. "Where did you get the cherries?"

"I didn't steal them, if that's what you're thinking." Pasquale gave him a handful of cherries. "I got them from my aunt and uncle. If you ever need food, just let me know. We have so much food now that we might need a refrigerator to store it all."

Biagino's jaw dropped. He avidly ate the cherries as he watched Pasquale stagger away under the heavy load.

Grazia was distraught by the notion of marrying a man she had never met, an unfamiliar man who would take her to an unfamiliar country where people spoke an unfamiliar language. The idea of leaving Italy terrified her. The sound of a whistle coming from the street made Grazia's heart beat faster. As she peered from the window, Grazia got a full view of Giorgio. She felt possessed by a frenetic desire to be with him. His kiss had made her shiver! Giorgio was someone she knew, someone who could offer her a future in her own hometown. Giorgio could be her savior! At night, Grazia fantasized about eloping with Giorgio.

Every day, Norina asked Grazia if she had made the decision to wed the American suitor. Grazia's reply was always the same: she needed more time to think.

Norina would say calmly, "Aunt Clotilde keeps asking me if you've accepted the marriage proposal. She has to write a letter to Ignazio with your answer."

Norina didn't want to upset her daughter. At the moment, Grazia was all-powerful. Grazia was like a magician who had the power to make their poverty disappear.

The story of Grazia's American suitor had become a real-life fairy tale. People were so eager to hear the next chapter that they would find excuses to pass by Saint Peter Street in hopes of running into Norina or Grazia and inquiring for more details. Grazia always managed to avoid the interviews. Norina instead was always willing to give out information. She loved to brag about her future son-in-law.

"He's an 'industralist,'" Norina would say. "If you saw the chandelier factory that he has, you aren't going to believe your eyes. The ceiling is filled with chandeliers. They light them up all at once when they have parties."

"Why would they have parties in a factory?" Concetta the Holy Water asked.

"Anything is possible in America," Lina the Warm House said.

"Grazia is lucky," Concetta said.

"You don't just need luck," Carolina the Good Life said. "You also have to be beautiful, because beauty attracts a wealthy man. I'm sure that if Grazia weren't so beautiful, she wasn't going to be picked by a rich American."

"Rich men aren't stupid. They pick the best girls." When Norina noticed Colombina the Farmer's Wife passing by, she raised her voice. "My daughter got a marriage proposal from an American and has no use for a farmer's son."

Colombina stopped in the middle of the street and placed her hands on her hips. "My son is young and good-looking. I wonder what sort of foreigner your daughter is marrying. He's probably an old man with a stiff leg."

"Looks are not important in a man. Your son can take his good looks and shove them up his ass."

Colombina showed her fists. "You're lucky that I don't pull your hair out."

Norina contorted her face. "Just try and lay a hand on me."

Colombina ran towards Norina like an infuriated animal. Concetta and Carolina managed to catch and restrain Colombina by grabbing her arms.

Colombina gave Norina a harsh look. "Your daughter is not married yet... anything can happen."

"I give you the horns." Norina showed her index finger and her pinky finger. "You're trying to give my daughter the *malocchio*? You can't give the *malocchio* to a person that doesn't deserve it. The *malocchio* is going to fall on you."

Concetta and Carolina dragged Colombina away. Many nosy neighbors gathered around Norina.

"When people spit into the sky it always ends up on their faces," Norina said. "Remember when Colombina told me that my daughter wasn't good enough for her son?"

Lina nodded.

"Now it's the other way around. I can proudly say that her son is not good enough for my daughter, because my daughter can do better."

"You can't compare an American with a farmer." Lina giggled. "The difference is like night and day."

Carlo the Broken Neck blamed himself for not proposing to Grazia before the American. He presumed Grazia was engaged, but he didn't lose hope.

"An engagement can always be broken. A beautiful unwed woman is like a bird without a cage. You have to catch it before another man does," Carlo's father used to say.

She's not in the cage yet. She's not married yet, Carlo thought with a trace of a smile.

The following morning, Carlo the Broken Neck paid Clotilde an unexpected visit. Clotilde gave him a gracious welcome.

"I'm here to ask your niece's hand in marriage," Carlo said all in one breath.

A rich man like Carlo the Broken Neck would have never proposed marriage to a peasant girl like Grazia. Grazia has suddenly been upgraded ever since she got the proposal from the American. Clotilde smiled at Carlo. "I would be happy to inform my sister-in-law about your marriage proposal. I'll give you an answer in two days."

Carlo gave Clotilde a kiss on the hand and walked out of the house.

Clotilde thought Carlo the Broken Neck deserved due consideration since he was a rich man. She wanted to sell her niece to the highest bidder.

Later in the day, Clotilde invited Norina, Ada, Rodolfo, Vituccio, and Marta to her house to discuss Carlo the Broken Neck's proposal to Grazia.

"I felt I had to consult the whole family before giving the Broken Neck an answer," Clotilde said.

"Carlo is one of the most affluent men in town," Rodolfo said.

"If Grazia marries him, she doesn't have to leave town and move to a far away country," Marta said.

Vituccio curled his lips. "The Broken Neck is a horrible man. I heard that he raped two women."

"I heard that story as well," Rodolfo said. "I also heard the two women were asking for it. Whores shouldn't complain when they get raped."

"I've been told the Broken Neck pretends to be generous but he's actually very stingy," Ada said. "I don't think he's going to help the family."

Norina twisted her face. "If he's stingy, he's not going to help the family for sure. I need a generous son-in-law."

"Americans have a reputation for being generous," Clotilde said.

Rodolfo raised an eyebrow. "If the American owns a factory, he must be far wealthier than Carlo the Broken Neck."

"The American could give the whole family a chance to go to America," Clotilde said.

"The American is the better suitor," Norina said.

They all agreed.

Clotilde didn't even bother to tell Grazia about Carlo the Broken Neck's marriage proposal.

Giorgio resented his mother for not allowing him to marry the women he loved. He presumed Grazia was already engaged to the American, but he didn't lose hope. Hope is the last thing that dies in a man's heart. Giorgio was confident he could convince Grazia to elope with him if he could just have a chance to talk to her. He firmly believed she still loved him. Giorgio stopped by Grazia's house and whistled repeatedly. Grazia's heart pounded at a roaring rate when she heard Giorgio's whistle from her bedroom. She promptly peered out of the window and got a clear view of Giorgio. She also saw her mother appear on the street.

"You shouldn't whistle when you pass by my house." Norina lifted her chin and placed her hands on her hips. "My daughter got a marriage proposal from a rich American. She's doesn't even think to look at the likes of you."

Giorgio stopped whistling. He attempted to talk, but no words came out of his mouth. Grazia imagined how humiliated Giorgio must feel. She remembered feeling the same humiliation when his mother had treated her like a worm. Giorgio walked away with his head down.

Two days later, Carlo the Broken Neck paid Clotilde a visit. He was eager to hear the response to his proposal.

"I'm deeply sorry, but my niece Grazia had another marriage proposal from an American at the same time, and has chosen to accept," Clotilde said. "These days, women are intrigued with America."

"I'm always available in case Grazia changes her mind," Carlo said.

"If my niece changes her mind, you'll be the first to know."

"Thank you for your consideration." Carlo kissed Clotilde's hand and exited the house.

Carlo the Broken Neck believed there was a solution for everything. *All I need to do is get Grazia alone and rape her. Once she's lost her virginity, she'll have no choice. Her relatives will beg me to marry her. And then, the best part is that I don't even have to marry her. I'll keep her as my lover, and I'll compensate her family with some unmarketable surplus fruits and vegetables from my fields. Her family is poor. Grazia will do anything to help her family.*

XXXIV

Grazia felt so dismayed at the notion of marrying the American that she had a hard time sleeping at night. One night, Caterina woke from her sleep and noticed her older sister was crying.

"There's something bothering you," Caterina said.

Grazia got up from the bed. "You know what's bothering me."

"You're not thrilled about marrying the American."

"How can you expect me to be thrilled? I don't even know him. He could be a drunk. For all we know he could even be a criminal."

"Don't exaggerate. You know that he's a decent person since he's cousin Ignazio's friend. You even know what he looks like because you got to see his picture."

"The picture is blurry. His face in the picture is so small that you can hardly see it. I can only see a glimpse of a man."

"He's a rich American. By marrying him, you could free yourself from poverty. You always hated being poor." Caterina adjusted Grazia's pillow. "You should try to get some sleep."

Caterina went back to sleep. Immersed in her thoughts, Grazia couldn't fall asleep. She needed to talk about her situation with someone who would understand her. The only friend she was comfortable confiding in was Patrizia. Grazia went back to bed and fell asleep comforted by her anticipation that her best friend would help her make the right decision.

Early the next morning, Grazia went to Patrizia's house. She immediately informed Patrizia that she didn't want to marry the American.

"I understand how you feel." Patrizia patted Grazia's shoulder. "It's not easy to marry a person you've never met in your life."

Grazia's lips quivered. "I wish my mother and Caterina would understand."

"I knew a woman who married an American man who didn't speak a word of Italian. They communicated through gestures."

Grazia widened her eyes as she realized there was a possibility that her American suitor didn't even speak Italian. "I have to go home."

"You don't feel good?"

"I'm fine."

"If you want to talk some more, I'll be at the Sewing School all day today."

Grazia nodded and ran outside.

Grazia didn't notice a man staring at her as she scurried down the street. The man was Carlo the Broken Neck. He followed Grazia from a distance and watched her walk into her house. Anna the Heavyweight, who was combing her daughter's hair on her balcony, noticed the scene.

"Carlo the Broken Neck is following Grazia," Anna said.

"Norina told me that Carlo proposed marriage to Grazia," Margherita said. "I heard that Grazia refused Carlo because she favored the American."

"Carlo cannot be trusted. He has a bad reputation. We have to keep an eye on him."

Margherita nodded. "I always hang out on the balcony. I'll tell you if I see anything wrong."

As soon as Grazia bounded into her house, she asked her mother if Sal spoke Italian.

"Clotilde told me that Ignazio's friends are all Italians," Norina said. "Sal has to speak Italian for sure."

"I hope he speaks Italian." Grazia bit her lip so as not to cry. "If he doesn't, how am I going to communicate with him? With gestures?"

"Clotilde says that Ignazio is a very intelligent man. Since Sal is his friend, he has to be intelligent like Ignazio. A proverb says: 'Tell me who your friends are and I'm going to tell you who you are.' If Sal doesn't speak Italian, he can learn Italian very fast because he's intelligent."

Grazia exhaled heavily. "I hope he's intelligent."

"Women want to marry anyone who can take them to America. My friend Rocchetta married an idiot she didn't even know because she wanted to go to America."

"How did it turn out?"

Norina shrugged. "I don't know. Rocchetta never came back to Italy."

"How sad! She had to give up her friends and family to marry an idiot she didn't even know."

"You don't know how lucky you are to get a marriage proposal from a good-looking and intelligent man. You don't know how to appreciate luck even when it's falling from the sky."

"I'm going to the Sewing School." Grazia rushed out of the house.

Once on the street, Grazia gave a sigh of relief. She was glad to get a break from Norina's increasingly determined campaign.

As soon as Grazia arrived at the Sewing School, Patrizia took her to the side.

"Giorgio begged me to give you this letter," Patrizia whispered, handing Grazia an envelope.

Grazia tore open the envelope and read,

Dearest Grazia,

I want you to know that I love you more than life itself. Please meet me tomorrow morning at eight thirty in the waiting room at the train station. Let's elope and get married. Have the courage to fight for your happiness!

Loving you forever,

Giorgio

P.S. Please show up even if you don't want to marry me. I want
to talk to you. If you don't show up, I'll do something crazy!

Grazia's eyes filled with tears.

Patrizia gave Grazia a hug. "It's never too late to follow your heart."

At night, Grazia had a hard time sleeping again. She couldn't get
Giorgio off her mind. Giorgio was offering her a last chance to seize
her happiness. Patrizia's words echoed in her mind: "*It's never too late to
follow your heart.*"

The following morning, the Voltinis had eggs, milk, and ricotta cheese
for breakfast. When they were done eating, Mario, Olimpia, and
Pasquale put on their new school uniforms and walked out of the
house.

Caterina decided to take Little Donato to Old Veronica's house and
spend some time with her boyfriend, Rocco. She led her little brother
out of the house.

Norina reached for her fishnet bag. "I have to go to the bottega."

As soon as Norina left the house, Grazia ran up the stairs. In
the bedroom, Grazia felt driven by a flicker of enthusiasm. She
took off her mourning dress and her worn undergarments. The
mirror framed her naked image. She had an elegant, lengthy neck,
a small waist, outstanding breasts, well-rounded hips, and long
straight legs. She reached for her new lingerie and put it on. She
then stepped back to take a full look at herself. She looked good!
Grazia slipped on her Sunday clothes and placed her flower print
dress in a small bag. She wished she could have taken some clothes
with her, but it would have required a bigger bag, and the neighbors
would have been suspicious. She grabbed the small bag and rushed
down the stairs.

Seated on her balcony, Margherita noticed Carlo the Broken Neck on the street. She ran inside the house and woke up her mother. "I saw Carlo the Broken Neck standing by Grazia's house."

Anna jumped out of bed and threw on her housedress . "What the hell is he doing on Saint Peter Street so early in the morning?"

"He should be in his fields with his workers," Margherita said.

Anna quickly hurdled onto the balcony. She noticed Carlo was staring at Grazia's front door. *He's up to no good.* She bolted down the stairs, out of the house, and sat on the steps of her side door.

In the meantime, Grazia walked out of her house and accelerated her pace. She froze at the sight of Mario emerging down the street.

"You were supposed to be in school," Grazia said. As she confronted Mario, she noticed that blood was dripping down his forehead. "What happened?"

"Three-three boys-boys ga-ve me a be-ating. They said-said that-that I'm-I'm too-too dumb-dumb to go to-to school."

Grazia escorted Mario inside the house. She reached for a cloth and cleaned the blood off of his forehead. "Thank God it's just a scratch."

Tears streamed down Mario's face. "The-the-the boys did-did-did that to-to-to me-me-me because they-they-they are smarter than-than me-me."

"They're not smarter." Grazia gave Mario a hug. "They are bad boys."

"These-these things are-are-are not-not-not going to-to happen to-to-to me-me when I-I go to-to America," Mario mumbled, drying his tears with his sleeve.

"When we go to America, you'll have a better life." Grazia expanded her eyes. She was shocked at her own words. She jumped up at the sound of the church bells, striking nine. She suddenly recalled Giorgio's note: *"If you don't show up, I'll do something crazy."* Grazia gave Mario a kiss on his forehead. "I have to go. I'll be back soon."

As soon as Grazia dashed out of her house Carlo the Broken Neck began walking quickly after her. Anna the Heavyweight followed Carlo from a distance, never letting her eyes off him.

Anna clenched her fists when she saw Carlo getting in his car. *I can't keep up with him now, no matter how fast I run.* Then she noticed that Carlo's car was going no faster than a walking pace. *He's following Grazia for sure.* She accelerated her pace. *That son of a bitch is up to no good.*

When Grazia arrived at the train station, she gave a sigh of relief. She went to look for Giorgio in the waiting room, but Giorgio was nowhere to be found. She had arrived too late. Grazia sank onto a bench and covered her face with her hands.

In the meantime, Carlo's car came to a halt at the train station.

Anna the Heavyweight watched carefully from afar as he got out of the car and peered into the waiting room.

He's looking for Grazia. He's going to offer her a ride for sure. I have to protect her. Anna bolted towards Carlo's car, scrambled into the backseat, and lay there low.

As a train passed by, Grazia's eyes filled with tears. It was as if she had missed her special train to the land of happiness. In her heartrending trance, she had no idea Carlo the Broken Neck was staring at her. As soon as Grazia began heading out of the train station, Carlo dashed back to his car and quickly got into the driver's seat.

His face lit up when he saw Grazia heading in his direction. He opened the car door and waved at her. "I have something important to tell you."

Grazia walked towards him. "What happened?"

Carlo manufactured a somber look. "Your mother was looking for you. She wants you home immediately. Something terrible has happened."

Grazia began to quiver. "What happened?"

Carlo snatched her by the hand and pulled her inside the car. He hurriedly slammed the door closed and revved the engine. "I'll take you home."

"Why does my mother want me to come home? What happened to my family?" Grazia kept asking.

"Nothing happened to your family," Carlo finally responded as the car came swiftly into a halt in a cherry field. In a quick motion, he lifted up Grazia's skirt and grabbed at her legs.

"Don't touch my legs. Let me out of the car," Grazia yelled, kicking the car door.

Carlo flashed a sardonic smile. "Relax. You're going to like it."

Grazia's skin crawled. His smile reminded her of Antonio the Devil's smile. "What are you doing?" she bellowed, as he ripped her panties off.

Anna the Heavyweight got up from the back seat and grasped Carlo by the neck. "Take your hands off the girl or I'm going to strangle you, you son of a bitch."

Carlo widened his eyes as his mouth fell open. He didn't even attempt to talk. He promptly took his hands off Grazia.

Anna turned to Grazia. "Get out of the car."

Immediately, Grazia opened the car door and leaped out of the vehicle. She was just catching her breath when she saw Anna punching Carlo in the face.

"You have to consider yourself lucky that I'm not in the mood to kill you." Anna wrinkled her nose. "But you never know. I may change my mind and kill you with my bare hands one of these days."

"Please spare me. I'll give you money." Carlo's whole body was quivering as he took lira bills out of his pocket.

"I deserve this cash, you cheap blood sucker." Anna snatched the money. "I've worked in your fields, and you paid me half of what you used to pay a man."

"Please don't tell anybody about this." Carlo clasped and twisted his hands together. "I won't tell anybody that you punched me."

Anna opened the car door. "If I hear that you take advantage of any girl in town, I'm going to cut off your balls," she shouted as she got out of the car and slammed the door.

Carlo the Broken Neck drove away as fast as possible.

"He's an animal, and he made me feel like one." Grazia was breathing heavily. "He made me feel like a worthless worm."

"Evil people make good people feel like worms, and then they even step on them." Anna hugged Grazia and patted her head. "Thank God he didn't get the chance to step on you."

Tears streamed down Grazia's face. Anna the Heavyweight had saved her from Carlo, but she still needed Giorgio to save her from the mysterious American, and she had arrived too late to their rendezvous.

I hope Giorgio hasn't done anything crazy, Grazia thought.

In the waiting room of the train station, Giorgio had waited for Grazia for a long hour. He was utterly devastated when he realized Grazia wasn't going to show up. He went back home, banged his head on the wall, and screamed desperately like a mortally injured creature. Colombina thought her son had gone completely insane.

Anna the Heavyweight escorted Grazia home. Anna informed Norina that Carlo the Broken Neck made an attempt to rape Grazia.

Norina banged her fist on the table. "That son of a bitch even asked for my daughter's hand in marriage to make us believe that he had serious intentions."

"He's a conniving bastard," Anna said. "He raped the Margassi Sisters while they were working in his fields."

Grazia's face paled. "That bastard ruined their lives."

Norina grabbed Anna's hands and held them tightly. "Please don't tell anybody that Carlo the Broken Neck wanted to rape Grazia."

"I swear on my husband's grave that I'm not going to tell a soul."

"People mix things up." Norina bit her tongue. "They can spread rumors that Grazia got raped. My daughter can't afford to lose her reputation. The American is never going to marry her if she loses her reputation."

Anna nodded.

"*I don't want to marry the American. I don't want to marry a stranger. I want to marry Giorgio,*" Grazia wanted to say out loud, but she remained silent.

"Stop thinking about Carlo the Broken Neck." Norina patted Grazia's shoulder. "Just make believe that he never existed."

That night, Norina lit a candle and placed it by the statue of Our Lady of Sorrows. She got down on her knees and blew a kiss to the Madonna. "Thank you for saving my daughter's virginity. I need one more favor. Make sure that Grazia accepts the marriage proposal from the American suitor soon."

Giorgio flirted with the hope that he still had a chance with Grazia. He continued to whistle every time he passed by her house. Norina would usually run him off afterwards, but regardless, the whistle gave Grazia the chills and made her heart rise to a frantic pace. It could have been his last whistle, his last attempt to take her away.

XXXV

A hand sticking out of a window caught Grazia's attention as she strolled down Saint Peter Street. It was Contessa Fiorella's hand waving vivaciously. In a fraction of a second, Grazia found herself standing in front of the opulent *palazzo*. When the door opened, Grazia rushed inside and closed the door behind her.

"I'm alone in the house. The maid went to visit her sick daughter, and my husband went to visit his healthy lover," Contessa Fiorella said. She looked Grazia in the eye. "There's something troubling you."

"My relatives want me to marry a man I don't even know, a man who is taking me to a foreign country." Grazia's face blushed. "I don't want to marry him because I'm in love with Giorgio. I was going to elope with him."

"Did you elope with him?"

"No."

"Why?"

"At the last minute, I changed my mind because I realized I couldn't take away from my brother Mario his dream of going to America."

"You don't love Giorgio enough to marry him. You love your brother more. Therefore, you should not marry Giorgio."

"I'm considering writing Giorgio a note and eloping with him."

"You've probably had plenty of time to write that note, but you haven't written it."

"But I love Giorgio."

"Be careful. You think you love him, but you don't. Giorgio is a challenge to you because of Colombina's disapproval. I don't think Giorgio loves you enough either."

"Why?"

"Because whenever his mother dragged him away from you, he didn't protest. I've seen the same scene many times. Giorgio wasn't taught to love his wife. He can only love his mother. Only when his mother dies will you have a chance to be loved by him. Men maneuvered by their mothers don't respect their wives. As a result, their wives are so frustrated that when they become mothers-in-law, they take out their frustrations on their daughters-in-law and make their lives miserable." The contessa took a pause and lowered her voice. "To love somebody, you have to be yourself."

"What do you mean?"

"Giorgio is not himself. He is his mother's puppet. He cannot love you even if he wants to. And you are not ready to love at the moment, because you cannot be yourself."

Grazia exhaled. "I would love to be myself."

"The foreign man will take you to America, a place where you'll have the freedom to explore who you want to be."

"What do you mean, 'explore?'"

"In America you'll have the opportunity to get a good job, to make something of yourself, to be independent and discover who you really are and what you really want. The Statue of Liberty, the greatest symbol of America, is a woman. If you marry the American, you'll be a free woman. You'll have the option to divorce your husband if he mistreats you. If you marry someone in town, you may end up incarcerated for the rest of your life. You don't have to be locked up to be imprisoned. You can be imprisoned in many ways. Remember that freedom is more important than life itself."

"Freedom is more important than life itself," Grazia said to herself.

"In America, the Statue of Liberty will be waiting for you." Contessa Fiorella held Grazia's hand. "It'll be the first thing you'll see once the ship lands in New York."

The corals and yellows of the sky became more intense when Grazia walked out of the *palazzo*.

As soon as Grazia got home, Norina said, "Aunt Clotilde wants to know if you decided to marry the American."

Grazia remained silent.

Little Donato waved at Grazia. "Chicken Grazia come back?"

Norina exposed a fake smile. "Chicken Grazia is going to come back soon."

Little Donato jumped up at the prospect of getting Chicken Grazia back. Grazia scrutinized his legs. They looked curved in such a miserable way that it broke her heart. She considered herself lucky to have straight legs. She was born under a better sky, because her father was still alive then. He was able to provide milk to strengthen her bones. Being the firstborn, she felt responsible for the well-being of her entire family.

Mario quietly emerged from the back room.

"Mario go and play outside," Norina said.

Obediently, Mario scrambled out of the house.

Mario has no future in this little town. No one is ever going to give him a decent job. He is destined to be a laughingstock. I'm the only one who can help him. If I marry the American, he could go to America, and I could give him a future, a better life. Mamma is right. I can't grant myself the luxury of refusing this opportunity. The fate and future of my family are in my hands. Grazia turned to her mother. "I'll marry the American."

Norina kissed Grazia on both cheeks. Grazia didn't show any emotion. She remained impassive to her mother's affection.

"I'm going to Clotilde's house." Norina scurried outside.

Little Donato tugged at Grazia's leg and asked her to sing him a *Ninna Nanna*. Grazia picked up the baby and sang for him until he fell asleep. She then carried the baby up the stairs. Once into the bedroom, she freed her arms from the weight of her little brother by placing him in his crib.

"Chicken Grazia," the baby murmured in his sleep.

"Chicken Grazia has been sacrificed for the family," Grazia whispered.

Norina headed to Clotilde's house, eager to give her the good news.

"I convinced Grazia, she's going to marry the American suitor," Norina said, as soon as she walked into the house.

Clotilde spread her arms wide open. "Saint Joseph has answered my prayers."

Norina pinched her fingertips together and moved her hands up and down. "What Saint Joseph? Our Lady of Sorrows did it all on her own."

"You think Saint Joseph didn't help?"

"Not one bit."

"Never mind, I don't want to start an argument. I'm not going to waste any time." Clotilde reached for a pen and a sheet of paper. "I'm writing a letter to my cousin Ignazio to inform him that Grazia has accepted the marriage proposal."

Norina was so excited by the thought her daughter was about to marry an American that she didn't sleep all night. She got up from the bed and stood by the window, contemplating the sky. As the dawn ascended, shades of pink and yellow emerged from the darkness. Enchanted, Norina smiled. She was enthralled and ecstatic that her fate had finally changed.

Grazia's siblings believed Sal was a hero who was going to take them to America. Olimpia spoke about Sal as if he were a character in a fairy tale book. She told Little Donato that Sal was a rich relative of *la Befana* and lived in a wonderland filled with chocolates and candies. Sal was going to bring him lots of goodies.

"Sal bring Chicken Grazia?" Little Donato asked.

"Of course, Sal is going to bring you the chicken from America," Olimpia replied.

Little Donato would jump happily every time he thought he was going to get Chicken Grazia back. No one had the heart to tell him that Chicken Grazia had been sacrificed for the family. No one thought to tell him that the real Grazia was also being sacrificed for the family. Grazia's siblings saw her as a fairy godmother that was going to grant them the chance to go to America.

Olimpia viewed America as a fascinating place populated by people who lived in gigantic houses surrounded by gardens filled with colorful flowers. The Americans smelled exquisite because they always carried chocolates and candies with them. They were very generous since they gave their children lots of goodies and toys. The American girls had the prettiest dolls. America was definitely the place where Olimpia wanted to be!

According to Pasquale, America was the land of opportunity where everyone got rich fast. He couldn't wait to go to America, get rich, and buy one of those big cars actors drove in the movies. Of course, he was going to come back to Italy and show off the car to his friends, along with plenty of dollars. He was also planning to be generous to his less fortunate friends. What good was it to have money and not be able to spend it on your mates?

Mario had seen what America looked like in movies he watched on Mrs. Fatti's television set. It was magnificent! The streets were wide and filled with big cars, and the people were dressed in colorful clothes. Everyone there was always polite. He loved the thought of being in another environment, surrounded by people who were kind. He was unhappy in his little town, where people made fun of him and made him feel worthless. America was definitely a better place.

Caterina believed America was some sort of lovers' Paradise that would open the door to her romance with Rocco. Since she had become a candidate to go to America, she had the magical power to grant Rocco and his entire family the chance to go to America. Caterina had a prosperous future to offer. America was the place where she could get rich and live happily ever after with Rocco, the love of her life!

The opportunity to go to America was worth a fortune. Grazia was granting her family that fortune. All the members of the family were so grateful to Grazia that they treated her with exaggerated benevolence, and pampered her like never before.

Norina made a cake for Grazia's 18th birthday. As Grazia cut the cake, her eyes gleamed with tears. It was the last birthday she was celebrating with her loved ones. Grazia gave one piece of cake to her mother and to each of her siblings, and watched them eat it with delight. They were celebrating the American dream.

Strolling down the street, Grazia ran into Saveria the Midwife.

"I heard you're getting married to an American," Saveria said.

Grazia nodded.

"I'm glad. In America, you'll have the chance to become a great designer. Aria the Maestra says you're one of her best students. You're too bright for this little town. You belong in a place where you can pursue your dreams, where women can be successful and make a difference."

Grazia flashed a half-smile. "I belong in America?"

"Yes, you belong in America with a special man who's going to appreciate you and honor your liberty to make you own choices. Most of the men in this town think they own their women." The midwife patted Grazia's shoulder. "Remember, no one should own another person."

As she headed home, Grazia kept repeating the midwife's words in her mind. *Most of the men in this town think they own their women. Remember, no one should own another person.*

Loud yells coming from Maddalena's house distracted Grazia. *Maddalena is getting another beating from her drunkard husband. She has to submit to his abuse because that despicable man provides for her.* Contessa Fiorella's words came to Grazia's mind. *There's no escape for women in this town. Women are trapped.*

Grazia thought about the poor women who had a child every year just to satisfy the sexual desire of their husbands. Only men were valuable. Men were the rulers. Women felt so powerless that they treated their men like kings. Even unsuccessful husbands who were barely able to provide enough food to feed their families were treated like royalty. Women had more respect for men than for themselves.

Grazia recalled that her mother shrieked with delight when she gave birth to her brothers, as if she had given birth to a Prince. "It's a boy!"

Her mother had a halfhearted expression when she gave birth to her younger sister. "It's another girl!"

The sky caught Grazia's eyes. She could trade that sky for another sky, an American sky, assuming it would be a better sky.

Ignazio's letter arrived from America. Clotilde rushed to the Voltinis' house and waved the letter in the air. Norina and Caterina promptly congregated around her. Clotilde wore her eyeglasses and read the letter out loud:

Dear precious and honorable cousin Clotilde,

I'm writing to inform you that my friend Sal was very happy to hear that Grazia has accepted his proposal of marriage. Sal is eager to come to Italy. He has already purchased his ticket. He will be arriving at Naples on August 22nd. From Naples, he'll take the local train that stops at Vocevero. He'll be wearing a red tie so Grazia will be able to recognize him from a distance. Make him feel at home. He's a family-oriented man who has lost his family. He's about to become an important member of your family.

An affectionate greeting filled with lots of respect and deep admiration from your dear cousin,

Ignazio

P.S. I made it clear to Sal that he'll have to take care of all the expenses of the wedding, and he has agreed. Sal has a lot of money. He has a big business and a big heart.

Clotilde smiled as she took off her eyeglasses. "What a man! Ignazio writes beautifully. He uses so many nice adjectives: precious and honorable cousin Clotilde… It sounds so erudite. He's so precise. I've never found a grammatical error or an improper adjective in his letters."

Norina nodded, though she didn't comprehend the meanings of the words, "erudite," "grammatical" and "adjectives." Norina understood what she considered to be the most important thing: "Sal had a lot of money!"

"Where is Sal going to sleep when he comes?" Caterina asked. "We have no room in this house."

Norina turned to Clotilde. "A man never sleeps in a woman's house before he marries her. Sal has to stay at your house."

"Sal can't stay at my house." Clotilde said. "I don't even have running water. He should stay at Ada's house. He comes from America, where he has all sorts of modern appliances."

"You're right," Norina said. "I didn't think of that."

"Lately you're too excited to think properly," Clotilde said. "I'll pay Ada a visit and I'll suggest to her to have Sal as a guest."

"What if Uncle Rodolfo doesn't want to have Sal stay in his home?" Caterina asked.

Clotilde laughed a little. "He won't refuse hospitality to the American nephew-to-be."

"You're right," Norina said.

"When Sal comes, you shouldn't show him your house," Clotilde said. "If he wants to see your home, don't invite him to dinner. Just invite him for a cup of coffee. You don't have a bathroom. You only have the sewer, and it would be shameful if he finds out. The less time he spends in your house, the lower the chance he has to go to the bathroom."

Norina nodded.

"A woman who is marrying an American should not work as a maid," Clotilde said. "Grazia has to quit her job."

"I can take Grazia's job," Caterina said.

Norina and Clotilde agreed. Caterina's eyes sparkled at the thought of taking over Grazia's job. She quickly planned on putting money away for herself.

"We've got to tell Grazia her fiancé is coming in two weeks," Norina said. "Where's Grazia?"

"She's upstairs in the bedroom." Caterina said. "She's taking a nap."

"Wake her up and tell her."

Caterina ran up the stairs. Once into the bedroom, she was surprised to see that Grazia was wide awake.

"Sal is on his way." Caterina flashed a smile. "He'll be in town in two weeks."

"I know." Grazia's eyes shone with tears. "I heard you, *Mamma*, and Aunt Clotilde talking downstairs."

Caterina rushed down the stairs. She didn't notice the tears rolling down Grazia's face.

Grazia was terrified by the thought that her whole life was about to change. She caught sight of the decrepit walls, which seemed to be falling apart. For the first time in her life, those walls appeared flawless to her. The chips of paint missing from those walls looked like inlaid gemstones. She didn't want to part with those walls. Those walls had witnessed her childhood. They had seen her grow up, and though they had gotten old and decayed, they had given her shelter. As she looked around, she felt distraught at the realization that everything would soon disappear: her little town, her family, her friends, her crumbling house and even her nosy neighbors. She was going to leave her entire world behind her. Though her life had been mostly miserable, it was the only life she knew.

How can you leave a life you know for a life you don't know, just because everyone tells you it's better? Grazia asked herself.

Grazia was tempted to rescind her acceptance to Sal's marriage proposal, but she didn't have the courage. It was too late. Sal was on his way to Italy, and most of all, she couldn't disappoint her mother and her siblings. They needed the American dream. Grazia patted her tears to her cheeks. She then took Sal's blurry picture and placed it on the night table. She had to get acquainted with that glimpse of a man. She had to convince herself that he was an exceptional person, a man who would love her dearly.

Grazia's siblings were so excited about Sal's arrival that they were making a countdown of the days. They couldn't wait to meet him. Grazia, on the other hand, did everything in her power to avoid thinking about it. She tried her best to keep herself busy. She dedicated her time to the Sewing School, where she was creating new dresses under the supervision of Ombretta the Maestra.

Clotilde suggested to Norina that it was the proper time to talk to Grazia about the facts of life. Norina summoned her daughter to the bedroom and explained to her how to have children, and how to fulfill her spouse's carnal desires.

"It's your duty to make love to your husband every time he wants to do it. You're not going to like it. Women don't like sex." Norina's face blushed as she spoke. "Only whores like sex. But to make your husband happy, you have to make him believe that you get pleasure from sex, otherwise, he's going to feel bad. Don't ever refuse to make love to your husband or else he's going to go to the whores for sex."

Grazia curled her lips and looked away. She couldn't face her mother.

Norina lowered her voice. "When your husband runs around with whores, it has very bad consequences."

Grazia scrunched her forehead. "Consequences?"

Norina exhaled. "Your husband can bring home a bad disease. I know a woman in town that died from a terrible disease like that. I think the disease was called 'syphilis.'"

Grazia widened her eyes. No one had ever told her about such "consequences." Sex was a matter of life and death!

XXXVI

The sun's rays shed light on them as they walked out of the house. They were like the leading characters of a movie shot on Saint Peter Street. Many neighbors stood at their front doors, at their windows, and on their balconies to get a better view. They seemed like three *signore*. Grazia appeared as beautiful as ever in her flower print dress, and Clotilde and Norina looked very refined in their black Sunday outfits.

"Here they come," they heard a voice whisper.

Clotilde and Norina enjoyed every minute of their fame. Grazia blushed out of embarrassment. Vituccio was waiting for them in his car at the corner of the street. As the *signore* look-alikes got into the car, some neighbors started to gossip.

"Where are they going all dressed up?" Maddalena asked.

"They're going to pick up the American from the train station," Titina the Alligator said.

Maddalena noticed Grazia had a sad look on her face. "The bride-to-be doesn't look pleased."

"I don't think she's happy to get married to the American," Carmela the Daughter of the Umbrella Repair Man said.

"She won't get the benefits of being an American Wife here because he's going to take her to America with him," Carolina the Good Life said.

Lina the Warm House twisted her lips. "The girls these days don't know how to appreciate the luck they get from the sky."

Giorgio watched the scene from his balcony. His eyes filled with tears as Grazia disappeared from his sight.

Immersed in her own thoughts, Grazia didn't say a word throughout the entire ride. Clotilde and Norina kept exchanging anxious looks. Once they arrived at the train station, Clotilde relaxed a bit. Vituccio got out of the car and asked a station attendant about the arrival of the train scheduled from Naples.

"It usually runs one hour late," the attendant replied.

Vituccio turned to the women. "You're better off sitting in the waiting room."

In the waiting room, Clotilde and Grazia sat on a bench. Clotilde drew a rosary out of her purse and began to pray. Norina paced back and forth.

"Norina, you're getting on my nerves." Clotilde huffed. "I can't concentrate on my praying. Why don't you pray with me?"

"I can't pray," Norina said as she sat next to Grazia. "I'm too nervous."

Grazia was sitting still. She was so petrified by Sal's impending arrival that she refrained from looking at the window that framed the train tracks. The arrival of that train was going to have a big impact on her life. She clasped her hands together to keep them from shaking as she pictured Sal's photograph in her mind. It was so blurry that she could only see a glimpse of a man. She feared what Sal might actually look like.

"A man who comes here to marry a girl he's never met must be desperate and unattractive. If he was good-looking, he would just find an American girl," Grazia overheard a friend at the Sewing School say.

Sal is a total stranger. I don't know anything about him. Would he beat me? Would he be a drunk? Would he be a madman who would lock me up? Grazia thought. She wished fervently to have a future in the land where she was born, in a town where everybody knew her name, with friends that would protect her.

All of a sudden, Grazia felt driven by the frenetic desire to escape the awkward situation. She could run away. She still had time. The train hadn't arrived yet. As she looked around, she realized her aunt and her mother were leaning forward, sitting like two solid columns on either side of her. It felt like those two columns were suffocating her. It gave her the sense of being behind bars. She felt hot flashes rising to her face.

The sight of a man standing by the entrance door distracted Grazia from her reverie. The man was tall, handsome, and had the aspect of an important person. He looked at her and gave her a smile as he walked towards her. Grazia felt comforted by his smile. His penetrating black eyes inspired trust and protection. He could have been her savior, some sort of saint in disguise, who could have helped her flee. She refrained from staring at him, fearing to give away her thoughts. She lowered her head and composed the pleats of her dress.

The handsome man asked, "Excuse me *signorina,* are you waiting for the train from Naples?"

"Yes," Grazia responded. "The train is running late. I've been waiting for over an hour."

"I thought I was late, but since the train is late, I'm on time." He exhaled. "I have to consider myself lucky."

Grazia flashed her magical smile. She had also considered herself lucky the train was delayed.

He stared at her, enchanted by her beauty. "Your face is not new to me. You look familiar. I'm under the impression that I've seen you somewhere, but I can't recall where. What is your name?"

"Graz-" her voice was overpowered by the screeching tracks. The noise was so earsplitting the man didn't comprehend her name.

Grazia felt a hand grasping her arm. As she turned, she was faced with Aunt Clotilde's stern look. "The train has arrived."

Grazia sneaked a last glance at the handsome man as her aunt dragged her away. He seemed like a false saint who had instantly disappeared.

"Let's go. You shouldn't talk to strange men. Don't forget you're about to get married." Clotilde indicated the train. "Sal could pop out of the train any minute."

To Grazia's eyes, the train appeared like a huge serpent, leering viciously at her.

As they walked out of the waiting room, Norina spotted Vituccio, who was talking to a taxi driver.

Norina waved at her brother. "Come here. Sal is going to come off the train any minute now."

Vituccio jogged towards them.

"We should look for a man wearing a red tie," Clotilde said.

Norina and Clotilde had their eyes set on all the men coming out of the train, but they didn't spot anyone wearing a red tie.

"Do you see him?" Norina kept asking.

"I don't see him," Clotilde kept responding.

Clotilde clasped her hands. "I hope Sal didn't miss the train."

Grazia gritted her teeth. She wished Sal had missed the train.

"I see a man wearing a red tie," Clotilde said. "It must be Sal."

Grazia lowered her head. She didn't want to look at Sal.

Norina's whole body quivered. "Where is he?"

"He's next to the man with the big mustache," Clotilde responded.

Norina tapped her feet. "We have to call him."

Clotilde shook her head. "It's not polite to call out to a man that we haven't met. He's the one who should walk towards us."

Norina huffed. "How can he walk towards us if he doesn't know us?"

"Stay still." Clotilde held Norina by the arm. "He'll spot Grazia since he saw her photograph. He should be able to recognize her."

They waited patiently for ten long minutes.

Sal scrunched his forehead as his eyes darted around the train station.

"Let's wave at him," Norina said.

"It's vulgar to wave at a man you haven't met. We should walk a little closer to give him a chance to notice us." Clotilde turned to Grazia. "You should smile lightly at him. You had a light smile in the photograph. I'm sure he'll recognize your smile."

Grazia slammed her eyes shot and forced a light smile as Clotilde and Norina led her to Sal.

He immediately identified Grazia. Sal thought she looked stunning in her flower print dress. She looked like the personification of spring. "Grace!" he whispered.

At the sound of his voice, Grazia opened her eyes. Her mouth fell open. She almost went into shock. Her body began to wobble. Her heart started beating uncontrollably. Her whole face gleamed with joy. She couldn't believe he was in front of her. She could hardly accept that he was real. It was like he had popped out of her dreams! She had admired him for so long! Lately she hadn't even dared to dream about him!

Sal wasn't a stranger wearing a red tie. He was a man she knew. He was the distinguished man she had met at Mrs. Zordi's house. She had the sensation of having been truly blessed by the sky! She felt like the luckiest woman on earth. Grazia was so overwhelmed that she could already feel her body responding to the physical attraction she had for him.

Sal kissed her on the cheek and squeezed her hand tightly. "I haven't been able to stop thinking about you since the day I met you," he whispered.

His words were like music to her ears. The sound of his voice was like a soft wind caressing her soul.

Sal looked at Clotilde and Norina. "I'm Sallustio."

Clotilde flashed a smile. "I'm Clotilde, Grazia's aunt. She's Norina, Grazia's mother, and he's Vituccio, Grazia's uncle."

Norina remained speechless. She didn't know what to say.

"It's a pleasure to meet you," Sal said, bowing and kissing the women's hands. He greeted Vituccio with a handshake.

They were all excited and a bit ill at ease. Norina kept biting her lower lip. No words came out of her mouth, though she attempted to speak. Vituccio couldn't find the right words to say. Grazia was too shocked to say anything. Sal was so exceedingly happy to finally be with Grazia that it didn't occur to him to start a conversation.

Clotilde decided to do the talking and asked, "Sal, how's my cousin, Ignazio?"

Sal didn't seem to comprehend. His eyes were fixed on Grazia.

Clotilde decided to throw in an English word. "Is my cousin Ignazio 'OK'?"

"Oh, he's fine. I saw him recently at the Italian-American social club." Sal chuckled as he placed his hands on his belly to indicate Ignazio had a big belly. "Ignazio eats a lot of spaghetti."

"Oh! Ignazio likes spaghetti?" Norina asked. She hastily covered her mouth with her hand as she recalled her sister-in-law had told her to talk as little as possible.

"Sal, do you like Italian food?" Clotilde asked.

"I like it very much. Italian food is the best food in the world," he responded, keeping his eyes on Grazia. She was like a vision to him.

"Where do you want me to put the suitcases?" the station attendant asked, wheeling a cart filled with suitcases.

Norina's eyes lit up as she counted eight pieces of luggage.

Vituccio pointed at his car. "Put them in my car."

"Your car is too small," Sal said. "We need two cars. We can use your car to carry the luggage."

Vituccio agreed. Promptly, the station attendant loaded the luggage in Vituccio's car.

"Where are the taxis?" Sal asked, tipping the station attendant.

The station attendant flashed a big smile. "There is only one taxi available."

The taxi driver was waiting in front of his car, hoping to get an American customer. The station attendant approached the taxi driver and whispered something in his ear. The taxi driver swiftly opened the doors of his spacious white Mercedes. Clotilde took the front seat while Sal sat between Grazia and Norina in the back seat. Sal was delighted to sit next to Grazia.

As the car took off, Sal wanted to touch Grazia's hand, but refrained from doing so because he felt intimidated by Norina's presence.

"Sal, your Italian is very good," Clotilde said. "Where did you learn to speak Italian?"

"My father was born in Palermo. He moved to the United States when he was twenty years old. He taught me how to speak Italian. I have many friends in Italy, and I love to visit them. I met Grazia at the Zordis' house. I wanted to ask her for her address but I didn't get a chance. When Ignazio showed me Grazia's picture at the social club, I realized it was fate."

Grazia was still so astounded that she could barely think. She remained silent because she could not find any words to say.

"This is the center of town," Clotilde said as the car passed by the *piazza*. She indicated the fountain. "It's a monument that was commissioned by Mussolini."

Sal scrutinized the fountain surrounded by many angels with water pouring from their mouths. "I like the fountain, even though I didn't like Mussolini."

"Mussolini was not a good-looking man. He was short," Norina whispered then covered her lips with her hands.

Clotilde gave Norina a stern look. To her relief, Sal didn't seem to hear Norina's remark.

Clotilde exposed a hint of a smile as she shifted her attention to Sal. "Mussolini did a lot of bad things, but he had his good side. He had appreciation for the arts. He used to call the Italians: *Popolo di artisti.*"

"A population of artists," Sal said, marveling at the sight of marble statues standing by the entrance of the castle.

"The castle needs to be restored, but the town can't come up with the money," Clotilde said.

"It's stunning." Sal thought the little town of Vocevero was enchanting, even though the streets were extremely narrow.

The cab came to a halt in front of Ada's house. The taxi driver got out of the car and opened the car doors. Clotilde was the first one to step out, then Norina.

In a split second Grazia looked into Sal's eyes and ever so quietly whispered, "*Sono contenta che sei qui con me.*"

She saw in his warm eyes that he was exceedingly happy to be with her. They longed to kiss, and might have if they were alone. The spell was broken, however, when Clotilde said, "And here is the family."

As Sal helped Grazia out of the taxi, she noticed her nicely combed siblings waiting on the street clad in their best clothes, and many people standing by their front doors. The Voltini children ran towards the white Mercedes, eager to meet their brother-in-law-to-be. They were followed by several other curious children.

Playing the role of the leading man, Sal attracted the stares of all the spectators. They inspected him from head to toe as he tipped the driver. The driver hopped, flashing a bright smile.

"The American gave the driver a great tip," a voice whispered.

"He looks much older than Grazia, but he's attractive. She's lucky to get a good-looking American man," another voice whispered.

"Sal," the Voltini children called out.

Clotilde turned to Sal. "I want to introduce to you Grazia's siblings: Caterina, Olimpia, Pasquale, Mario, and Little Donato."

"Big family," Sal said.

Pasquale watched the white Mercedes until it disappeared into the distance. "That's the car I want to get when I go to America," he said to his friend Biagino.

Caterina searched for Sal's luggage. She took Pasquale on the side. "Where's the luggage? How can an American come to Italy with no luggage?"

Pasquale contorted his face. "Sal can't be rich if he hasn't brought any suitcases."

Vituccio's car caught Caterina's and Pasquale's attention.

As soon as the car came to a stop, Vituccio poked his head out of the window. "I need some help with the baggage."

Pasquale and Caterina ran to the car. Their friends followed them.

"Look," Pasquale said to his friends. "The car is filled with American luggage."

Caterina grinned as she tapped her feet. They were all astonished at just how many pieces of luggage there were.

"Sal brought a lot of American chocolates and candies for sure," Pasquale said.

Biagino patted Pasquale's shoulder. "Don't forget about me."

"I'll give you some American goodies in exchange for your blessing to go out with your sister," Pasquale whispered.

As soon as Biagino nodded, Pasquale beamed.

Rodolfo welcomed Sal into the house with a handshake and a charming smile. "I'm Uncle Rodolfo. This is my wife, Aunt Ada, and my daughters, cousin Mariella and cousin Catia."

Sal bowed and gave the women a hand kiss. "It's a pleasure meeting you."

Rodolfo forgot all about introducing Marta.

Clotilde turned to Sal as she noticed that Marta was clenching her jaw. "I want to introduce to you, Marta, Vituccio's wife."

Sal bowed and kissed Marta's hand. "I'm delighted to meet you, Aunt Marta."

He's a real gentleman, Marta thought, flashing a light smile. *He pays me respect. He calls me aunt already.*

Vituccio, Mario, and Pasquale carried the luggage into the main room. Marta's mouth fell open. She had never seen so many pieces of luggage. Caterina, Olimpia, and Little Donato bounded into the room. Little Donato stamped his feet and burst into tears.

"What happened? Did he get hurt?" Sal asked.

"He's crying because he thought you were going to bring him a chicken from America," Olimpia said.

Sal widened his eyes. "A chicken?" He then indicated a suitcase. "I didn't know Italian kids wanted chickens. All I have are American chocolates and candies."

Olimpia patted Little Donato's head. "Sal is going to bring Chicken Grazia another day."

The children gathered around the suitcase. As soon as Sal opened it, their eyes sparkled. They had never seen so many chocolates and candies. Little Donato practically leaped into the suitcase. The children grabbed the sweet treats as if they were digging for gold.

Clotilde gave them a stern look. "Get away."

"Let them have their fun. They're children." Sal drew an envelope from his handbag and gave it to Clotilde. "I have a letter from Ignazio."

Norina fixed her eyes on the envelope. "Open the letter."

"It's not proper to open a letter in front of everyone," Clotilde whispered.

"Dinner is ready," Ada said.

They all went into a large dining room. There was a banquet table set with an embroidered tablecloth, matching napkins, fine dishes, glassware, and silverware. They all sat around the table.

Before they began eating, Clotilde said, "Thank you Lord for bringing us together to honor You. Bless this food. Amen."

Vituccio got up from his seat and raised his glass of homemade wine. "To America!"

"To America," they all said in unison, raising their glasses.

They had grilled vegetables, prosciutto, and mozzarella for appetizers, and lasagne and *braciole* for the main course. Sal relished the sumptuous meal. He had never tasted food so delicious in his life.

Norina watched Sal as he ate. *He doesn't eat fast. You can tell that he's rich.*

Rodolfo gave his attention to Sal. "Cousin Ignazio tells us you are a businessman."

"I own a garment factory," Sal said.

Norina didn't quite understand the sort of factory Sal had mentioned. She didn't bother to ask. She wasn't in the mood to learn another line by heart. She had grown quite comfortable saying Sal owned a chandelier factory.

As Ada brought the cake to the table, the children congregated around her. Clotilde cut the cake and served a piece to everyone. The children ate the cake voraciously.

Sal drew his hand in his pocket and pulled out a small box. He got down on one knee and handed the box to Grazia. "Please accept this ring and all my love."

Grazia froze with the box in her hand, not knowing what to do.

"Open the box," Clotilde whispered.

As Grazia opened the box, her eyes expanded at the sight of a sparkling diamond ring.

Clotilde flashed a smile. "It's absolutely spectacular."

"It's such a big stone," Ada said. "I've never seen such a ring."

Norina was a little disappointed that the ring didn't have a lot of gold around the stone. She thought gold was more valuable than stones, but didn't dare express her opinion.

"It's a stunning ring," Grazia finally said.

Sal got up from his knee and slipped the ring on Grazia's finger.

"You're officially engaged," Clotilde said.

Vituccio drank another glass of wine all in one shot. "It's time to go home," he mumbled.

Marta gave him a harsh look. *He's had too much to drink. He's not happy if he's not doing something bad.*

Clotilde informed Sal that since he was not married to Grazia yet, he wasn't allowed to sleep over Grazia's house, and therefore he was going to stay as a guest in Aunt Ada's house.

"I made reservations in a hotel in the city," Sal said.

If he's staying in a hotel, he must have a lot of money, Clotilde thought.

"I can make arrangements with Uncle Vituccio to drive me to the hotel," Sal said. "I'd rather hire him than hire another taxi driver. I'll come tomorrow morning."

"I'll be happy to drive you," Vituccio said. "You don't have to pay me. I don't charge relatives."

Marta gritted her teeth.

"I'll be offended if you refuse to accept my money," Sal said.

Marta relaxed.

"What about the suitcase filled with the goodies?" Pasquale asked.

"Take more candies and chocolates, please," Sal responded.

The children jumped up and down. They hastily filled their pockets with the chocolates and candies before Clotilde gave the children a severe look. "You've taken enough."

The children ran out of the house, eager to share the American treats with their friends. Norina took plenty of chocolates and candies and dumped them into her fishnet bag. As she did so, she turned her back on Clotilde.

Norina has no manners. She's just like her children, Clotilde thought, twisting her lips. As she shifted her attention to Sal, she exposed a smile. "We have to leave now. We'll see you tomorrow."

Sal ushered Grazia, Norina, and Clotilde to the door. He gave Grazia a kiss on the cheek and whispered, "I'll see you tomorrow."

Grazia responded with her magical smile. She stumbled as she walked out of the house escorted by her mother and her aunt. She was still in a state of shock. She kept smiling to herself as she evoked that Sal was not a stranger but the attractive, distinguished man with piercing eyes, who she had found so sensitive and intelligent. She had admired him for his values and his ideals. He was a real gentleman!

On their way home, Clotilde opened the envelope and drew out a letter and a fifty-dollar bill.

Norina tapped Clotilde's arm. "Give me the money."

Clotilde reached for her eyeglasses and put them on. "Take it easy. I want to know what the money is for." She skimmed through the letter. "The fifty-dollar bill is a wedding present for Grazia."

Norina grabbed the American bill. "Grazia can use the money. She needs nice dresses."

Clotilde bobbed her head in agreement. "Grazia is marrying an American. She has to look her best now."

Saint Peter Street was crowded with inquisitive neighbors awaiting Sal's arrival. Many neighbors were standing on their balconies, by their windows, or by their front doors to get a better view of the scene.

"I wonder what's taking them so long," Lina the Warm House said "We've been waiting for hours."

"The trains are always late," Giacomino the Blind Man said.

Finally, Norina and her children emerged down the street.

"They're coming," Lina shouted.

"Where's the American?" Titina the Alligator asked.

"I don't see him," Margherita replied.

"Can it be that he didn't come?" Titina raised an eyebrow. "Many Americans have changed their minds at the last minute."

As the Voltinis got nearer, Ninuccio the Painter took a closer look at them. "They look happy. The American must have come to town."

Pasquale smiled at everyone on hand. "The American had a whole suitcase filled with chocolates and candies."

Norina swung her bag as she waved to the neighbors. They all waved back at her and watched her as she entered her house.

"I guess the groom-to-be is staying at Norina's sister's house," Lina said. "Tomorrow we should pass by the house and check him out."

"We better go to Norina's house now if we want to have a taste of the American treats," Anna the Heavyweight whispered to Lina.

Lina agreed.

Minutes later, Anna the Heavyweight and Lina the Warm House paid the Voltinis a visit.

Norina welcomed them with joy. She promptly placed a plate of American chocolates on the table. Norina recited another line she had learned by heart. "Grazia's fiancé is a gentleman. You can tell he comes from one of the best families in America."

Grazia remained silent. She sneaked into the hallway and climbed up the stairs. Once she stepped into the bedroom she unwound. She wanted to be alone with her thoughts. She wasn't in the mood to talk to the nosy neighbors. She felt so happy that she didn't want anyone to distract her from her happiness.

In the meantime, Lina and Anna were enjoying the American chocolates voraciously.

"Norina, you don't mind if I take one for my brother, do you?" Lina asked.

Norina shrugged. "I don't mind at all."

Lina treated herself to a whole handful of chocolates.

"Let me get some for my daughter too," Anna said, taking two handfuls of chocolates and placing them in her pockets.

Lina turned to Norina. "Is Sal staying at your sister's house?"

"No, he's so rich that he's staying in a hotel in the city," Norina said. "He gave Grazia a big gold engagement ring with a stone. I don't know the name of the stone."

"I asked Aunt Clotilde," Caterina said. "She said that the stone is called diamond."

"What kind of stone is that?" Anna asked.

"The diamond is a special stone that shines a lot," Lina said. "Can we see the ring?"

"Grazia has it on her finger." Norina realized her daughter wasn't in the room. "Where's Grazia?"

"I saw her going upstairs," Caterina said.

Norina shifted her attention to her neighbors. "Meet me outside. I'm going to get the ring. I want to show it to everyone."

Norina dashed up the stairs. Anna and Lina grabbed more American sweets and scrambled outside.

As soon as Norina bounded into the bedroom, she hastily slid the ring off Grazia's finger. "The neighbors want to see the ring."

Grazia didn't protest. She didn't want to take away from her mother the glory of showing off a precious ring.

Norina ran out of the house and presented the ring to everyone on the street.

"The stone shines so much that it looks like it has a little light inside," Anna the Heavyweight said.

"It's splendid," Lina the Warm House said. "I've never seen such a thing. We should show it to Mrs. Fatti. She's an expert when it comes to American jewelry."

Mrs. Fatti was standing by her front door. She was rarely seen outside.

Norina handed her the ring. "This is the ring that Grazia got from her fiancé."

"It's fabulous," Mrs. Fatti said. "He must be a very wealthy man to give her this ring."

Norina recited one of the lines she had learned by heart. "He's an 'industralist' who owns a whole factory where they make chandeliers."

More and more curious neighbors gathered around them.

"Look, the diamond shines in the dark," Lina said.

Giacomino the Blind Man pictured the stone dazzling in the dark like a star in the sky.

"It must be a special stone if it shines in the dark," Titina the Alligator said.

Ninuccio the Painter nodded. "I heard that these special stones are very expensive."

"I usually get nice jewelry, but I never got a ring that shines in the dark," Maddalena said.

The neighbors took turns looking at the ring. Colombina the Farmer's Wife passed by and asked Old Veronica what was going on.

"They're all looking at Grazia's engagement ring," the old woman said.

Colombina wrinkled her nose. "How can a lowlife like Grazia marry an American?"

Old Veronica folded her hands. "God manages to help the poor people out."

Colombina walked away, whispering curses.

The sound of Baronessa Rosa's voice saturated the street. She sang the aria "Love is a Rebel Bird."

Hypnotized, many people turned their attention to the opera singer.

As Baronessa Rosa sang, Giacomino envisioned white pigeons dancing in the navy blue sky. *They are celebrating Grazia's engagement*, he thought flashing a smile.

XXXVII

The Voltinis' feasted on sumptuous meals at Ada's house. Rodolfo brought home the best and freshest, fruits and vegetables. He did everything in his power to impress Sal, the American nephew-to-be. Sal amazed his in-laws-to-be by buying the finest cuts of meat. Rodolfo gave the leftovers to Norina to bring home. Norina had so much food that she ended up giving it away to her friends. She always gave double portions of food to the Dumb Brothers and the Margassi Sisters. Neighbors often sat by the Voltinis' front door, flirting with the hope of getting some food.

"When the farmer prospers, so do his chickens," Lina the Warm House would say.

"Then Norina's chickens are lucky," Giacomino the Blind Man would say.

Norina felt highly respected. Whenever she joined a gossip group on Saint Peter Street, the neighbors offered her a chair to sit on. Her sisters-in-law, Marta and Clotilde, welcomed her with joy when she paid them a visit. The Dumb Brothers and the Margassi Sisters ran to her whenever they saw her roaming down the street and gave her grateful hugs. Even the White Flies nodded hello to Norina when they bumped into her.

Sal escorted Norina whenever she went on shopping sprees. From the merchants, Norina received the same reverence as the White Flies, since Sal paid cash for everything she purchased. Sal derived gratification from all the looks of admiration and praise he received. No one had made him feel so important in his entire life. Sal felt like a champion.

Sal wasn't aware that Norina had made a deal with the merchants. They were to overcharge Sal to pay off the debts she had accumulated from when she had showed the marriage proposal letter to obtain credit. By having Sal pay her debts, Norina had gained the trust of all the merchants again. Their trust meant credit for the future thanks to Sal.

Norina was planning to use that renewed credit line after her daughter left Italy. She was confident that Sal would continue to help her out financially. She believed she didn't have to worry about the future. Her future would be prosperous. Many hundred-dollar bills were going to fly over from an American sky!

On one of their shopping sprees, Sal bought multi-colored fabrics for Norina. This was to encourage her to wear bright clothes instead of solid black.

"You're too young to wear black," Sal said.

"I'm a widow," Norina said. "I have to wear black."

"How long have you been wearing black?"

"For the past two years, since my husband died."

"Well you're not dead. You're alive. You have every right to enjoy colors."

"But people are going to talk."

"Forget about them. People will always have something to say."

Norina remained silent. She loved flashy clothes.

"You should also cut your hair and style it. Old ladies pull their hair back in a bun." Sal flashed a light smile. "I'll pay for a hair stylist."

Norlina's eyes lit up. She had always wanted to wear a nice hairdo like the White Flies.

After Norina had her hair cut, she felt ten years younger in her new coiffure. With the vibrant new fabrics, she made lots of outfits for herself.

When Norina promenaded on the street wearing her hew hairstyle and her colorful new dresses, she sensed looks of admiration from everyone. She felt like an American Wife. When Domenico the Butcher bumped into her on the street, he bowed and kissed her hand. Tonino the Baker couldn't stop looking at Norina when she brought cookies to be baked.

Tonino delivered the baked cookies to Norina's house personally.

"You're still a beautiful woman," he whispered.

Norina beamed. She felt she was no longer a wretched widow. She felt like a woman, a beautiful woman!

Sal took the Voltini children to the only toy store in town and bought them whatever they wanted. The children were exhilarated beyond belief.

"Sal is better than *la Befana*," Olimpia said to her friends as she hugged her magnificent porcelain doll.

Pasquale liked to ride his flashy bicycle. He enjoyed the looks filled with amazement mixed with envy that he received from his friends.

Mario loved his toy truck with real lights. It was similar to the one Robertino, Mrs. Fatti's son had. Mario actually believed that Sal was a saint, just like Santa Claus.

Little Donato was fond of his new tricycle. His friends cheered when they saw him riding the tiny vehicle. He got so attached to his tricycle that he no longer played with the chickens, and forgot all about Chicken Grazia.

Sal enjoyed the happiness Grazia's relatives derived from his gifts. Their happiness was so intense that he thought it was worth every lira he spent.

"Sal bought jewelry for Grazia from the best jewelry store in town. He bought pearl earrings and a pearl necklace for Caterina, and gold necklaces with crosses for Ada, Clotilde and Marta. He also bought gold bracelets for my nieces. And for me..." Norina showed her neighbors a thick gold necklace and a pendant with the image of a Madonna engraved.

"Your future son-in-law is a real gentleman," Lina the Warm House said.

"What did he buy for Grazia?" Titina the Alligator asked.

"A bracelet, earrings, and a necklace with the stones that shine in the dark."

"Those stones are called diamonds," Carolina the Good Life said. "Only millionaires can afford to buy diamonds."

"He's a generous millionaire," Lina said.

Norina's eyes coruscated. "Sal also wants to pay for the trousseau and all of the expenses of the wedding reception."

The neighbors expanded their eyes as they exchanged looks.

Giacomino the Blind Man turned to Norina. "Your sky got so bright."

Norina beamed. She was grateful to Sal for brightening her sky, and bragged about him to whomever she spoke.

A week before the wedding, Norina had Grazia's trousseau on display in the house. The trousseau astounded everyone.

"These are high quality linens," a *signora* from the Catholic League said.

"Grazia's outfits are couture," Mrs. Fatti said.

"I wanted to pay for the trousseau, but Sal insisted so much. He bought it all," Norina said. "I didn't have to put up a lira."

Titina the Alligator nodded even though she thought that Norina didn't want to pay for the trousseau.

"Norina has saved a lot of money," Clotilde said.

"Some people spend a fortune on their daughters' trousseaus," Maddalena said.

"My cousin sold a piece of land to pay for her daughter's trousseau," Carolina the Good Life said.

Norina indicated Grazia's portrait. "I only spent the money for the portrait."

They all looked in unison at Grazia's portrait standing on the mantle of the fireplace.

"The portrait has changed Grazia's sky," Clotilde said.

They all smiled in agreement.

When Grazia and Sal went to dinner at the Zordi residence, Mr. and Mrs. Zordi welcomed them with good cheer. Grazia felt awkward being served by her sister Caterina in the house where she had been a maid. Caterina didn't mind. She was happy to have a job, since she was able to put money away. When the meal was over, Caterina brought out the champagne and scurried into the kitchen, eager to enjoy the leftover dessert.

Grazia had never had champagne in her life. She only drank half a glass.

"Champagne is my best friend," Mrs. Francesca Zordi whispered. "It makes me feel good."

"My wife always tells the truth when she drinks champagne, *in vino veritas*," Mr. Tiziano Zordi said.

"Champagne gives me a feeling of freedom." Mrs. Zordi downed her champagne. "I tell the truth when I feel liberated."

"Tell the truth about Grazia and Sal," Mr. Zordi said.

Mrs. Zordi giggled. "The minute I introduced Grazia to Sal there was something magical. It looked like he had been struck by lightning. Sal couldn't stop looking at her, and he couldn't stop thinking of her afterward. Since all the letters he wrote to me were about Grazia, all my letters to him were also about her. Grazia has been the lead character of our correspondence."

"It's funny you should say that," Sal said. "I got to know Grazia through Francesca's letters. Sometimes I feel like I've fallen in love with a character from literature."

Mrs. Zordi lit up a cigarette. "You have to give me credit for being a good writer. I always search for genuineness, and I'm able to discover the real essence of people."

Sal clapped his hands. "Francesca, you're a great writer."

Mrs. Zordi puffed smoke into the air. "I note the good and the bad about people. I even wrote to Sal about the incident when I caught Grazia stealing pasta."

Grazia's face blushed. "I'm still so sorry about that."

Mrs. Zordi scrunched her cigarette into the ashtray. "You apologized more than enough. It broke my heart you were in such need. I could see you felt so embarrassed you wanted to disappear. Tears were streaming down your face."

Grazia placed her hands on her cheeks. "Stealing was the last thing I wanted to do."

"I know that." Mrs. Zordi poured more champagne into her glass. "I can read you like a book. Due to your poverty, you couldn't be yourself. You did things you considered wrong for the sake of your family's survival."

Grazia turned to Sal. "Were you shocked when you heard I was a thief?"

"You're a gorgeous bandit, who apologized and didn't do it again." Sal patted Grazia's hand. "That's not a real thief in my book."

"How do you know I never did it again?"

Sal gave Grazia a bear hug. "Because the following day, you didn't take any leftovers from the refrigerator, even though you were entitled to take them. That's a sign of nobility and integrity."

Grazia felt good in the comfort of his arms. She felt released from the guilt of having stolen.

"I felt so bad when I heard you got very sick," Sal whispered into her ear.

Grazia raised her eyebrows. "Very sick?"

"Caterina told Francesca you were seriously ill. I was ready to come from America to see you. I thought you were going to die."

"I was not ill. Caterina made up those lies to get my job."

"I actually believed those lies. I wrote to Francesca every day to find out how you were."

"That's when I knew for sure that Sal loved you," Mrs. Zordi raised her champagne glass. "To true love."

Sal, Grazia and Mr. Zordi raised their champagne glasses. "To true love," they said all together.

Sal and Grazia were one of the most sought-after couples in town. People turned their heads when they saw them on the street. The Margassi Sisters got excited when they ran into them, just as if they had seen a celebrity couple.

"I want to present to you my special friends, Gina and Giovanna Margassi," Grazia said to Sal.

The Margassi Sisters were so overwhelmed to be introduced to a classy American man that they were speechless. They both smiled with their lips sealed, to avoid exposing their rotten teeth.

"They're happy to meet you," Grazia whispered to Sal.

Sal bowed and gave the women a hand kiss. "It's my pleasure to meet you."

The Margassi Sisters had never been treated with so much kindness by such a sophisticated man. Inebriated by the scent of Sal's cologne, they stared at his bright white teeth. Enchanted, they waved and walked away.

"Why are they so shy?" Sal asked. "It seemed like they were afraid to talk."

"The Margassi Sisters are not themselves." Grazia pursed her lips. "Their lives have been ruined."

"Ruined?"

"When they were young, they were raped by a landowner while they were working in the fields."

"That's terrible."

"People blamed them for being raped."

"Why?"

"Because the Margassi Sisters worked in the fields. Ignorant people believe men are hunters, and unwed women have to protect themselves by avoiding situations and places where men can take advantage of them."

Sal's eyes flashed. "The landowner behaved like a monster. No man has the right to ruin a woman's life."

Grazia wrinkled her nose. She was tempted to tell Sal about her experience with Carlo the Broken Neck, but as she gave it some thought, she decided not to. The deserved beating Anna the Heavyweight gave Carlo had forced him to leave town. "The landowner is a pig. Through the years, the Margassi Sisters got nothing but more abuse.

Men didn't take them seriously. Men pretended to be in love with them, but they only used them for sex."

"Unbelievable."

"It's a shame." Grazia's eyes became gloomy. "The Margassi Sisters had so much talent. They had the potential to become the best dress-makers in town, but ever since they were raped, they've never been treated with respect. They picked up a bad reputation. They were called whores since they had so many affairs, and women wouldn't give them work as dressmakers, fearing they would ruin their reputa-tions by associating with them. The poor sisters ended up working as maids."

Sal frowned. "That's so tragic." His frown turned into a smile. "I want to hire them for my garment factory in America. I can always use dressmakers with talent."

Grazia stared at Sal with her mouth open. "You can give them work?"

"I'm an employer. I can request visas for them in America as employees with special skills."

Grazia jumped up. "That would be wonderful."

"People should be where they belong. Talent is a terrible thing to waste."

Grazia's face radiated warmth. *If Sal can help the Margassi Sisters, he can help many women in town who need work and freedom.*

She took a look at Sal and realized there was something special about him. He had a big heart! Grazia closed her eyes and gave Sal a thankful kiss.

Even though Grazia appreciated the gifts she received from Sal, what she treasured most was the love she received from him. She loved to be loved by him. She couldn't believe how in the past, men had made her feel like a worthless worm. Most of the destitute women from Vocevero considered themselves inferior beings. Sal had the power to make her feel important and precious. She no longer felt like just another miserable small-town girl. She felt just like what she was meant to be… like what she was supposed to be… like what she wanted to be… She felt like a real woman!

Now, as they passed by Giorgio's house, she didn't even bother to look at it. Even if she had been walking alone, she still wouldn't have glanced at Giorgio's house. As the moment she first saw Sal's red tie, Grazia crossed Giorgio out of her mind and forgot she ever felt anything for him. Giorgio belonged to the past, a past she had buried and didn't want to remember.

The Margassi Sisters stared at Grazia with their eyes wide open when they heard Sal could give them jobs in America.

"Is it true?" Giovanna Margassi kept asking.

"Tell me again that it's true," Gina Margassi kept saying.

"It is true." Grazia raised her voice. "Your sky is about to change. You two are candidates to go to America."

Giovanna shut her eyes and grinned. "Maybe I'm going to get lucky and find true love in America."

"I like American men," Gina said. "They have nice teeth and they smell good."

"American men are also gentlemen," Giovanna said.

"They're respectful." Gina sighed happily. "They kiss women's hands."

The Margassi Sisters were ecstatic. When they sauntered on the streets, they told passersby they were candidates to go to America. People's jaws dropped. The news that the Margassi Sisters were going to America spread as fast as the wind. People instantly forgot all about the sisters' bad reputations, and saw them as lucky human beings. People loved to associate with lucky human beings. The two sisters were treated like small-town celebrities.

Sal and Grazia's upcoming wedding was the talk of the town. Everyone was looking forward to it. Many neighbors on Saint Peter Street paid Norina visits and begged her to be invited. Norina ended up with too many people on her guest list.

"Norina is having an American style reception for Grazia's wedding," Titina the Alligator said to Colombina the Farmer's Wife.

"The lowlifes get all the windfalls." Colombina contorted her face. "They even get blessed by the sky."

Old Veronica looked up in the sky. "The colors of the sky change. They can't always be dark. I'm glad that Norina's sky got brighter."

"Norina is very generous to us," Lina the Warm House said.

"When the farmer prospers, so do his chickens," Titina said.

Colombina placed her hands on her hips. "Have you become one of Norina's chickens?"

Titina nodded.

Colombina curled her lips. "You should be ashamed to be Norina's chicken. Don't forget that Norina was a night payer. And don't forget that she's a happy widow. Norina has no respect for her late husband. She wears colorful clothes. She's looking for a lover for sure."

Titina remained silent. She felt privileged to be Norina's chicken. She didn't want to be dethroned. Norina's chickens were all invited to the wedding.

Colombina walked away clenching her fists.

Clotilde wanted to have the wedding reception in a catering hall, but Rodolfo insisted on having it at his house.

"My house is more elegant than a hall," Rodolfo said.

Clotilde smiled in agreement, as she knew Rodolfo's residence was indeed more modern than the two catering halls in town.

The impending wedding kept many people busy. Norina, Ada, Marta, and the Margassi Sisters sewed ensembles for themselves and for the children. It was an important event. Everyone had to look their best and reflect *la bella figura*. Many spectators would be looking at them. In the kitchen, Clotilde prepared kilos of cookie dough with Olimpia's and Caterina's help. Pasquale and Mario made many trips carrying pans of cookies to the community oven. The Voltinis' house had become the most aromatic house on Saint Peter Street. The poor loitered by the Voltinis' front door to smell the delicious scents diffusing into the air.

XXXVIII

Clad in their tailored outfits, Grazia and Sal looked like a White Fly couple. As they strolled on Saint Peter Street, they greeted their neighbors and acquaintances. Mesmerized, Serafina the Maid couldn't keep her eyes off them. To give the poor maid a feeling of importance, Grazia introduced her to Sal.

"I'm pleased to meet you." Sal bowed and kissed Serafina's hand.

Serafina grinned wide, exposing her bare gums. No one had ever paid her that kind of deference. "Go to Our Lady of Sorrows' feast. The Madonna is going to bless you for sure."

"We'll go to the feast," Grazia said.

Serafina kept looking at Grazia and Sal as they walked away.

"She's so cute," Sal said. "Who is she?"

"She's Serafina the Maid," Grazia said. "She walks her employer's son to school every day, and she insists on carrying his school bag. She always goes to church to see the brides and grooms, even though she actually never gets invited to the weddings."

"Well, then we should send her a proper invitation to our wedding."

"Yes, I'll send one to her. Serafina is going to be thrilled."

Sal spotted a group of little children dancing and singing in a circle. They were having a lot of fun. "Who's watching the children? Where are their mothers?"

"The mothers are in their houses cooking or cleaning. The children are supervised by the elderly women. They're the guardians of the street." Grazia indicated many old women seated by their front doors.

Old Veronica was singing a *Ninna Nanna* to a baby lying on her lap. Grazia blew a kiss at the baby. "Is he Carolina's son?"

"Yes, he's Little Gianni." Old Veronica hugged the baby. "He's getting attached to me. This morning Carolina and Carmela had a big fight."

"Why?" Grazia asked.

"Carmela wanted to watch the baby, but Carolina preferred me over her." The old woman flashed a bit of a smile. "I have more experience with children than Carmela."

They love babies so much that they even fight to take care of them, Sal thought. He realized the street was a safe playground for the children, since it was so narrow that cars could not get through. He wished he had a playground guarded by kindhearted old women by his house when he was a kid.

Though they were sauntering on Saint Peter Street, Grazia didn't indicate her house to Sal. Her mother made her promise not to show Sal the house. Norina was too ashamed of her home.

Grazia noticed Contessa Fiorella's hand sticking out of her window. The hand waved for them to enter the *palazzo*.

"We've been invited to visit the contessa. She's the woman who has been imprisoned in her house by her husband."

"I would love to meet her."

Promptly, Grazia led Sal to Count Torre's opulent *palazzo*. As the door opened, she dragged him inside. They were faced with Contessa Fiorella, who hastily closed the door behind them.

Sal bowed and kissed the contessa's hand. "It's a pleasure meeting you."

"I'm happy to meet the man Grazia is marrying," the contessa said. "I'm writing a novel, and since Grazia is the leading character, you are an important character as well."

Sal's eyes sparkled. "Really? I'm a character in a novel?"

The contessa flashed a glint of a grin. "Yes. I find you fascinating as a character."

"I can't believe a beautiful and intelligent *signora* like you is kept a prisoner in her own house," Sal said.

"A person can be imprisoned in many ways." The contessa exhaled. "I realized that I have always been a prisoner."

Sal tilted his head. "Always?"

"I've been a prisoner because I couldn't be myself. Through my writing, I've been able to fight my demons and find out who I am." Contessa Fiorella leaped at the sound of the church bell. She counted the rings in her mind. "My husband could come home any minute."

"I don't want to run into him." Grazia swiftly escorted Sal out of the house.

"Your friends are remarkable people," Sal said.

Grazia bobbed her head in agreement.

The *piazza* was adorned with garlands of lights forming a succession of arches to celebrate the town's annual feast in honor of Our Lady of Sorrows. The sidewalks were filled with chairs and tables topped with colorful umbrellas and food stands selling the best of the local gastronomy. People were having espresso, cappuccino, pastries, and many other delicacies. Thousands of people parading in their best attire promenaded up and down the *piazza* under a starry blue satin sky.

Sal noticed four mature ladies wearing long black lace dresses and lots of sparkling jewelry. Grazia waved at them. They waved back.

"You know them?" Sal asked.

"They are called the Four Seasons Contessas. They are named after the four seasons: *Primavera*, *Estate*, *Autunno,* and *Inverno.* Even though they had many suitors, they refused to get married because they never found true love."

"What interesting women you have in this town. Each one seems to have an incredible story."

At the sound of music blasting, Sal turned his head in its direction and spotted a gazebo filled with musicians. People were seated around the gazebo enjoying the music.

"They're playing Verdi," Sal said. "He's one of my favorite composers."

Baronessa Rosa appeared on the stage and began to sing the aria "Sweet Name."

"She's the best opera singer in town," Grazia said.

"Her voice is commanding," Sal said.

Grazia saw Anna the Heavyweight in the audience. "You see that big and tall woman?"

Sal nodded.

"She's nicknamed the Heavyweight. She's the strongest woman in town. She fights to defend the underdogs. She's given beatings to a lot of bad people. She's the one who punched Antonio the Devil for what he did to me."

"She's an extraordinary woman."

"The brunette standing next to Anna is her daughter, Margherita. They call her the Lover of Saint Peter Street because she's in love with Franchino the Bird's Nest. He's a married man who sold the cart he used for his business to save her life."

"That's true love."

Grazia pointed to the life-size statue of Our Lady of Sorrows standing triumphantly in front of Saint Maria's Church. The statue was clad in a black lace gown covered with many layers of jewelry and lira bills pinned to her gown. Sal stared at the statue.

"The people here are so devoted to Our Lady of Sorrows that they give her money and jewelry. Some people claim they've received miracles from her."

As they walked towards the statue, Grazia noticed the Dumb Brothers. They were standing at each side of the Madonna.

"Sister Felicia told us to pray to Our Lady of Sorrows," the elder Dumb Brother said. "We did a lot of praying."

"I hope the Madonna forgets all about our sins," the younger Dumb Brother said.

"What did you do?" Grazia asked.

The elder brother lowered his head. "We've cursed a lot."

"Sister Felicia came to visit us in the fields," the younger brother said. "She yelled at us and told us that cursing is a bad sin."

The elder brother's lips trembled. "I'm afraid that Sister Felicia is going to yell at us again."

Grazia stifled her laughter and walked away, dragging Sal along.

"They seem to be afraid of Sister Felicia," Sal said.

"Sister Felicia was the mother superior of the orphanage where they grew up. She was very strict. Anna the Heavyweight pulled a prank on them not long ago. She pretended to be Sister Felicia and told them not to curse."

"They believed her?"

Grazia shrugged. "They're the dumb brothers of the town. They believe anything people tell them."

Sal laughed heartily.

The pier was occupied by many rides and more food stands. Grazia saw her siblings having the time of their lives on the rides. She figured Sal had given them the money for the tickets.

"You're spoiling my siblings," Grazia said.

"They're children. They deserve to have fun." Sal noticed a woman with white hair dressed like a homeless bum, handing out candies to children. "Who is that woman with white hair?"

"She's Olga the Scared Cat. She's a fruit vendor who spends all her money on poor children."

"That's incredible."

Grazia spotted the Lucky Widow. She was clad in a white suit and a black evening hat, and was surrounded by many children. Grazia recognized them. They were Laura the White Flower's children.

"Do you see that lady wearing the black hat?"

"I see her. What about her?"

"Her nickname is the Lucky Widow."

"Why do they call her the Lucky Widow?"

"On her wedding day, she was kidnapped and raped. Her husband sent her back to her mother because he couldn't deal with the shame of having a wife who wasn't a virgin."

"That's terrible. She was a victim. He should have loved her even more."

"Luckily, after her husband died, she found real romance. A great man fell in love with her and married her. From that point on, people called her the Lucky Widow."

"That's an appealing love story." Sal revealed a light smile. "She looks like a character out of a novel."

As they continued their stroll, Grazia saw Angela the Crazy Head and waved at her.

"Who are you waving at?"

"That's Angela the Crazy Head. She's the smart woman who did the readings of Contessa Fiorella's novels. She also defended my brothers when they were accused of stealing, and won the case."

Angela waved back and walked towards them.

Sal greeted Angela with a bow and a kiss on the hand. "I'm happy to meet you. I've heard so many wonderful things about you."

"I heard wonderful things about you as well," Angela said.

"We went to visit Contessa Fiorella," Grazia said.

Angela beamed. "I'm thrilled for her success."

"What success?"

"I gave her novels to the notary public to read, and he gave them to a publisher." Angela did a little jig. "I just spoke to the notary public and he told me that Contessa Fiorella's novels are going to be published soon."

Grazia's face brightened. "I'm happy for the contessa. I hope she makes a lot of money."

Angela turned to Sal. "I've been looking for my brother who lives in America for the past ten years. Can you help me find him?"

Sal nodded. "Of course. I'll hire a private investigator as soon as I go back to the United States."

"Thank you." Angela waved as she walked away.

As they watched Angela blend into the crowd, Grazia saw Pino the Red Eye. She led Sal to the vendor's small stand. Pino was selling fresh octopus. Lisetta was standing by his side. Grazia introduced her fiancé, and Pino introduced his. Sal bowed and kissed Lisetta's hand. While he did so, many people exchanged looks filled with astonishment. It was strange to see a gentleman kiss a whore's hand in public.

Pino appreciated Sal's gesture. No one had treated his Lisetta with such finesse. "You're a-a real-real gentle-man. You de-serve a-a-a girl like-like-like Grazia. She's a-a-a star in-in-in the sky."

Sal gave Grazia a bear hug. "She's the star in my sky."

In the comfort of his arms, Grazia felt like a star in the sky, since Sal treated her like one.

"Lisetta is-is-is the-the star of my-my-my sky. If-if-if I play the-the *to-rero* again-again in-in-in the-the circus, I'm-I'm-I'm going to-to-to make-make-make money and I'm-I'm-I'm going to-to-to marry m-m-my star Lisetta."

Lisetta beamed.

"I hope you get married soon," Grazia said, walking away with Sal.

"He played the *torero* in the circus?" Sal asked.

Grazia giggled. "Yes, he played a *torero* that kept falling off the donkey. My family and I had to pretend to be related to him so we could get free tickets."

Sal looked Grazia in the eye. "Your life is so rich."

Grazia scrunched her forehead. "Rich?"

"Your life is rich because it's intense, and it's filled with so many emotions and many events that create excitement: live comedy, live drama, live theater…"

Grazia widened her eyes. "I've never thought of any part of my life as rich."

Sal flashed a hint of a smile. "You can be rich in many ways in life."

XXXIX

Saint Maria's Church had never been so crowded. People were standing in the back and every nook and cranny. They were all eager to see Grazia, Norina's daughter, marry Sallustio Solvi, the American. Norina felt like a White Fly in her pink lace dress and her puffy hairdo. She enjoyed the looks filled with admiration she received from people and scrutinized the outfits the other women were sporting. Mrs. Matilde Fatti was pompously clothed in a couture turquoise satin dress. She felt honored to be seated next to Mrs. Francesca Zordi, who was dressed up in a stunning maroon lace suit and a black hat. Angela the Crazy Head looked comely in a burgundy ensemble she had borrowed from an American Wife.

All the girls from the Sewing School were seated in the second row with the Maestre: Aria and Ombretta. They all looked their best in their colorful couture designs. Serafina the Maid was clad in her baby blue lace dress. She was staring at the main entrance, eager to see the bride. She was ecstatic to have been formally invited. Anna the Heavyweight was proudly dressed up in a purple lace dress. She waved happily at people. She felt like a White Fly in her new frock.

A White Fly kept gazing at Sal. "The groom is a refined man."

"The groom looks like the happiest man on earth," a voice whispered.

"Who is the best man?" another voice asked.

"It's Mr. Tiziano Zordi, an important lawyer who lives in the city," Lina the Warm House responded.

"Grazia used to be his wife's maid," Titina the Alligator said.

"A maid that marries an American… it's a fairy tale story," the White Fly said.

At the sound of the nuptial march, the spectators turned their heads to look at the stars of the day walking down the aisle. In their navy blue suits, Mario and Pasquale were the groomsmen. Olimpia and Caterina were the flower girls gliding in their white gowns. Little Donato was carrying the pillow with the wedding rings in his white suit. Norina couldn't help but wave at her neighbors when the bride appeared, escorted by Vituccio. Sal stared at his bride flashing a bright smile.

Giacomino the Blind Man asked, "How is the bride's dress?"

"It's breathtaking," Lina whispered. "I've never seen anything that compares to it."

Giacomino tapped Lina's arm. "Describe the dress to me."

He received no answer since everyone was hypnotized by Grazia. The blind man had to rely on his imagination. He pictured a stupendous satin dress, hand-embroidered, with a cloud-like train that floated behind it.

Norina exhaled, relieved, as soon as Vituccio gave Grazia away to Sal.

"You can fall in love with a person just by looking at that person's portrait," Father Camillo said. "When something is meant to be, it happens because it's predestined from the sky. Everything is written in the sky."

Many in the audience nodded.

"It's very romantic," Margherita whispered, directing her gaze at Franchino the Bird's Nest. To her, he looked like a groom in his black suit.

The Margassi Sisters, dressed in their own designed flower print outfits, smiled with their lips sealed to avoid exposing their rotten teeth. They were also smiling at the prospect of a better sky.

Norina stared at her children. They looked picture perfect in their brand new clothes and mirrored *la bella figura*. They seemed like a vision to Norina. She felt like she was living a dream. In her intense excitement, she feared their images would disappear. From time to time, she glanced at Sal and her children to reassure herself they had not vanished.

Clotilde dried her tears with a cross-stitched handkerchief when the priest pronounced Sal and Grazia man and wife. Baronessa Rosa's rendition of the "Ave Maria," resonated in the church as the bride and groom walked down the aisle and exited out. The Dumb Brothers gave away little bags filled with rice to the guests. It was their wedding present to the newlyweds.

"Hurrah to the newlyweds. *Viva gli sposi*," many guests shouted, showering the bride and the groom with rice.

Ubaldo the Photographer snapped lots of pictures of Grazia. "She's a great subject," he kept saying.

The spectators watched Grazia and Sal as they got into a white convertible car. The Margassi Sisters blew kisses at the newlyweds.

"Good luck to the bride and groom," Gina Margassi said.

"God bless them for giving us the chance to go to America," Giovanna Margassi said.

Serafina the Maid wished she were younger. Grazia may have given her the opportunity to go to America, too. She gazed at the bride and the groom. They looked like a couple straight out of a television box.

A procession of children and a cloud of white pigeons followed the car as soon as it took off.

"Marriage can change your luck," Lina said.

"I heard they're not just having sandwiches," a passerby said. "They're having an American style reception."

Giacomino nodded with a light smile. "I've been invited to the reception."

Serafina the Maid beamed, exposing her bare gums. "I got invited too."

Titina narrowed her eyes. "Are you sure you got invited?"

Serafina pulled a card from her brassiere and waved it in the air. "It's the first time I got invited to a wedding."

They all stared at her, unable to hide their shock.

It was a custom to start any wedding reception with the recital of a poem. Clotilde took Olimpia by the hand and led her to the middle of the room. Olimpia recited a long poem dedicated to the newlyweds. The girl wrung her hands together as she stomped and stuttered. Though Clotilde was disappointed and embarrassed, she forced a smile at the spectators. When Olimpia finally finished reciting the poem, all the onlookers applauded. Olimpia and Clotilde were relieved that the spectators were kind.

While raising his glass of champagne, the best man, Mr. Tiziano Zordi, said, "Best wishes to Sal and Grazia. Their love made me believe in true love."

The newlyweds and guests all raised their champagne glasses.

"*Salute*," the best man said, inviting everyone to drink.

"*Salute*," the newlyweds and the invitees replied in unison.

They all drank their champagne.

Rodolfo curled his lips as soon as he noticed the neighbors of Saint Peter Street among the guests. He turned to his wife and whispered, "I don't understand your sister. Her daughter becomes a White Fly and she invites a bunch of lowlifes to the wedding. She should give herself some airs. She should stay away from those people. They make us look bad."

"Norina is so happy that her daughter has married a good man that she wants to share her joy with everyone," Ada said.

Rodolfo gritted his teeth. "She should share it with the right people." His voice was overpowered by the sound of Giacomino the Blind Man's accordion.

The sound of the music blasted through the whole neighborhood. A group of boys cheered and amused themselves by dancing in the street. It was an opportunity for them to learn how to dance. Rodolfo peered out the window and noticed that Lisetta was dancing with Pino the Red Eye.

Rodolfo wrinkled his nose. "There's a prostitute dancing in front of my house."

Clotilde shrugged a shoulder. "She's on the street, where she belongs. She's not in the house."

Ada took Rodolfo aside and gave him a harsh look. "You're an ungrateful creature. You should be nice to Lisetta."

Rodolfo scrunched his forehead. "I should be nice to a prostitute? Are you out of your mind?"

"You should be thankful to Lisetta because she gave you great sex in the past. Once, you were drunk when you came home, and you told me Lisetta is a woman and a half because she knows how to please a man. You're the last person who should be ashamed of her. If you're ashamed of her, you should be more ashamed of yourself, because she became part of you when she had sex with you," Ada said, knowing her husband would never smack her in public.

Rodolfo narrowed his eyes and flared his nostrils. "How dare you speak to me like that?" He lowered his voice. "You're taking advantage of the fact that it's your niece's wedding, and I can't punch you in the eyes in front of the White Flies. As soon as everyone leaves, you'll be sorry."

"You'll never ever lay a hand on me again, because if you do, you'll never see me again. I'll go to America. I'm a great dressmaker. In America, I'll be able to support myself. I'm not going to need your money or your abuse. Do you know how bad you'd look if I left you? Rodolfo the Great Shoulders, dumped by his wife?" Ada flaunted a bit of a grin. "People are going to laugh at you."

Ada pranced away. Rodolfo remained speechless with his eyes wide open.

Mario stood in the rear corner of the room and enjoyed the party scene. He felt as if he were watching a movie on the big screen. Many waiters wearing nice uniforms undulated through the room carrying their trays piled with lasagne, tortellini, cannelloni, meat, and fish. Mario noticed the guests had different eating habits. Some people asked for small portions. On the other hand, the neighbors of Saint Peter Street asked for big portions. Mario thought his neighbors must have had larger appetites. Titina the Alligator and Anna the Heavyweight brought their own paper to wrap pieces of meat. They hid a lot of food in their big bags.

As Baronessa Rosa's booming voice sang the "The Tango of the Jealous Lovers," Maddalena and Arturo danced passionately. They were such great dance partners that everyone smiled at them. When they finished dancing, people clapped their hands.

Angela the Crazy Head walked by Maddalena and said, "You look so happy when you dance."

Maddalena showed a half-smile. "The bird in a cage doesn't dance for love, she dances for rage."

Mario couldn't figure out what Maddalena was talking about. Enchanted by the music, he watched people having a great time dancing. Deep in his heart, he wished he could dance with his sister Grazia, but he didn't have the courage to ask her. He had never had the audacity to dance in his life. Saveria the Midwife was swaying with a handsome young man, who Mario figured had to be her son.

Mario spotted Uncle Vituccio and Aunt Marta. *They smile at everyone while they dance. They look happy. They must have decided not to fight for the day*, he thought.

The Margassi Sisters were dancing with two well-dressed men. Mario recalled that he had always seen the two sisters with men who were poorly dressed. He figured the well-dressed men must be the sisters' rich boyfriends. He was glad for them. The two sisters had always been good to him.

Caterina and Rocco, the son of the shepherd, were hopping around staring at each other. *They must like each other a lot*, Mario thought.

Pasquale was talking to Biagino's sister, a pretty brunette. *Pasquale must like her a lot because he smiles at her a lot*, Mario thought.

Carolina the Good Life's husband rocked his baby boy in his arms. The baby giggled as his father spun him around. Mario realized the baby must like his father a lot.

Mario looked at his sister, the bride, and noticed Sal beaming like a car headlight at Grazia. *He likes her very, very much.*

Mario noticed that a tall man approached Carmela the Daughter of the Umbrella Repair Man and asked her to dance. Carmela shook her head. Mario wondered why she refused to dance with him.

"I can't believe that Carmela refused to dance with her lover," Mario heard Titina say.

Mario figured that Carmela must no longer like her lover.

Mario flashed a light grin when he saw Mrs. Francesca Zordi, the blond woman who drove the car. She was very beautiful, as beautiful as Contessa Fiorella. He wondered why Mrs. Zordi was dancing with the old man who had made the speech. He was the same man who was standing next to Sal in church. A beautiful signora like Mrs. Francesca Zordi should have been dancing with one of the good-looking actors he had seen on television.

All the guests shifted their attention to the bride and groom when they cut an enormous cake.

Mario stared at the cake. He had never seen a cake so big.

It must be an American cake, he thought. His focus was distracted by Olimpia wandering around the room.

Olimpia kept pointing to the ceiling, saying: "Hi!"

Mario thought Olimpia was very happy. Aunt Clotilde realized Olimpia was drunk. She took her by the hand and dragged her out of the room. The bride and the groom withdrew from the room as well.

"Where did they go?" a girl asked.

"They went to change their clothes," Titina replied.

The newlyweds returned twenty minutes later in their honeymoon attire. Grazia looked splendid in a beige tailored outfit and a matching hat. Sal looked like an authentic American in a blue suit and white shoes. The bride and the groom said their farewells to the guests and gave away favors and small baskets filled with almond cookies.

When Grazia and Sal walked out of the room, the guests followed them outside and blended in the crowd. People applauded and cheered as the newlyweds got into the car. Many people followed the car until it sped away, disappearing into the distance.

The newlyweds spent their first wedding night in the high-class hotel in the city. Grazia undressed herself in the bathroom and donned a white lace nightgown. Surprised by her image reflected in the mirror, she covered herself with a towel. She was reluctant to come out of the bathroom. Her eyes gleamed with tears as she recalled the way her mother described sex to her. Sex was a duty. A duty couldn't be fun. Sex was something women didn't enjoy. Only whores enjoyed sex. Women had to pretend to get pleasure from sex lest their husbands feel bad. Grazia wished she didn't have to have sex.

A knock on the door startled Grazia. She cringed as she thought Sal was pressing his right to consummate their marriage. Her face blushed when she stepped out of the bathroom. Sal picked her up, held her in his arms and placed her gracefully on the bed. Grazia felt awkward. She covered her face with the sheet. When she poked her head out of the sheet, she was hit with the realization that she was in bed with a man. She had never been in bed with a man! She felt so embarrassed that she wished she could vanish. She felt relieved when Sal turned the lights off.

Sal made love to her with tenderness. When Grazia reached her orgasm, she had the sensation of touching the sky. It was a grand feeling. She had freed herself from all her fear of sex. Sex was phenomenal! Sal caressed her face and her body all night long. He loved her. She was the woman he had always dreamt of. When Grazia fell asleep, he watched her, completely and totally enamored.

The following day, Grazia and Sal had a deluxe breakfast at Aunt Ada's house. They had fresh *zabaione*, fresh ricotta cheese, almond cookies, *zeppole*, and plenty of espresso.

Sal relished Norina and Ada's homemade food. "You two are great cooks. Your meals are so fresh and exquisite. In America, not even millionaires eat the quality of cuisine you cook."

Ada and Norina widened their eyes as they exchanged looks. They thought Sal was exaggerating, and going out of his way to give them compliments.

"Sal, you're very sweet to say that," Ada said.

"The newlyweds have to respect the tradition to visit their relatives," Norina said "Since Aunt Clotilde is the oldest aunt, you have to visit her before Uncle Vituccio and Aunt Marta."

"I'll be happy to wear one of my new outfits," Grazia said, heading to the bedroom.

Grazia returned ten minutes later in a magnificently tailored hand embroidered yellow linen suit. She spun around to give Sal a better look.

"You look like a Park Avenue lady," Sal said.

A Park Avenue lady must be some sort of American peasant woman, Norina thought. "I made the suit and Ada did the embroidery."

"I love it," Sal said. "It's a couture suit that money can't buy. Mussolini was right when he said Italy has a population of artists."

Ada raised her eyebrows. "Mussolini wasn't talking about us. He was talking about real artists."

Sal flashed a light grin. "He was talking about you and your sister as well, because you're both great designers and great artists."

"Thank you for considering us artists," Ada said. "Do they like suits like this in America?"

"In America, a custom-made hand embroidered suit would cost a fortune."

"Why is it cheaper here?"

"Because in this little town, people with talent are underpaid," Sal said.

"You're right," Norina said, even though she didn't understand the word "underpaid."

"I'd like to open a garment factory in town and import the 'Made in Italy' products to America."

Grazia's eyes sparkled. "That's a fantastic idea. You could employ a lot of the women in town."

Sal beamed. "I would be honored to give work to these great women artists."

Flashing a bright smile, Clotilde welcomed Sal and Grazia into her house. She had set the table with a hand-embroidered tablecloth, a tiny crystal glass, a fancy bottle of homemade liqueur, and a plate filled with almond cookies. Grazia only ate one cookie. Sal ate plenty of cookies with gusto.

"The cookies are mouth-watering," Sal said.

Clotilde's face radiated. "I made them."

"You're a talented baker."

He's a gentleman, he gives out compliments, Clotilde thought, pouring the liqueur slowly into the tiny crystal glass. She handed the glass to Sal.

"What about Grazia?" Sal asked.

"Grazia is not allowed to drink," Clotilde said.

"Why?"

"Because... she's a girl."

"Grazia is no longer a small-town girl. She's going to become an American. In America, women drink just as men do. They have the same rights as men."

Clotilde didn't dare contradict Sal. She promptly reached for another tiny crystal glass and poured liqueur for Grazia. Sal drank his glass of liqueur all in one shot. Grazia felt as powerful as a man when she sipped the liqueur.

"The liqueur is out of this world," Sal said.

Grazia smiled in agreement.

The newlyweds enjoyed more lemon liqueur when they paid a visit to Uncle Vituccio and Aunt Marta.

XL

White pigeons flying around Count Torre's *palazzo* caught Grazia's attention as she strolled on the street with Sal.

"Contessa Fiorella has finally left," Grazia said.

"How do you know?" Sal asked.

"The shutters of her window are open. They used to be closed all the time." Grazia looked at the pigeons swirling cheerfully in the bright sky. "She's as free as a bird."

"I'm so glad she finally set herself free," Sal said.

People couldn't bear the shock when they saw Contessa Fiorella walking out of the opulent *palazzo*. Angela the Crazy Head was the only person who was aware the contessa was going to escape. She watched the scene with delight. Contessa Fiorella looked stunning in a white suit and a matching hat.

Angela flashed a radiant smile. "She looks so beautiful. She looks like she's getting married to herself."

Carmela the Daughter of the Umbrella Repair Man smiled in agreement. Ninuccio the Painter, Arturo, and Carmine the Shepherd couldn't keep their eyes off the contessa. They kept staring at her. Passersby stopped to look at her.

"Who is that *signora*?" a passerby asked.

"She's Contessa Fiorella," Arturo responded.

"She's a breathtaking woman," Ninuccio said.

Carmine exhaled heavily. "I finally got to see her."

"She looks like the Lucky Widow," the passerby said.

"She's not that lucky. Her husband is still alive," Angela said.

Count Torre went out of his mind when he realized his wife had left. He squealed like an infuriated animal while he punched the wall. He frantically went looking for her, like a predator in search of his victim.

"Have you seen my wife?" Count Torre kept asking people.

The neighbors of Saint Peter Street didn't dare tell him they had seen the contessa. Count Torre searched everywhere for his victim. He even went to the *carabinieri* and asked if someone had seen his wife. No one knew her whereabouts.

As they strolled on Saint Peter Street Sal asked Grazia to indicate him her house.

Grazia's face drooped as she pointed at a tiny house. "My house is old and decrepit. We don't even have a wet sink." She stopped herself from saying they didn't even have a bathroom. "My mother is ashamed of the house. She begged me not to show it to you."

"Your mother should not be ashamed. No one should be ashamed of their poverty. Poverty is not a disease. It's simply a condition. A condition can change for the better. Poor people can become rich. Tomorrow morning, I want to see your house."

Grazia shrugged. "I guess I have no choice. I'll just have to show it to you."

Later in the day, Grazia informed her mother that Sal wanted to see their house.

"Just tell Sal that you're going to show him the house and don't show it to him," Norina said.

"*Mamma*, I can't do that. He's my husband. I have to be honest. He wants to see the house tomorrow morning."

"I hope he doesn't have to go to the bathroom when he comes to the house. Did you tell him that we don't have a bathroom?"

Grazia shook her head. "No, I didn't."

Norina gave a sigh of relief.

Norina and Caterina spent the entire night cleaning the house. The following morning, they welcomed Sal and Grazia into the house. The kitchen smelled like the essence of cleanliness.

"It's nice. It's cozy, and it's very tidy," Sal said. As his eyes darted around the room, he realized there wasn't a refrigerator. "Where's the refrigerator?"

"We don't have a refrigerator," Caterina said.

"Very few people in town have a refrigerator," Grazia said Norina indicated the stove with two burners. "But we have a brand new stove."

"The stove doesn't have an oven?" Sal asked. "How do you bake the delicious cookies?"

"We send them to the community oven," Caterina responded.

"You go to all that trouble?"

"Very few people on the street have a stove with an oven," Grazia said.

Norina indicated the new flower print curtain that screened off the back room. "There's another room where my sons sleep."

"I thought you kept the television in there," Sal said. "So where do you keep the television?"

Norina pursed her lips. "We don't have a television, but we see a lot of movies on Mrs. Fatti's television."

As they moved to the second floor where the main bedroom was, Norina showed the statue of Our Lady of Sorrows, standing triumphantly on the dresser.

Sal gazed at the statue. "It's spectacular. The dress is embroidered with gold thread. It's definitely a work of art."

Norina blew a kiss at the Madonna. "I pray to Our Lady of Sorrows when I have a problem. She helps me a lot."

"Praying is good for the spirit," Sal said. "It gives you strength."

Norina spread her arms wide open. "I wish I had a better house, but this is all I have."

Sal patted Norina's shoulder. "You have other things that are more valuable than the house."

"What other things?" Norina shrugged. "I have nothing else."

"You think you have nothing, but you have the universe."

Norina narrowed her eyes. "The universe?"

"You have a lot of love around you."

Norina raised her eyebrows. "A lot of love around me?"

"You are surrounded by people that love you. There is a passionate bond between you and your children."

Norina bobbed her head even though she didn't quite understand the word "bond." "Oh yes… my children are good to me. They pay me respect a lot."

Sal beamed. "There is a passionate bond even between you and your relatives and friends. You are filled with passion even when you fight with each other."

"Oh, I do my best not to fight with anybody. I try to get along with everybody."

"You deserve respect and admiration for raising six children without a wet sink, a refrigerator, an oven, and a television set. You should be proud."

Norina bit the inside of her lip. *If he finds out about all the debts I had, he's going to lose respect for me for sure.*

Sal turned to Grazia. "Tomorrow, we're going to go shopping, and I'm going to buy your mother a refrigerator, a new stove with an oven, and a television set."

"Are you sure you want to buy all those things?" Norina asked.

Sal nodded. "I also want you to have a wet sink. I'm going to hire a plumber to install the sink and the faucet."

Caterina jumped up as she flashed a bright smile.

Norina beamed. "Oh Sal... Thank you so much. God bless you. I think Our Lady of Sorrows sent you."

Grazia gave Sal a warm hug. "Thank you."

At the sound of the church bell, Norina counted the chimes on her fingers. "We have to go to Ada's house to have breakfast."

As they scurried out of the house, they bumped into Titina the Alligator.

"Titi, whenever you want to watch television, you can come over to my house," Norina said.

"You have a television set?" Titina asked.

"My son-in-law is going to buy it for me tomorrow. He is also buying me a refrigerator, a new stove with an oven, and he's going to pay a plumber to put in a sink with running water."

Titina's mouth fell open. "The only people on the street who have a wet sink are Maddalena, the American Wife, Contessa Fiorella, Baronessa Rosa, and Colombina the Farmer's Wife."

Norina winked. "Tell Colombina about all the new things that I'm getting."

"When I have the time, I'm going to go to Colombina's house and I'm going to tell her." Titina hurried away. She steered herself towards Colombina's house.

"She's going to tell Colombina right now," Grazia whispered to Sal.

Sal giggled.

The following day a refrigerator, a television set, and a new stove with an oven and four burners were delivered to the Voltinis' house. The neighbors were dumbfounded.

"I hope they share their bright sky with us," Giacomino the Blind Man said.

"They will," Lina the Warm House said. "When the farmer prospers, so do his chickens. Don't forget that we're the Voltinis' chickens."

"It's a big privilege to be a Voltini chicken," Titina the Alligator said.

Lina and Giacomino nodded in agreement.

The Voltini children loved the refrigerator. They called it the magic box. They kept opening the magic box's door to feel the cool breeze. Norina didn't yell at them for the horseplay. She felt her children had the right to have some fun. Often, the children gave Giacomino the Blind Man and their friends a treat by allowing them to enjoy the cool breeze.

The Voltini residence became the movie theatre of Saint Peter Street. The Voltinis had plenty of spectators at night eager to watch their television. Mrs. Matilde Fatti had been dethroned. The neighbors no longer went to watch her television set by her house. They claimed they got a better view of the movie at the Voltinis' house, because Norina kept the front glass door open.

Sal loved to see people gathered by the Voltinis' home to watch television. He thought it was an amazing scene, because the degree of enjoyment of the audience was tremendous. The viewers showed Sal lots of respect, since he was the one who had provided the television set. Sal relished their attention. When he received appreciation and gratitude from people, it gave him a feeling of importance and intense joy. He was not accustomed to such an experience.

Sal was enchanted by the narrow streets of Vocevero, where the poor children had fun playing all sorts of games. He believed having fun was something wonderful and amazing that didn't have a price in life, because it was the kind of intense happiness money could not buy. Even though he was wealthy during his upbringing, he never had as much merriment as the poor children in the little town. Sal hardly had any playmates when he was growing up.

While Sal and Grazia were roaming along on Saint Peter Street, they bumped into Carmela the Daughter of the Umbrella Repair Man.

"Grazia, I have something important to tell you," Carmela said. "My relatives are out of town. Can you come over to my house?"

Grazia patted Carmela's shoulder. "Of course."

"Would you like me to wait outside?" Sal asked.

"You can come too," Carmela said. "I trust you more than any man in this town."

Sal's eyes sparkled. "I'm honored to have your trust."

Carmela led Grazia and Sal to her house. Once inside, they all took a seat around the table.

Carmela looked Grazia in the eye. "You know my situation."

Grazia nodded. "I know. Your boyfriend will never marry you because his family doesn't think you're worthy of him."

"You're the only people I can rely on." Carmela paused and took a deep breath. "I have a dark secret."

"What secret?" Grazia asked.

Carmela placed her hands on her cheeks. "I gave my baby away."

Grazia's jaw dropped. "You gave him away to an orphanage?" Carmela remained silent.

"What happened to the baby?"

"I gave my baby to Carolina the Good Life. I thought he would be better off with Carolina than in an orphanage. I was glad because I could see my baby every day." Carmela sighed. "But things have changed."

"What happened?"

"Carolina got jealous. She thought the baby was getting too attached to me." Carmela covered her face with her hands. "Carolina has forbidden me to visit my Little Gianni, my baby."

"That's terrible," Sal said.

"I'm a bad person." Carmela burst into tears. "I feel guilty I didn't keep my baby."

"You had no choice," Grazia said. "Your boyfriend should feel guilty."

"He doesn't feel guilty," Carmela cried out. "He's a beast. He's self-ish. He cannot love anybody besides himself… I dumped him."

"*Brava* Carmela, you did the right thing," Sal said.

"I'm glad you realized what an animal he is," Grazia said.

Carmela grabbed her hair. "I didn't do the right thing for my baby."

"You gave him to people who can take good care of him," Grazia said. "You'll keep an eye on him. You'll watch him grow up."

"At least I'll get to see him from a distance." Carmela dried the tears with her sleeve. "My boyfriend wanted to give the baby away to an orphanage."

"That's the worst thing he could have done," Sal said. Grazia turned to Sal. "Carmela is a great dressmaker."

"Sewing is my passion in life," Carmela said.

"I'm going to open a garment factory in town," Sal said. "I'll give you work."

"If I get work, I'll save money until I can afford the legal fees to get my baby back. You're an important man who can make a difference in women's lives." Carmela bounced out of the chair and gave Sal and Grazia a hug. "Friends like you are precious."

Grazia's eyes coruscated. *I would never have dreamed in a million years that I was going to marry a man who would make a difference in people's lives.*

Sal and Grazia sauntered out of the house and meandered down the street. Grazia noticed that Sal's eyes gleamed with tears.

Grazia tilted her head. "What happened? You look sad."

"I feel moved that Carmela wants her baby back," Sal said. "Carmela's story brought back so many sad memories."

"What sad memories?"

"My mother left me when I was a kid. She went to live with her millionaire lover... and she never looked for me."

"I'm sorry to hear that. Who raised you?"

"My father raised me, but he was more interested in his business than me. He wanted to become richer to compete with my mother's lover."

Grazia tucked her head on his chest. "You didn't get any affection from your parents."

"That's why I told you your life is so rich. In life, you can be rich in many ways. Even though you didn't have money, you got affection from your family. I never got any affection from my father. Maybe it would have been different if my mother had been around. I resent my mother for leaving me. Every time I came to Italy, I never had the guts to visit my mother. Deep down in my heart, I wanted to see her, but I couldn't bring myself to pay her a visit."

"I thought your parents died a long time ago."

"My father died two years ago. My mother died in my heart as far back as I can remember."

"You have to visit your mother." Grazia gave Sal a warm hug. "You have to make peace with your past. I'll come with you."

Sal exhaled heavily. "I could use your support when I visit Mrs. Isabella Solvi."

"You should call her *Mamma*."

Sal's face blushed. "It's painful for me to even say that word."

In order to emigrate to America, a medical checkup was mandatory. Sal escorted Grazia to a doctor in Naples.

After examining Grazia, the doctor turned to Sal. "Your wife is as healthy as a fish. She's ready to have lots of children."

"We'll have children when my wife feels ready," Sal said.

"Most people have children as soon as they get married. I get a lot of complaints from husbands when their wives don't get pregnant on their honeymoon."

"A woman is not an incubator. A woman has to conceive a child with her mind before she conceives it with her body."

Grazia flashed a bright smile. Sal was no ordinary man. He gave her the freedom to make choices. He treated her like a real woman!

Grazia and Sal walked out of the doctor's office holding each other's hands.

"We have to visit your mother," Grazia said.

Sal squeezed his eyes shut. "I don't have the guts to face my mother."

"You have to do the right thing. Otherwise, you'll regret it for the rest of your life."

"You're right." Sal expanded his eyes, surprised by his own words.

When the morning approached, Sal and Grazia took a boat from Naples and went to Capri.

Grazia was enamored by the island. "Capri is a fabulous."

"It's a place where people fall in love. My mother fell in love with her lover on this island and has never left ever since, not even when he died." Sal sighed. "I can't believe she didn't even look for me after he passed away."

Grazia caressed Sal's face. "We should visit her and ask for an explanation."

Later in the day, Sal led Grazia to an opulent villa surrounded by a spectacular garden.

"This villa is magnificent," Grazia said.

"My mother has been living here for the past twenty-five years," Sal said.

Grazia rang the bell. Minutes later, a plump maid opened the door.

"We are looking for Mrs. Isabella Solvi," Grazia said.

"May I please have your names?" the maid asked.

"You don't need our names, just tell Mrs. Solvi her son and her daughter-in-law want to see her," Sal responded.

The maid stared at Sal. "You're her son?"

Sal lowered his head. "Yes, I'm her son."

"Your mother has been dying to see you for years. She always wrote to your father and asked about you. Your father always replied in his letters you didn't want to know anything about her."

Sal's eyes bulged as his mouth opened. "My father always told me it was my mother who didn't want to see me."

"Come in," the maid said. She guided Sal and Grazia into the living room.

Isabella was seated on the sofa sipping a drink. She was a fine-looking woman in her late fifties with a deep set of green eyes.

"Mrs. Isabella, I have a surprise for you," the maid said.

Isabella's eyes sparkled as she looked at Sal.

"*Mamma,*" Sal mumbled, giving her a bear hug.

Isabella's eyes filled with tears. "I've been dreaming of this moment for years. My dream has finally come true."

"My wife, Grazia, made this a reality," Sal said. "She convinced me to come."

"God bless you." Isabella kissed Grazia on her forehead.

Sal and Grazia spent a whole week in Capri. They had a great time. Isabella enjoyed their company so much that she didn't want them to leave. They promised Isabella they would visit her again soon.

When Sal and Grazia went back to town, they paid Angela the Crazy Head a visit and told her Isabella's story. Angela was fascinated by the story.

"I didn't want to tell the townspeople the story because I'm afraid it will be distorted by the rumor mill," Grazia said.

"The story should be narrated by a great writer like Contessa Fiorella," Angela said.

"I heard the contessa's husband is still looking for her. Do you know where the contessa lives now?"

"I'm the only one who knows where the contessa lives. I'm her best friend," Angela said. "I'm going to tell her Isabella's story. I'm sure she's going to be willing to write a novel about Isabella."

"My mother is a great character," Sal said. "She deserves to be the heroine of a novel."

Angela exhaled. "Sometimes I feel like I'm a character who popped out of a novel."

"I feel I'm living a romance novel," Grazia said.

Sal smiled in agreement. "At times, I get that feeling too." Sal held Grazia's hand. "We're the leading characters of our own romance novel."

The day of Grazia and Sal's departure to America finally arrived.

Norina invited her relatives to a special dinner in honor of the newlyweds.

Before they began eating, Vituccio raised his glass of homemade wine and said, "To America."

"To America," they all replied in accordance with the toast.

They all drank with gusto and relished the sumptuous food.

Clotilde turned to the children. "It's time to say good-bye."

Grazia's eyes became gloomy as she looked at her siblings.

"I'm going to miss you," Caterina said, giving Grazia a hug.

Pasquale's face blushed as he gave Grazia a kiss on the cheek and whispered, "I never told you this, but you're my favorite sister."

Little Donato grabbed Grazia's legs and didn't want to let go, as if he knew she was leaving for good.

Caterina picked the baby up in her arms. "We're going to see her in America."

Mario stood still with his head down. He had stayed up all night rehearsing what he wanted to say to his motherly sister, but he refrained from talking, knowing it would take too long to express himself. He summoned his courage and approached Grazia.

Grazia patted Mario's head and whispered in his ear: "You're my favorite brother. I'm going to miss you."

"You are my favorite sister. I'm going to miss you a lot," Mario wanted to say, but he remained silent. His eyes welled with tears.

Pasquale gave Mario a stern look. "Stop crying. You have to learn how to behave like a man."

Mario covered his eyes with his hands. He was ashamed he couldn't quell his tears.

"You are the princess of the family," Olimpia said, gripping Grazia in a bear hug that seemed to last forever.

Rodolfo gave Sal a handshake and a charming smile. "I'm glad my niece has married a fine man." He kissed Grazia's hand. "You've grown into a fine woman. I'm proud of you."

Ada took Grazia aside and said, "You made a big difference in my life. Thanks to you, my husband treats me well now. He's afraid that I'll leave him and go to work in America."

Grazia beamed. "You're finally getting the respect you deserve."

Marta gave Grazia a tender cuddle. "Don't forget to write to me when you arrive in America."

"I won't forget," Grazia said.

Clotilde tapped Grazia's shoulder. "It's time to go."

Many friends and neighbors on Saint Peter Street lined up to send off Grazia and Sal.

Old Veronica enveloped Grazia into a warm embrace. "You deserve luck. You've been a good girl."

Margherita's eyes gleamed with tears when she gave Grazia a good-bye kiss on the cheek. "I'm so glad you are living a fairy tale."

"Grazia's story is a fairy tale; a poor girl from a little town who marries a rich American," Lina the Warm House said. "It's like one of the novels that Angela the Crazy Head reads."

The Margassi Sisters gave Sal and Grazia hugs.

"You are the best people that I've met in my life," Giovanna Margassi said.

"I never thought that people like you could exist," Gina Margassi said. "You are changing our sky."

"See you in America," Sal said.

Angela the Crazy Head stamped a kiss on Grazia's forehead. "Contessa Fiorella wants you to say hello to the Statue of Liberty on her behalf once you arrive in America. She also said not to forget that the statue stands for women's freedom."

"I want you to tell Contessa Fiorella that she has touched my life and helped me find myself, because she knew me better than I knew myself," Grazia said.

Angela smiled. "I'll tell her."

"I always took your side when people talked bad about you," Titina the Alligator whispered, patting Grazia's arm. "People were jealous of you."

"My husband treats me well now because he's afraid that Sal will give me the opportunity to go to America," Maddalena said.

Grazia grinned. "I'm so glad."

"Don't forget about me," Carmela the Daughter of the Umbrella Repair Man said. She grabbed Grazia's hands and held them tightly.

"I won't forget about you," Grazia whispered. "You'll be the first woman in town to work in Sal's garment factory."

The screeching noise of an engine grabbed everyone's attention. It was Vituccio's car, which had come to a halt at the corner of Saint Peter Street.

Olimpia indicated the car. "Uncle Vituccio is driving them all the way to America."

Pasquale chuckled. "They can't get to America by car. It's too far. Uncle Vituccio is driving them to Naples, where they're going to take the ship that will take to America."

"Though we're all going to Miss Grazia, we have to understand that she's going away for our own good," Caterina said. "Thanks to her, one day, we're all going to go to America."

Pasquale flashed a bright smile. Olimpia beamed, swinging her arms. Mario revealed a contented grin.

The Dumb Brothers made their appearance. They turned to Sal and Grazia.

"I hope you have a lot of American children," the elder Dumb Brother said.

"All our friends who went abroad forgot all about us," the younger Dumb Brother said. "They never bothered to send us their regards. I hope you don't forget about us too."

"We won't forget about you," Grazia said. "You and your brother are unforgettable."

The younger brother scrunched his forehead. "Unforgettable?"

"You and your brother are so special that we'll always remember you," Sal said. "We'll never forget you. You're unforgettable."

The Dumb Brothers' faces coruscated. It was the highest compliment they'd ever been paid.

"People will never forget how stupid you are," Anna the Heavyweight whispered, pushing the Dumb Brothers aside. She raised her voice. "Now it's my turn to say good-bye." She looked at Grazia. "I want to pick you up for one last time. I used to pick you up when you were a child."

Anna held Grazia by the waist and elevated her up in the air.

Grazia giggled. "My head is spinning."

The fortress of a woman plopped Grazia on the ground and whispered, "Carlo the Broken Neck is so afraid of me that he's still out of town."

"Thank you. You're a great woman. I'll never forget what you did for me. You helped me in the most difficult situation in my life. Please, continue to fight for the underdogs and for women who don't have a voice."

Anna smiled, even though she didn't know the meaning of the word "underdog."

As Giacomino the Blind Man readied his violin, Baronessa Rosa emerged from her balcony and sang,

You always visit me in my dreams
I miss you so much when I'm awake
I hope I get to see you soon
I'm afraid I won't see you again…

Sal grinned as he noticed the white pigeons swirling in the sky. "There are birds in the sky."

"The white pigeons are dancing in the sky," Giacomino the Blind Man said. "They're breathtaking. They look like angel wings coming out of the clouds."

How does he know that if he can't see? Sal thought.

"We have to go," Clotilde said.

Sal and Grazia gave more hugs to friends and relatives. They gave a special embrace to Giacomino and waved vivaciously at Baronessa Rosa.

Baronessa Rosa waved back at them. "I hope I see you soon."

The spectators watched Vituccio as he opened the door and settled Norina, Clotilde, Sal, and Grazia in his car. As soon as Vituccio got in too, he revved the engine.

"God knows if we're ever going to see Grazia again," Old Veronica said. "A lot of people who have gone abroad have never come back."

The Voltini children ran towards the car waving their hands, in an attempt to say good-bye to their sister one more time.

Grazia's eyes filled with tears at the sight of her siblings dashing towards the car. She noticed Mario was running as fast as he could, but couldn't keep up with her other siblings. Their images became smaller and smaller until they completely disappeared into the distance.

The car window seemed to frame images running in quick motions. Grazia saw the Sewing School, Saint Maria's Church, the *piazza*, the old castle, the cemetery... A memory was attached to each image. She stared at each image as if she were looking at it for the last time. As the car sped, the images that comprised her past slipped away from her sight. Her heart pounded as she realized that those images were attempting to greet her for the last time. Those images were all settings of important scenes in her life. Now that she was about to leave them, she was finally appreciating them. Never before had those images appeared to be so wonderful, so spectacular, and so precious!

For the first time in her life, Grazia perceived how enchanting the trees in the fields surrounding her town were. Those trees were remarkable. Their leaves didn't look solid green. They had many shades of green, because the golden rays of the sun pelted them. Those trees looked like powerful giants that gave protection to the tiny houses painted in pastel colors. The rock walls that divided one property from the other looked multicolored. Light shades of pink, yellow, and purple undulated on those rocks.

As the car slowed down, Grazia noticed an old woman tending goats in the vicinity of a large farm that looked like a castle. The would-be castle was surrounded by a mantle of vineyards full of green grapes that looked like emeralds as they glittered in the sun. Grazia looked at the sky, her sky. That sky was magnificent! It was the sky of her hometown, the sky that had witnessed her life, her ancestors' lives.

Aunt Clotilde's voice interrupted Grazia's reveries. "Don't be sad. One day soon you'll come and visit. Sal loves Italy."

As Sal smiled in agreement, Grazia gave a sigh of relief.

When they rode by the old section of the town, Grazia saw Pino the Red Eye and Tommasino the Donkey Ears and waved at them. They cheerfully waved back at her.

"You shouldn't even look at them, Clotilde whispered. "They're nothing but lowlifes."

Those "lowlifes" had never looked so precious to Grazia's eyes. "I'm going to miss them."

"They're the last people you are going to miss," Norina said.

"They were part of my life." Grazia flashed a glint of a smile. "They made my life colorful."

The ship at the port of Naples was colossal. Clotilde and Norina marveled at the sight of it.

"It looks like an enormous *palazzo*," Clotilde said.

"How can a big *palazzo* like that move?" Norina asked.

"It moves thanks to the propeller."

"The propeller?"

"The motor, that's the most important part of the ship. Grazia, for example, is the propeller of our family."

Norina scrunched her forehead.

"Grazia is the propeller of the family because she will allow everyone to move to America."

Nodding, Norina flashed a bright smile.

The colossal ship made a screeching noise.

"What's that noise?" Norina asked.

"It's the signal that the ship is about to depart. The passengers should board now," Vituccio said, giving hugs to Grazia and Sal.

Sal gave a kiss on the hand to Clotilde and Norina.

Norina patted Sal's shoulder. "You are a great son-in-law."

Clotilde gave Grazia a warm embrace. "I can't believe you're actually going to America." She then turned to Sal. "Give my regards to my cousin Ignazio and my Aunt Elvira."

"I will," Sal said.

Bursting into tears, Norina clenched Grazia in her arms and whispered, "You are the propeller of our family."

On the ship, Grazia's tears streamed down her face. She stood on the balcony and watched her loved ones waving at her on the pier. As the ship departed, her loved ones got smaller and smaller until they became invisible.

"Where did they go?" she asked herself.

How strange! People who had been part of her life had disappeared suddenly in the immensity of the sky. It seemed they had been swallowed by the enormity of the sky. She had the sense that all those people had been part of a dream, because she could no longer see them or touch them. Grazia wondered who they really were...

They were part of Yesterday's Sky.

Grazia's eyes lit up as she envisioned the Statue of Liberty rising in the American Sky...

The End

Made in the USA
Columbia, SC
28 March 2018